The Vicar's Deadly Sin

A Lady Jane Bartholomew and Miss Margaret Renard

Mystery

Book One: The Seven Deadly Sins Series

Miguelina Perez

ACKNOWLEDGMENTS

To God for all my blessings; to my Mother: Myrta, siblings and friends whose faith in me made this possible, thank you!
To my friends gone before their time – your faith and love will always be with me.

Cover by: The Killion Group

All rights reserved.
No part of this book may be reproduced in any form, without permission of the author.

Copyright © 2014 Miguelina Perez
ISBN-13: 978-1463551575

Prologue

September 1815
Coast of Dover, England

At half past midnight, the entire village was fast asleep, and only those who use the night for illicit activities were out and about. A mild breeze blew in from the village's seaport. Facing France across the narrowest part of the English Channel, Dover's inhabitants depended on the port for their livelihood—which mainly consisted of fishing and trading. The moonless sky hid the cloaked figure as it crossed the cemetery toward the chapel.

Once inside Vane crept cautiously forward between the pews closing in on his prey. Tonight the chapel, with its protective comfort and arched stained-glass windows, could not protect the sole occupant. That his prey was a man of God made no difference to Vane. He was sure no mercy would have been shown if he had been the one stalked. The village vicar had allowed greed to get the best of him. Vane had become weary of those who stood in his way.

He could hear the vicar murmuring words from the book he was reading, perhaps in search of a theme for his next sermon. Vane wanted to laugh at the paradox. The vicar's mission was to bring people closer to God, and now it was up to him to send the vicar to meet his Maker.

He had worked hard for what he wanted and would be damned if he were going to hand it over on a silver platter. The vicar was a fool to think he could blackmail him and get away with it—an unfortunate and fatal error, in fact. Quiet steps brought him closer to his prey. To his right as he advanced into the nave he noticed a small marble statue of St. Francis. He smiled. Irony had a cruel way of introducing itself in life. Before him was a man of the cloth who wanted more than what God offered him, while St. Francis had given up everything to serve God.

Sensing him, the vicar lifted his head from the notes he had been writing from the Bible, and turned, relaxing a little. "You are early, but I'm glad nonetheless," he said. "Must be getting back to the house, and the sooner we get this over with, the sooner I can leave."

Vane slowed his approach, staring at him. The vicar was a short man with a belly that protruded out of his jacket. Tonight he wore a white linen shirt that had been wrinkled from the day's activities. The shirt was open all

4

the way down his chest, hanging loosely around his waist.

"You don't have to be gloomy about this," said the vicar, a smirk on his face. "Pay up and I will keep quiet for a very long time." He turned back toward the book and continued putting the notes for his next sermon in between the chapters he would be reading from.

The pristine smell of the church sickened Vane. The vicar's eyes, reflecting his greed, and his demeanour of cockiness was all too much for him.

Vane picked up the small statue. The muscles in his right arm tensed as he tightened his grip, the stone digging into his palm. Before the vicar could turn back to face him the heavy statue of St. Francis came down upon his head. He thought how St. Francis—physically disabled, lover of nature and animals, a holy man— would probably be turning in his grave at this very moment, horrified that his image had been used for such an unholy act. It pleased him. He let the statue fall from his hand and stood for a moment to watch as it landed on the floor with barely a chip to it. Vane stared at the scene before him, his eyes settling on the cross. He thought of one final act, before turning to leave. Task done he mused how his father had tried to stop him from his goal and met with the same fate as the vicar. Killing had become a necessary need for him. Nothing and no one could stop him now from achieving his goal.

Chapter One

Having awakened earlier than usual from a disturbing dream, Margaret shed any thought of going back to bed. The lingering tension from the dream prevented sleep. It was the same dream, always. Her father trying to tell her something, but he would die before he could utter the words. She settled instead for ringing her maid and requesting a hot bath.

She stood a little longer at the window. The fog might ruin the day but she hoped for the best. Returning to her bed, Margaret picked up the book she had been reading before she'd drifted to sleep. "Pride and Prejudice" was her favourite novel; so much so that she could not remember how many times she'd read it. She often found a comparison between herself and Lizzie Bennet, as they were both witty and outspoken, not to mention spirited. At least that was what Mrs Roth, her housekeeper, had accused her of on several occasions.

Mrs Roth, hearing the bell from her mistress' bed chamber, went up to see to the bath, bringing one of the new maids with her.

"You are Ellie?" asked the ancient housekeeper.

"Yes, Mrs Roth," the girl responded, wringing her hands.

"Well come now, the miss called for a bath. She likes her tub filled with hot water."

"Yes, ma'am," said the girl, barely in a whisper.

They headed from the kitchen toward the front of the manor where the steps led toward the upstairs bed chambers.

"You will find life here never a dull moment," began Mrs Roth. "Though my miss lacks a title, and may be a young lady of no consequence to the uppity social hooligans, she is well to do—her fortune coming from lands, in England and Antigua, thanks to my dear boy Richard. Her father took care of everything. God rest his soul. Killed himself, he did—could not handle losing Abigail. That would be Miss Margaret's mother." Mrs Roth took a deep breath and made a sign of the cross with one hand tracing the cross from her forehead to her breast and reaching one shoulder and then another.

On reaching the upstairs landing, Mrs Roth turned toward the right side of the house and the bedrooms.

"You will see she is a pleasant-looking girl. A curious and insightful young lady she is and does not shy from her opinions," another breath. "She is well-versed in many topics ranging from war to politics to gardening and is fiercely loyal to those she adores. She has a surprisingly solid constitution for someone of good breeding." Mrs Roth ended her praises with great pride as they came to a halt in front of her mistress' door.

"I think it is going to be wonderful working here, Mrs Roth."

Mrs Roth smiled and quickly ushered the young lady into her mistress' room.

Tub filled and rose salts added, Margaret was left to her own. Lowering herself into the warm bath, the sweet smell of the roses from her garden swirled around her. She felt the disquiet evaporating out through the pores of her skin to be carried away by the steam. All things considered, other than the nightmare, she had no worries in the world. Though sometimes the memories were just hiding, waiting for the right moment to come and torment her. She thought of her family—at the age of twelve; she'd lost her mother and infant brother during childbirth.

After her father's death she was left as ward to her aunt, Lady Marguerite Harrison, wife of the Earl of Strathmore. It proved, however, not to be an agreeable arrangement. Lady Strathmore, believing her brother married beneath his status, had never fully accepted Margaret and her mother as members of the Renard family. As a matter of fact, her brother's death led her to believe, with great joy, that an opportunity had arisen to reverse the family fortune for her only son Carlton.

But as quickly as she had arrived at Cheetham Manor in the hopes of acquiring the family fortune and introducing Margaret to society, Lady Strathmore departed just as fast. The moment the reading of the will revealed that Margaret's fortune was non-transferrable Lady Strathmore dispatched a coach back to Norfolk and acquitted her responsibilities of the young girl.

So with the guidance of her father's solicitor and the family servants, Margaret's life was as happy as it could be, though society might argue it was an unconventional life.

Other than a family, Margaret lacked for nothing. She was fortunate, for many girls of gentle breeding were forced to seek employment either as a governess or schoolmistress, while others resigned themselves to a "civil contract," polite but without overmuch affection. She loved Dover and was content with never leaving it. Dover afforded her the sea, which her mother loved dearly. Why, even Shakespeare had written about the white cliffs of Dover in his play, *King Lear*.

Dressed and having done away with her breakfast of eggs, toast and a hot cup of tea, Margaret ventured out to get her errands done, without chaperon. Fiercely independent she cared not for social constraints. She was not a foolish girl either, giving way to fancies like love or marriage.

Knowing their mistress' penchant for breaking the rules, the staff always made sure she was always followed by one of the footmen.

The morning had improved much—blue skies, birds singing and gentle breezes were in abundance. Arriving at the market, Margaret was disappointed at the lack of patrons. Dover was a beautiful village, and became more so when it came alive with its inhabitants buzzing about getting their errands and shopping done. People knew each other and watched out for one another.

Looking over the vegetables, Margaret bumped into the town's most fervent gossip.

"Good gracious," declared Mrs Appleby, a tall and thin woman of five and sixty with streaks of grey hair on each side of her head. "How have you been, my dear?" she asked as she none too surreptitiously surveyed Margaret's dress and hair. Mrs Appleby loved memorizing what people wore. No doubt to report back to her neighbours.

Before Margaret could reply, the woman added in a low whisper, "Have you heard about the vicar?"

"Good morning, Mrs Appleby. I am well, thank you for asking, and no, I have not heard about the vicar." Margaret answered the woman in order of the questions she posed, hoping to annoy the older woman, but without success. Margaret detested gossip.

"Oh, dear, dear," Mrs Appleby said, looking around to see if she'd acquired an audience. A disappointed sigh escaped from her thin lips at not finding one. Turning back to Margaret, she stated ominously, "Murdered he was. The vicar's been murdered. Dark dealings, it was."

"What?" Margaret exclaimed, dropping the carrots back onto the table. *A murder and in Dover?*

"Horrible, from what I heard." Mrs Appleby dropped the eggplant she had been surveying prior to Margaret's arrival, "To be murdered in the very place where he preached to us every Sunday. Can you imagine? I mean, is nothing sacred these days? Of course, one never likes to speak ill of the dearly departed, but I found him a tad self-righteous."

"What happened?" All sorts of questions busied Margaret's mind, including who would want to murder a vicar? "When did it happen?"

"It happened late last night. He was hit with the statue of St. Francis, from what I heard."

Margaret's thoughts spun widely out of control as Mrs Appleby rambled on about the strength and violence it would take to kill a man with one blow. "Goodness!" Goose bumps running up her arms, Margaret pulled her shawl closer to her. "Pray, how did you come to hear such news?" A flush of heat rising to her cheeks when Mrs Appleby giggled with delight at knowing things others did not.

"Come now, Margaret, surely you would understand if I do not reveal my sources. I did hear a cross was found stuffed into his mouth."

Margaret's thoughts quickly shifted to the anguish of the vicar's widow. Goodness, she must pay her respects to his wife. Though she was most anxious to tell Jane what had occurred, Margaret knew what society demanded of her. Vegetables forgotten, she murmured her excuses to Mrs Appleby and rushed away.

13

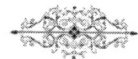

Entering the vicar's home, Margaret was not surprised at the entourage of village dowagers fluttering about the widow. All wanting to be of assistance, but instead finding one another at odds over who would prepare the tea, arrange the biscuits, and perform similarly important tasks.

The vicar and Mrs Bostwick had been part of the community for a little over ten years. Though they were never blessed with children, they were sensible of the orphans and made it their mission to help those in need.

Margaret knew some of the villagers considered the vicar a little too sanctimonious. However, she felt that was not sufficient enough reason to murder a man. Not that there was ever justification for murder. Even in war, she could not justify the carnage that came with it.

Curious, she had to ask, "Mrs Bostwick, do you have any thoughts about who could have done this? And why?"

The widow, who had come to know Jane and Margaret, shortly after their mothers' death, loved the girls. While she knew their love for crime solving was not a hobby of young ladies of good standing, she had made allowances because of their losses. When Margaret asked who would do such a thing, she did not mind the insensitivity of her question. But there was no reply.

Margaret found herself staring into glazed eyes. She felt sorry for the widow. She knew too well what it meant to lose a loved one. *Who would want to kill the vicar?* Regardless of his often self-righteous attitude—she agreed with Mrs Appleby on that account—he seemed to be a good man who loved God's children. It was beyond reason as to why anyone would want to murder him. But perhaps the vicar was not what he had seemed. He certainly must have angered someone enough for them to commit murder.

Margaret reached over to Mrs Bostwick and placed her warm hands around the woman's cold fingers. She recalled the times she and Jane had visited the vicar's cottage. Memories of sweets made by Mrs. Bostwick and the vicar practising his sermons would always remain dear to her. "Has the magistrate been here?"

Mrs Bostwick continued her blank stare. It reminded Margaret of tales she'd heard of people reportedly leaving their physical bodies and slipping into other states of being. She repeated her question.

"What?" Mrs Bostwick jumped slightly, as if just realizing that Margaret had been speaking to her. "Oh, dear, pray do forgive me."

"Please, it is I who should be asking for forgiveness. For here I am plying you with questions when you have lost your dear husband," Margaret said, keeping Mrs Bostwick's now warmed hands in hers.

The recently widowed woman smiled warmly at her guest. "Did you say the magistrate? Oh, yes, yes. He came with others and asked a few questions and then left. They did say that they might be back, but I doubt they will give it another thought."

"Did they look in your husband's study?" Margaret asked, unable to help herself.

"I...I believe so," was all Mrs Bostwick could muster, bursting into tears.

"There, there," Margaret soothed her. "Did the vicar say anything to you prior to his death, anything out of the ordinary?"

"All I know is that one evening he had gone off for a walk, for he usually liked walking in the evenings. He felt communing with nature helped him with his sermons." She reddened at the notion she was babbling.

Margaret waited patiently for her to continue.

"When he came back, he had a strange look about him. As if he was pleased with himself. I took it to mean that he had found his next sermon topic. When I asked him about it, he merely replied that opportunities sometimes presented themselves when you least expected them. I of course thought it strange, but you know how he was sometimes with his sermons."

"I know my husband was self-righteous, but he was a good man and did not deserve to die in such a horrid manner."

"You are right; he did not deserve to die so horribly and before his time."

As if a brilliant thought hit her, Mrs Bostwick seemed to come alive; "Margaret, would it be too much to ask if you and Lady Jane could find out those responsible for my husband's death?" asked Mrs Bostwick. More tears streaming down her face.

What Mrs Bostwick was asking of her was a little over hers and Jane's experience. Margaret found the loss of human life, through such a horrible act deplorable.

She remembered the first time they had gotten into trouble for sleuthing. Their proclivity for solving crimes had begun with small crimes, as in the case of the missing horse. What a debate she had with the

17

magistrate when she tried to convince him of the identity of the guilty party.

Indeed it had been a touchy situation, for the perpetrator was the Duke of Lancashire's younger son. It had required all of Jane's finesse to smooth the magistrate's ruffled feathers and convince him to question the party. The boy claimed it was a prank he played on his father's old friend. With the horse returned to its rightful owner, the magistrate grudgingly thanked the girls in private, with no public acknowledgement made concerning their help with the case. But the villagers knew, of course. Jane's father even appeared to be more than a little proud of his daughter's sleuthing abilities. But that was a matter altogether—a matter of theft and not murder.

Margaret merely nodded for she knew too well. The vicar was known for his self-righteous sermons—with the exception of his very being, everyone else was a sinner. The real question here was what had excited the vicar so that got him killed?

Mrs Bostwick and the vicar had been very kind to her and Jane when they were growing up. Days of summer were spent in their gardens as smells of cinnamon cookies and apple pies sifted through the air. The girls excited in their anticipation for a bite.

"I cannot promise anything, but I will see what I can do," said Margaret.

Several seconds passed, and then Mrs Bostwick said, "Thank you, Meggie," she had always called her that, and Margaret did not mind at all. Rising from her seat, Mrs Bostwick added, "I must go and lie down." She straightened her skirt. "Please make my excuses to the other ladies." In a whisper she added, "Feel free to look around, if you wish." With a slight smile, she kissed Margaret lightly on the cheek and left her alone with more questions than she'd had when she arrived.

Indeed she would take advantage of this opportunity to search the vicar's office. Locking composure sternly over her excitement, she ran into the kitchen. The ladies were still buzzing about. When she managed to get their attention, she told them Mrs Bostwick had retired to her bedroom with the hopes of having some chicken soup for dinner. The well-meaning women bustled out of the vicarage on their new mission to the market.

"We need sage," one of them said as she passed through the door.

"We do indeed and we mustn't forget the chicken," another exclaimed.

Margaret closed the door and, as soon as they were out of sight, she headed directly to the vicar's office. She stood for a moment, surveying the room with its masculine taste. The wide windows behind a large mahogany desk and leather chair shed enough light even on overcast days. Today they allowed her a good look at the built-in maple bookcases lined up along the rest of the walls, housing thousands of books neatly catalogued in alphabetical order. Not at all sure what she should be looking for, Margaret searched, hoping to find something out of the ordinary. Finding even the smallest clue about what the vicar had gotten involved in, causing his untimely death, would be very helpful.

Chapter Two

The fluttering of the servants did nothing to ease Lady Jane Bartholomew's disquiet. Her only consolation was the expected return of her father on the morrow. She imagined herself walking beside him, laughing away the silliness of her sensitivities, but for today she would be content with Margaret's visit later in the afternoon. She could hear the servants' cheerful bustling, for they too adored her father and wanted everything to be perfect upon his return.

He had been gone for weeks, and she missed him frightfully. Jane had spent the evening before wrapping small gifts she got him during his absence, knowing well he would be doing the same for her. She cherished the small tokens he brought from all parts of his travels. She looked at the bracelet she now wore, with its small golden flowers and centred rubies, a gift from Italy.

He'd even brought one for Margaret, but instead of rubies hers was adorned with sapphires—her favourite gemstone.

She and Margaret often joked about being sisters. To Jane's father, she might truly have been another daughter.

During her father's absences, Aunt Petunia journeyed from Shropshire to stay with her. Though she loved her aunt, Jane always counted the days until her father returned home. She missed the peace and tranquillity of the house. Having grown up without a mother, she and her father created their own private routine. Falling into a comfortable habit, every evening they retired to the drawing room after a light supper to read and talk about the events of the day. However, unlike her pleasant conversations with her father, Aunt Petunia's incessant gossip quickly became tiresome. Hence, when she announced she would be visiting her sister in Fullerton, Jane happily ordered the carriage with great haste. She was thrilled that she had escaped from accompanying her aunt because of the expected visit with Margaret. Aunt Petunia agreed to allow her to remain under the care of the servants and Biltmore, the family's trusted steward and his lordship's personal manservant.

Soon she would send one of the more experienced stable boys to fetch Margaret in the family carriage. She often worried about her wandering out alone and without proper chaperone. The wooded areas were unsafe, an no doubt Margaret would argue that she could handle herself.

The shrill whistle of the kettle had Jane abandoning the window for the settee. A cup of tea would be very welcome, and help settle her nerves. Her mind went back to Margaret's whereabouts. Her friend was stubborn indeed. It had taken much coercing on her part to convince Margaret to allow Biltmore to come by with the carriage to fetch her.

"Come in?" she said, still unsure if she'd actually heard a knock.

"I beg your pardon, my lady." A shy housemaid carrying a tray with the tea carefully walked into the room and placed the tray on the coffee table.

"Thank you, Eloise. Please don't forget to bring us some fresh cakes and more tea once Ms Renard arrives."

"Yes, milady."

"That will be all."

The maid curtseyed before leaving the room.

Several minutes later, Jane felt much better. Looking around the drawing room, she realized how deeply it was in need of painting. She decided the soft blue walls would do well in a sage green. In fact, she couldn't recall the last time the room had been painted. Taking the chair by the mahogany writing table, she began making a list of things she wanted to do to the manor. Besides the painting, different pillows would be required to match the new colour. And then, perhaps, a changed variety of prints to adorn the walls, or tapestries, and maybe a different rug or two.

"There," she exclaimed an hour later. "That should take care of the sitting room." In her excitement she had ignored the rest of the house. To rectify the situation she decided to continue adding ideas in the hopes of acquiring a complete list of renovations. Several hours later, engrossed in her thoughts Jane had not heard the coach approach until it pulled up to the courtyard.

List temporarily forgotten, Jane jumped her seat and ran to the window in time to see John, the footman, open the door to the coach to assist Margaret down. While working on the renovation ideas she had forgotten all of her troubles and had begun to believe that perhaps she had confused the sense of impending doom with loneliness. Now that her friend was here she felt her old self.

"Good day, John," Margaret said.

The footman bowed. "And a good day to you, miss. Milady would be in the parlour."

Margaret thanked him and proceeded under the arched entrance to the house. Jane had done a wonderful job in decorating and maintaining it. She loved coming to Wellington Manor, named after Jane's father's hero, the Duke of Wellington, and definitely thought of it as her second home. She halted, admiring the painting of Jane's father in the front hallway, and the door to the sitting room burst open.

Jane literally flung herself at her friend, hugging her. "Oh, thank goodness you've come. I have missed you awfully, and I will be selfish now and hold you here for a few moments. I am glad to see you."

When she was finally led into the parlour, Margaret furrowed her brow. "Jane, is everything all right?"

"Oh, I am being silly. I'm anxious for Papa to come home, not to mention missing my dear friend."

"I'm sorry, love. I should have insisted you come and stay with me for a few days. That dreadful fog had me crawling up the walls."

Jane was relieved to hear she was not the only one to feel the uneasiness that had been looming over everything. The fog created an effect on her friend too. "Oh, it is nothing, really. Besides, I couldn't have abandoned Aunt Petunia. But now you are—"

"Where is Aunt Petunia?" asked Margaret

"She's gone to Fullerton. You know how I feel about her, but I will be overjoyed when she's returned home and my dear papa is here safe and sound," Jane said as she poured the tea, her hands shaking slightly as she held the teapot.

"Jane, what is the matter?" Margaret asked.

"Oh, nothing really," Jane said, trying her best to sound as if she was merely out of sorts from lack of companionship.

Margaret, however, knew better and gave her friend a look that conveyed that thought.

"Oh, all right." Jane moved from her chair and settled back down on the settee by the window, Margaret following her. "I've been a little uneasy. I wrote a list of things I would love to do to the manor and instantly began to feel better. Then when you arrived, bringing me much happiness, the heaviness I felt suddenly lifted. Therefore, I deduce I suffered from a touch of loneliness. But here I am rambling. What would Papa say if he could hear me?" She gave a small laugh. "I know. He would tell me to stop reading those gothic novels."

Margaret felt terrible for her. She really did look a bit on edge. She made a mental note that next time Jane's father went away, she would insist on her dear friend staying with her or perhaps come to Wellington Manor for the duration of his absence. "Don't worry. I have always maintained you have a sixth sense about things like this," she said. "Really, it's no surprise you feel an impending doom for something terrible has indeed occurred."

Suddenly the excitement of detecting had lost its appeal to Margaret. Her friend was in terrible need of a distraction. Perhaps a walk and some reading would help Jane relax a bit.

"You really are frightening me, Margaret. What's happened?" Jane asked taking her friend's pelisse and bonnet.

There was a certain firm self-possession about her, and Margaret should have known that her friend would catch the change in her disposition. There was no easy or delicate way of putting it. Besides, she abhorred the very male notion that all women were the wilting flower type. "The vicar has been murdered," she said calmly.

"The vicar murdered! My goodness, who would do such a thing?"

"I haven't a clue. But I did as society demands and paid my respects to Mrs Bostwick. While there she asked if you and I could help in finding out who committed this horrible act. She even allowed me access to the vicar's office. Unfortunately, other than his arriving home one night excited about something, I found nothing to aid us in solving the mysterious misfortune that befell him. Based on the facts, whoever killed him must have been quite strong. It would point to the murderer being a man. I am told a cross was found inside the vicar's mouth."

"What did you say to Mrs Bostwick?

"I told her that we cannot promise anything but we would try to do our best."

"Margaret, you are talking about murder." Jane rose from her settee and began to pace around the room. "I believe that is way out of our miniscule expertise."

"I know, but it would be great if we were to solve the murder, could you imagine what it would do for us in society?"

"No, but I can imagine what society would do." Jane said stopping in front of Margaret. "Pray from whom did you hear about the vicar's death?"

"Why, from Mrs Appleby."

"Mrs Appleby? Oh really, Margaret, that woman never learns," an exasperated Jane declared. "She has naught better to do than go around soliciting gossip."

Unfortunately, there were others, who were only too happy to comply. These were the sacrifices of living in a small town where everyone knew everyone's business and some relished in knowing. Margaret ignored Jane's outburst and continued, "I believe the vicar discovered something that got him killed."

"But what? I really think that this is beyond our scope and should just let it be. Let the magistrate find out who killed him." Jane said, gazing into a corner of the room, a shudder tracking her from head to toe.

Margaret felt a small stab of excitement. Her friend seemed to have left her earlier nervousness behind and, instead of the horrid circumstances, found herself thinking about the facts pertaining to the murder. *Who would kill a man of the church, and why? Is the murderer a resident of Dover?* And while she was ready to get started on the search for a killer, she knew Jane needed some time to think about other things. "Jane, let's drink our tea and take a walk around the gardens. We can say a prayer for the vicar and clear our thoughts.

The smell of your mother's beautiful flowers always work wonders on me."

"I agree, but first there's something we should do."

"What needs—?"

"Biltmore!" Jane yelled out. The intensity of her voice made it sound as if their lives were in some sort of danger.

Margaret covered her ears, Jane's screech catching her by surprise.

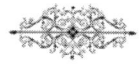

Biltmore Krowkowski, Bilty to the girls, burst into the parlour, his new land cavalry pistol in hand, ready to do battle with whoever had accosted his charge.
Having been her ladyship's father's valet and a trustworthy fellow, Biltmore was as proud of his Polish heritage as he was of his position under the service of Lord Bartholomew and no doubt would give his life for Margaret, as he would for Jane or her father.

Discovering young master Charles surrounded by a group of highwaymen, Biltmore showed his talent for easing the unharmed out of dangerous situations. Grateful for having saved his son's life, Jane's grandfather offered Biltmore a job as her father's valet, but in reality to guard his headstrong heir. He came to live with the family when her father was just a teenage boy.

With his knack for telling wild stories, they often imagined him to have been a pirate prior to coming to work for the Bartholomew family. He was known to be swift with a blade and even faster with a pistol.

Biltmore found Margaret with her hands over her ears and an excitable lady Jane pacing. God help them all when the two got together—it did not take much to see that they were up to something.

"Put the gun down, Biltmore." Jane rolled her eyes at the dramatics. "I need you to bring the horses and carriage around. The vicar of Dover has been murdered."

He knew better than to argue with her, but at the same time knew too well to just give in to her requests without asking some questions. "Do we have a place in mind?"

"Yes, of course, we're going to the scene of the crime," Jane said, noting Margaret had remained silent. Jane silently praised Biltmore for not showing any emotion and accepting commands with ease.

"Very well, my lady," he said as he bowed to the command. Nodding, he turned to leave.

"Oh, and Biltmore—"

"Yes, my lady," he responded, turning to face Jane again.

"Bring your gun."

"Yes, my lady." He agreed for the third time. Swearing to his lordship that he would protect them at all costs, he had already determined to bring his weapons. He always did when he travelled with his ladyship. Bowing again, he crossed the entrance of the room and closed the door behind him.

Leaning against the door, Biltmore took a deep breath, steadying his heart. Then he gave a small prayer for the adventure on which they were about to embark, praying that they'd find nothing, and at the worst, their adventure would turn out to be just an uneventful trip through the countryside. Tomorrow his lordship would be back and he could take back the responsibility of watching over Lady Jane.

It wasn't that he didn't love the child. Actually, he had been there to see her born and grow up, but she was high spirited, and he must own up that he was not as young as he used to be. When the misses got together, trouble usually followed them, which meant more work for him as he worked harder to keep them safe and out of trouble. He feared these two would be the death of him yet. Taking a deep breath to steady his nerves Biltmore left the young ladies to their plans.

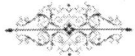

Back inside Jane turned to Margaret, "Come, we must change our clothes."

"We must?"

"Yes, you would not want to be tromping about the grounds in your lovely gown. Would you? I know I wouldn't..."

As it was in most cases, Jane's voice of reason always won their disputes.

"Besides, it would look less conspicuous if we were to dress like the villagers," added Jane.

Arm in arm, the girls headed upstairs to Jane's bedroom where they changed their clothing before joining Biltmore and the waiting carriage.

Since they were off to perform a sombre task, the girls rode in silence. Finally, the carriage pulled up in front of the vicarage. Fortunately, the area seemed void of any occupants, giving the girls the opportunity to do their investigation without any interruptions. Descending from the carriage with Biltmore's assistance, they set out to work.

"Jane, did you notice all of the chapel windows are closed and none broken?"

"Yes, I did, which could imply the assailant must have entered through the front door."

"It would be the most logical approach. The church being a place of refuge and solace, it was always left open," Margaret agreed.

They were about to enter when Biltmore stopped them. "If you do not mind, my lady, I would like to go first, just as a precaution."

Jane wanted to wave him away but knew if she did not cooperate with him, he would insist on leaving at once. "Very well, but be careful and quick."

The girls waited patiently as Biltmore turned the door knob, and found it locked. Pulling a long, narrow piece of metal from his sleeve, he placed it into the hole of the lock and wiggled it with little effort until he heard the latch give way.

They gasped in astonishment. "What is that?" they asked in unison.

"Something I acquired in one of my adventures."

"It is amazing. Can you teach us how to use it?" Jane asked.

"I would—"

"It would come in handy during other investigations," added Margaret.

"I would most certainly not. You young ladies are in so much trouble already. When his lordship hears about this—" Biltmore said, retracting his offer.

"Well now, I do agree with you, Bilty. However it would be more difficult to discuss why you let us come. Don't you think?" Margaret said, obviously pleased with herself.

As Biltmore was about to retort, the girls in their eagerness to start investigating the premises, pushed forward and entered the church, leaving him standing alone in their wake.

Once inside, Jane and Margaret felt the force of the severity and sadness of the vicar's death. Slowly they made their way to the altar. They immediately found the place where he had fallen. Blood stains still remained.

"Look, Jane that must've been where his head lay."

They stood for several seconds in silence.

Jane tried picturing how the vicar's lifeless body would have lain after he was struck.

"I have an idea. I will be right back," cried Margaret running outside.

Jane took careful steps to the pulpit. The Bible he had been working on rested there, closed, with notes placed at different sections throughout.

Several minutes later Margaret returned with seamstress chalk in hand.

"What are you doing?"

"Watch and you'll see." Imagining how the vicar fell and how his body landed on the floor, based on the blood stains, she traced his form on the stone with the chalk. It gave them a view as to how the vicar had fallen once he had been struck. It also showed them where the killer had let the statue fall.

"Brilliant, Margaret!" Jane squealed, forgetting for a second where they were, but quickly recovered lowering her voice once more, "Just brilliant."

"He must have been leaning over the altar reading the Bible when he turned to welcome the intruder or visitor. That means the killer was standing from behind. The vicar then turned his back to the killer to close his Bible—and…then bang!" Margaret smacked her hands for effect. Vicar falls, blood gushing out—"

"Oh my..." uttered Jane, as she paled and swayed at the imagery of the horrible scene. *Murder was a nasty business indeed.*

"Jane, dearest, what is wrong?"

Biltmore appeared at his ladyship's side. His stiffness told the girls that their time had run out.

"I am fine. But we should leave this place soon." There was a need in her to go back to the safety of her home. She would have to think things through. It could be that both she and Margaret were getting into something that was beyond their abilities.

"Very well. In conclusion, the vicar falls dead. The statue is let go, and the killer walks out, disappearing into the night. However, somewhere out there he is walking around with either shoes or boots containing dust from the statue. Also, because the vicar turned to close the Bible after he greeted the killer, this tells us that he knew his killer."

"And so we, too, may know this person," Jane said incredulously. It was one thing if the killer was just passing through town. But it was disconcerting to think that many of the villagers, whom they had known since they were little girls, could be the killer.

Once back from their dismal trip, Margaret and Jane decided to finish the day with their planned walk in the gardens.

Afterward the girls returned to the manor, where they ensconced themselves in the drawing room with a fire. They read for a while, drank some more tea, and finally settled for a small dinner prepared especially for them by the cook. Through dinner the girls continued with more talks about books, fashion, and perhaps visiting Bath the following spring. Their conversation touched many subjects, but never the murder. It was still there, in the back of their minds, as if they realised their involvement in the vicar's death would not end with merely paying respects to his widow.

The tete-a-tete ended with talks of marriage.

"Are you sure?" asked Jane.

"Yes, I will never marry. I will never allow myself to self-destruct over losing someone."

"You are not your father, Margaret. You are strong. Think all you will miss not marrying," Jane reasoned.

"I have all I need. I have a fortune and I have you."

Jane giggled, though disturbed by Margaret's declaration of marriage.

"I shall marry," declared Jane.

Margaret laughed. "Of course you shall. I on the other hand, shall be a biddy old aunt to your spoiled children.

They both laughed.

Chapter Three

After Margaret's departure, Jane enjoyed the rest of the evening in serenity. Thoughts of their trip to the chapel and the vicar's murder were set aside for the time being. As always, their visits lifted her spirits. While Biltmore drove Margaret home, Jane retired to the parlour, where she continued to wrap her father's gifts, occasionally stroking the silky fur of her four-year-old tabby, Bessie.

Jane ached to have her father home so she could talk things over with him. His presence always lent a sense of normalcy to her world, yet she admitted her anxiousness wasn't merely due to his absence. She was momentarily distracted when she heard Bessie purr.

"Oh, Miss Bessie, you are such soothing company. What would I have done in this big old manor without you?" In reply, the cat rose from her place and scampered over to the kitchen where Cook no doubt was preparing her own evening meal. "Well, I never!" declared Jane, pretending to be insulted, as she chuckled at Bessie's audacity. Cats had a way of knowing their own self-worth. Sighing deeply, she went in search for another cup of tea.

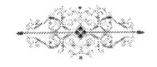

The visit with Jane had gone well, relieving Margaret's tension and her own gloomy mood caused by the vicar's death. But during the ride home, she kept finding new questions. *Did the vicar see something he shouldn't have?* If that was the case, then it must have been serious enough for someone to kill him. Perhaps retracing the vicar's steps in the days before his death would help shed light on a few clues.

The sudden stop of the coach brought her back to the present. Biltmore jumped, with great agility, from his seat. Opening the door to the carriage, announced, "Here you are, miss, safe and sound, as I promised her ladyship."

Margaret looked up and smiled at the big man. "Thank you, Bilty." Rising on her toes she planted a kiss on his cheek.

Biltmore reddened at this display of affection. He bowed, closed the door behind her and bade farewell as he climbed back into the outside box seat. With a snap of the whip in the air, the horses began to move back toward their snug stable.

Margaret stood for a moment outside in her manor's courtyard, waving good-bye to Biltmore. The moment she walked into the house she was besieged by the scullery maid, Evangeline, who seemed overwrought. Clearly something out of the ordinary had happened in her usually peaceful home.

"Good Lord, miss. I'm glad you're home. It seems you have a visitor." Evangeline was a sweet girl, but often gave way to exaggerations. Not in an untruthful way, but certainly tending more toward the dramatic.

"A visitor?" Margaret repeated in disbelief, "at this late hour?"

Since her father's death there had been three visitors: the vicar to offer his condolences; her father's sister, Lady Marguerite Harrison; and Jane's father, Uncle Charles. She knew she had cousins, but never had one bothered to write or contact her, though truthfully this did not bother her in the least.

"Yes, miss. It is your father's solicitor, Mr Latham. He's in the parlour and insisted on waiting until your return."

"Very well, Evangeline. Do bring us some hot tea and biscuits."

The maid seemed unsure about leaving her alone with the solicitor, as if the man was a stranger, but bobbed a curtsy before hurrying to get the tea.

Margaret wondered what was so urgent that Mr Latham would feel compelled to show up unannounced and at such an unsociable hour. Not that it mattered to her for she wasn't one to keep up with the rules society imposed on her because of her gender.

Still, she possessed enough feminine vanity to glance at her reflection in the hall mirror. Several strands of hair had pulled loose from her tight bun. She hurriedly tried to remedy the problem, but the curls refused to cooperate. Drawing in a long, deep breath, Margaret pinched her cheeks, and decided it would have to do.

She turned the knob of the door and then stopped. *Goodness, what if he's come to inform her that she is no longer rich? What would she do?* The thought of working as a governess for some lord's bratty children did not sit well with her. *Perhaps I could stay with my father's sister. No! That would never do. Her aunt was impossible and not once has she accepted her or her beloved mother as a Renard.* Maybe the prospect of becoming a governess was not as dark as she first believed. Not wishing to keep her solicitor waiting any longer, Margaret resolved to put her concerns aside for a moment. Opening the door, she stepped into the room projecting self-confidence.

There was a rustling of papers and a tall figure rose from one of the settees. Margaret's breath caught, for standing in front of her was the most handsome man she had ever seen. Then her breath, which she seemed to have been holding, left her lungs ever so slowly. She noted his height. He was taller than anyone she'd ever known. His skin had seen the sun, yet it was a pleasant colour; bringing about the dark parts of his watery blue eyes. His jet black hair had been combed neatly toward the back, and he was dressed impeccably. What was more striking to her was the fact that he seemed familiar, yet surely she would have remembered him if they had met before. Now Margaret wished she'd taken time to fix herself properly, though the thought of her wanting to look pleasing for a man surprised her, in fact, shocked her to the core!

What's come over me? These ridiculous ideas happened to silly girls with nothing better to do than hope to form an attachment to a man. She needed no such attachment, she reminded herself.

"Miss Renard?"

"Yes," she answered, as she curtsied, finding herself incapable of further speech at the moment. The man in front of her was breath taking and not her father's solicitor, though he seemed vaguely familiar.

Feeling uncharacteristically shy and insecure, Margaret struggled to pull herself together before she appeared daft for she hated feeling weak especially in front of strangers. The man stood staring at her, seemingly unaware of her inner turmoil.

"Please forgive the unannounced visit and allow me to introduce myself. My name is Phillip Latham, solicitor, at your service. I was most recently made executor of your estate. My father, the late Edward Latham, was originally hired by your father, the late François Renard, to manage your inheritance and estate."

"Did you say the late Edward Latham? I wasn't aware he had been ill." She had known the older Latham since she was a little girl. "I'm sorry for your loss. How terrible it must have been for you and your family." Margaret was taken aback at this sudden announcement of yet another death.

"Thank you, Miss Renard. It was unexpected, even though he had issues with his heart. We were thankful he died peacefully in his sleep."

45

Margaret noted the ease in which the young man related the news of his father's death, as if they were merely discussing the weather. Such decorum was no doubt to due to society's frowning on the overt display of emotion. "Please accept my deepest condolences," said Margaret. A death was a death, and by natural causes or not it was painful for those left behind. She remembered her father's death since it was more recent than that of her mother and felt a slight pang. She did not agree with time healing all wounds, but it did lessen the pain. Life was strange. And as it always seemed to go on, death lurked about, like an unwelcome guest. She wondered if Mr Latham's loss of his father affected him much like her father's death did to her.

The colour drained from Margaret's face.

"I am sorry, Miss Renard, I had no idea my father was more to you than a solicitor. Would you like for me to call your maid, or instruct her to bring you a small glass of brandy?" He went over to assist her to the sofa.

"No, but thank you, sir, it's nothing really. I have recently learned that our dear vicar was murdered and now I learn of your father's passing. All this dying, I must admit, can fray one's nerves."

"I do concur it was most disagreeable upon hearing of the vicar's death," said the young solicitor. Margaret sensed his choice of the word 'death' was to protect her female sensitivities, though not necessary.

"Yes, it was," Margaret agreed wondering if Mr Latham knew more on the matter. "Do you have any ideas or thoughts on who the culprit might be or why anyone would murder a man of the cloth?"

"No, I am afraid not," he said, eyes studying her closely.

"I was rather fond of your father," she said, hoping to distract him from thinking of her, no doubt, peculiarities. "He was not like most men. Not only was he an excellent solicitor, but he showed genuine concern for my well-being, especially after my father's death. He was a man of unconventional wisdom, who thought for himself and was rather proud of it. He didn't bow to what society expected of him, and therefore, earned my father's as well as my deepest respect. He shall be terribly missed."

She had learned from the vicar's wife just last year that the senior Latham had inherited his title as Duke of Stanton upon his father's death, the same way the man standing in front of her now had.

Like her, the senior Latham had detested English society and had a love for the law, very much against his own father's wishes. But Edward Latham had been fortunate, for where other men would have been disowned, his father adored his only son and upon his death passed on his title, good name, lands, and wealth to him. It seemed now Edward Latham was doing the same for his son. She fleetingly wondered if he realized how much she knew about his family's history.

The thought put her more at ease, but only for a moment.

Mr Latham gave her a brave smile. "I had no idea you knew my father so well. But I thank you, for your condolences and kind words. I shall convey your thoughts to my mother. She and my sisters have taken to the country during their period of mourning. My younger sister, Penelope, is fifteen, and was to have entered society this season. Indeed, if her being spared from such an ordeal had been caused by anything other than our father's death, I daresay she would have been practically giddy with relief."

Margaret could not help, but smile, recalling a similar incident with Jane and Uncle Charles where she begged him not to put her through the agonizing trial of entering society. She thought it disgusting, and loathed the idea of being paraded in front of eligible bachelors in the hopes of making a suitable marriage. She would have preferred chasing after frogs and butterflies instead of spending an evening with a bunch of dandies and fortune-seekers, for her inheritance was more than that of many young men in the district.

Under normal circumstances, Margaret believed she would have enjoyed meeting Phillip Latham's sister. "I can relate to your sister's feelings, having long endured society's expectations of young ladies. I too had difficulties with being presented. You mentioned another sister?"

Mr Latham relaxed at the silkiness in her voice. "Yes, two, the eldest is Susan."

"Is your eldest sister married?" she asked, a teasing tone creeping into her voice.

It was obvious that Mr Latham was becoming uncomfortable with the level of her questions. He was most likely a man who did not mix business with pleasure, not even pleasurable conversation.

"No. No, she is not. She is but seventeen."

"Perhaps instead of living by society's rules, she'd prefer to marry for love," Margaret said. "I'm sure she is as a beautiful as she is smart." Margaret spoke as if she was a woman of great age delivering words that come from wisdom through experience.

Latham was torn for a moment between his curiosity of the chit and the invasion of his privacy. The young lady truly was as peculiar as he had heard. *She spoke freely without thoughts of decorum.* He supposed this was due to be having been raised without a woman's influence. "What would lead you to think her a beauty, since you have not met her, or have you?" he asked. He studied her red hair cascading in curls down to her ivory shoulders and emerald green eyes. He found her to be taller than most of the women he had met, but she was still shorter than him. Her soft cotton dress accentuated her small breasts. The empire waist of the dress expanded further down as the loose fabric caressed her hips. She was a beauty indeed.

"Your father claimed your mother a great beauty, which stands to reason that her beauty would have been passed down to her daughters."

He frowned, and then cleared his throat—she presented a good argument. But what troubled him most was that it seemed Miss Renard spoke as if she was unaware of her own beauty. Not sure why he would think such a thing, he brought the conversation back to business, "Yes, well, I wanted to call on you immediately and make you aware of the recent changes with my father's law practice. I wanted to reaffirm your finances are still in good hands. I did not want you to worry that the services my father had been providing would come to a complete stop."

She watched him go on, but then he stopped talking, looking at her intently. A piece of paper slipping from his hand drifted to the floor. He blamed her breath taking beauty for his momentary lapse. Dover being a small town had been prone to gossip. While eccentric, she was rich and no doubt grateful she could do as she wished. Though society was not kind, for she was seen as an anomaly and other than a fortune hunter, most men shied away when she was brought up in conversation as one of Dover's beauties.

"Mr Latham, please have a seat. My maid should be here shortly with tea and biscuits."

He picked up the piece of paper he had let fall before choosing the seat opposite the large sofa. She noticed again how tall he was for he looked rather uncomfortable in the small, feminine chair.

"Thank you."

She took the sofa. Though she was tall for her sex, she seemed small and fragile, dwarfed by the ornate piece of furniture.

Mr Latham continued to gaze at her, then caught himself and looked down at the papers around him; shuffling through them. "I feel responsible for you now. For your well-being, I mean, for your estate's well-being."

Margaret smiled, trying to regain her composure. She briefly wondered which one of them would manage to do so first.

"Tell me about your younger sister. Does she prefer to play with frogs and chase butterflies?" Margaret wanted to know more about his family and welcomed the opportunity to leave off thinking about the recent murder and focus on a safer subject. She was perplexed at the unusual power he had over her to make her feel so open?

"How did you ever guess?" Latham seemed genuinely surprised and appeared to relax a little.

She smiled. Evangeline chose that moment to make her appearance with the tea and cakes.

"Ah, finally our tea has arrived," Margaret said with a playful smile. Thanking Evangeline when she began to pour the tea, she playfully shooed her away, declaring that she would pour herself. The maid gave her a curious look, curtsied and exited the room.

Sensing Latham's discomfort at discussing aspects of his personal life gave her energy while simultaneously making her feel relaxed. A thought came unbidden into her head, for, despite his momentary lack of composure, he reminded her of Jane Austen's Mr Darcy—stiff and proper.

"Regarding your younger sister, I, too, hated the thought of coming out into society. The thought of those silly girls looking for a husband, as if that is what they are meant to do in life, did nothing for my disposition. I would say both your sisters are very smart young ladies." She took a tea cup and handed it over to him. Margaret was pleased she and Jane were not the only women in the town who believed that there was more to life than seeking the bonds of matrimony, especially because society deemed it appropriate.

"Why the interest in my family?"

She gazed meditatively into her teacup, "Merely making polite conversation, sir. As a woman, I can appreciate the rules set by society. We are as smart as most men, if not smarter. Men have their private clubs, while we women have a mutual bond in spirit and intelligence." But she had apparently opened some door in his mind, for he did not let the conversation diverge easily.

"I understand women have their own places for the opportunity of bonding, and if I am correct, there is Almack's. Besides, it's expected of young ladies born to privilege to be introduced to society," he said. "It's their duty in life."

She stopped midway from taking a sip of her tea. *Had she heard him correctly?* "I daresay Almack's a joke, Sir. It's managed by a bunch of snobbish old biddies. Your comment suggests to me you believe women are born to shackles?" Margaret asked, her voice turning to ice.

"And I daresay being 'born to shackles' versus being born to high society is not a very decent comparison. To someone like you it may be shackles, but to my family it is a small payment for living in a civilized society," said Mr Latham.

Margaret stood up. "Indeed, sir, are you implying that I am uncivilized?" she asked stiffly. His aloofness after such a comment irritated her.

Mr Latham rose as well, looking a bit worried. "Of course not, I am merely stating that society sets up rules separating itself from the animal kingdom and—"

Her temper ignited by his comments; the young man stood no chance against her retort. "Oh, so now I am an animal?" She swallowed hard to control the tone of her reply.

"Please forgive me. I did not mean to offend you. I merely stated—"

"I think, sir, you should take your leave. Any future communications may be carried out via post."

"Surely you are not serious, madam. You are letting your sensibilities get the best of you." Mr Latham fought back.

"Well, now you are accusing women of being prone to emotional outbursts?" Margaret's voice carried out into the hall. She had no doubt that the servants were beginning to form a group outside the door to the drawing room, being able to hear her overwrought voice.

Mr Latham sighed, releasing the indignation that had worked its way up from his toes to his face, and before he caught himself, he blurted, "Yes! That is exactly what I am saying, madam. Women are highly emotional, and some have a propensity to give opinions freely on matters that do not concern them. Furthermore, when vexed, you all become judge, jury and executioner." He bent to gather his papers believing a quick exit was to his best advantage. He turned around once more to look at her. He barely retained his manners, resulting in a distinct hardening in his eyes.

He felt as if the room had suddenly become overheated, even the young lady's breathing had become forced and deep, no doubt, as a result from no one having spoken to her in such a manner.

"Take care, dear lady, you look about to faint. A pity I don't carry the salts with me as my father always advised me to do. Good day, madam." He started to bow, but instead ducked quickly to avoid being hit by a cup the headstrong young woman had thrown at him.

Albeit surprised; he couldn't help but laugh. Having two sisters and a mother, he was never one to retreat. But not knowing the young woman, who was now his client, a promise he made to his late father, he thought it best to do so this time. The things he'd heard about her were clearly true. She was the most infuriating woman he had ever the misfortune to meet. Opinionated, head strong and quick tempered. No wonder she wasn't married. As he closed the door, he hoped he would not come to regret his promise to his father.

He then heard her scream from behind the door, "Neanderthal!"

He chuckled, forced to admit she had fire. Though he pitied any man she married. He turned and came to a complete halt against a group of her servants who had gathered on the other side of the door. He hadn't meant to insult her, but she was making it difficult for him. Confounded girl had a way of twisting his words around. *It was a pity women weren't allowed to practice law, she would have made a great solicitor.*

The old butler who had let him in earlier, handed over his coat and hat. Mr Latham assumed an air of dignity as he took his belongings. He bid them a stiff farewell and strode rapidly out the door to his waiting barouche.

Eager to check in on her mistress, Evangeline found her in near hysterics, "Miss, what is wrong? I've never seen you so upset."

57

"That is the most insufferable man I have ever met. He had the nerve to come into my home and insult me!" Margaret hoped never to see him again but knew this was impossible. Her father and his had been the best of friends, and prior to the senior Latham's death, Margaret knew her estate was in good hands.

"I beg your pardon, miss, did he take liberties with you? I could have Munson call him out." Evangeline stood with her hands on hips.

She could not believe what Evangeline had just said. The image of old Munson—stooped over when he walked—duelling with Mr Latham, immediately produced a most restorative effect on Margaret's mood. Throwing herself onto the sofa, she wrapped her arms around her waist, and laughed until tears streamed down her face.

Chapter Four

The next morning Jane rose in greatly improved spirits, certain that her father's imminent arrival had much to do with it. The staff bustled happily about as they finalised the preparations for a festive welcome for his return.

By midday, she had completed all of her tasks. Carrying a basket of heather, she entered the dining parlour, contemplating for several seconds where to place it. Settling on the dining table, she moved back for a final look. Happy with the success of all the preparations, she headed back to the drawing room. Halfway there she heard a coach approach. Nearly jumping with excitement, she dashed to look out the front window in time to see the coach pull to a full stop at the front entrance of the house.

Jane ran toward the main doors, on the way quickly glancing at the hall's mirror for a last inspection of her appearance. She was a little pale but better than yesterday. Rushing out the door, she practically threw herself into her father's arms. Demonstrations of affection were usually restricted in society, but she and her father had never stood on formalities.

"My darling girl, I see you have missed me as much as I have you," her father said. "Let me look at you." He pulled her away gently and stared at her face. "Dearest, have you been ill? You should have sent word. I would have come right away."

"Oh, Papa, now you're here, all is well. A slight cold, but as you can see I am none the worse." Jane did not like to lie to her father, but knew that business called him away for long periods of time, and if he were to discover what went through her mind at times, he would insist on staying behind for her benefit. She took a good look at her father and noticed a glow about him.

Charles Bartholomew, Earl of Crittenden, was but five and fifty, and considered one of the most handsome men in the county with his youthful countenance and hair yet to reveal any signs of aging. All in all, he was in excellent health and form. Jane was always proud of her father and often spent time with Margaret discussing all the widowed ladies who might claim his affections. With a sigh of contentment, she and her father entered the house and walked side by side with arms around each other toward the parlour.

The parlour had always been her father's favourite place. Often it was the first place he would insist on entering and relaxing after one of his long journeys. The room, though masculine in its décor, still harboured enough feminine touches throughout to honour Jane's mother. Walls of dark cherry wood surrounded the room. A large mahogany desk—her father's favourite place to sit to either write or manage the estate business—sat by the far left corner of the room by the windows. Jane could see that it had been recently polished, and fresh flowers had been placed in its centre.

Several chairs filled out the room, including two huge ones covered in yellow fabric that sat in front of the fireplace. According to her father, this had been a favourite place of her mother's. During her pregnancy, she often came here after dinner to take short naps while he worked on estate matters.

His lordship looked around the room, his eyes finally resting on the yellow chairs. One guess and Jane knew where his thoughts had wandered. But instead of finding a sense of sadness in his eyes, she acknowledged that there was no doubt he did indeed have a special radiance about him.

One of the maids followed them in pulling a tea cart and port. Jane agreed readily to a cup while her father chose the port. She raised a brow, indicating the earliness of such a request, eliciting a laugh from her father.

With a glass in hand Lord Crittenden revealed the nature of his good mood. "It is time to celebrate. Jane, I've met someone and well, we've married." Noting the incredulous look on her face, he quickly added, "But I took great pains to keep you in mind before making my choice. I do hope you will love her as much as I do."

When she made no comment, her father began to worry. "Please do say something, dearest."

Jane desperately tried to make sense of things before she replied. She did not wish to hurt his feelings, and yet she wanted to yell or scream, which would be, of course, unacceptable. But the look on his face told her he needed assurance from her, and this was one of those situations where she could not merely say something polite and then retreat to her room. *What does one say to a parent when they have gone off and eloped? Should it not be the other way?*

Freeing a deep breath she hadn't realized she'd been holding, Jane answered, "Papa, I am merely surprised. I had no idea you were courting anyone. Please tell me about her."

In truth, she didn't want to hear any details about the new Countess of Crittenden, but she feigned interest for her father's sake. Perhaps in time she would learn to tolerate the woman. She felt a sudden shock. Was she jealous? It would not do for her father to think that.

"Come, Papa, I am most anxious to hear all about her," Jane begged, praying her voice conveyed enthusiasm and sincerity.

"Well, my dear, Amelia and I met at a ball hosted by the Duke of Stonewall. The moment I laid eyes on her, I could not tear myself away. She danced the quadrille with me, and I was smitten, absolutely smitten." He paused and then smiled.

Jane noted her father's excitement, and it sounded more like true happiness. He had always been a man of good constitution, but this was bliss. Yes, he was blissfully happy.

Her father came to her and put his hands on her shoulders as to assure her that he'd thought of her in his decision. "Jane, Amelia is very excited at the thought of having a daughter to spoil. She is widowed and has no children of her own. Although she has a young cousin she cared for after his mother died when he was still a child, leaving him to an overbearing father."

"Papa, I am nineteen and not a child anymore."

His lordship noticed his daughter's pout. Her father's countenance changed seeming to understand her disquiet. "I know, Jane." Smiling her father reached for her hands. "Please do not think I am trying to replace your mama. That can never happen. Amelia is a good woman with a wonderful heart, and she will love you if you but let her."

She took a deep breath. What could she say without hurting him? She asked, neutrally she hoped, "When shall I have the pleasure of meeting her?"

Her father searched her face for any varying emotions, as if trying to discern any hidden inflections or meanings in her words or movements. Jane could see a semblance of her mother in her own reflection staring back from her father's eyes.

"She is waiting in the carriage. She thought it best, that I shall have privacy with my daughter, while I delivered the news of our nuptials. I shall go and fetch her." Her turned to leave.

"Papa?"

"Yes, dearest?"

"This cousin of her ladyship, is he with her as well?"

"Oh no, he rode in another carriage. I think you both will get on very well. He is a loyal and trustworthy fellow with excellent manners."

They had never had a child stay with them. Her father said something about an abusive father. Well, she and her father would do their best to make him comfortable and perhaps even spoil him a bit.

"How old is he?"

"Oh, I believe he is not more than seven and twenty."

"What?" Jane cried. This was too much for her. Perhaps her father was taken in by flimflam? "Papa, I do not understand. Why would this young man attach himself to an elderly cousin?"

Her father was taken aback. "Well, I daresay I am thankful to have a few years still left in me, before I am considered elderly or dead." He teased his daughter, trying to bring her back into good humour.

"Oh, Papa, don't be foolish. You're in your prime," she said, approaching him, and then ran her fingers through his hair. "See, here," she commanded him to look at his full set of black hair, "not one strand of grey."

Her father laughed. "Please remember to be as kind to your step-mama. A woman's vanity could be hurt a lot easier." Changing the subject, he added, "When I first met Amelia, I remember her saying he was quite the charmer. I must say, she was right. I met him at the wedding. He is quite a good looking young man, a bachelor and a wealthy baronet, at that."

Jane was no longer listening. *How can her father consider having a seven and twenty-year-old grown man living with us? Why it is unacceptable—even if he is related to his new wife.*

Her father continued, "As a baronet, Sir Hugh Cameron is wealthy and quite the catch. If I were you, dear, I would snatch him up as quickly as you can. Once word gets out he is here, the mothers with single daughters will be breaking their necks, making certain their daughters have a chance to meet him in the hopes of forming an attachment."

The last thing Jane wanted, or needed, was for her father to play matchmaker. "How convenient for Sir Hugh, as there are indeed many young ladies of the town in need of a wealthy husband." Jane found comfort in her sharp reply, regretting it when she saw the pained look flit across her father's face.

She forced her mouth into a smile. "But enough of that." Quickly stepping over to him Jane took his hand in hers. "I am very happy for you. You have been alone for a long time. It was about time you wed."

Jane realized she had never seen her father so light-hearted and agile. It was as if a new man had come home, a man in love and happy in wedded bliss. A thought occurred to her that maybe she should visit Margaret for a few weeks and give the newly married couple some time alone.

Just as she opened her mouth to make this proposal, for she knew Margaret would be amenable to it, her father tightened his hold on her hands.

"My dear, we both have been alone far too long. I have faith you and Amelia will get along splendidly. Now, please stay here. We will meet you shortly. Please excuse me for a moment."

Jane noticed a skip in his walk as he left. Once her father closed the door to the parlour, she wandered over to one of the settees and sat to wait for the instrumental change about to come.

She found no solace in the ticking seconds as the clock calmly proceeded. Rising, she began to pace, finally stopping by the window in time to see her father help a woman from his carriage.

Careful not to be caught spying on them, Jane hid behind the curtain as she watched her father and his new wife come toward the house, the servants curtseying and bowing their heads in welcome. She stayed by the window until she heard their footsteps in the hall. Moving to the centre of the room, Jane clasped her hands together, to quell her fidgeting only to decide that perhaps she should sit. She hurried back to the settee, putting her left hand on the arm, only to decide she would rather stand.

At that instant, her father and the new Lady Crittenden entered the parlour. Jane straightened her shoulders, lifted her chin, and clasped her hands together once again.

Lady Amelia Bartholomew's blue eyes were sharp, but instead of an icy greeting; they were warm and bright as a summer day. She gave Jane a gaze that was steady, but not unkind, and then she smiled.

Lord Crittenden cleared his throat. "My love, this is my daughter, Jane."

Her ladyship held out her hands and Jane slowly walked from the settee to take them. "I have heard so much about you, my dear. It is with great pleasure that I finally make your acquaintance."

Jane curtsied. "I am most happy to meet you." She paused, glanced at her father, who was observing her anxiously, and smiled.

Her reservations began to slowly dissipate, when her new step-mama said, "I have a feeling we are going to be great friends. I have not had the blessing of children, but if I did have a daughter, I am sure she would have been as lovely as you and with your sweet disposition."

Overwhelmed by Amelia's kind words, Jane believed her to be most sincere. Only a remarkable person could make her father content and happy. And while Jane had enjoyed the task of being his hostess and the lady of the house for many years, she knew there were other sorts of relationships between men and women she could not fulfil. Her father was deserving of everything that was good, whatever her own feelings were. For his sake, she would try to warm to her new stepmother, who did seem to have good qualities.

The family chose to remain in the parlour for their tea, Amelia filling Jane in on her first thoughts upon meeting her father. Her father blushed, clearing his throat as the ladies laughed at his discomfort.

At the sound of the arriving coach, Amelia jumped to her feet shivering with excitement.

"Darling," said Charles, "I believe Hugh's arrived."

Her ladyship turned to Jane her face alight with joy. "Sir Hugh Cameron is my cousin. He has been knighted by the King for his bravery in the war under Wellington against Napoleon," she said with pride. "I do hope you are comfortable with the idea of his staying with us for the time being."

"Step-mama, this is your new home, and as lady of the manor and a member of this family, any of your extended family are always welcome here." There! She'd said it and meant it, as well.

Amelia hugged Jane warmly, a glistening of tears forming. "Thank you."

Jane was about to say something else when the door to the drawing room opened to Biltmore.

"I beg your pardon, my lord. Sir Hugh Cameron has arrived."

Eager to make the acquaintance of the young man, Jane moved toward the door and then stopped. She had no interest in him as a potential suitor. Her father would have to deal with the disappointments of matchmaking, for when she married it would be for love and not

70

because society dictated she must marry. In that respect, she and Margaret felt alike.

"Come...come, Cameron. Welcome to our home and pray consider this your home always and for as long as you wish to stay."

Striding in, Sir Hugh bowed and thanked his lordship.

Lord Crittenden introduced his daughter. "This is my lovely daughter, Lady Jane Bartholomew."

"Lady Jane." Sir Hugh bowed again as Jane curtsied. "It is a real pleasure to make your acquaintance. I feared you were but a figment of your father's imagination."

Jane felt a strange thrill at his deep rich baritone followed by a handsome smile. Now why would she care for his smile, Jane wondered continuing to take measure of the man. He was not as tall as her father, although taller than she. His brown hair was combed in waves and pushed to the back accentuating the one feature that had trapped Jane's attention, his eyes. They were the most astonishing different shades of green that shifted in the light.

Her father laughed. "You jest, Cameron. I told you I had a lovely daughter."

Sir Hugh Cameron, knighted by the King for his services to his country was of foul disposition. He had been ordered to find out who had been responsible for the smuggling going on between his country and France when all he craved is to be at sea. The coast of Dover was rumoured to be the place, and so here he was. Fortunately for him, his cousin had met the Earl of Crittenden, Charles Bartholomew and it was love at first sight. Finding out that his lordship was a good man and faithful servant of the crown, he could not have asked for a better husband for his dear cousin, whom he considered a second mother.

Despite his irritation with the assignment, he now saw there might be benefits. He'd found himself facing the loveliest angel his eyes have beheld. His lordship had indeed not exaggerated on his daughter's beauty. It was unfortunate indeed that he would not have time to find out more about her, for his visit here was of a business nature and he had but a brief time to accomplish his mission. As far as he was concerned, in his line of work, king and country would always come first.

Having received his orders, he had been in the middle of settling his plans when he learned from his cousin that she was marrying the Earl of Crittenden from Dover. A blessing in disguise, he thought. Dover was where he needed to be, and what better guise than that of accompanying his recently married cousin, a widow who had a little over a year ago lost her husband in the war, to her new home.

Fortunately this meant he wouldn't have time to give consequence to rich, spoiled, unattached young ladies of society.

He had seen enough of his parents' marriage to avoid the matter altogether.

Sir Hugh ambled over to where the port stood and, without invitation, poured a drink.

"Pray forgive me, Cameron," said his lordship. "I fear I am neglecting my duties as host. Please help yourself and make yourself at home. I will have Biltmore prepare your room."

Biltmore, who remained after showing Sir Hugh into the parlour, acknowledged his new orders with a bow and left.

He could see the young chit eyeing him from the bottom of his glass, her blue eyes sharpening at him, no doubt wondering if his time in the military had blunted his manners as he'd walked into her home in a commanding attitude as if he it was he who was lord of the manor.

Jane turned to see if her stepmother disapproved, but to her dismay she found her beaming at Sir Hugh. Goodness, as far as Amelia Bartholomew was concerned, Sir Hugh could do no wrong.

"My love," Amelia turned to her husband, "did you not promise a dinner as a way of introduction to your neighbours?"

"Yes, of course. Jane, would you be so kind to assist your stepmother in putting together a dinner party?"

"I would be delighted, Papa." Jane turned to her stepmother and smiled tightly. "Would you like to go over the list tonight after dinner?"

"After dinner would be wonderful," said her ladyship. Turning to her husband in absolute bliss, "I believe I should retire to our room for a quick repose. Would you accompany me?"

Jane's father looked pleased with the suggestion and was a tad too quick to respond that yes he too could do with a good rest. Jane felt a strange stab in her chest. How could her father just...? Caught in the sudden confusion of her emotions she nearly missed their departure. Just before the doors to the parlour closed, Jane heard her ladyship compliment her father on his lovely home.

"I daresay a party would be a tremendous idea, do you not agree, Lady Jane?" Sir Hugh asked. "I hear Dover is infamous for its beauties. Do make certain my cousin includes some of these ladies in her invitation."

"I shall personally see that all of the eligible ladies are invited. After all, why should it always befall young ladies to find a suitable match? One would presume that men do find themselves in situations that would call for them to secure a marriage with a large dowry, don't you agree?"

Her new stepmother's cousin blanched and turned the slightest shade of green

Good! Jane thought. *It should serve him right if I invited the Misses Smiths—both past their prime and in the matrimony market.* Jane silently chuckled. *They would eagerly entertain him in the hopes of forming an attachment.*

Sir Hugh lifted an eyebrow. "Do you disapprove of pleasing entertainment, or is it marriage you fear, my lady?"

"I fear nothing, Sir. I merely gathered, by the manner of your arrival, that you would indeed enjoy a good party. Though I believe the parties we usually have may not meet your expectations." As Sir Hugh was about to reply, Jane quickly continued. "If you will excuse me, I must talk to the cook." Without waiting for a reply or acknowledgement, Jane curtsied and glided out of the room.

Oh, how she appreciated that stunned look on his face! Most certainly he was unaccustomed to women speaking their mind.

On the way to the kitchen, Jane decided that she would have to break the news of the vicar's death to her father and stepmother later. At this moment, they were lost in the joy of being married, and who was she to kill that joy? This is the happiest she could remember seeing her father in a very long time.

Deep in thought Jane nearly collided with Barnaby, a recently hired servant, who seemed relieved at having found her.

"A letter has arrived for you, my lady," he barely finished saying as she hastily snatched the paper from his hand and turned away from the kitchen to her private room.

Sir Hugh watched in astonishment as the door shut behind the young lady. *My God, the chit was an absolute terror!* He thought one second, but then after his initial

76

shock, he found himself smiling and being damned if he had not begun to like the spitfire. She was wholly different from any other debutante he had the fortune of escaping. His smile grew as he realized life here just might be anything but dull.

Chapter Five

Relieved to have made it to the safety of her room without encountering anyone, including her new stepmother's cousin, Jane opened Margaret's letter as soon as the door shut behind her. She took a deep refreshing breath as she headed for her settee. This was her place of serenity in the often tumultuous world. She loved the calming light pink hues which covered the walls, the crisp white linens and colourful fresh lilies and daisies from her mother's garden. This was without a doubt her favourite room in the whole house. And today the sun's rays cut through the glass pane windows to make the room brighter than most days.

My dearest Jane,

I have much to tell you. Upon arriving home, I discovered I had an unexpected guest. It seems my father's solicitor, Mr Edward Latham, has passed away, and his son is now handling my affairs. At first I was very pleased to meet him, for he seemed an agreeable young man.

He then insulted not only me, but our fair sex. He had the nerve to say that Almack's Assembly Rooms were a wonderful place for women to convene in partnership. I told him Almack's was a sham, and it was managed by a group of snobbish old biddies. He also believes being presented to society is a woman's duty. Jane, I believe when Miss Austen created Darcy she had him in mind. He is not only proud, but of a stubborn constitution. The impossible man vexed me to the point of succumbing to the vapours, which I took great care not to let him know.

I then asked him to leave. He even made me break one of Mama's favourite tea cups.

Jane giggled. It did not surprise her that the highly emotional Margaret had not remained calm, especially after being insulted by a man. "Oh, my goodness," Jane cried out. It must have been awful if she did that. She read on:

I pity his sisters. Well enough of the man, I promised myself not to let him ruin my letter to you. I cannot wait until we see each other again. I hope your dear papa's arrival is all you hoped it to be. I trust Cook will be preparing his favourite dishes.

Affectionately yours, Margaret

Jane rose and moved to her writing desk. She would gladly wager a large amount of money that her letter would be of more interest to Margaret than pondering about the son of the late Edward Latham. As she took pen to paper, she made a mental note to make sure to include the family of Latham's father in her prayers before going to bed tonight.

My dearest Margaret,

I cannot begin to tell you how excited I was for Papa to come home. I had revelled in the pleasure of having him all to myself. However, you could never imagine what news he brought.

Almost immediately, he informed me he had married! I must admit I was highly upset, but you would have been proud of me for hiding my feelings. Upon meeting his wife Amelia, I am glad to report that I could see they were besotted with each other, and though I would like to have believed I was all Papa needed, I will be the first to admit marriage may do him much good.

My step-mama seems to possess a kind disposition. I not only see my father's deep feelings for her, but feel she indeed returns them. I find myself exceedingly content for him. He finally has someone to love him, as a daughter cannot. Their wedded bliss engrossed my attention, so it was rather upsetting when in stormed my step-mama's obnoxious cousin. Can you imagine he is *seven and twenty and has attached himself to her as a child would to his mother?*

He drinks and mocks me at every opportunity and to think Papa has invited him to stay with us for as long as he chooses! Oh, Margaret, how I do wish you were here. Papa is wishing to plan a ball to introduce his new bride. I have agreed to help, so please be on the watch for the invitation. Yours will be the first to leave here, and I expect the first to return with a reply. I must rest for now; I seem to be developing a headache.

As always, all my love, Jane

Margaret was so engrossed with Jane's letter that she did not realize Evangeline had entered the drawing room until the girl announced the unexpected visit of the vicar's widow, Mrs Bostwick.

Rising from the sofa Margaret carefully hid the letter underneath a stack of books and wondered that whatever brought Mrs Bostwick out to see her must be of great importance. Straightening her dress to be sure she was presentable, Margaret refocused her thoughts from the excitement over Lord Crittenden's marriage to the sombre aspects of the vicar's murder investigation. Perhaps Mrs Bostwick had brought information that would aid them in the search.

The door to the reading room opened. Mrs Bostwick, in her mourning clothes, entered very slowly as though she was unsure she was welcome, however, when she saw Margaret her steps quickened, the tension sliding from her frame. Taking Margaret's hands in hers she expressed her relief, "My dear Meggie, thank you for receiving me on such short notice."

"Mrs Bostwick, please have a seat. I had hoped to visit with you again and see if there was anything you needed," Margaret said. Walking over to the seat opposite Mrs Bostwick, Margaret straightened her skirt prior to seating. A pang of guilt coursed through her. It was obvious that the older woman was in pain over the loss of her husband, while she and Jane were busy gossiping about the new Lady Crittenden and her cousin.

"Thank you so much," Mrs Bostwick murmured, "but I do not require anything at the moment. You are very kind. Why just the other day I was commenting to the vicar what sweet children you and Lady Jane were." She hiccupped as if the memory of her husband threatened to overwhelm her. "Please do not worry on my part, I am, or should I say, I will be fine. I have even managed to straighten out the financial affairs with the help of our solicitor, Mr Phillip Latham."

Margaret was surprised to hear Latham's name again. Fresh memories of his insults brought colour to her cheeks. "Mr Latham, you say?"

"Yes. It seems my husband solicited his services just days before he was killed. Almost as if he had known something horrible was to befall him."

Willing her expression to remain blank, Margaret was successful in not showing her excitement, and continued looking steadily at Mrs Bostwick. *Perhaps he was involved in something that he knew could kill him.*

Margaret took Mrs Bostwick's hands into hers and giving them a comforting squeeze, asked, "Did Mr Latham discuss with you the reason your husband required his services?"

"He could not say much because of client confidentiality, but he did say my husband wanted to invest some money," Mrs Bostwick admitted, wringing her hands.

Giving her a moment to settle down, Margaret waited several seconds before asking another question. "Did Mr Latham say how much?"

"No, only that it was a large sum."

"Could your husband have acquired the money as a loan or from a relative?"

"Well, no. You see, we barely made ends meet. How he came to this money I do not know. I'm afraid it was the reason he was killed." She began to cry softly.

Margaret moved closer, taking the overwrought Mrs Bostwick into her arms. The fine fabric of her mourning dress slid against Margaret's hands. *Silk?* She had no idea that silk was being made available since the trading between France and England had been at a halt.

"Do not worry, Mrs Bostwick," Margaret soothed, "I promise you whoever murdered your husband will atone for his crime."

Mrs Bostwick swallowed, calmer now. Shortly after having a good cup of tea, she took her leave.

Margaret pondered over the recent information. *Where or from whom had the vicar acquired a large sum of money? And perhaps even more importantly—how is Mr Latham involved?* She huffed out a breath of consternation; Mr Latham could definitely pose a problem.

With a nod Margaret decided that Latham was now her sworn enemy, and worthy opponent. The Neanderthal was a stickler for society and its rules; making it difficult to ascertain any information from him, hence hindering the investigation. That meant she and Jane had but one option—to acquire the information in another manner. She hoped Jane would agree that they had no other choice but to break into Mr Latham's office.

Chapter Six

"Ashes to ashes, dust to dust," began the Vicar of Farthingloe as the late Vicar of Dover was laid to rest. Margaret and Jane took the opportunity to survey their surroundings for clues or guilty suspects. Despite the overcast skies, and a lingering chill in the air, most of Dover's occupants were in attendance.

It was not the weather or the circumstances that turned Margaret's mood. Although she was standing close to Jane, her uncle and his new wife, she was disconcerted to have Mr Latham at her left.

To Jane's right, Margaret noted a solemn Sir Hugh. He seemed a pleasant and reputable fellow, though quite the opposite of Jane's description of him. Jane had developed an intense dislike of him and while both felt annoyed at the men's presence they each had a right to attend: Mr Latham as the vicar's attorney and Sir Hugh as a guest of the Bartholomews. However, it did not give them the right to stand so close.

Prior to the start of the funeral start Margaret and Jane noted his lordship's introduction of Mr Latham and Sir Hugh. And while the men acted as though it was their first meeting, both girls had the feeling that the men

87

were previously acquainted with each other. Whether this was a pertinent observation or not was yet to be seen. The most logical reason would be that perhaps Sir Hugh had sought out legal advice from Mr Latham. It struck Margaret this to be too much of a coincidence for it to be otherwise.

Margaret's thoughts wandered to earlier that morning when she had been properly introduced to Jane's new stepmother on their way to the church. Jane had been right; she found Lady Crittenden to be quite amiable and extremely in love with her husband.

"I must confess our meeting, while under sad circumstances, brings me the pleasure of knowing that his lordship, who I've considered as a dear uncle, is the happiest I've ever seen him. I, too, find comfort in knowing that as I may not be around as often as Jane wishes, she now has the guidance of another woman."

Amelia Bartholomew's eyes watered at Margaret's words, "Thank you," her ladyship agreed as she extended a hand to Margaret. "While this is truly a sad occasion, I am pleased to have made your acquaintance and hope to see more of you."

Margaret feeling Jane's fidgeting, returned her wandering mind to the sombre surroundings and glanced at her friend, but she seemed fine. Refocusing her attention to the burial, Margaret felt an elbow stab her in the ribs. Exasperated with her friend's antics, and at a funeral no less, she turned slightly toward Jane to inquire what was amiss. Jane inclined her head imperceptibly to the far right. Margaret's eyes followed Jane's signal—a figure dressed in dark clothes, further away from the gathering crowd, moved cautiously in and out of view.

Excited at the prospect for clues, Margaret's first instinct was to see if anyone else had seen the figure, but found all with the exception of Sir Hugh focused on the Vicar of Farthingloe's words.

Margaret felt a flash of anger course from the tip of her toes all the way to the top of her head. How was it that she, Jane, and even the flippant Sir Hugh could notice something amiss and Mr Latham did not? But, then wondered why she should care.

Once the coffin was lowered into the ground, Margaret and Jane checked to see if the mysterious figure remained hidden or had it gone. It was gone. They shared a glance—this was their signal in their investigation.

As the crowd began to disperse, they headed to the widow's cottage. It was time to find some answers and searching the vicar's study once again was on their agenda. Heads held high the girls walked slowly towards the Bartholomew's carriage.

At the widow's cottage several of the village ladies were in attendance, bustling about the sitting room, fetching cups of tea and making sure smelling salts were at hand. Some of the men shuffled their feet, clearly uncomfortable and bored, while others talked as casually as if they were attending a normal social occasion.

Margaret nodded to Jane, putting her hand to her throat. Another signal they had agreed upon the night before.

Each found it easy to slip away from the group, and once in the hall, they moved quickly and silently down the hall to the vicar's study.

Jane closed the door softly behind them.

"Remember, should we be discovered, you felt faint and we came in here for you to rest," Margaret said, as usual taking the lead.

"Agreed," Jane nodded but made a face.

As Margaret well knew, Jane detested always playing the part of the weak female, hiding a smile, Margaret

90

moved to the vicar's desk, leaving Jane to look through the bookcases.

"Do we know what we're looking for?"

"No, we do not. I suppose anything that looks out of the ordinary," replied Margaret pragmatically.

Involved in their search, neither one of them heard the click of the door's lock.

"Well, well," Sir Hugh said. "What have we here? It appears the woodworm has gotten out of hand in the study." He strolled in, followed by Mr Latham. Both men's expressions were disapproving as they eyed the two young women, knowing well the implications of their presence in the library.

"Do tell, ladies, what are you doing here?" Latham asked in a cold voice, much like one of the church deacons whose nose had resembled a hawk's beak, frightening them as children.

"I was feeling a little faint," both said in unison. *Oh, dear!*

The men looked at them dubiously, not believing a single word.

"Lady Jane, you do not seem the sort to fall prey to the vapours," said an unconvinced Sir Hugh.

91

"That reveals how little you know of me," Jane said defiantly. "What Margaret meant to say was that since I was feeling unwell, we decided to come in here, away from the crowd for a chance to recover."

The men looked at each other and then Sir Hugh strode up to Jane. "Why do I find that hard to believe?" he asked, looking her right in the eyes.

"Are you calling me a liar, Sir Hugh?" Jane retorted, her tone an octave higher. One thing she was not, and that was a liar. Yet here she was doing just that.

"Do not play games with me," Sir Hugh said. "I'll tell you why you're in the late vicar's library. You hope to find a clue to his murder. Am I right?"

Jane opened her mouth, only to shut it quickly when she was promptly cut off before the words forming on her tongue had a chance to leave her mouth.

"So proud as to believe you can do better than the magistrate's office in tracking down the vicar's killer? You both need to stay out of this and stick to needlepoint."

Temper rising, Jane looked up at Sir Hugh, gaze unwavering. "We are *not* unfamiliar with investigations, sir. In fact, on several occasions we have assisted the magistrate's office. We've provided a fresh perspective on solving crimes."

Sir Hugh studied her face, no hint of amusement in his expression. "What types of investigations?"

When she didn't answer, he pressed his lips together and frowned. "*This* is not a case of missing animals, like my cousin told me about."

"You may wish to be very careful what you insinuate, old chap," Latham warned. "I recall a similar conversation with her friend the other day that ended rather badly. Words tend to take a different meaning around here."

Margaret who had remained silent could no longer. "It ended 'rather badly', Mr Latham, because you are a very rude social stiff. A stiff, mind you, that believes women should be kept in shackles. That women—" Margaret drew in another breath, "—have no right to think, let alone decide what is best for them, and therefore, should abide by the dim-witted rules set by society." She pointed a finger at him. "A society, mind you, ruled by men."

Latham took a step back, looking at Sir Hugh, for assistance. When he saw none coming, he merely replied, "Society is ruled by men, Miss Renard, because

93

someone has to remain sensible in order to protect it. Women gallivanting about without proper escort and meddling in business that does not concern them is viewed as unbefitting and a discord in the normal happenings of our culture, and not to mention a safety hazard."

Margaret's cheeks took on a red hue. *How dare he accuse them of being the bringers of society's downfall?* "I am terribly sorry if we are putting a dent in your vision of society. If you are going to accuse my sex of such an idea, I suggest you first look at our monarchy. Prinny, the Prince Regent, and his escapades have made a laughing stock of our monarchy and society."

Sir Hugh made an effort to come to Mr Latham's rescue, when Jane intervened. "I agree with Margaret and I'll have you know that we already visited the scene of the crime and discovered that whoever killed the vicar knew him."

"Really, how did you come to that conclusion?" asked Sir Hugh.

"Simple. Margaret traced where the body had fallen with seamstress chalk, which I thought was brilliant. Anyway, we could determine by the way he fell that he had turned his back on the killer to close the bible. And his notes were left out," Jane ended with a curt nod.

Sir Hugh remained silent.

Seeing her chance to inquire about an idea that had been plaguing her since the funeral Margaret queried, "Sir Hugh, there is a matter which has interested me of late. Did you know Mr Latham prior to this morning?"

"I have but recently become acquainted with Mr Latham, Miss Renard," he answered stiffly. "Why do you ask?"

"Really, and yet here are the two of you together," said Margaret ignoring his question.

"Are you accusing me of being insincere?" Sir Hugh began to turn red around the collar.

"Not any more than you are accusing us. I will wager my entire fortune," Margaret added with a smile, "that you and Mr Latham have known each other longer than just having met this morning."

Margaret continued, "I will even include Cheetham Manor in the deal." She watched them closely, trying to capture the same expression they had earlier when her uncle had made the introductions. Seeing she was not going to get an answer to her question, she turned away toward the windows. The sky had maintained its grey

95

hue with the wind picking up, as if something malicious and wicked headed their way.

Mr Latham, unfazed by Margaret's words, followed her to the window. "Miss Renard, do you take us for fools?" he asked in a whisper.

"I can hardly pass judgment on your character for we've only recently met," Margaret whispered back. Realizing there was no need for whispers, she said out loud, "However, you appear suddenly, and offer little input or explanation about your reasons or motives for being here. Therefore I find it a bit odd you should question my presence when I am trying to find some answers and you leave nothing but questions in your wake."

Left alone with Lady Jane, Sir Hugh turned to her, "So it was more than a spell of indisposition that drew you and your friend to the library?"

"Sir Hugh, you must remember we are used to a quiet life in our little village, and the strange and wicked happenings of late have been upsetting. More to the point, why would it interest you? After all, are you not merely a visitor in Dover?" Jane asked.

He ignored her question. He had no intention of justifying himself to this *little girl*. His acquaintances were of no one's business but his and his superiors. "You are correct, I am merely a visitor. However, if there is a murderer afoot, and in my dear cousin's newly home town, then it is my duty to make sure she and her family remain safe."

"We really do appreciate your concern, but Margaret and I can quite handle what is to come."

Sir Hugh thought her stubborn, but to insist that she and her friend were going to get involved in a murder was ridiculous and stupid indeed. They could only end up getting hurt, or worse, killed.

"I guess there is no way of talking you and your friend out of this crazy notion, but then understand this, both of you: Latham and I shall be watching you whether you like or not." With that said, he turned and walked away.

Mr Latham sighed in frustration. Margaret could sense his gaze upon as if he read her inner thoughts.

"So you are telling me that you and Lady Jane will continue with this ridiculous notion of trying to solve a crime that is best left in the hands of the magistrate?"

"What you really mean is in the hands of a man!" Margaret accused. At this moment she detested him even more than she had thought possible and found it hard to look at him. She turned to where Sir Hugh and Jane stood. She could tell by the way Sir Hugh continued to shake his head at her, often raising a pointed finger that Jane hadn't given up her debate either. Margaret could tell by the way Sir Hugh shook his head and raised a pointed finger at Jane that she hadn't given up her debate either.

"Well now that you do bring it up, it is a man's job. I know the magistrate, and he is quite capable of the investigation."

Margaret was about to reply to his silly notions about what constitutes a man's job when Sir Hugh was upon them.

"Come, Latham. I believe we have overstayed our welcome. We also have a murderer to catch."

"We do?"

Sir Hugh ignored his question, "Miss Renard, it was a pleasure to meet you. We shall see each other again and very soon."

On their way out, Latham led the way with Sir Hugh closely following. But at the door he turned to the girls once more, "I caution you ladies to be careful. You have no idea with whom you are dealing. A person who commits one murder will surely find it easy to commit another." Bowing, he left them to ponder what he said.

"The nerve of that man," cried Margaret. *What did he mean by seeing each other very soon? Did he mean to say they were now investigating the murder? Just what they needed!*

"I believe it is called the dramatics." Jane huffed

"Well, whatever it's called," Margaret began pacing the room, "we need to continue with our search. The hunt has now turned into a contest of wills. We must now not only discover who killed the vicar, but do it before they do and, in turn, prove to them that we are as capable as any man in finding a murderer. Needlepoint, ha!"

"Quite correct," said Jane, looking around the room.

"Jane, what were you and Sir Hugh talking about?"

"Oh, it was really nothing," Jane answered picking up a book and flipping through the pages. "I asked him why he was suddenly interested in the vicar's murder, when he was merely a visitor, but he ignored the question."

"Really?" Margaret thought about her reply for several seconds, and then re-joined Jane in their search of the room.

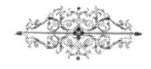

"I don't believe they heeded your warning, Cameron," declared Latham once they'd securely shut the library door.

"I'm afraid you are correct. The ladies are determined to place themselves where it does not concern them and perhaps ruin the whole operation."

"Perhaps we should discuss this with his lordship," Latham added as he led the way back to join the rest of the Bartholomew party.

Sir Hugh knew from the beginning that Lady Jane was going to be a problem in more ways than one, but he never suspected Miss Renard's perceptiveness. Suddenly he had a very bad feeling about the whole thing—the war front was looking rather pleasant right about now.

"Oh, well," Margaret said jumping down ungracefully from one of the chairs she had used to reach some of the higher books. "This has been a waste of time. Come let us return to the others before our absence is noticed." She picked up Jane's reticule from where it had been left by the door. "Goodness, what have you in your bag? I can literally use this as a weapon."

Looking through the lower shelves, her friend raised her head and grinned. "That's the point. I, uh, appropriated a small statue of Venus from Papa's desk. Ever since the vicar's death I've been feeling a little uneasy and thought perhaps I could use it as an inconspicuous weapon."

Margaret laughed, handing Jane the bag. "What would I ever do without you?"

Hooking their arms together, they turned to leave the study. A strong gust of wind slammed the window open, startling the girls. Papers from the desk scattered, flying around the room.

Margaret ran to close the window as Jane chased the papers, stacking them back on the desk. Noticing a sheet of paper had fallen underneath the table, Jane knelt down and began to crawl toward it. Stretching to reach the paper, she noticed an envelope lodged between two pieces of wood.

"Margaret!" she cried. "I've found something." She felt for the envelope and scrambled back from under the desk.

Margaret ran to her friend and craned over her shoulder, watching eagerly as Jane opened the envelope. Inside was a brass key with a fleur-de-lis motif. "Look at the design," Margaret whispered.

"I see it. A fleur-de-lis," Jane said.

Margaret stamped her foot, Had Jane gone daft? "It might be a clue."

"It *is* a clue, otherwise why would it be hidden?"

Realising they were running out of time, the girls acted quickly as they tried the key on the desk drawers and the one door in the room but found no match.

"Jane, we really must get back," Margaret called out, stepping swiftly toward the door.

"I agree. Let's go." Jane placed the key in her reticule.

"There has to be something that we're missing. Something that will tell us more about why the vicar was murdered," Margaret whispered in frustration.

"Agreed, and I have a feeling the key is a clue. Once we find the lock, we'll find answers. At least we've eliminated his study, for now."

Margaret was the first to see Jane's father. She could tell that he had been anxiously looking for them, for as soon as he saw them he waved at them. He took his wife's hand and, excusing himself from the village butcher, pulled her with him to where Margaret and Jane were standing.

"There you are," he said. "We're ready to leave. Sir Hugh and Mr Latham are waiting outside for us."

Both girls agreed they too were ready to leave, though Margaret had private reservations. This seemed such a good opportunity to search the premises. But then again, perhaps with so many people present, this was not the time. Besides, to stay behind would seem rude, and she might find herself walking home under heavy, wet, grey skies. The air suddenly had an ominous stillness, as if a storm might be brewing.

Chapter Seven

Outside, the girls walked behind his lordship and Lady Crittenden. Mr Latham and Sir Hugh followed close behind them. Both seemingly tense and alert.

Suddenly a loud bang shattered the quiet. Margaret at first assumed a storm had begun. Instead she found herself caught in a different storm, the kind that happens very quickly and brings death to those in its path.

The frightened neighing of horses echoed around her just as the ground began to vibrate. Margaret felt herself being pulled back and down as two immense horses rushed past them. A heavy weight landed on top of her. Struggling against the unfamiliar presence, she turned her head and to her shock, discovered Mr Latham had thrown himself on top of her. Before she could react, Mr Latham was on his feet, pulling her up toward him. Without so much as a "by your leave" he took her face in his hands and looked her over to make sure she was unharmed. At that moment, she felt a sense of tenderness between them—his concern for her melding with her own surprise in the way he had thought of her safety first over his own.

A sudden awareness that they were not alone struck Margaret, as it apparently did Mr Latham. She noticed him tensing. "Oh my," she murmured catching her breath.

"Are you hurt?" Despite his attentions, his voice was stern.

"N-no, I am fine. What happened?" To her consternation, her voice was shaky and, though she dared to ask, there was no doubt in her mind that what had just happened was no accident. Someone wanted to either seriously hurt or kill them.

"I believe something startled the horses into charging."

"Jane?" Margaret whispered. Remembering the rest of their group she and Latham set out to find them.

In the aftermath of the accident there were screams and people rushing about. Men were trying to calm the horses, as others tried to help those that had fallen or were pushed out of the way, mostly women.

Among the chaos, Latham found Sir Hugh's semi-unconscious body. Sir Hugh had used his body to shelter Lady Jane from serious harm.

As Latham assisted him up, Sir Hugh began to recover, but remembering Lady Jane, Sir Hugh returned to his

105

knees as he pulled her up from the ground. With a pale face and laboured breathing, he asked if she was well.

"Yes," Jane said, trembling in shock. "I ... thank you," she managed to add. Realizing the seriousness of the situation, she immediately turned to look for Margaret. Untold relief swept through her as Margaret and Mr Latham stood close by unharmed.

For once she was grateful for both men's presence. If it hadn't been for Sir Hugh holding her up, she would probably have crumpled to the ground, as one of those weak-minded females who often used such tactics to their advantage as a way to attract a man.

"Jane, are you well?" Margaret asked walking to stand by her friend.

Jane smiled weakly, "Yes. If it hadn't been for Sir Hugh, I—"

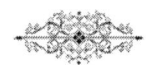

"Amelia!" the pained cry of Jane's father cut through the commotion causing Jane's heart to skip several beats in fear. She turned to see her father about to lift his wife's inert body. She and the others raced to him, their own shakiness gone. Latham reached him first and gently pulled him away from her ladyship to give Dr

Harrison, who had heard his lordship's cry, a chance to examine her.

"It is my fault. Confounded it! I wasn't quick enough," railed his lordship.

Heedless of her black dress covered in mud, Jane put her arms around him. "Papa, I know she will be fine. You'll see." She wanted to cry at the unfairness but knew she had to be strong for him. Her father had finally found a smidgeon of happiness, and to lose it all again, she feared, would be the end of him.

Fortunately for the Bartholomews, one of the village doctors had been in attendance at the funeral, so he was summoned immediately.

The doctor first checked for a pulse; Jane sighed when he confirmed that he had found one. As the little group stood in tense silence, he carefully continued with his examination of her ladyship's head. Withdrawing his hand covered in blood, he looked up at Lord Crittenden, who grew paler at the sight, probably fearing the worst.

"She is alive, but has suffered a severe cut when her head hit a rock. We must take her inside and tend to it," he said. The doctor began to lift her ladyship, when his lordship intervened.

107

"Since I couldn't protect her, I'll be damned if anyone is going to carry her but me."

The doctor looked at him intently. "Very well," he said, as he gently handed the Countess over to his lordship. "I expect she will make a full recovery, my lord."

"Oh, please Papa, you mustn't blame yourself. You did all you could." Jane hurried alongside her father, helping to clear curious people out of the way.

Focused and getting through the crowd, Jane barely registered that Sir Hugh had caught up with them and had taken a place opposite her at her father's side until he spoke. "Charles, please do not blame yourself! I took the liberty of examining the scene, and if you had not pulled my cousin out of the way, the results would indeed have been far worse, perhaps deadly. She was directly in the line of the frightened horses. Sir, I owe you for saving my cousin's life. She's the closest thing I have to a mother." Sir Hugh laid his hand on his lordship's shoulder. At this, his lordship's pained face relaxed a little.

Jane took note of the interchange, grateful to Sir Hugh for providing the words of comfort her father desperately needed. She then did the unthinkable. She locked eyes with Sir Hugh and gave him a silent thank you.

Inside the vicarage, her ladyship was afforded a makeshift hospital room opposite the late vicar's study. As his lordship was still distraught, the doctor recommended he remain outside while he cleaned and dressed her ladyship's wound.

The girls assisted the doctor, and once the wound was cleaned and bandaged, they moved to a corner of the room to allow the doctor to perform a final examination.

"Oh, Margaret, what if she were to die?" Jane let the tears fall freely now that they were in private.

"Don't say such things," Margaret gasped. "Besides, you heard the doctor—she is expected to recover fully."

Jane smiled through her tears. "It's that I'm worried about Papa. As strong as he is, I fear he couldn't handle another loss."

"He's not the only one. In the short time you've known her you've come to care for her, haven't you?"

Jane could not dispute the question. Margaret was right. In the short time, she'd come to know her stepmother she had grown to care for her deeply and was not ready to lose the woman she now thought of as the mother denied her by fate. Life, though good, had become routine and perhaps a little dull before Amelia Bartholomew had come into their lives.

"I have," declared Jane, "and I must admit I have been somewhat envious of her at times, but she has been so very giving and loving to us both. Since she has been here, the loneliness Papa and I shared no longer lingers at the manor."

"That's wonderful, Jane. I'm very happy for you and uncle." Margaret hugged her friend. "We must pray for her swift recovery. And you'll see she will be up and about in no time."

"You're right. She's now a Bartholomew and will pull through," declared Jane, hugging her friend.

Jane pulled away abruptly. Goodness! She had forgotten about Sir Hugh. He, no doubt, would be very upset at the thought of losing his cousin. She'd heard him tell her father that Amelia was the closest thing he'd had to a mother. "Will you stay here and watch over them? I shall be back shortly." Gathering her skirts, she turned to leave.

"Of course," Margaret said, looking at her friend with concern.

"It is all right, Margaret. There is someone I must find. Please excuse me."

Margaret nodded with a supportive smile as her friend rushed off.

Outside, cool drizzle had begun to fall and with it the temperature, making Jane wish she had worn her green pelisse instead of the wrap she had chosen. She quickened her steps toward the chapel. With one look at the skies, she could tell the storm still loomed ahead. It was as if the very heavens were commenting on the day's event.

Before entering the chapel, Jane had the distinct sense of being watched. Stopping, she looked around, finally settling on the wooded area on the right side of the chapel. Listening with intent, she heard nothing, not even the creatures of the woods. Quickening her steps, she moved to the door, stopping one last time just before entering. This time instead of the quiet she was rewarded with the sounds of bird song and crickets. If someone had indeed been hiding in the woods, they were now gone.

A chill ran through her. This was not the first time she'd had a feeling she was being watched. Back then she had set it aside as part of her imagination, but now there was no doubt, she was certain that the surveillance was indeed connected to the vicar's death.

She needed to tell someone, but first she needed to find Sir Hugh.

Jane found him in the smallest of the chapels within the church. And even though the evidence of the vicar's murder had been swept away along with the chalk marking Margaret had made Jane could still envision the bloody body lying by the altar. Her first instinct was to run, to forget all about the investigation, but too much had happened. No. To run now would give the killer pleasure. Worse it would prove to Sir Hugh and Mr Latham that she and Margaret couldn't deal with a situation where only men dared to tread and that was not acceptable.

And while Sir Hugh could often seem self-absorbed, the man deserved compassion and consolation. He had come close to losing the only person he thought of as his mother. A situation Jane could well understand. She thought of pity as well, but it was quickly discarded. Sir Hugh was not a man who would have cared for, let alone tolerated, any kind of pity. His male ego would simply not allow it.

Sir Hugh sat in back of the first pew facing the altar, in prayer.

Odd, I would never have thought him the kind of man to pray—one who believed in a greater power, Jane thought, walking slowly and quietly down the aisle. As she took a seat next to him, Sir Hugh's head remained bent in prayer. Jane didn't want to disturb him, yet she wanted him to know she was there should he wish to talk. She bowed her head as well and prayed for her stepmother. She was young and had a second chance with a man she adored and a full-grown daughter to worry about. Jane then prayed for her father who would be totally devastated to have found a second chance at love only to have lost it so soon. And finally for Sir Hugh, who loved Amelia as a mother.

"Thank you," he said in a sincere yet solemn voice which echoed throughout the church carrying with it a sense of pain.

Jane lifted her head, reaching over to take his hands in hers and quickly releasing them when shyness overcame her. He had been touched that she was here with him. She smiled. "Please, you don't need to thank me for being here for my stepmother." *And for you,* she wanted to add realizing that this was only the second time she had smiled at him since meeting. And to think it took her stepmother's brush with death for it to happen.

"I know we have had a difficult start," he said, "but it pleases me that my cousin has won a place in your heart."

Taken a little aback by his declaration Jane felt herself flush. It was the first time she had ever heard him say something sensible and personal. Her stepmother had indeed won a place in their hearts, including Margaret's. At first Jane had convinced herself it was just for her father's sake, but now it was clear that it was also for her own happiness. She'd had no idea how much she was in need of a mother, even if she was all grown up. Jane made a promise to make it up to her step-mother as soon as she was well again.

"I must admit I have come to think highly of her. And I can never remember my father being this happy." The thought of her father and the happiness he had found with his new wife made Jane's insides feel warm and safe—a smile playing sweetly on her face. Perhaps this is how it would have felt had her mother lived. In that moment Jane felt the sudden urge to share part of her past with Sir Hugh, though she was not entirely sure why.

His hands were warm as they covered hers. "Thank you for loving her and for being here. But, should you be here alone with me?"

A blush coloured her cheeks as Jane turned to the altar. "Nonsense, we're family," she said shyly, turning back to him.

Sir Hugh was about to say something else when he heard footsteps hurrying toward them, and reluctantly let go of her hands.

Margaret rushed into the chapel. "I'm glad I found you both. I've come—" she cried out, abruptly stopping, "—Pray, forgive me…" A look of indecision played across her features.

Jane shifted her body away from Sir Hugh. "It's all right Margaret."

"Aunt has recovered, but Uncle is still beside himself and has been asking for you both."

Sir Hugh and Jane stood as one at the good news. And in what she could only describe as a temporary lapse of propriety, Jane took hold of Sir Hugh in a hug.

"Oh, my…" Jane stammered and dropped her arms. She could feel the colour and heat rising in her face and found it matched Sir Hugh's. Quickly looking away, she turned to her friend instead. "We should return to them at once."

Sir Hugh led the ladies from the chapel, glancing once in a while at the nearby woods.

The three returned to the makeshift sickroom to find his lordship and his wife in private conversation. Passing by Mr Latham without any greeting Jane ran to her stepmother's bedside, and planted a kiss on her forehead.

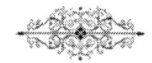

"I'm sure of what I saw," Latham said grimly a moment after he ushered Sir Hugh to the side.

"I am too," Sir Hugh answered. "It was the same figure that was watching us during the vicar's funeral. There is definitely something going on, and I'm convinced it's connected with the vicar's murder." With his cousin and her family in the line of fire, the mission had now become personal.

Latham tensed, "What figure? Care to explain?"

Sir Hugh hadn't been certain until this moment that Latham had missed the figure lurking at the vicar's funeral. A figure he was sure had startled the horses into a stampede as he tried to escape notice, nearly killing them all in the process. Sir Hugh braced himself. He hadn't survived countless of wars and battles just believing in the simplest of reasons for someone's actions. His hunches had never abandoned him, and this one was telling him the stampede was no accident.

It was time to approach the situation from another point of view.

"Let's say I'm not a mere captain in the King's army," he started, looking at Latham very intently, "and therefore cannot declare myself unemployed at the moment. I must admit I am in need of your help."

"I accept your invitation to join in on your investigation," Latham said.

"Just like that?" Sir Hugh asked, eyebrows rising in surprise.

"While I have no knowledge of having met someone in your, uh, unique position, I have heard of men working for the Crown, sworn to duty on behalf of England to protect her from her enemies." Latham smirked. "And that you are my friend, although the man who stands before me is a different man than I had known at school. I'm still trying to puzzle out how you managed to pass the classes with the highest grades when you hated to study."

Sir Hugh smiled mischievously. "I must admit, I miss those days. It was the only good thing my father ever did for me. We did not have a lot of money, but he insisted his sons would have the best education money could buy."

"I too miss them. Life was much simpler those days," declared Latham. "I promised my father that I would look out for Miss Renard. As much as I have come to detest such a promise, if there is foul play, then I must do whatever it takes to make certain she remains safe."

Sir Hugh was not a fool. There was something more in Mr Latham's promise to keep the red-headed beauty safe. Though truth be told, Latham would rather die than admit any such feelings or entertain such thoughts. From the corner of his eye Sir Hugh spied Margaret watching them.

Yes, Latham's assistance in solving the mystery surrounding the Bartholomews would be most welcome, especially since Amelia was now an integral member of the family. If there was danger, he would do his utmost to protect his cousin and her new family.

"Now that we are in accord, I need you to do an errand for me. If we are to work together, then I need you to report this to my superiors," said Sir Hugh. With a covert glance he noted Margaret leaving her perch and returning to the others and wondered how much she had heard.

Chapter Eight

Within a short time, life at the manor settled once again into a quiet routine, though the Countess' injury was still on everyone's mind. Lady Crittenden had proven to be a good patient, never complaining or demanding. Not that she had anything to complain about aside from her husband's hovering. The moment they had arrived back at Wellington Manor his lordship had insisted on carrying her up to their rooms where he immediately ordered one of the maids to tend to her every need. A needless request, thought her ladyship, since her husband stayed by her bedside to make sure she had everything she needed.

With her ladyship's care well in hand, Margaret found herself and Jane with more free time than they had originally calculated.

Mr Latham, who had left the village the morning after the accident, still remained gone. As well as Sir Hugh, who had also vanished without a word and has yet to return.

Their sudden and mysterious departures left the girls to wonder how deeply the two men were involved with the investigation. Margaret filled Jane in on the mysterious conversation the men held, and Jane mentioned to Margaret being watched on the way to the chapel when she had gone to seek Sir Hugh.

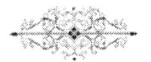

Several days later, after having brought his wife her breakfast, his lordship settled into his usual place beside her, content that she was on the mend.

Jane had come by to check on her stepmother and seeing her father had taken care of everything, left them alone, setting out in search of Margaret for a quick walk around the gardens.

She found Margaret reading in the library and without waste of time suggested they take a walk. She wanted to discuss the accident with Margaret without interference. Her friend readily agreed. It seemed to Jane that the book she had been reading offered her friend little entertainment, so the suggestion of a walk was as readily received.

"Why would someone be lurking near the vicarage?" Jane asked once she knew they were a safe distance from the house. She and Margaret walked side by side, arms interlocked.

"I don't quite understand it either. Everyone knew it was the day of the vicar's funeral. The figure was near Uncle's horses where Wilson was tending them."

"I spoke with Wilson," Jane said, "and he neither heard nor saw anyone suspicious on the grounds the day of the funeral."

"It is clear their intentions were to scare the horses into charging at us," Margaret said, unlocking her arm from Jane's. She motioned to a nearby bench that backed several white and pink rose bushes—their lovely petals falling gently as they bid farewell to the summer air. Taking a seat Margaret scooted over, leaving room for Jane to join her. "The real question then becomes who was their target?"

Jane nodded; she too wondered who their intended target was. She had to face the fact they did live in an ever-changing world where murder and crime occurred even in the safest area of the English countryside. What are decent people to do? "I fear you're might be right. Someone murdered the vicar in the church, which seems extremely wicked to me. I don't see why attempting to kill another person would give them any qualms."

"Glad you agree. Unfortunately, it does bring us to a dilemma," Margaret said. Rising from her seat, she began to pace.

"Which is?" Jane asked, watching as her friend stopped rather dramatically. She always did have a thing for the dramatics.

"I could only think of three intended victims," declared Margaret, taking back her seat next to Jane.

"Three? Besides Mr Latham and Sir Hugh, who else could it be?" Jane had a bad feeling she already knew of whom Margaret spoke, and found it difficult to want to hear anything further on the subject.

Shaking her head in disbelief, anger began to surge through her. She stood and began to pace in the same manner Margaret had done earlier. Jane detested being a coward; it was not part of her nature. Surely she could be unnerved by unnatural things, but that did not necessarily mean she was a coward. If her father was in danger then she would do whatever she could to make sure, he knew about it. Summing enough courage she asked incredulously, "Who would want to hurt my father?"

Margaret rose to stand near her friend. "Men, good men like Sir Hugh, Uncle and even Mr Latham," she paused before continuing, "often makes enemies. You must consider the possibilities."

"Perhaps they are after Sir Hugh," claimed Jane. "After all you do make enemies in the war front."

"Truth be told, I believe it is Mr Latham who has enemies. Perhaps he is not as good a solicitor as he would like us to believe—most likely has lost a case or two." Margaret added.

Jane dismissed her friend's opinion, "He is not the sort of solicitor, Margaret. He deals with property and taxes."

"Well," Margaret huffed with disappointment, "I suppose there is no sense in possible scenarios for his involvement then."

Jane, who was still having difficulties that her father was a possibly the intended target, ignored the comment. "No. I won't hear of it. Father could not be the target. I fear we've read too many of Anne Radcliff's gothic novels the vicar warned us about. Now they're clouding your imagination." But even as she denied it, Jane could see Margaret's point of view. Hence, she had a choice: either refuse to believe what Margaret had implied, and risk her father or one of the other gentlemen getting hurt or killed, or join her in finding out what was going on. If they discovered their ideas were unwarranted, then just, as well.

Resuming their walk, the girls continuously looked around the gardens as if expecting some malignant force to appear. As if a horrible sense of darkness loomed ominously over Dover. Instead they found singing birds and a brightly shining sun on the fine greenery of the garden.

They had not gone far when Jane suddenly felt as if they were being followed. Turning to check, and not seeing anyone, she picked up her pace along the privet-lined path, Margaret at her side. "We need to tell them."

Margaret abruptly stopped. "Have you lost your senses? What makes you think they're going to believe us? They'll accuse us of extreme propensity to wild imaginings. Why, they'd laugh at us. We'll only prove to them that detecting is indeed a man's business and not something a woman is capable of."

"Let them laugh," Jane cried, "they deserve to know someone may be out to kill one of them."

"Then it will be our job to protect them," Margaret said proudly.

Jane frowned. "Protect them?" her voice an octave higher. "What do we know about protection? I'm afraid all I know is how to needlepoint or how to be an excellent hostess. Margaret, the more I think about it the more I am convinced that what you are asking for, is not within our scope."

Margaret readily interpreted Jane's thoughts and realized that perhaps it was an insane task to take on, when they could barely protect themselves. Their bond was eerie at times, as if their minds worked as one. "Very well," she said, caving in to Jane's determination.

As much as she detested it, Margaret felt her friend was right. It did not change the fact, however, that doing things her way was far more dangerous since it would put the life of one of the three men in grave danger. She didn't care what happened to Mr Latham, stiff and pompous as he was, even if he did have beautiful blue eyes. *Good heavens did she think he had beautiful eyes?* Nonetheless, she did not wish him ill, but a little drama in his otherwise stuffy life would do him good. Margaret grabbed her friend's trembling hands into her own. "Very well, we will both tell them our theory."

Obviously relieved, Jane nodded.

Margaret laughed and then sobered quickly. "Of course, regarding the vicar's murder, we still have no proof of anything, as Mr Latham would quite accurately point out. No proof, save for the key we found. I keep asking myself where the vicar would hide any proof of involvement in something so nefarious that it got him killed. Since we looked at the vicarage and found nothing, I daresay we must look elsewhere. Turn our search to the meaner places and think like someone who has something to hide."

"Perhaps this is where Sir Hugh and Mr Latham might prove useful," Jane offered.

Margaret gave a decidedly unladylike snort. "Sir Hugh may be a help with that sort of thing; I grant you, but Mr Latham? Oh, he'd be of no use, other than perhaps to check his law books."

"I don't know whether to take that as a compliment or an insult."

Both girls screeched in fear at the male voice.

Mr Latham stepped out from behind a hedge where the path turned.

Jane was the first to recover. "Oh dear, you gave us a start, Mr Latham. I had no idea you were back and about the grounds today."

"I apologize for frightening you," he directed his apologies to Jane. "It seems I've arrived just in time to hear my good name sullied."

"... and eavesdropping no less," Margaret accused him.

"Women eavesdrop and gossip, not gentlemen. Although I did happen to hear the vicarage no longer serves its purpose for your search of clues," Latham stiffly revealed. "Oh, yes and something about a key." Hands on his hips he stood with the wind in his hair and a smile on his face, projecting good spirits.

The girls exchanged looks and then stared back at him standing in his usual rather commanding pose.

Margaret was the first to speak, "Fear not, sir. We're merely trying to find out who committed a terrible crime, though Jane and I seem to be doing more than the magistrate. We are convinced the stranger lurking about is a nefarious sort." Margaret then hastily added, "Even you and Sir Hugh must agree."

"No doubt," admitted Mr Latham. "Are we to argue again? Indeed I believed saving you from the startled horses would have allowed us the opportunity to move toward a more amiable relationship. Unfortunately, it doesn't seem to be the case."

128

Jane interjected, "On the contrary, Mr Latham, we are very grateful to you for saving our dear Margaret's life. If it had not been for you, I daresay the outcome would have been fairly grim. I shudder to think what my life would be like should something horrible happen to her."

"I merely did what any other person would have done given the opportunity," he declared, looking directly at Margaret.

Margaret's natural rosy cheeks were beginning to darken. "Yes," she agreed through clenched jaws, "we wouldn't want you to act out of character."

"Oh, goodness," said Jane, all colour draining from her face.

Mr Latham, suspecting the vapours, was by her side in an instant.

"I am afraid all I had for breakfast was a cup of tea," Jane declared.

Concerned for her friend, Margaret surrendered, though she was touched by his genuine concern for her friend. Why she disliked him so, she didn't know. True the man was stubborn at times, especially when it concerned his responsibilities to society. So he was a bit stiff, but other than that he was amiable about others.

"Would you like to have a seat and rest for a minute?" he asked Jane, looking around for a bench.

"Perhaps I should return to the house. You and Margaret can continue with the walk. We were headed toward the pond. There's a statue there that Papa had commissioned, and I wanted Margaret to see it. I think you both will find it beautiful and peaceful."

Margaret, who had taken Jane's hands into hers, frowned for a moment.

"It would be my pleasure to escort your friend," Mr Latham said pleasantly, no hint of dread, "but I believe you shouldn't be walking around alone either, even in your own gardens."

"He's right, Jane. Please, let him accompany you back to the house, and I shall continue with my walk. Besides, if I am accosted, I am sure Mr Latham will be there again to act with his male instincts or may simply decide to watch my demise hidden from behind the hedges so that he is rid of me once and for all."

Mr Latham reddened, his temper rising. "I believe you have an over-active imagination, and that may be your undoing for all this running around without proper chaperon—a pity I am sure as a result of all those wasted hours of reading romances."

"Very well, Margaret. Once your mind is made up, it cannot be changed. But pray do be careful and do not stay out too long, for I will send Mr Latham to fetch you," threatened Jane.

Margaret smiled, looked at Mr Latham, smile gone, curtsied and moved toward the path leading to the pond.

"See you back at the manor," Jane called after her.

As they walked away, Mr Latham glanced at the petite young woman. She looked exceptionally pretty this morning. The walk and breeze heightened the colour in her cheeks, golden curls hidden by the yellow bonnet she wore. He had to admit he always found the opposite sex a mystery. In comparison, Margaret's haughtiness made him want to scream. He had to admit a spirited woman like Miss Renard was alien to him. He was accustomed to the young ladies he often met with no minds of their own, for they were bred at a young age to feign ignorance in the hopes of attaining a husband under the assumption it would please their male counterparts. And he found them boring. Miss Renard, on the other hand, was intriguing. And he believed a woman with her own mind could present some interesting challenges, much to society's chagrin.

"I'm glad to see you have recovered from one of your unusually timed fainting spells," Mr Latham declared, keeping his eyes forward.

Jane stopped in her steps.

Sensing her no longer by his side, Mr Latham also came to a stop. Turning to face her, he found her gazed looking up at him, a gentle smile on her face. He walked back to where she stood; offered his arm and she took it. They continued their walk back to the manor.

"I must admit feeling faint at times does come in handy," Jane jested.

"You are rather a contradiction, which I believe is an attribute very much awarded to the female persuasion. However, I might add you are also an exception, for I find you able to handle situations with great decorum and refinement. Your friend, on the other hand—"

"I must admit Margaret can be free spirited," interjected Jane. "But she is very loyal and fair. She was practically raised an orphan. Oh, she had relatives, most of who were only interested in her fortune. They popped in every so often, in their attempt to acquire her wealth, but then abandoned her. Her servants were very protective of her and have taken care of her since she was not quite six and ten." Jane responded brashly.

"Margaret was fortunate she didn't have to seek employment as a governess. Your father saw to it that she became an important part of my family. He asked my father to be her next guardian should anything happen to him. My father was honoured to do so. She may seem a little out of sorts staying within the bounds of acting as a lady, but she finds society too constricting. She's not one to conform so easily."

Mr Latham was pensive for several seconds. "Thank you for clarifying things a little. You and Miss Renard are as alike as any sisters could ever be, yet different in many ways. I believe, Lady Jane, you would fit nicely in the London ton."

"Margaret and I get on well, and together we are an unstoppable force. We were entertained on several occasions by my aunt Charlotte in London, so we are not strangers to the London scene," Jane said in defensive.

"It would certainly be agreeable to show you and Miss Renard about London, but I am afraid your friend would most definitely feel different about such an endeavour. As for you, I am sure it would be a pleasurable undertaking."

"Margaret may seem difficult to understand or become acquainted with, but once you get to know her, she can be an invaluable friend."

"Ah, this then is where you both differ. One can win your trust and loyalty early on, whereas with Miss Renard, I think a person would first have to win her loyalty, no matter how long it takes, before they could be called a friend."

"True, sir," Jane gasped.

Mr Latham smiled taking pleasure in rattling her usual calm nerves.

"You mustn't let Margaret's blustery manners frighten you off. She is a dear. I do hope you give her another chance."

"My lady, I would be perfectly willing to be her friend. But how do you propose to get her to agree to such an arrangement?" he queried with a cocked brow.

Appearances of propriety vanished, Jane said, "You must approach her differently than other ladies. She doesn't easily take to flattery, and she prizes her independence and judgments. After all, for many years she has proven she can handle herself."

Was her ladyship suggesting that Miss Renard be treated like a man? "Yes, I can see, but don't you think that to be unnatural in society? I mean, a young lady should respect and follow the rules set forth by society. At her age, Miss Renard should be wed and preparing for her future. She would be cared for and want for naught."

"Margaret cares for naught, Mr Latham—."

"Lady Jane?"

"Yes."

"Will you please call me Philip?"

"Yes, of course."

Mr Latham seemed pleased.

"As I was saying," continued Jane. "Margaret wishes to be treated as an equal, a real person—as if you would treat your fellow man. Do not discuss any instances of the so-called weaker sex around her. She is intelligent and would warm to you quickly, I am sure, if you adopted a different approach..." Jane let the idea trail off.

"Why, Lady Jane, it does seem you might be attempting to play matchmaker." Latham jested taking pleasure once again at her reddening cheeks.

"Oh no, not I. It's only that I dislike seeing those close to me in discord," she explained.

"So you admit I am close to you then," Latham teased.

"Well, I—"

"I jest, Lady Jane. However and for reasons unbeknownst to me I sense Miss Renard detests me. Besides, I would have thought you'd consider Sir Hugh a more suitable match for her."

"Sir Hugh? While I am grateful to him for saving my life, I find him incorrigible. He has no respect for anyone or anything and is quite spoiled. I would not wish my friend with someone of his countenance and impediments. The use I have for him at present is to help us in our investigation. Someone of his ilk would certainly be familiar with the meaner places we need to explore. And by the by, Margaret does not detest you."

Mr Latham chuckled. "Ah, he does elicit a strong reaction from you,"

"Well, of course he does. He insults me relentlessly."

"Perhaps he, like Miss Renard, is unused to conversing with certain types of persons. He is used to getting his own way, and when someone challenges him, he kicks out, like an untamed stallion," he offered.

Jane pursed her lips. "Are you comparing us to horses, now?" she teased.

"Of course not!"

"Well then, I would not know of those things."

"Oh, I imagine you know of many things, Lady Jane. By the way, how deeply do you and Miss Renard plan to carry on with this investigation?"

"Why, we intend to discover who killed the vicar, spooked the horses at the funeral and watched me as I walked to the chapel," she gasped. "Oh dear," she swayed.

Stopping in his tracks, Mr Latham turned to steady her. "What do you mean watching you? Have you told anyone about this?" then shaking his head, added, "No of course not."

This bit of news was not going to go well with Cameron. The last thing they needed was to attach themselves as the young ladies' guards. This could hinder their investigation.

He sensed the horror of having revealed something that she didn't want anyone to know. "Sir, it could have been my imagination, after all that has been going on. As a matter of fact, just before you appeared I felt as if we were being followed, and it happily turned out to be my imagination."

"Sometimes our senses are attuned with our surroundings. I fear that with this bit of information, I will have to apprise your father and Sir Hugh. The more

137

reason you and your friend should not be venturing out alone," he added.

If Lady Jane feared any repercussions she did not show any signs of it.

"Tell me something, Mr Latham, did you by any chance happen to see a cloaked figure hiding in the trees at the vicar's funeral?" she asked.

Mr Latham grunted. "Sir Hugh noticed the person doing a terrible job at trying to remain inconspicuous."

"Well then it would seem we are all being watched?"

He laughed, "That may be. However, someone watching Sir Hugh or I is a different matter than someone watching you or Miss Renard."

"Why?" she cried, "Because we are women?"

"There is that, but men are more adept at protecting themselves."

Pouting, Jane retorted, "Margaret was right about you."

Latham felt sorry for hurting her sensitivities, but he was right. What did women know about protection? "I am sorry, Lady Jane. Please know that Sir Hugh and I really do care what happens to you both. Besides, there are other members of your family that I am sure you do not wish to see any harm come to. So you do need to trust us and tell us should anything else occur out of the ordinary."

"Of course you are correct." Jane agreed.

Addressing the issue of the intruder at the funeral, Mr Latham felt it best to change the subject a bit. "I will give you an important investigative technique, Lady Jane," he said. "Had the person at the funeral been a professional assassin, neither Sir Hugh nor anyone else for that matter would have been able to see him. The fact that he was seen tells us that this person lacked expertise—"

"Are you saying we are dealing with an amateur?"

He was impressed. It took an extensive explanation from Sir Hugh for him to understand the differences between an expert killer and an amateur one. Yet, Lady Jane knew, once she realized there was a concern.

"I believe you are correct, but just so you both know, Margaret and I shall continue to work on this investigation until we get to the bottom of this horrible incident."

"You are both high-spirited," he sighed. "Promise me something."

"It depends," Jane said carefully.

"Should you discover anything, would you please come to me or Sir Hugh and share the information?"

"I shall promise, because I think you a sensible man and an excellent solicitor. But I cannot speak on behalf of Margaret."

It pleased him that she thought highly of him.

"However, as far as Sir Hugh is concerned, I shall not promise to do anything of the sort. The man has an ego the size of Italy."

Mr Latham laughed. "You have given me advice on how to win over Miss Renard. Perhaps you might like me to return the favour with information on how to approach Sir Hugh."

Jane was appalled, "I most certainly do not. I find him disconcerting and quite proud; tigers do not change their stripes."

He laughed whole-heartedly knowing if Sir Hugh had heard what she thought of him, he would take her words as a compliment. Tigers were powerful creatures, claiming great speed and strength. "Are you comparing us to animals? Besides, Lady Jane, I believe you have chosen a wrong analogy. Sir Hugh might easily be a chameleon for all you know of him. I beseech you not to write him off as useless. At the very least, please feel free to confide in me. I will handle your communications with discretion and help you, however, I can."

"Thank you," Jane said stiffly.

They walked the remainder of the way in companionable silence. Arriving at the kitchen door entrance Jane bid him thank you and good bye but Latham would not hear of being dismissed until he had walked her to the foyer. Once he was sure in her security he bowed and strode away.

"Come in!" barked Jane's father, who had been sequestered in his study for over an hour. Since the murder and the most recent accident that nearly killed his wife and the girls, his lordship had become a bear. His wife, refusing to tolerate his foul mood any longer had dismissed him to the study to calm his temper. As the door opened he looked up to find Jane and Margaret standing hesitantly at the entrance.

"Ah, look who has come to visit me. Sorry, dears, for growling at you. Her ladyship has accused me of being unfit company. I can't say I blame her, for I have reasons to be exceedingly out of sort, but that is of no importance to you. So come, tell me what brings you here?"

Margaret, who had never seen her uncle lose his temper and wished not to become part or privy to it, remained silent. Since it was Jane's idea, she felt it was appropriate that she should be the one to tell him that he may be the killer's next victim.

Jane looked at her father and then at Margaret.

Margaret became aware of Jane's resolve melting away and did not blame her. She was having second thoughts, as well.

"Well? Out with it." His lordship growled again.

"Cook said dinner would be served fifteen after the hour. Pray excuse us." Grabbing Margaret's hand, Jane pulled her friend out of the study, closing the door behind them.

"What now?" asked Margaret, not blaming her friend one bit for choosing not to tell her father their theory.

"We'll figure something out." Jane said leading the way down the stairs.

For once Margaret hoped for an uneventful evening.

The next morning Margaret returned home, but not before promising to return. Since the vicar's murder, she had neglected her duties as a landowner and been remiss on checking on those less fortunate. She had Cook prepare several baskets filled with food and remedies for the ill before requesting Aloysius to bring the carriage around.

Most of these families she would be looking in on had been living on the land for several generations and had been very loyal to her family. Having spent several hours visiting a total of five families, Margaret returned home completely exhausted. Promptly she wrote herself a reminder, not trusting her weary mind. She had promised two of the families to send several items she had forgotten to bring in her rush. Silently Margaret swore to be more diligent; hence promising herself to visit tomorrow another five families.

After a much needed hot bath, Margaret had dinner in her drawing room. Between bites she wrote letters to the butcher, the market owner and one to Mr Latham, requesting an increase for those employed by her father's estate. She found it disturbing that the vicar had resorted to an unbecoming and eventual deadly course of action because he needed money. Here she was far richer than ever and foolishly lived her life as if she had no cares in the world. Starting today, she vowed to concentrate on giving and making sure those who worked for her were properly taken care with food and medicine. She had a feeling that once she told Jane of her plans that her friend would want to do the same for her tenants.

Chapter Nine

A fortnight had passed since the day of the mishap with the horses, and the night of the party had arrived.

Feeling more like herself, her ladyship refused to remain in bed any longer, much to her husband's dismay. He would have loved nothing more than to keep his wife locked in her room away from all harm. Eventually, it was her logic and reasoning regarding the welcome diversion from the recent accident which wore down his objections. Although it took a bit more patience to convince her husband that she was strong enough to handle the preparations, for the party.

Jane provided her stepmother great assistance with the preparations and while she appeared to be calm and in control, her thoughts were troubled. Despite the excitement of the upcoming ball, Jane couldn't forget the macabre events plaguing them recently.

By dusk, music and laughter could be heard spilling from the manor. And yet Jane had to make a conscious effort to enjoy the evening and hold back the negating thoughts of the vicar's murder.

Festivities were well underway when Margaret arrived. In awe of the decorations, she let one of the servants take her pelisse. Once relieved of it, she felt a gentle touch on her elbow and turned to see her friend.

Although attired beautifully in a light blue dress of the season's most current fashion, Jane's eyes lacked their usual brightness, and there were shadows under them. Her full lips curved in a smile, but Margaret could see her friend was troubled.

Grasping Jane's hand, Margaret gushed, "Everything is beautiful, Jane. Everyone who is anyone is here. This will be the ball of the season. It will be talked about at tea for months to come."

Jane returned Margaret's pressure on her hand and acknowledged the compliment but remained silent.

The silent response spoke volumes to Margaret, who pulled Jane aside, "Come tell me what's troubling you."

Jane's eyes were focused somewhere beyond Margaret, as she shook her head. "It's just that I worry so about Papa. I haven't been able to talk to him about our theory."

"You know, I've been thinking. It could be a theory and nothing more. What if the person merely upset the horses by accident, when he or she only intended to look and nothing more? Or perhaps they were just trying to scare us away from the investigation?"

The heavy cloud surrounding Jane began to lift, "I must say, it never occurred to me. Oh, Margaret, if it is true, then my father is safe."

"Yes, dearest and so are Mr Latham and Sir Hugh."

Jane hugged her friend, the relief coursing through her evident on her face.

Although to Margaret, Jane appeared sensitive and breakable at times, underneath she was strong, with a steely confidence nothing could shake. One of the great elements of their friendship was the way they balanced each other out—Jane's sensitivity and intuitiveness with her bold actions. She now made an effort to help Jane focus on the moment at hand.

"Please try to relax. Your father is safe, and your stepmother has healed nicely. You are safe among family and friends. We will get to the bottom of the vicar's death, and when we do, we can put all of this behind us. But, for now, let us rejoice over your father's newfound happiness. And speaking of happiness, where are they?"

Jane took Margaret's hand and pulled her to the east side of the room where his lordship and ladyship stood drinking punch.

"You have outdone yourself, Jane. I adore how the four halls are decorated in seasonal themes."

Ignoring Margaret's compliment, Jane pounced out of character in front of her father and stepmother. "Papa, look who has come."

His lordship smiled warmly. "Margaret," he said, holding out his hand to her. "It is good to see you again."

Margaret curtsied and took his hand. "Uncle, I cannot express enough how delighted we are in having you back home. It's good to see your healthy colour has returned."

His lordship laughed, "See, my sweet. I am surrounded by your fair sex. As you tolerate my moods so do my girls."

Margaret turned to take her ladyship's hand. "It is good to see you again. You are looking much improved." Margaret then gave her a kiss on the cheek.

Her ladyship returned the kiss. "Dearest Margaret, I am so glad you are come. Jane has been lost without you, as I am sure you've missed her as well."

148

"Indeed I must admit I do miss her terribly when I'm home. I would have returned sooner but was inundated with neglected duties and errands. Simply knowing she now has you, I don't worry as much."

"It is very kind of you to say, my dear. But Jane really needs someone her own age around and so it is settled."

"Thank you. Would you mind terribly if I were to call you 'Aunt'?" Margaret asked a little shyly.

A few tears appeared instantly, threatening to roll down her ladyship's cheeks. Beaming at Margaret, she replied. "Of a certainty you may! I should like nothing more. I am truly blessed not only to have gained a daughter but a niece as well."

"Jane is as dear to me as a sister could ever be," Margaret said. "Thank you for your generosity. And be assured, you shall see much of me in the future."

"Excellent," his lordship said, turning to his wife. "Darling, Lord and Lady Carlsford have arrived and I want you to make their acquaintance." With another smile to the girls, they strolled off to greet more of their guests."

"Let's go out onto the balcony where we can talk," Margaret suggested nudging Jane.

"Agreed," Jane said, glancing about.

As they exited, Margaret was tempted to ask her friend for whom she searched.

Once out on the balcony, Margaret wasted no time in discussing her recent discovery. "I have had an epiphany. While visiting the families on my property and bringing them some food and other necessities, I realized here I am with more money than I care to count, and these people are struggling. We take each day for granted and for what? I think the vicar was killed and money was involved, there is definitely more here than what little clues are suggesting."

"Pray, do calm down. You're on the verge of hysterics."

"No, I am fine. I feel as I have been offered a chance to give back. I mean, I have been generous in the past, but I've realized it was not enough. I wrote to the butcher and market owner to provide these families with whatever they need. I even gave my entire household staff an increase in their wages. Of course I could tell they were thinking I may have gone mad. But I tell you—"

"Splendid! And you're correct. Life is indeed too short, as we have witnessed with the vicar's death.

Tomorrow I shall speak with Papa about doing the same. Perhaps you and I can even go and visit some of the elderly," eagerly declared Jane.

"I'd like it very much," Margaret said as she eyed her friend. "How are you adjusting? Tell me the truth, you look well, but I sense you are a bit strained."

"Oh, I'm well enough. Stepmother is generous, kind and a good woman. If she can make Papa happy, then I am happy. And with our initial theory no longer valid, it makes me much happier, as well."

"Still," Margaret said, "it must be different—a new feeling having her around."

"Granted—there have been no arguments or raised voices. Not even a minor disagreement." Sir Hugh's deep voice suddenly close to them made the girls jump. In their enthusiasm to speak privately, neither had seen him watching from the shadows, or heard him quietly approach them. "And I have been watching and listening."

Sir Hugh appeared looking very dashing in his uniform. Coming up, he bowed to their curtsied greeting.

"Glad to see you again. I did wish to thank you for saving my friend the day of the vicar's funeral,"

Margaret said. Before Sir Hugh could reply, she added, "I hope you are enjoying his lordship's hospitality."

"Indeed, I have been," Sir Hugh jested, smiling mischievously at her before looking at Jane. "Your dress becomes you, Lady Jane. So happy we are not related."

Margaret noted Jane's reaction to him. Her cheeks turned a soft hue of pink as Sir Hugh continued to stare.

"Your interest in women's fashions is a rare commodity in men," Jane said. "You do them justice, does he not, Margaret?"

"I believe a gentleman's interest in our fashion proves men have the capability to be in touch with their feminine side," Margaret teased.

Sir Hugh choked on his drink. "Truly, Miss Renard, men do not have a feminine side. More probably, the moment women took to reading during idle times have further confused the entire gender."

"What do you know about the types of books women read?" Margaret questioned.

Before he could reply his lordship returned for his daughter.

Lord Crittenden's face showed that he was pleased to see the young people conversing. He chuckled as he approached. "Sir Hugh, I see you have found the young

152

ladies and have met our Margaret. May I remind you; she is like a daughter to me, so please be on your best behaviour."

"I assure you, my lord, I shall exude the ultimate in gentlemanly behaviour," Sir Hugh finished with a dramatic bow toward his lordship.

Margaret giggled as Jane rolled her eyes.

His lordship turned to his daughter. "The Marquis de Faucheaux has arrived. He has begged to make your acquaintance."

Jane turned to Margaret as if unsure of her abandoning her.

"I'll be fine, Jane," Margaret said. "Go with Uncle, and I will trust Sir Hugh to keep me company until your return." It had not escaped her notice how Sir Hugh's body changed from relaxed to stiff, almost challenging at the mention of the marquis. There was a story there.

Sir Hugh bowed. This time there was a serious and alert manner to his composure.

A look of confusion appeared on Jane's face as her father escorted her back inside to the party, Sir Hugh's gaze following them.

"Tell me, do you like gardens?" Margaret asked, sensing there was more to him than he allowed others to see.

"I do, Miss Renard. However, at this moment, my interests lie elsewhere."

"Do you have a good sense of character?"

"Why would you ask that?" Sir Hugh turned away from the ball's festivities to face her.

Margaret chose her words carefully. "I see before me a man with two personalities." She sensed him stiffen again. "I first met a man who chose the cover of a rogue. And now before my very eyes, at the mention of the Marquis, I see an intriguing man who I suspect has previously met the Marquis or knows of his character."

"Are you always so perceptive?" Sir Hugh gave her a measuring look.

Margaret was pleased to have discovered she was precise in her deduction about the mysterious Sir Hugh.

"Then you are acquainted with the Marquis de Faucheaux?" She tried again, for he hadn't answered her question.

"Miss Renard, you strike me as a lady of good breeding, hence I understand such a lady tends to keep to matters that concern them and not others."

"See there, it is those kinds of comments that get you and your sex in deep trouble," she said, all teasing gone out of her.

"I am sorry if I offended you, Miss Renard," he answered sharply.

"I would be offended only if the remark you had made been true. It may exist in a man's world but not in a woman's. Though I must agree women tend to be much more emotional than men, we do, however, make decisions based on them. And before you say that it is a female weakness remember all of the wars that were started over a silly argument that questioned a man's ego."

Sir Hugh sputtered.

Sensing that she had caught the braggart off guard, Margaret continued, "I normally do. However, when my dearest friend, who has been through much lately, is involved, then I will do my utmost to keep her safe. If the Marquis is of no good consequence, then I should like to know." Concern for Jane's safety and happiness was always a primary mission for her.

"Would you trust my opinion? Several minutes ago you thought me a rascal without good breeding."

"True, but it is Lady Jane who thinks you lack in so-called 'good breeding'. Though I must admit you play your role well. For whatever reason, which I intend to find out, you are playing a game with my friend and her family, and that makes it my concern."

"My word, do the women in the countryside have such unbecoming manners?" Sir Hugh chuckled.

"Trying to insult me, again, Sir Hugh? It won't work, for I have had my share of rude behaviour from another gentleman. I assure you I do not flinch as easily as some silly young ladies who feel they should appear weak so the men may thus show themselves stronger and in control."

Sir Hugh laughed openly.

Margaret found the sparing match most enjoyable. In fact, she corrected herself, the more time she spent with him, the more she liked him. Enigma or not, she did fancy herself a good judge of character. And Sir Hugh was a good man, although one with a hidden agenda, which made him a very dangerous man.

"Would you have this dance with me?" His question distracted her momentarily.

He placed her hand on his arm and began guiding her indoors, where couples were engaged in a waltz. A minute into their dance, Margaret had to admit he was an excellent dancer. And very soon, he would prove himself a good companion, as well.

"Tell me about your family," Sir Hugh asked politely. "Were both your parents French?"

"My father's great-great-grandfather was from France." Margaret answered easily, though, at war with France, it was not uncommon to find one's neighbour was French. England benefitted from the many delights of the French culture, with fashion and entertainment enjoying a boost in English society. "He married an English girl, and the rest is history. He made his fortune in farming and owned various lands here and in Antigua. Though we didn't acquire a title, my family was quite well off." She thought how the elegant and reserved Jane would perhaps be shocked at how easily she was discussing her family's history with this stranger.

She smiled and then added, "My father amassed a fortune and left me with enough money to support myself several times over. Upon my death, my fortune will revert to male relatives, whom I am certain will spend it most expeditiously—bankrupting themselves in no time."

"Do you ever intend to marry?"

Margaret felt decidedly uncomfortable, certain she was blushing from her head to her toes. "Normally, I would say it is a rather personal question, that is had I been one of those stiff young ladies of society. But as I care none for society, I will say that I find marriage a state of being shackle to another human being. Love does that to you, know."

"That is rather cynical for someone so young and pretty."

Margaret's blush deepened.

"I am sorry," said Sir Hugh. "I did not mean to pry. I was just curious as to why a lovely young woman such as yourself, or even Lady Jane, have remained unwed."

She was not about to tell him about her father and the devastating loss that led to his death. "I—," she began, but then spotted someone she had hoped to avoid seeing ever again. Standing near Lady Farnsworth was Phillip Latham, or the Duke of Stanton, as he was probably being introduced.

Sir Hugh followed her line of sight to where Latham stood.

"I see your interests lay elsewhere, Miss Renard."

"Nonsense! I know he is your friend, but he counts as nothing," Margaret snapped, purposely moving around to face the other direction.

"The lady doth protest too much," Sir Hugh raised an eyebrow, daring her to protest again.

Margaret was saved from a response as the music came to an end. Sir Hugh escorted her back outside for some air. She fanned herself. "Would you mind fetching me a glass of punch?"

"It would be my honour," Sir Hugh bowed, a smile quirking at his lips. "However I hesitate to leave you unchaperoned."

Teasingly Margaret insisted she would be safe but promised to scream should she require rescuing. She watched him walk away and immediately found herself comparing him with Mr Latham. Sir Hugh, harbouring an affinity for playing games, nonetheless had a mature and responsible approach. He was less inclined to care what society thought of him, contrary to the solicitor's cool exterior which exhibited a proud man who played by the rules of a male-dominated society which she, as a woman, was reminded of every single day.

Chapter Ten

"A penny for your thoughts," the words came from a recognizably deep baritone. Margaret whirled around, coming face to face with her nemesis.

"Mr Latham! Or should I address you as your Grace?" she asked as she executed a slight curtsy.

Bowing, his eyes lingered for a moment longer than was sociably polite. "Come now, must we always be on guard? I would be honoured if you called me Philip, and before you ask, I was invited by his lordship. Yours are not the only affairs I handle."

"Believing that I would ask you such a question, sir, would suggest something to the effect of rudeness. Is that what you are implying?" She hoped for Sir Hugh's speedy return. The thought of being alone with this insufferable but dashing man was ruining her evening.

Clearing his throat Mr Latham changed the direction of their talk. "I saw you dancing and—"

"I believe, sir, with whom I dance is of no consequence to you."

Latham's stance became suddenly stiff. "Ah, Miss Renard, I believe we are finally in agreement over something." Drawing a deep breath he walked away, but then stopped and turned back to her. "I am more perplexed at the thought of you ever acquiring anyone to dance with at all, seeing as you are always so highly emotional." Without a backwards glance he resumed his retreat allowing the crowded ballroom to swallow him, laughter bellowing from deep in his throat in response to something said to him as he passed a group of men.

Margaret heard the laughter coming from inside, rising far above the gaiety and voices of the crowd—surely Latham laughing at her expense. Margaret wished she had something to throw. Her violent feeling lasted for a moment until she remembered him saving her life. She was confused and felt wretched for being ungrateful and rude to the man. Damnation to men!

The Marquis bowed low over Jane's hand. "Mademoiselle," he said in a low but surprisingly strong voice.

Jane noted he was a very handsome man of about five and thirty, though he looked much younger. His jet black hair was combed straight to reveal an agreeable forehead and dark blue eyes, along with a well-shaped nose and square jaw. He was very tall and well built. She'd wager (and likely win) the other girls would indeed find him handsome and quite the catch. Yet she felt an odd sense of unease about the elegantly aristocratic man standing before her.

"Marquis de Faucheaux," Jane said, participating in the usual social graces, as she made a disturbing observation. While he was exceptionally good-looking and quite eligible, none of the unattached young ladies were vying for his attention. She found this quite puzzling, but instead of being intrigued, she was troubled even more.

"It is a rare delight to meet a young woman of such beauty and intelligence," he said. "The renown of your great wit is eclipsed by the stories of your beauty."

Goodness! Suddenly feeling uncomfortable, Jane turned to look around the ballroom, her eyes finally settling on Sir Hugh and two young women with whom he was flirting. The man had no sense of propriety.

As though he had heard her thoughts, Sir Hugh turned and locked eyes with Jane. He then had the audacity to smile and bow at her.

Jane flushed and turned back to the Marquis.

"Sir," she said, smiling warmly, "do you visit England often?"

"Rather often," he said. "I have several homes—one in London, another in Brighton, and one here in Dover. I am fond of English society and find it quite agreeable."

"Dover is quite small, so I wonder, then, why we have not met before," Jane said.

"Unfortunately, mademoiselle, business matters have kept me abroad for long periods of time, but I feel we shall be meeting again, especially since we now enjoy similar circles."

Jane stared at him, trying to fathom any hidden meanings in his dark eyes, though she could not help but feel an odd twinge of fear, a deep unease which this stranger's charming words could not alleviate. There was something sinister about his dark looks. She couldn't shake the feeling and glanced about the room. Surely there was nothing to fear where the Marquis was concerned. There were times she imagined things which weren't there and preferred to think of it as having a keen sense of perception, though she had to remind herself constantly that this was the case.

As if by magic, Sir Hugh suddenly materialized at her side.

"Sir Hugh, there you are. I had hoped you would come and allow me the honour of introducing to you the

Marquis de Faucheaux." Jane hoped her overly enthusiastic greeting would not shock him. He was no fool. Normally she would have greeted him with a sharp retort, but this once she was glad for his company.

"The Marquis and I are well acquainted," said Sir Hugh, bowing at her curtsy and then bowing to the Marquis.

Jane watched the men, noting a darkness creeping into the marquis' eyes as the air thickened with tension around the two men. Their wary eyes on one another reminded her of the eyes of a hunter, as if each man viewed the other as prey.

"A pleasure to see you again Jean Claude, will you be staying long?" Without waiting for a response Sir Hugh turned his attention to Lady Jane. "I have come for our dance."

The change in attitude was so complete, that it didn't take Jane long to figure out the possible cause of the animosity between the two. Perhaps the Marquis, being French, would have a hard time moving in social circles with a man who played a role in Napoleon's defeat.

"Sir Hugh is correct, Lady Jane. We walk in similar circles." The French man finally spoke.

"I beg to differ, Marquis," Sir Hugh said stiffly. "You see, I fight for England. Whereas you? Well, no one truly knows but can only imagine where your loyalties lie."

Her first deduction had been correct. Their animosity began with the war, but she sensed Sir Hugh knew more about the Marquis than he let on.

Wishing to avoid a scene Jane tapped her companion playfully on the arm, "Sir Hugh, the music is about to start. Marquis, will you please excuse us?"

In a daring move prompted by the sudden desperate need to be away from the Marquis, Jane curtseyed and then took Sir Hugh's hand, waiting for him to lead her to the dance floor and inwardly praying he would play along with this masquerade.

Sir Hugh smiled and fell into the role without further prompting. Jane had no clue why he would be amenable to helping her, but she was grateful nonetheless.

With one eyebrow raised, Sir Hugh nodded at the Marquis, "Marquis, as always a pleasure to see you again." Swivelling away, he escorted Jane to the floor, glancing back at the Marquis one last time before giving her his full attention.

Jane did not miss the expression of a dangerous look on the Marquis' face.

As they danced the quadrille, Sir Hugh asked, "What was that about? I'm sure you could readily handle the Marquis' attentions. You seem quite, ah, capable."

"I am. I do not frighten easily. I was fine, although you two seemed ready for battle. I merely wanted to prevent an unfortunate scene between the two of you. Whatever did you do to him to create such hatred towards you?"

"Then why the sudden frown, if you had been doing well? You should not crease your pretty face so," he said teasingly taking a finger and tracing the crease above her nose.

Although Jane felt a little tingling sensation run from the tip of her toes to stomach, she was shocked at the intimacy of his touch. "You did not answer my question," Jane chided hoping no one had seen what he had done—for rumour of an attachment would follow.

As if realizing what he had done, Sir Hugh said in a serious tone, "The Marquis and I have had our own discords, but nothing I can't handle. I assure you. There, I have confided in you, as you asked."

Lady Jane looked as she might lean forward toward, her eyes cast to the crowd as though she were about to confide something to him, but then pulled away.

Sir Hugh frowned. "You can tell me anything, you know." He glanced again toward where the Marquis had been standing moments earlier and no longer there.

Jane gave her head a slight shake.

His face changed from a concerned frown to a haughty smirk. "Fine, if you do not wish to tell me what is wrong, I am certain you can take care of yourself. I do not see you as the type to be afraid of anything, my dear. By the by, I have had a conversation with Latham about you being watched the day of the funeral."

Jane shivered slightly, and her cheeks flush a delightful pink. Seemingly disarmed, she made no comments regarding his talk with Latham.

He smiled, satisfied with the effect his words had. Though it pained him to watch how she abruptly became angry and then closed off. They didn't speak for the rest of the dance.

When the music ended Sir Hugh remained close at her side—a fact that was not missed by the eligible ladies trying to catch his attention.

Eventually, Sir Hugh found Margaret talking with some elderly dowagers and escorted Jane back to her friend. He bowed a greeting to the ladies and then excused himself.

Chapter Eleven

Jane tried to shrug off Sir Hugh's slight as she and Margaret quietly made their way back to the terrace where they could sit and drink their punch, catching up on the evening's events. Indeed, the man was a chameleon, one moment he was flirting with her and then the next she might as well been an annoying fly he was attempting to swat away.

Having danced a set, they found the gently scented breeze a welcome delight. The area was lit with small table lanterns, the full moon adding to the glow of the evening. They were more than content to rest a bit before going back to the party. Small tables and chairs were aplenty, and guests had yet to make their way to the terrace. Glad for the solitude, they chose the table furthest from the double glass doors, away from the loud music and laughter.

"I love your dress, Margaret. Alba did a splendid job." Jane sighed as she took a seat

It pleased Margaret to hear such praise from her friend. She always considered Jane the one to set the trend of fashion for Dover. "Have you seen what she did with the pearls around the cuff of the sleeves and the lace hem?"

she asked unceremoniously lifting up her right leg to show it off.

Jane gasped softly at Margaret's blatant exposure then released a set of giggles. "Yes, I agree Alba does have a certain talent for designing unique pieces."

Remembering Mr Latham, Margaret said, "I saw your father invited Mr Latham to the party. I find him insufferable. Why, he even had the nerve to tell me he was surprised any of the gentlemen present would want to dance with me." Still appalled as when he first said it she tightened her hands clasped around her cup of punch

"The audacity of the man!" cried Jane.

"I agree. I hope not to run into him again. Your father would do well not to invite him again," Margaret huffed.

"That may prove difficult since he is staying with us."

"Mr Latham is staying with you, whatever for?" Margaret cried, her voice raising an octave higher.

"Mr Latham?" Jane asked a bit confused, "Why would he be staying with us? Her mind drifted toward her dance with Sir Hugh—her friend temporarily forgotten.

"We were discussing Mr Latham's impertinent demeanour and you said...you are obviously distracted...who did you think I meant?"

"Why, Sir Hugh, of course," Jane said guiltily.

"Sir Hugh! Heavens no, why should you not wish to see him again? I found him to be most amiable, and a charming gentleman."

"Really, I think for the first time since I've known you, you have lost all senses. Need I remind you Mr Latham saved your life?" Jane asked.

"I assure you I have not lost my senses, and Sir Hugh saved yours. By the way, I had a wonderful time with him in the garden after you left me."

Margaret giggled at Jane's bewilderment, "I find Mr Latham of great consequence, humour and sensibility."

"That is odd, indeed," Margaret said chewing her bottom lip.

"Whatever do you mean?" Jane asked incredulously.

Margaret raised her cup and took a drink of her punch while she gathered her thoughts. "Well, Sir Hugh is not all he presents himself to be. You will find him quite the opposite, as a matter of fact the same way I perceive Mr Latham."

"I see what you mean." Jane giggled. "We are in quite a dilemma."

"Perhaps you should marry Mr Latham," teased Margaret, "and I shall marry Sir Hugh." Shortly, thereafter the girls found themselves in a fit of laughter.

171

"It could be a possibility, or we can agree these men are more of an enigma than we first thought," Jane said bringing herself under control.

As their conversation ended the girls realized that the ballroom had suddenly grown quiet. Had the ball ended without them realizing? Deciding they'd been absent long enough, they made their way inside. A commotion near the entrance of the ballroom explained the unexpected silence. The long-absent Mr Gerald Huntington, Earl of Roxburgh, had returned from his travels abroad. Rumours circulated he had left to visit America, Spain, and Russia. Lord Roxburgh was not only handsome, but a rich bachelor and the talk of society. Last summer Jane had suspected him of being infatuated with Margaret but found her friend had not been impressed.

"I can't believe my eyes," whispered Jane, as the music began once again, and people resumed their dancing.

"Unbelievable," cried Margaret noting the young single ladies standing aside anxiously waiting to see whom Lord Roxburgh would honour with a dance. "They should be ashamed of themselves," she added with annoyance at the women simpering over the man.

She remembered his attempts at courting her, and although she did like him, she found it was not enough to tolerate his stubbornness and cockiness. He had expected Margaret to swoon over him as the other young ladies did. Perhaps in time she could have grown to love him, judging by her own reaction to him now, but it wouldn't have been a long happy union and ultimately would have proved disastrous.

Much to her mortification, he headed their way, sauntering elegantly through the room causing the ladies to stare or swoon as he passed them.

When Lord Roxburgh finally stood in front of the girls, he towered over them, exuding power.

"Ladies," he acknowledged them with a bow. "Margaret, you have grown even lovelier."

Margaret quelled the need to roll her eyes. He had been gone for over half a year. *How much could she have changed since then?*

"And you, handsome as ever," she replied with a brief curtsy.

"Does it show?" he mocked.

"I could tell by the number of ladies pining for your attention."

"All of them, Margaret, but neither you nor Lady Jane seem the swooning type. Unless, of course, you tell me differently now," he said.

"I am afraid not, my lord," Margaret replied sharper than she intended, her hope, to end the conversation colouring her words.

She couldn't miss the sudden darkness in his eyes. He certainly had changed, but maturity had nothing to do with it.

"But do not despair," Jane interjected. "I wager you shall not be without a lady to escort to any given ball this season."

Lord Roxburgh turned to her as if he was seeing her for the first time. "Lady Jane, as always you are not only the beauty of the ton, but the one with the most sensibilities. You do your fair sex great justice." He lifted her hand to his lips. "You will make an excellent wife someday."

Not giving Jane a chance to respond to Roxburgh's remark, Margaret interjected, "I was sorry to hear about your father, Gerald." It had been a long time since she had addressed by his given name. They were kids once and often spent time running wild through the forests, playing pirates and fairy tales.

A brief flash of darkness returned to his eyes. "Thank you. It was sudden; he went in his sleep."

"I trust your trip to America was a welcome respite." Margaret said, hoping to draw him from the sadness.

"Thank you. Yes, America was an interesting respite, though I found it rather barbaric. I find English society to be the heart of civilization," he said, his eyes settling on Jane, the melancholy from his father's now gone.

Jane blushed and shifted nervously.

Margaret noted Roxburgh's amusement at Jane's reaction as he asked if he could fetch them some refreshments.

"Thank you, no. We just finished some of punch." Margaret said.

"Well then, off I must to dance. It is difficult being a handsome, rich young bachelor these days." He bowed dramatically. "Damn near dangerous if you ask me." With a wink he was off.

Jane and Margaret both laughed. This was the Malcolm they remembered.

In response to their laughter, he turned back to face them, "Do not fear my ladies, I shall return for a dance with each one of you."

From across the room, Sir Hugh and Latham watched the exchange. Sir Hugh's eyes narrowed as Lord Roxburgh kissed Jane's hand.

"Easy there, my good man. We don't want to draw any attention," Latham said. "That is unless you are ready to claim the young lady's attention and declare your intentions toward her."

"Nonsense, Latham. I have no intentions of declaring anything with anyone. As soon as this whole business has been dealt with, I shall happily go back to my life as a confirmed military bachelor," Sir Hugh said, noting that Latham had also been intensely watching the exchange. Nodding towards Roxburgh, he asked, "What do you know of him?"

"Afraid all I know is one day he was in debt and then mysteriously the next day he inherited his title and thirty-thousand pounds a year."

"Interesting, let me guess, you are his solicitor as well?" Sir Hugh asked in jest.

Mr Latham ignored it. "No, I am not, though my father tried but with no success."

The men watched Lord Roxburgh move away from Jane and Margaret and walk back to the other ladies anxiously eying him for his attention and an opportunity for a dance.

Settling for Lord Riechert's daughter, Lady Angelique Stonewall, Roxburgh gracefully led the girl to the dance floor.

Looking back Sir Hugh caught Jane watching him and Latham observing Roxburgh and for a moment worried that she might question how a man who so recently arrived in Dover seemed to be wildly acquainted with some of the more distinguished inhabitants.

The ball ended just after midnight and after bidding their last guests good night, his lordship and ladyship retired to their chamber.

Jane and Margaret stayed up late talking about Malcolm's return. Jane then talked about her introduction to the Marquise de Faucheaux. "Something about the way he spoke sent chills down my back," she said, as another set of chills ran down her spine.

"Gerald seemed to show interest in you, but I couldn't exactly determine if he was being courteous or truly interested," Margaret said.

Jane blushed but dismissed the idea as complete foolishness. "You really are beginning to enjoy this."

"I must admit you both did look to be an excellent match, while dancing."

"I could say the same when I watched you and him dance," Jane teased. For a moment, she thought of mentioning how she had spied Sir Hugh and Mr Latham watching them, but pushed the idea away knowing that Margaret would probably react badly to Latham's attention.

They continued their talks until complete exhaustion came over them. Bidding their own goodnights each of them headed to their own rooms.

Chapter Twelve

The next morning, as Margaret, Jane and her parents were breakfasting and talking over the previous evening's festivities, they heard several male voices outside the dining room.

"Ah, here come the rest of our guests," his lordship announced before taking a bite of his toast.

Margaret looked inquiringly at Jane, who shrugged her shoulders.

Other than Sir Hugh, Jane had no idea which of the many guests had stayed for the night. The thought of not knowing when guests spent the evening under her roof was a bit unnerving.

Sir Hugh was the first to enter. "I am telling you, Phillip, I'll wager a week's wages Second Hand Rose will come in first."

Latham followed. "You're on, old man."

Jane's father cleared his throat. "Gentlemen, there are ladies present."

At once, they took the hint and bowed. "Pray, forgive us, my lady, Lady Jane, and Miss Renard," Latham said.

A shocked Jane couldn't believe her eyes. *Was there no shame in the man?*

179

"We trust you are all well on this fine fall morning," Sir Hugh added, before they both headed to the buffet table.

Jane gave Margaret a look that instructed her to compose herself. Shrugging her shoulders, Margaret rolled her eyes at her friend.

Her ladyship gave a contented sigh, "It was a wonderful ball, my dear," smiling at her husband as she took a bite of toast, blushing slightly as he smiled back. "I did enjoy meeting Lord Roxburgh, dearest. What a pleasant young man, such a cheery constitution," she added taking a sip of her tea her eyes gleaming as they settled on Margaret.

Sir Hugh took note of his cousin's meaning. "Take great care, dear cousin, one must never judge a book by its cover."

Mr Latham quietly placed his fork on the plate, seemingly no longer hungry.

Margaret who had been hungrily enjoying her toast stopped. "What know you of Roxburgh, Sir Hugh?"

Pushing his plate aside, Sir Hugh leaned back into his chair. "Personally, I know nothing of the man. But then unless you know a person well, one must never assume knowledge of that person on the first meeting."

Jane opened her mouth to respond when a servant entered and approached his lordship. "Excuse me, my lord. This has just arrived," he said, handing him a white envelope sealed with gold wax, the initial "D" pressed distinctly over it.

"Thank you, Alfred." His lordship took the letter and opened it immediately. "Ah, it's an invitation from Lord and Lady Dalton for dinner. It includes any guests staying with us."

His lordship turned to his wife who was busily enjoying her eggs. "Lord and Lady Dalton have been our neighbours for over fifteen years. Their daughter Sophie and Jane made their debut at the same time." He went back to reading his letter. "Interesting," he continued, "the invite mentions you specifically, Cameron."

"Dinner sounds lovely," responded her ladyship, not keeping up with the conversation.

Jane caught the excitement in her stepmother's voice. She loved the prospect of attending another social gathering, as she was eager to become acquainted with all of their neighbours. In fairness to her stepmother, the Daltons had turned down their invitation to yesterday's ball because their two youngest daughters had been ill.

181

Now that she'd settled in as her father's wife and had become acquainted with the running of the manor, there seemed much to her ladyship's dismay, little time for entertainment. Jane knew her father would see it differently, especially since they just had a ball and her ladyship was still recovering from the injuries incurred at the vicar's funeral. Recalling that day sent shivers down her spine. Immediately she felt Margaret's eyes on her, as though her friend had felt her disquiet. With a slight nod Jane, returned her attention to the conversation.

"Lord George Dalton?" Sir Hugh asked, returning his plate to its previous position in front of him.

"Yes. Have you made his acquaintance?" Jane's father asked.

"I haven't had the pleasure of meeting the viscount directly, but if he is the father of a George Harrison, then I am acquainted with the name. I served with George. He was an impressionable young man and a quick-tempered one. On occasion, I've had to bail him out of undesirable situations."

Nodding thoughtfully, his lordship placed the letter on the table and continued with his breakfast. "Well, apparently George has spoken highly of you. He must have heard you were in town."

"No doubt through Mrs Appleby. The woman has no bounds where gossip and rumours are concerned," Margaret declared.

Normally Jane would agree with her, but she seemed busy staring at Sir Hugh. She looked at him as if she was seeing him for the first time. Sir Hugh played the perfect gentleman for Margaret, gallantly intervened for her with the Marquis, and now he'd saved a knight's son from leading a wayward life. She wondered if there was truly more to him than he let on. She had a feeling that no matter how long she would come to know the man, he would always remain a mystery.

For a heartbeat, she had the sinfully thrilling thought of delving into that mystery.

Having decided the evening before that she needed to return home to take care of her landlord duties, Margaret took advantage of the momentary silence to rise from her chair and excused herself. "Uncle and Aunt, I've had a wonderful time, but I do believe I must get back home. I hope to have you and your guests over for dinner soon."

She turned to Sir Hugh, who, along with Mr Latham and Jane's father, had risen from his seat.

Her ladyship stood as well and extended her hands to Margaret, who ignored them, instead giving her hostess a warm hug. Amelia, rather than being shocked at this display of affection, became teary-eyed.

Jane too rose, "Will you come back tomorrow so that we can ride together to the Daltons?"

Sensing her friend's unease, Margaret turned to Jane with one of her best smiles. "Yes, of course. I shall have Aloysius bring me over. So you needn't worry on my account."

"Very well, I'll see to it that one of the stable boys takes you home."

Mr Latham shook his head and smiled. "Nay, Lady Jane. I would be very happy to escort Miss Renard home in my carriage."

Margaret immediately protested. "Mr Latham, I do thank you for the offer, but it isn't necessary. The walk home will do me good."

"Nonsense, English roads are often unsafe. Besides, I have urgent matters to deal with at home, which so happens to be on the way to yours."

Around the table everyone, swivelled back and forth between the exchanges as if watching a game of racquet.

Jane cleared her throat nervously.

Margaret held his gaze. "I fear nothing, Mr Latham." However, inside she didn't feel at all as brave as she pretended, especially with the recent attack at the funeral and her conversation with Jane about her being watched.

"Ah, yes," Latham said, breaking the uncomfortable silence, that settled after her statement. "I do recall a recent conversation where you made very clear to me that you were quite fearless. I am merely trying to save Charles the use of his carriage, when I am myself heading home."

With that reasoning, Margaret was left with no choice but to acquiesce. She certainly didn't want to inconvenience her uncle.

"Then I accept. Thank you, sir," Margaret said stiffly before bidding the others a final farewell.

Jane walked her friend out to front of the manor. "Margaret, it's not a problem for us to have someone take you home."

"I'll be all right." Margaret resolutely straightened her shoulders. "Surly I can endure his presence for a few more minutes."

Any further conversation ended when Margaret entered Mr Latham's waiting carriage. Though she was ready to partake in a verbal duel, she was pleasantly surprised when he chose to ignore her and read his paper instead. However, it wasn't long before her mercurial tempered surfaced, annoyed that the paper provided more interest than conversing with her.

Margaret did not miss the slight smirk he directed at her as he turned the page.

Such disregard of her presence was extremely rude of him, no doubt a form of punishment for the earlier verbal jousting at her home. Margaret began to shift in her seat, and cleared her throat several times. By the time she'd composed a tart observation on his lack of manners, the barouche swayed to a full stop outside her manor.

Margaret, now furious with herself and Mr Latham in particular, practically jumped out of the barouche before it came to a complete stop. This daring move made to prevent Latham from assisting her down.

Margaret all but dove out the door before they had come to a full stop, she tilted her chin up, obstinate as ever. "Thank you for the ride. I am greatly obliged."

"You are most welcome," Latham said. "I trust you enjoyed the ride, Miss Renard. My goal was to give you the peace you seemed to desperately require. Did I do wrong?" he asked innocently. He tipped his hat negligently, a mere formality, and signalled to the driver to go on, leaving Margaret standing in the drive.

She stamped her foot and cried loud enough for the footman to hear her, "Insufferable and beastly man!"

Latham waved lazily out the window.

She stamped her foot once, this time wounding a toe, "Confounded man." Upon entering her home, she was besieged by Evangeline.

"Not now, Evy, I've a headache," she said. "I will be in my room. You may advise Mrs Roth to surprise me with dinner, and would like some tea brought to my room in the meantime," Margaret commanded, leaving a confused Evangeline to ponder whom or what had caused her mistress distress.

Chapter Thirteen

Shortly after Margaret's departure, Jane sought solace in her mother's gardens. This was a place that always seemed to provide her the sanctuary she craved when pondering troubling things. In just three months' time they would be celebrating Christmas, a time for rebirth, yet all around her was death and discourse. The death of the vicar, the near fatal accident that could have killed her stepmother and the uneasiness of a stranger lurking among them all weighed on her.

Her spirits lifted somewhat when she considered Sir Hugh becoming bored and thus departing her home. She wondered why he felt the need to linger. She always heard stories of young men desiring adventure and travel through Europe. Why this was not happening in Sir Hugh's case, she couldn't fathom.

"Hullo there, Lady Jane. Mind if I join you?"

Astonished to see the subject of her contemplations coming toward her; caused Jane to skip a step heightening her irritation. Clearly the man took pleasure in vexing her, so had he now taken to following after her? Then she remembered their encounter in the chapel and how he had seemed different. In fact, since then she had grown a bit more tolerant of him. Truthfully, she did want to get to know him a little better.

"Sir Hugh. What are you doing here?" She asked, trying to sound indifferent. Once he caught up with her she continued with her walk toward the gardens.

"Certainly not the greeting I was hoping for. However, I'm a resilient man and shall recover sufficiently, given time. I truly would like to accompany you. Since my arrival, I've longed to see the grounds and gardens. Last night during the dance I caught a glimpse of the gardens in the dark and imagined them to be more beautiful in daylight." He smiled.

She was taken aback by his sudden interest in the gardens. He didn't look the kind of man who would find anything as tame as horticulture high on his list of hobbies; hence her impression of him following her had not been a false fancy, after all.

"Thank you, Sir Hugh," Jane answered cautiously, wondering what game he was playing. "The gardens are very dear to me, for my mother's hands and talents are evident in everything you see here."

Sir Hugh nodded appreciatively towards a flowering bush. "I have heard much about your mother from Amelia."

"It must be hard for a newly married bride to listen to her husband praise his deceased wife."

"See, Lady Jane? This is where imagination can get one into trouble," he said teasingly.

She turned toward him, expecting to read more, but his face wore a neutral expression.

"On the contrary, my cousin is insecure and ponders whether she can measure up to your dear mother."

Something about the way he said, "Dear" warmed her heart. There was no sarcasm or jest in his voice. *Sir Hugh was clearly becoming quite the dilemma. His ability to unnerve her strong constitution was refreshing if not annoying.*

"I have no idea why she would feel the need to measure up to my mother. She is a gentlewoman of good countenance, wit, and one who is willing to be a mother to an already grown daughter. On that point alone she has won my esteem, not to mention the way she glows when she speaks of my father or when in his presence. Such love and devotion is truly a testament to marriage."

"I agree with you, marriage's success is solely dependent on the couple." Sir Hugh seemed to be lost in thought, as if the comment had brought forward some kind of sad memory

Before she knew it, Jane blurted out, "I am sorry for your loss."

"Nay, I was merely thinking of my parents," he said.

Jane noticed a sudden shift in his mood. A sadness she'd never thought he would exhibit, especially to her.

Sir Hugh continued, "Unlike your father and mother, my parents' marriage fell early on into disillusionment, gradually sinking into a union of intense dislike. I wasn't at all surprised my mother died before my father. She most certainly wanted to get away from him and, through death, found a permanent way to do so." He bent to caress a rose. Straightening, he quickly looked at her. "I must say he didn't look altogether heartbroken after her death. In fact, I think he was rather glad to see me off to war, leaving him free to live his life as he pleased."

"My goodness, it must have been horrible for you." *That certainly explained his scorned view of life and perhaps marriage;* she grimaced. According to her stepmother, Sir Hugh was not known for staying in one place for very long, and his career has kept him from becoming attached to anyone. His heart only had room for England. Jane thought how sad it must be to love something that could never love you in return. "I am truly sorry for what you went through," she said. A sudden sadness squeezed her chest, but Jane swallowed it down. "It is a shame you didn't have any siblings."

"Ah, but I do. I have four," he said with a laugh, his countenance brightening.

In that moment Jane could see how the memories of his brothers and sisters brought him joy, but she could tell it came with a sense of longing.

"Oh, excuse me. I assumed you were an only child." Jane blushed at her assumption.

"Ah, well let me correct that. The eldest is my brother Frederick, who lives in Scotland. He and my sister-in-law, Abigail, have three little ones. Then there's Paul, still in the military. My eldest sister Harriet is married and expecting her first child, and last but not least is the youngest, Mary, who currently resides with my brother Frederick." He picked up a petal which had fallen from a pink rose and absently played with it between his fingers. "I'm sure when Harriet has her child, Mary will stay with her. I know that she will be a comfort to her sister during her confinement."

"Your mother was blessed to have five children." Jane's throat constricted her words becoming a mere whisper as the old sorrow, and lifelong sense of loss, suddenly descended upon her. With great effort Jane took a steadying breath. *You will not cry in front of this man*, she ordered herself.

"Lady Jane, pray forgive my insensitivity. I should not have mentioned family."

Sir Hugh's declaration of compassion disconcerted her, the compassionate look in his eyes more so.

"Nonsense!" Jane took another breath and let it out slowly as she stopped to examine a rose "I think having lots of brothers and sisters is a wonderful blessing. As you know, I am an only child and would have loved siblings. Thankfully, Margaret is like a sister to me, and she makes up for this lack."

"I find it hard to believe, you lacking in anything." He smiled.

She felt her cheeks grow scarlet. There had been such honesty in his words that she was once again put off by the unexpected.

How was it possible that such an irritating man had the ability to pull her out of her doldrums? She knew she tended to brood at times. Jane lifted her chin; she could not allow this man to charm her. "There is something I would like to share with you."

His eyes narrowed, "Pray, tell."

"Margaret and I suspect there is more than one killer involved. What say you?"

He sighed, annoyance clear in the breath. "I had hoped you and Margaret would leave the investigation to us."

"We agreed to no such thing," Jane said frankly. "From what I remember, you merely said you would be watching and left the room. Margaret and I only assumed neither of you were interested in finding out who killed the vicar."

"And I assumed my hasty retreat that day spoke of action."

"Action? We have yet to see any action coming from you or Mr Latham." Jane huffed in a rather un-lady like manner.

Sir Hugh stopped walking and stood with his arms crossed. "Well, we do have our own way of investigating. Just because you do not see something does not mean it's not there."

Jane wondered at his comment. "Oh, yes, indeed, there are many details where men are useful, such as visiting seedy establishments where villains might be lurking." She paused, toyed with the fan in her right hand, and then continued. "You do visit seedy establishments, do

194

you not? There has to be someone you can talk to and find out what is going on around the town."

Sir Hugh stared at her and then burst out laughing. *My, oh my, was she a spit-fire!* "I must agree that in my younger days, I daresay I visited a few, ah, seedy establishments, as you call them. But I have become much more responsible since then, so I am afraid frequenting such establishments has been few and far between for me.

"Well I am afraid this will not do." Jane tapped her fan against her chin. "Margaret and I may need you and Mr Latham to enter some shadowy public house to gather information. Information, we, as you can understand, cannot easily gather because of our sex."

"You have quite an imagination, my lady. No doubt from the many novels you and Miss Renard have read." Sir Hugh found it exhilarating to think that, should he spend the rest of his life with her, she would never cease to amaze him. Though at times her tenacity was annoying, he could not help but admire that quality in her. He gave himself a mental shake. Now such thoughts were dangerous, indeed.

He then found himself comparing the ladies. He had to admit he liked Margaret. She was pretty, and shared similar manners to his; whereas Lady Jane, was not only a beauty, but had fire "I believe that you may mock us, sir," her voice became hoarse with annoyance, "but I assure you that seedy establishments do exist and not just in novels!"

"Pray where should I find these seedy establishments?" Sir Hugh tried to pull an innocent look and could tell he had failed miserably when Jane turned on her heel and walked away from him.

"If you do not know that, sir," Jane said over her shoulder, "then Margaret and I fear all is lost with the investigation."

"I am sure you have your own sources," he said, his voice resigned. These two chits were not going to make things easy for him and Latham. If they didn't watch their step all of them could be in for trouble.

"I do my best to stay on top of things, which is why I am surprised and shocked this wickedness has entered our village. After all, are we to do nothing but become pawns in a game of chess? Being in the dark, as we are, about whom the villain, or likely villains, might be, does very little to ease our nerves."

"I assure you, you are all safe. You are safe." Voice low and deep, automatically taking her hands in his, he assured her.

He could see the effects of holding her hands register on her pretty face, as her cheeks turned a rosy pink. He was more surprised when she took a step closer to him. Shocked, he released her hands, and directed her back to their walk which started out in silence.

After a few moments Jane cleared her throat. "Margaret and I have developed a theory. Suppose a band of smugglers were doing business on our coastline. What would—"

"Here we are," Sir Hugh interrupted Jane as he stopped at the arched entrance to the gardens. "It's truly lovely, my lady."

From the entrance of the garden, beds of flowers bloomed enthusiastically around the cobblestone walkway. Large enough for two people to pass through, they walked side by side. A light breeze rustled the leaves above them.

"You are trying to distract me, Sir Hugh. Don't you want to hear our theory in full?" she asked.

"I would prefer, at this moment, to hear about the flowers that meant so much to your mother." Yes, he was trying to distract her from the most dangerous venture she and her friend had set themselves upon, but he was also meant what he'd said about the flowers.

Jane sighed, giving in to the tour.

They continued slowly for a while, discussing the different varieties, Jane often relating to him stories her father told her about each flower and its particular meaning to her mother. Sir Hugh watched in candid delight as pleasure brightened Jane's eyes and she became more animated moving from one planting to another.

A house sparrow landed on the branch of a plum tree above and then bothered by the walking couple, took flight. Sir Hugh watched as Jane's eyes followed the creature's flight until it vanished into the higher branches. For a moment he could read her mind as it seemed to have taken flight as well.

Leaning a little closer to her, he whispered, "You are far away."

Jane jumped startled and embarrassed.

"Forgive me," she said. "I was thinking about how dry it's been of late and that I should advise the gardener to take special care to water the flowers. They do suffer when it's so warm."

Moving forward of him Jane pointed to a grouping ahead of them. "Papa told me stories of how proud my mother had been of this area of the garden. She designed it herself."

"I see," Sir Hugh said with a smile. "You certainly have much to say about these gardens, but I wonder if that was really where you were a moment ago."

Jane stared straight ahead. "Really, there is no reason why you shouldn't take me at my word. If I say I was pondering the state of the gardens, then indeed, that is where my attention was. Would you prefer if I declared I was concerned about the state of affairs of the monarchy? Which would you believe?"

"I meant no offense," he assured her, his tone nevertheless amused. The gardens were too important to Jane for his irreverent nature and for her sake; he would try to keep the peace.

"Please forgive me," Jane said. "I was rather rude just now." She looked briefly into his eyes, and quickly turned away. "Tell me, why did you go off to war?"

At her glance, as brief as it was Sir Hugh felt his heart stutter and it took him a moment to gather his thoughts. "It was my way of getting away from my father. I got to join forces with Wellington during his campaign against

Napoleon, and was there when he defeated him. Sadly, many of our soldiers didn't come back." He suddenly stopped.

"Are you well, sir?" Jane placed a hand on his arm.

Shucking off the grip of melancholy, Sir Hugh resumed walking. "Yes, my lady," he said, not offering details. He would never discuss with her or any member of the fairer sex the ugliness of war. "Wellington is a great man and leader. He did England a magnificent service by ridding the world of a dictator."

"Papa always envied the officers. He wanted to go off to war, but—"

"Why didn't he?"

She smiled, "He didn't dare leave me and Margaret orphans. I found that to be very gallant and selfless of him."

"I would perhaps do the same thing if I had children. I would find it difficult to leave them. Yet, I know I would not hesitate to do so for the sake of England and her people." Sir Hugh gave a rueful shake of his head. Until he'd met Lady Jane, speaking of having a family had been out of the question. *The confounded woman had an effect on him.*

When Jane became unusually quite Sir Hugh touched her elbow and turned toward her. "Is something wrong? I am sorry, if my stories bring painful memories," he said, believing talks of family were painful for her, as well.

Jane looked at him, as if she was seeing him for the first time.

"Lady Jane?"

Jane blinked and snapped open her fan. "I believe I have had too much sun for today. I am afraid I haven't recovered completely from the party. Perhaps repose is called for. Let us, please, turn back."

He stared at her for a moment. Obviously he'd upset her sensibilities discussing family. The moment to make things right passing, he settled for a smile, before giving her his arm, a strictly neutral act of gallantry dictated by societal rules.

She linked her slender arm in his and allowed him to escort her back to the manor.

"Another day then," Sir Hugh said. Showing no signs of relenting, he added, "I am sure there are many secrets here for me to discover."

Jane merely kept her eyes forward, focused on keeping up with his firm, long stride.

Bringing her to a complete stop, Sir Hugh spun around, "May I ask you and Margaret to limit your outings? And when you do go out, always have someone with you, preferably one of the footmen should you find me or Mr Latham unavailable."

To his surprise Jane didn't rebuff him; instead she smiled and gave a simple nod. Seemingly pleased with himself, he turned, directing her back to the manor.

Chapter Fourteen

The next day the sun shone brightly, even though a cool breeze lingered into the afternoon mirroring the chill of unease in Jane's spine.

Waiting for Margaret in the morning room, Jane paced back and forth as she sometimes did when something bothered her. She faced the day with a mixture of confusion and trepidation as she relived her walk with Sir Hugh and worried about the vicar's murderer. When thinking of Sir Hugh, she experienced funny somersaults in the pit of her belly. However, the opposite was true when thinking of the poor late vicar. She felt cold and numb never imaging such chaotic emotions.

She hoped that tonight's dinner at the Daltons' would do them all some good. Life always seemed a little easier when Margaret was around. A better friend or sister she could not have asked for. Jane realized for the umpteenth time how fortunate she was to have people who loved her.

Amelia walked into the room and quickly excused herself when she realized the room was occupied. But before she could make her escape, Jane called her over.

"Stepmother, how lovely to see you please come in." Jane motioned for her to sit.

"I didn't mean to disturb your solitude," her ladyship declared, looking grand and beautiful in a dress of muslin sprigged with lilies of the valley. No one would have ever guessed that three weeks ago she had been in a serious accident that could have taken her life.

Jane smiled. "You could never do that. In the short time I've known you I've come to value your presence. Besides, any woman who can make my father happy is a rare gem, indeed." She wondered if there would ever be someone out there for her. An image of Sir Hugh popped into her mind. And as quickly as the image came, she pushed it away.

As if intuitively sensing what had passed through her daughter's mind, Lady Crittenden said, "I am sure your equal is out there, and perhaps you have already met him, hmm?"

Jane noticed a gleam in her eyes. *Oh, dear*, she recognized that look. To change the subject, she immediately asked Amelia's thoughts on putting together a small party. "We could invite a few special guests for an elegant evening of dining and conversation."

"I think it is a wonderful idea," declared her ladyship.

"Of course, I speak with father and insist on card playing to be off limits. I would prefer to have an intimate evening of pleasant conversation." Jane decided she would discuss the plans with Margaret.

"I agree. I have always enjoyed intimate dinners. It gives one the opportunity to get to know your guests better."

"Are you sure you will be up to it?" Jane asked. She did not want to over extend her step-mother, but they needed to get the investigation moving. With all of the parties and dinners they'd attended of late, it was no wonder they had not discovered any new clues or come close to solving the vicar's murder.

"Certainly, since our ball the other evening, I haven't myself had chance to plan a small dinner. It would most certainly give me great joy."

A twinge of guilt poked the ever-sensitive Jane. After all, it was now her stepmother's role to plan and head up such events. She must give way, even though the party was her idea. Though having her stepmother busy with the details of menu and seating arrangements, would give her and Margaret a chance to plan their strategies on how to go about testing Sir Hugh's and Mr Latham's knowledge of the murder investigation.

Lady Crittenden rose from the sofa. "If you will excuse me, I must find your father. He promised me a walk in the gardens, and in return I promised him to take my rest before leaving for the Daltons this evening."

Jane rose as well and kissed her left cheek.

"You are welcome to join us," she said, but Jane graciously declined the offer.

On her way out, her stepmother turned. "Will you promise not to venture on the grounds alone or allow Margaret to do so?"

Perplexed at this unexpected request, first from Sir Hugh and now from her stepmother, Jane took a step forward. "Why? Is something amiss?"

"The attack on our family has your father and I concerned for both your safety."

As childish as it seemed, having another woman, aside from Margaret, worrying about her well-being gave Jane a tiny thrill. Giving her stepmother another kiss, she said, "I promise we won't walk alone and will always make it a point to be in company with another."

Entering the hall, Amelia ran into her impatient cousin, who seemed to have been pacing anxiously while waiting for her report.

"Did she promise?" Sir Hugh asked upon seeing her.

"Yes, she did. Now quit worrying about the child." Amelia patted him on his arm.

"She is not a child. She is an over-confident woman who enjoys infuriating me."

"Are you developing feelings for her? I mean it when I tell you this, Hugh, I will not have you hurt her," his cousin threatened in a motherly fashion.

"I have no intentions of doing so, I promise—"

"I know you would not do so intentionally," she interrupted his retort. "But I know you, cousin. When it comes to king and country your job comes first, and promises are easily broken."

For once in his life, Sir Hugh couldn't respond to a threat—a threat that was no less plausible having come from his dear cousin. He took a deep breath. "Do not worry, my dear. I promise I will not hurt her." He kissed her gently on the cheek and headed out for some air.

Even a man was entitled to fresh air when things got complicated.

Margaret greeted Sir Hugh as he passed her on the front stairs, but he did not seem to notice her presence. Perplexed as to his attitude she meant to query Jane but found herself immediately caught up in the plans her friend had made for the dinner. She was also quickly privy to Jane's walk with Sir Hugh and her stepmother's strange request about not walking alone.

When Margaret didn't immediately respond, Jane said, "Yes, you can tell me, you told me so, although, gloating doesn't become you."

Margaret knew Jane didn't take well to teasing. In a carefully moderated tone she asked, "Are you then telling me you're beginning to trust Sir Hugh?"

"What I'm saying is you were correct about there being more to him than I first assumed and decidedly disliked."

Margaret had to hide a snicker by pretending to sneeze delicately into her handkerchief. One thing Jane despised even more than being wrong was admitting that she had made an error.

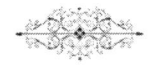

By four o'clock in the afternoon his lordship, elegantly attired, waited for the ladies in the grand hall. Married twice and with a young daughter, he was not a stranger to the length of time it took for women to get ready. He turned to the open door as a chilly draught wound its way inside declaring winter would soon be upon them.

The walk with Amelia refreshed and energized him. After Eliza's death, he never truly believed he could ever be happy with another woman until he'd met Amelia. For the longest time, he thought all he needed was his life with Jane, and for a while, it had been sufficient. But if truth is told, there were times when his life, while not unhappy, had lacked a sense of fulfilment.

Giving his appearance a final look in the mirror, he heard a coach approach. That would be the gentlemen, he wagered, and right on time. It should not have surprised him to see the two men together—they had become thick as thieves and a single coach would give them the opportunity of riding with the young ladies.

He called to one of the servants to check on the ladies.

The coach swayed into a halt in front of the manor. Sir Hugh was the first to step down, followed by Mr Latham.

"Gentlemen, as always you are welcome. As you can see, the ladies have yet to make their appearances. Not that I have been counting the minutes mind you, having been married twice I have developed the patience of a saint. A virtue you will soon discover vital, once you are wed." He chuckled as the younger men blanched at the thought of matrimony. "Now, now, gentlemen, be at ease. There are other benefits to marriage providing us the stamina to withstand feminine frailties."

They mutely agreed with his lordship's declaration when her ladyship entered the hall in a light blue gown trimmed in dark blue lace.

"Gentlemen, I apologize for being late."

"Nonsense, Amelia, apologies are unnecessary and might I add, you look breath-taking," her husband replied with devout sincerity.

She smiled, blushed and turned to Sir Hugh. "Hugh, you are looking the respectable bachelor without your military uniform, and you, Mr Latham, are truly dressed as the lord you are. I think the young ladies will be pleased."

The gentlemen looked at each other, dark dread looming over them. A happily married woman with matchmaking ideas made a lethal opponent, indeed.

"Papa—" Jane, wearing a pink gown trimmed with white bows, swept in to apologize for her tardiness when she realized four pairs of eyes staring at her.

"Jane, you look very lovely. Your mother would have been proud at the young woman you've become," her father said.

With a wide grin, Mr Latham politely bowed and elbowed Sir Hugh whose mouth was hanging open like a fish caught in a net.

With a jump, Sir Hugh snapped his mouth shut and bowed as well, quietly mumbling, "Yes, beautiful, indeed," under his breath.

Lady Jane blushed more than she care to.

Before his lordship could ask what Sir Hugh had said, Margaret made her appearance and looking equally as lovely.

"I'm sorry for keeping everyone waiting, but I—" Margaret stopped in her tracks, as all eyes turned to her.

His lordship felt for the young lady he'd come to think of as his niece was very becoming in an ivory gown trimmed with lace and it was obvious that she was overcome with shyness at being the centre of attention. To spare Margaret further anxiety, he broke the silence. "Well, since we are all here, I think it best, if we be on our way."

Sir Hugh nodded and glanced over at Latham. "Easy, there, old man. Do try and look a bit more natural. You'll frighten the poor chit," he whispered

Latham quickly shot a hard look at his companion.

Before Sir Hugh could comment further, his lordship decreed that the young ladies would ride with the gentlemen, and the group set out to the Daltons.

Chapter Fifteen

The Bartholomews, his lordship's party, arrived at the Daltons' manor at precisely half past six. Once introductions were made, and everyone had a chance to get reacquainted, guests and family retreated into the drawing room to wait for the announcement to dinner.

Lady Ella Dalton was a petite woman with greying hair and a stout figure. Though not yet five and fifty, she looked older, having born five children, now all grown with the exception of her two youngest, Lady Sophie, age eighteen, and Lady Cassandra, seventeen.

Lord George Dalton, Sr., who inherited his title from a distant male relative, resembled his wife in stoutness, though taller. His greying hair had been combed to the side and back from his round face, his gravelly baritone voice telling one he favoured the port.

Lady Sophie was considered the beauty with fair hair that bounced with full curls, and her porcelain complexion that no doubt was envied by angels. Others would argue that it was Lady Cassandra whose beauty was surely to surpass that of the Angel Jophiel. Younger than her sister Sophie, she was far taller and more curvaceous. Her bosom was accentuated by a revealing low collar, leaving little doubt of the young woman's awareness of her own femininity.

Margaret and Jane learned from Lady Cassandra that the two youngest Dalton boys were serving in his majesty's navy and were currently out of the country.

As for the infamous George, the oldest of the Dalton children, he had remained in London during his tour of service with the Royal Guards.

"Sir Hugh made a real difference in George's life," Lord Dalton said. "Without your guidance, sir, I fear our George would have been lost to us forever."

Sir Hugh inclined his head briefly. "No need to thank me, your lordship. George is to be commended for having the sense to undertake the changes needed in order to make his family and country proud."

"We are proud of our Georgie," Lady Dalton confirmed. "It is a pity he's not here, for he would most surely cause a rift between you, Lady Jane and Miss Renard. He is considered the most handsome of any young men you would ever meet. When visiting us, mothers throughout the town beg to make his acquaintance in the hopes of forming an attachment with one of their daughters."

Margaret somehow had difficulties imagining being courted by someone called Georgie, she turned in time to see her friend roll her eyes on Lady Dalton's going on about her son's handsomeness, while Latham seemed solemn at the idea that Georgie no doubt sounded like a flop, at least that is what Margaret wanted to believe. She looked at Jane in time to see her roll her eyes, as if wondering if Georgie was really that handsome. But one look at Hugh and she had her answer: He seemed in dubious thoughts to the young man's good looks. A mother's love was truly blind, Margaret finally deduced.

During the introductions, the mention of Mr Latham's title caused Lady Dalton great excitement. She visibly perked up at the prospect of two eligible bachelors for her daughters. When the families settled in the drawing room, the hostess began reciting a long list of her daughters' attributes. Fortunately, before any of the guests could comment, a footman had entered the room to announce dinner.

Lord Dalton, as host, escorted Lady Crittenden to the dining room, and as hostess, his wife was escorted by Lord Crittenden. The others followed closely behind.

"Tell me, Sir Hugh," Lady Cassandra began, leaning over to the right. "Did you and my brother serve with Wellington?"

Glancing around the table, Sir Hugh noted the girl's mother deep in conversation on the latest fashion and gossip; while Lord Dalton downed his fifth sherry; and much to his dismay he found the others, eagerly awaiting his response. As a man of the military, he often found it difficult to talk about himself.

"I did have the honour of serving with Wellington. He was instrumental in the defeat of —"

"How exciting, tell me how many Frenchies did you kill?" Lady Cassandra's angelic features hardened with the idea of death. The candles played upon them, almost turning her features into a ghoulish mask. "I've read *The Scarlet Pimpernel* many times. I found it quite romantic and thrilling," she said speaking quickly, causing her bosom to rise and fall with each breath she took.

There was fear amongst the guests that the girl was in danger of exposing her bosom if she didn't take great care and composed herself.

Attuned with a mother's ear, Lady Dalton registered the word "kill" over her tirade about the Royals' latest indiscretions and quickly intervened before Sir Hugh could reply.

"Now, Cassie, such questions are unbecoming for a young lady of good breeding," Lady Dalton lovingly reprimanded her daughter. "Please disregard the question, Sir Hugh. I am afraid my daughter is very young and quite naive."

If only she would reprimand her on the way she insists on exposing herself, Margaret thought with a grimace. She was appalled at the girl's behaviour, especially where the men were concerned. Margaret occasionally watched Mr Latham from beneath her lashes, hoping to catch him staring at her, but to her surprise, he kept his eyes focused on Lady Dalton and her talk concerning legal affairs. To his credit, she detected he loved his profession and realized while he had no need to practice law; he obviously did so because he enjoyed it. An interesting question came to her out of nowhere. *What would he do for something or someone he loved regardless of what society dictated?*

She remembered her father talking about the young men who wasted their fortunes, and once penniless, had no other choice but to marry heiresses for the sake of money. Miserable in their marriages, they drank and squandered their wives' fortunes. She had to acknowledge Latham was a sensible man of good breeding. His father would truly have been proud of him.

"And to what do we owe that beautiful smile, Margaret?" Lord Crittenden asked.

Blushing, she suddenly found herself the centre of inquiring eyes and to her dismay, Mr Latham, among the others, save for Cassandra, waited expectantly for an answer.

"Well, with all this talk about legal issues, I recalled with great fondness his lordship's father, the late Duke of Stanton. He attended my father's personal affairs and served him quite well. Lord Dalton, if you ever find yourself in need of an excellent solicitor, you would be wise to consider Mr Latham. I mean his Grace."

"Thank you, Miss Renard," Latham managed to say.

"Is this true your Grace? Was your father a solicitor as well?" Lady Dalton asked.

Margaret turned to him.

Mr Latham appeared to bear the title with ease, yet without undue pride. "Yes, it is true, my lady."

"Oh, my!" she let out a huge sigh, lifting a hand to her heart in an overly dramatic fashion. "I was just telling my husband, this very morning, how we were in need of a solicitor, for our very own Ashworth has recently retired. Was I not, dearest?" she asked her husband, whose face had become as red as the wine he was drinking.

Taking into consideration the lateness of the hour, the two families passed on the routine of separating the sexes, but chose instead for all to return to the drawing room. Conversations circulated from history to fashion, the men uncomfortable whenever fashion took the centre stage by the Dalton girls. Not wishing to encourage them, Margaret and Jane merely nodded their agreements when asked about dresses or ribbons, strategically disguising their boredom.

The conversation then took a turn toward the upcoming holidays. Lady Dalton asked her husband to confirm that his favourite holiday was Christmas.
His lordship only raised his glass in agreement. "Here, here." He then burped, downed another class of wine and soon fell asleep on the couch. His head falling to his rising chest; gentle snores could be heard.

Looking as if nothing was out of the ordinary, her ladyship yelled for a male servant, "Harrison!"

A young male servant came into the room, "Yes, my lady."

"His lordship has done it again. Please see to it that he gets to his rooms."

The servant bowed, "Yes, my lady." He walked over to his lordship, "Come along, your lordship." Lifting the man was no small feat, yet the young man was able to accomplish the task without any incident.

As Lord Dalton was being removed from the room, Jane's father used the opportune moment to thank their hostess and absent host for a wonderful evening. Since his wife was still recovering from an accident, he thought it best to leave before it grew too late. Agreeing, Lady Dalton reluctantly bid her guests farewell, but not before acquiring an invitation for dinner from her ladyship.

The mother of two unmarried and beautiful daughters was on a new mission of acquiring matrimonial proposals for them, and what better way than to expose them once again to the eligible bachelors currently staying with the Earl and Countess of Crittenden.

Chapter Sixteen

The first few minutes of the ride home passed in silence. Margaret, harbouring a headache, laid back and closed her eyes.

Jane, exhausted, wished she could just close her eyes and fall asleep, but the sway of the coach on the rocky road jolted her more than she cared to admit. When they hit a bump she'd grimace, casting a worried glance at her friend. All of the jostling was surly making her friend's headache worse.

To their credit the gentlemen remained quiet. Jane surmised that was due more to the disputes between them than the lateness of the hour.

Since sleep eluded her, Jane broke the silence, "Can you believe how Lady Dalton just yelled out for one of the servants to come and fetch her husband? I nearly dropped my fork."

"Yes, I can," said Margaret, her eyes remaining shut. Ignoring the gentlemen, she added, "It's true, there is a difference between someone who's inherited a title and those born into it. That is why I refuse to bow down to society. Its imperfections deserve to be mocked at all cost."

"It was clear that Lady Dalton was not born into it," Jane declared.

Mr Latham chimed in, "It is not society that is imperfect, Miss Renard, but the people in it. There are those who are led by greed and materialism, ruining a perfectly civilized society."

It was highly inconceivable that Mr Latham would insult his peers, but he'd just done it.

"Please don't misunderstand my meaning," he continued "The foundational rules of society are such that it is perfect. But because of the increase in wealth for those categorized in the middle class, they now are able to buy their way into society, as the Daltons, no doubt had done."

"The Daltons did not buy their title. It was inherited," Jane corrected Margaret.

"True," said Sir Hugh, joining in on the conversation. "While theirs is an inherited title, they now face the same dilemma as someone who had purchased their title. They are not educated in the etiquettes of the society that they now find themselves in and are therefore creating an unsavoury image of society."

"Why would you care, Sir Hugh? I rather thought you didn't care a shilling for society," Margaret accused.

"After all, once the vicar's murder is solved, off you will go to your next assignment."

At Margaret's declaration, and thankfully in the darkness of the coach, no one noticed the array of emotions coursing through Jane's body, threatening to make her sick.

"True, I don't care, but order is important and when a lack of it exists, chaos is sure to follow. What assignment, do you speak of?" asked Sir Hugh tilting his head at the question.

Margaret chuckled, "Spoken like a true soldier. Come now, Sir Hugh. We are aware that you are not whom you pretend to be, a man of the royal army, are we?"

Impressed with her friend, Jane remained silent, noting that Mr Latham also chose to remain quiet. She smirked inwardly wondering if he did so perhaps out of fear in getting into another argument with Margaret. Jane hoped no one had felt or seen her reaction to the idea of Sir Hugh gone forever. Well perhaps, not forever, for he would surely come and visit his cousin. All this time she had been wishing for his departure and now that she was reminded that he would go someday, the thought troubled her. Perhaps she was coming down with a cold.

It also did not skip Jane's notice that Sir Hugh blatantly did not answer the question Margaret had posed, and instead turned his attention to the dark outside the window with a knowing smile.

That seemed to be the end of any conversation, and the entire party then slipped into silence for the duration of the trip home.

When they arrived, the gentlemen quickly assisted the ladies from the coach. Nothing beyond a few hasty farewells was spoken before Mr Latham continued on his journey home and the others entered the manor and retired to their rooms.

As she closed her bedroom door Jane fretted slightly about Margaret returning home in the morning. But as her friend had previously pointed out, she wanted to make sure she continued with her tithing to her renters. It was slight comfort that Margaret promised to return as soon as she could. Realizing that fatigue was making her emotional, Jane put everything from her mind and prepared for bed.

True to her word, Margaret returned within a few days, this time to assist her aunt and friend with preparations for their dinner party. This was to be the last party before winter set in and the roads would be covered in snow making it too difficult and dangerous for traveling.

Stepping back to view the results of Jane's work, Margaret was impressed. "You are quite the artist," she said to Jane, watching her wind another piece of ivy around the staircase banister. The dining and living rooms were already decorated with large candles, their cheery flames brightening the rooms. The rugs had been given a good dusting, the wood furniture and silver polished, and Jane's mother's china gleamed. As the evening air had brought slightly cooler temperatures, the servants had been asked to light fires in all the bed chambers as well as the parlour. Even the gardener had joined in the preparations, bringing in green ivy with berries to place on the buffet and dining room tables as her ladyship had requested.

"Thank you," Jane said. "But so are you. Actually, some of my greatest ideas come from you. Remember the time I was visiting and you had taken a beautiful tablecloth and draped it over one of your chairs? I've often followed that example."

Margaret did. It was a piece of linen her own mother embroidered when she had been newly married to her father.

"Besides," continued Jane, "it's you who is so good at devising a well-sorted out plan on how to get the men to show their true characters. Any ideas since we last talked?"

"Well, really! That's tantamount to calling your friend devious," Margaret teased, and the girls laughed. They proceeded to retire to Jane's bedroom to discuss further strategies.

Chapter Seventeen

At the edge of town, by the east side of the coast Dover, silhouettes of men loading and unloading small boats of smuggled goods could be seen from where he perched. It was imperative he kept his distance, should they get caught. Vane was no fool, but it paid to have informants. Already they had confirmed his suspicions that Sir Hugh Cameron had been asking questions and was more than just a relation of the new Lady Crittenden. Cameron could be a dangerous opponent, but Vane wanted more facts before deciding what to do about the man.

And then there was Binet who came in handy when it came to the men; he made sure orders were carried out. Vane clenched his fist. His time was better spent courting a future bride. He looked at the welcome surprise in his hand. He'd received an invitation from Lord and Lady Crittenden to a small dinner at their manor. Vane had to admit he was looking forward to seeing the young ladies again. However, he wasn't too pleased when he heard Sir Hugh and Mr Latham were going to be amongst the guests.

But from what his inside source told him, he ascertained the young ladies were none too pleased with the gentlemen.

He smiled smugly at his own knack for investigating, a skill his future bride would surely appreciate as he courted her. However she would have to give up her little adventures after they were married. He would see to it.

Looking back to the coast, Vane noticed two men arguing, and then shoving began and within seconds fists were flying. He was just beginning to wonder where Binet had gone to, when a stout form approached the two men. The fight stopped. One of the men, on Binet's order, began to walk away. The other man yelled something at the retreating figure that Vane did not catch over the sounds of the sea. Whatever was said caused the Belgian to raise his hand and fire his pistol at the hostile man.

The other men stopped what they were doing to see what had occurred and gawk at their now deceased comrade. Once their curiosity had been satisfied, they thought it best to mind their own business and get back to the work at hand.

Vane would have to speak with Binet. Though the man may have had good reason to shoot the fellow, they could not afford to lose any more workers, not when the Italians had been so difficult in their demands. Vane had no allegiance to England or France, though he would be quick to thank them for making him a very rich man. Glancing at his watch Vane realized that he'd best be going otherwise he would be late for dinner.

That smug grin returned—he could not wait to see her again.

Hours later, Jane and Margaret, dressed in velvet gowns, joined his lordship and ladyship in the front hall. Jane wore a dark hunter green that complimented her blonde curls and green eyes, while Margaret's red gown was considered an admirable choice that complemented her pale skin, dark eyes and auburn hair.

Jane noted that her stepmother stood strong and rested, her arm linked with her father's.

"You two look beautiful," announced Lady Crittenden. "And I have never seen such gorgeous flowers. What a wonderful job you've done with the decorations, Jane."

"Thank you, Mother."

It was the first time she had called Amelia mother. Jane had always wondered what it would feel like to call someone "Mother" and now that she had done so, it felt wonderful. Besides, her stepmother made it easy, for she had been very loving and selfless, just as a mother should be.

Her ladyship's eyes visibly misted over and his lordship gave her hand a squeeze, "Now, now. What would our guests say if they arrive to find their hostess weeping?"

Amelia turned to her husband, eyes wide open. "Charles, sometimes I do believe you do not understand women at all," she said in exasperation.

"Oh, but I do, my dear. Otherwise how could I've been so fortunate as to acquire a beautiful and witty wife who unconditionally adores me and all of my faults?" he declared.

Jane blushed as her parents continued with their declarations of love. She thought it odd that everyone milled about in the front hall, since the only guest to be arriving was Mr Latham. Surely the butler could show him to the parlour when he arrived. A formal greeting line was not necessary.

"Papa," Jane said, "should we not retire to—" Her words were interrupted by the loud clatter of carriage wheels.

"Oh, that must be the rest of our guests," her mother said, "and quite punctual."

Other guests? This was not at all what she and Margaret had planned. "Excuse us for a moment," Jane said, gently pulling Margaret toward the parlour.

"Did you know there were other guests invited?"

"Of course not!" shrieked Jane. "It is highly improper. My mother must have intercepted my invitation list and invited them. What are we to do? This spoils everything. I need a minute to speak with my mother. Please make my excuses if anyone should ask," Jane commanded, leaving her alone to wonder what was going on.

Jane thought carefully in her recollection of a conversation with her mother about the guest list and was certain that there had never been a mention of an invitation for additional guests. Passing the dining room she counted nine settings as oppose to the six she had requested. Who the other three guests were, was a mystery to her and one she was determine to find out. But first she had to tell Margaret what she has discovered.

Margaret having known Jane for so long knew her friend was pained at having her plans disrupted. It was Jane who had been the perfect one for upholding a general appearance of good manners, at least on formal social occasions, but having her plans wayward, was the exception.

She stood alone in the parlour for several more uncomfortable minutes wondering where Jane had gone. *Maybe I should go after her?* Frozen by indecision, she stayed where she was.

Sir Hugh sauntered into the parlour, apparently disregarding whatever social niceties were happening in the front hall, and Margaret couldn't help noticing how his navy coat set off his light hair and eyes. She smiled, wondering what her friend might think of his military attire.

He went straight to the liquor cabinet and poured a glass of sherry, asking amiably, "Would you like a glass? It might help you relax. Latham is coming, you know."

Unaffected by Sir Hugh's saturnine manner, Margaret smiled. "No thank you. I shall trust my own wits to protect me. Have you seen Jane? She disappeared a few moments ago."

"The devil if I know," he growled setting his glass down a little harder than needed.

Margaret didn't know what to make of Sir Hugh's ill temper. She was relieved from any further wondering when Jane wandered back into the parlour.

"Good evening, Sir Hugh," Jane said suddenly finding herself flustered by the sight of the dashing young man in his uniform. She felt another surge of anger course through her—the man was impossible and infuriating. The man lived to unsettle her nerves. Remembering she had other concerns she turned to Margaret in her usual stiff composed countenance.

Sir Hugh gave her a mocking bow.

"Good evening, Lady Jane. How lovely you look tonight. What a great effort you've made. Surely it could only be because the Marquis de Faucheaux is among the guests tonight."

Jane felt as if a bucket of ice water had been thrown at her, her face suddenly paled.

"The Marquis?" she repeated slowly. "How do you know?"

Sir Hugh smirked. "I overheard my cousin and your father discussing the guest list earlier this afternoon. There was another guest who had also been invited, but I couldn't hear without seeming to invade their privacy. It should make for an interesting evening, don't you think?"

Jane felt her cheeks being to flame, slowly losing her composure. "I was not told. Pray excuse me." She whirled and left the room. Margaret moved to follow.

"Ah, going to the rescue of your friend?" asked Sir Hugh, studying the small amount of sherry left in his glass.

Margaret turned to face him. "Jane, on the whole, does not need rescuing. But I am going to support her, pray excuse me." Turning away, she went after her friend.

Margaret found her friend in the front hall confronting her parents.

"But why did you not tell me, Papa?" Jane asked, quite putout. Her face was flushed, yet her voice was carefully controlled. "Why should he be invited into our house for a family celebration?"

Other than the time her friend argued with her father about her entrance into society, Margaret had never seen

Jane so agitated. Concerned, Margaret slipped quietly over to her friend's side.

"And, pray, why invite Miss Nelson?" Jane snapped. "She only recently moved to town, and while I do agree we must be sociable, this evening was to be more of a family celebration than a gala event."

The girls had counted on the evening being in a personal setting to study Mr Latham and Sir Hugh in more detail. They were hoping to focus on how the gentlemen reacted in speech and manners, once certain questions were asked. They were going to determine if the men had any additional information on the vicar's murder. With other guests in the equation, Margaret fretted that they would not be able to accomplish their goal.

"My dear, I invited her," Lady Crittenden interjected, a slightly commanding air to her voice. "We must reach out to the community, and since the poor young woman has only recently arrived, she is likely in need of some social activity. Naturally, we should extend the hand of courtesy to her and her mother."

"I understand but—."

"Dearest, I meant to tell you that I had altered the guest list, but I simply forgot." Her stepmother seemed genuinely distressed over the matter.

Jane was no fool. What her stepmother really meant, regarding Miss Nelson, was that there was an available young woman in need of meeting an eligible bachelor in the hopes of forming an attachment. Admitting defeat Jane softened to her mother's plead for forgiveness.

"It's all right." Jane smiled slightly to prove to her mother all was forgiven.

Lady Crittenden released a sigh, "Mrs Nelson is under the weather, but sent her daughter, Beatrice and her companion, to us. The companion will be dining with the servants."

"Of course," Jane said. The redness of her face now turning to a soft pink hue, "I certainly agree, and I had hoped to visit her later this week. I am simply concerned you may not be up to entertaining a large group. You are still rather weak; I am sure."

"You are very sweet to be concerned over my well-being, but believe me when I tell you that I am up to the task. Three extra guests will not tax my health."

Jane held her breath as Sir Hugh sauntered into the front hall. She scarcely dared to breathe as she glanced from her parents to Sir Hugh and back, looking quite vexed.

Lady Crittenden was about to reveal who her third visitor was when the last coach approaching the manor's entrance was heard.

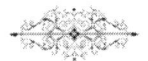

"Besides, I think of long sleeves as an instrument restricting movement when one is dancing," said Miss Nelson. "I mean, we have our shawls and coverlets for that." Her eyes roved from one of the ladies to another. Margaret had been seated to Miss Nelson's left, whilst Jane had taken the seat to her right.

Margaret leaning a little could see Jane's smile had been forced. As for herself, she quickly looked down, covering her mouth to hide a laugh. Miss Nelson's talk of fashion and the weather was proper for a young woman of society. At least it seemed to her, she was not prone to gossip and that should please Jane somewhat.

Her aunt, having mistaken the sound for a cough looked at her in concern. "Are you unwell, my dear?" she asked.

"I am fine, thank you, aunt." Margaret replied, *except for the fact I am seated next to Mr Latham!* She wanted to yell. While she could care less of fashion and weather, she was pleased for Miss Nelson's talk. Latham had been discussing banal subjects with her all evening, or rather, trying to. She had offered no more than a vague "Yes" or "Is that so?" throughout dinner.

Margaret was pensive and could sense Latham's confusion over her lack of interest. It no doubt was quite the opposite from the other night at the Daltons. She suppressed a chuckle.

Sir Hugh had taken the seat across from Jane. He tried offering comments that one could construed as either witty or rude. Margaret could also sense her friend's attitude toward Sir Hugh by the way she pushed her food around her plate, appetite gone.

The Marquis had taken the seat to Jane's right and was quite attentive, although she looked acutely uncomfortable.

"I really can't quite understand it, Margaret," Jane had declared about the Marquis, earlier in the evening while they were dressing.

"I should not fret so, Jane. You walk in different circles." Margaret had tried to assure her friend as her placed the last curl on top of her head.

But now, here was the blasted man, and her friend was ever so uneasy. Fortunately she was surrounded by her family.

In reality it was sad for the Marquis was quite handsome, and one of the most eligible and wealthy bachelors in the county, but every courtesy he extended to her friend seemed to be false, an act, she sensed, to hide something sinister. What frustrated her most was that no one else seemed to understand or comprehend this duality.

Jane turned to her friend and smiled.

Once in a while, Margaret would catch Sir Hugh giving the Marquis hard, unfriendly looks from across the dining table when the Marquis spoke to Jane, which much to her friend's dismay, was quite often.

Then there was Miss Beatrice Nelson, a plain, mousy-looking young woman, seated beside Sir Hugh. She repeated throughout dinner she was single and with some fortune. To her utter surprise, Sir Hugh was very attentive to the young woman, not only with insipid conversation but by making sure she wanted for naught. Confused, she could not believe he was concerned with the length of ladies' sleeves this season. That he fell so easily for such obvious feminine wiles disappointed her more than she wished to admit.

Sir Hugh found Miss Nelson to be a humble young woman. She only did what she was raised to do—to make herself visibly eligible for marriage by exposing her best attributes. For now, it seemed to him that she had set her sights on him. While he was flattered, he was not a cad and, therefore, treaded with great care, for any wrong word or action would and could be construed as a potential attachment, and he had no intention of letting that happen, not now or ever.

He turned from Miss Nelson to steal a glimpse of Jane and found the Marquis leaning over to whisper something into her ear. He could see that Jane was uncomfortable at the proximity of the Marquis. To know she feared the nefarious rake made his blood rush to his head, threatening to pour out of his ears. He took comfort in knowing should the man step out of bounds he would take care of him once and for all. Had the Marquis been any other man, perhaps he would not be so concerned. After all whom Jane formed an attachment to was not any of his concern. However, he found himself wondering about Jane and her future—feeling troubled at the thought of seeing only himself as part of that future. And, yet, while he wished her well in her plans of matrimony, he couldn't picture anyone but himself. Blasted woman…he needed to get back to civilization and women.

He turned his attentions back to the Marquis, and became more annoyed that the man knew no bounds. Sir Hugh could feel the rush echoes of his blood rush rising from the bottom to the top of his head, the pressure causing pain and the feeling the blood threatening to pour out of his ears. He willed himself to stay calm.

Seated at opposite ends of the table, Sir Hugh could see that both host and hostess seemed happily unaware of the seething emotions and ploys being enacted around the dinner table.

The third guest turned out to be Lord Roxburgh. The man exuded gallantry, charm, and confidence. In his usual manner, he praised them, including Miss Nelson, who blushed every time he smiled at her.

Unsure as to why, he felt committed to keeping Miss Nelson's attentions away from Roxburgh.

Margaret took a stab of her lamb chop.

Everyone seemed to be enjoying themselves, but there was some underlying tension between the men—and she wondered why, but could not come up with anything, other than perhaps they know each other from previous dealings—dealings that somehow had gone wrong.

After a seemingly interminable time, the dinner dragged to a close. The women promptly left for the drawing room while the men proceeded to the smoking room.

"Please excuse us for a moment," Jane said, and taking hold of her friend's hand ushered her out through a side door into the semi-dark hall.

"What's wrong?" Margaret asked. She had hoped to talk to her aunt.

"Why, only that we're going to listen to the men's conversation," Jane said.

Margaret almost rejected Jane's idea, but listening to Miss Nelson gossip about her recent trip to London, fashion always taking centre stage—who wore what and who did it justice—was not how she'd planned to spend the evening. Personally she could care a whit about which was the lesser of two evils, pelisses or bonnets. For Jane and Margaret, fashion was not on top of their choices for conversation. With a sigh she chose to go with Jane.

"Very well, but don't be surprised if all they end up doing is talking about the different types of snuffs or men's fashions," Margaret warned, "Or the war."

"I know, but if we don't listen, we may not learn anything. We must determine which of them is to be trusted and which should be turned away from our circle."

"Excellent idea, though, at this point, I think that Sir Hugh can be trusted." Margaret whispered. Perhaps the evening wasn't a total loss after all.

"What of Mr Latham?"

"What of him?" Margaret asked a headache threatening to rear its ugly head.

Jane shook her head in disbelief. "It is safe to say, that we can trust Mr Latham."

Margaret was about to argue differently, but they arrived at a rough, wooden door. There was a crack at the doorjamb, allowing them to hear the conversation. Jane was tall enough to peek into the room through a knothole.

Chapter Eighteen

Latham sat on a comfortable chair by the fireplace; Sir Hugh leaned against the mantel, while Jane's father caught the butler's attention to ask for a sherry.

"Tell us, Marquis, what still keeps you in England? I'd have thought you would have returned to France by now," Sir Hugh said.

The Marquis, who had taken the blue velvet seat across from Jane's father and Roxburgh, seemed rather surprised. "I cannot fathom why you would concern yourself with my travels, sir. We are not at war anymore, *n'est ce pas?*"

"The other day I heard rumours of a group trying to pick up where Napoleon left off," Sir Hugh replied with underlying sarcasm.

"Rumours do not concern me, monsieur. Napoleon was a great leader. It was a tragedy to hear of his defeat."

Mr Latham decided he didn't care for the Marquis. "A tragedy for whom?" he asked. "I've read the French were finally relieved to have got rid of him."

Defensively the Marquis responded, "I am merely saying he was while an emperor, a capable leader who wanted what was best for his country."

"Right, old chap, and conquering was an excellent exercise for the outdoors," Latham added. Sir Hugh and Crittenden laughed.

"I too happened to think him brilliant, Marquis," Roxburgh said radiating confidence and gallantry, smiling as Latham bristled.

The girls looked at each other. The conversation was taking on an interesting tone.

Sir Hugh couldn't figure it out, but he just did not like the man. He turned to Roxburgh. "Well, there you go, Marquis. We have someone here who seems to appreciate the love affair between England and your France."

The Marquis, previously relaxed, now stiffened.

"Come now, Marquis, please ignore the young rogues," Lord Crittenden finally interjected.

"I am not that naive, your lordship. I am aware not all of England enjoys the so-called love affair with the French, as our young friend here stated," the Marquis shot back.

Amusement now gone, his lordship's tone stiffened, "It appears, Sir Hugh, that you have overstepped the boundaries. The Marquis is a guest in my house, and on that merit alone he deserves to be respected."

Sir Hugh reddened at the reprimand, but did not retaliate. "You are correct, Charles. Marquis, pray forgive me."

The Marquis rose from the settee and bowed. "Apology accepted, sir."

Roxburgh, turning to his lordship, said, "I hear you have lately been having a bit of bad luck. I heard of the vicar's murder. Has the magistrate found anything that would tell us who did it or why he was murdered?"

The Marquis tensed at the mention of murder. It may have gone unnoticed by the others, but not by the girls.

Jane and Margaret strained to hear every word.

When Jane's father had reprimanded Sir Hugh, they both felt a bit sorry for Sir Hugh.

And the more they heard from Lord Roxburgh, the more Jane realized he was a mystery to her. He did not seem at all like the young man Margaret had known growing up. The Marquis was another mystery. The dashing Frenchman was playing at something, but exactly what or with whom, she had no clue. Perhaps they should keep a watchful eye on him. She had to admit, however reluctantly, that adding the Marquis to their list of suspects made things unnecessarily complicated. With too many variables in the equation of who murdered the vicar and why, failure seemed unavoidable.

Biltmore, on his way to the drawing room, stopped and raised an eyebrow at the girls. Ashamed at having been caught listening but unwilling to leave, they straightened and smiled at him. He frowned slightly at them, shook his head, and continued on his way.

As soon as he entered the drawing room, where the other ladies were, Margaret bent down once more to listen, while Jane returned to spying the crack in the knothole knowing that Biltmore would not give them away.

Drawing on a cigar, Lord Crittenden blew out a puff of smoke. "Murder is a nasty business, Roxburgh. You are lucky to have just recently arrived back from America." He shook his head and took another puff of his cigar, "Quite a nasty business indeed."

"Who would kill a man of the cloth?" The girls heard Roxburgh ask as he brushed something from his trouser leg, a disdain look about his face.

"We have no idea," Sir Hugh said. He glanced at Latham and then back to Roxburgh.

"I heard a cross was placed in his mouth," Roxburgh said in a manner similar to discussing the weather.

"Where would you get such information, sir, having only just arrived?" Latham asked.

Roxburgh laughed. "We're in the country, Latham. What is there but talk to be made among the landed gentry?"

"That is all too correct," Latham agreed. "I am sure you regret coming back at this time."

"Nonsense—Dover offers many opportunities. I wouldn't have stayed away too long."

"Opportunities?" interjected Sir Hugh

"Why yes," Roxburgh said, smiling as he picked up his glass. "There is always great port, of course, and beautiful women. But come, Sir Hugh, I am not vain. I concede Dover offers us its beautiful White Cliffs, excellent seafood, and lovely ports for sailing, *n'est ce pa*, Marquis?"

Latham surveyed Roxburgh as though he were seeing him for the first time. With a quick glance he noticed the same look of confusion flash across Sir Hugh's face.

"I believe it is time to join the ladies," the Marquis said, abruptly rising from his chair and heading toward the door, leaving Latham to wonder what had suddenly made the man so obviously uncomfortable.

When the men rose to adjourn the girls scurried up the hall and into the drawing room, explaining to the other ladies that their absence was due to Margaret's sudden stomach upset but assured them she was now much better. Taking their seats Margaret wondered if they could use that excuse again to escape if the conversation became tedious. She and Jane could barely contain the excitement over their discoveries and were looking forward to discussing them later when they were alone in their rooms.

As it was, without the men around, Miss Nelson's conversation became more intelligent and her conduct more relaxed.

"Lady Jane, I do adore your dress. Who is your dressmaker?"

Jane lifted her eyes to meet those of Miss Nelson, smiled, and said, "I have the good fortune of having my own dressmaker."

"Oh, how wonderful it must be to have someone at your beck and call, always ready to design at your every whim." The words came out pleasantly enough, but Margaret caught a hint of envy in them.

More so she could hear a touch of sarcasm as well as if Miss Nelson wished she too had a personal dress designer and not that Jane had an excellent one. Hoping that Jane had not caught the tone Margaret interjected, "I've no doubt, if you wish to have Alba design something for you; she would do it for a small commission." She knew Alba, who had six little ones, wouldn't mind the extra money.

Before Miss Nelson could reply, the men returned to the drawing room causing Miss Nelson to return to her previous behaviour—that of a single woman in pursuit of a husband.

Inwardly Margaret sighed, slightly worried as to how the conversation was going to move. She had Jane had questions to ask, questions that needed answers, and could not be asked in the presence of the current company without drawing attention to their investigation.

True to his lordship's promise, no whist tables were set so the company was left to their own devices. For the rest of the evening, the party broke into groups, and muted tones could be heard throughout the room. Jane took the opportunity to observe her guests.

Sir Hugh was flirting with Beatrice, who by the end of the evening Jane hoped never to see again.

Latham had tried to engage Margaret in conversation but having been rebuffed ended up nursing his sherry.

Jane noticed her friend's sulkiness and decided that it was attributed to the fact that Miss Nelson had now turned her attentions to Latham.

Feeling as if she was being watched, Jane turned to look around the room. Her feeling was confirmed as her gaze happened upon to fall upon the Marquis. He was openly watching her. Why his presence unsettled her so much was puzzling. Jane nodded to him politely, but inwardly couldn't wait to see the back of him.

After a moment the Marquis moved off to engage Roxburgh in private conversation leaving Jane slightly relieved without knowing why it should matter.

Miss Nelson's giggle broke through the quite, obviously thrilled beyond belief to have the undivided attention of both Mr Latham and Sir Hugh.

Margaret sat with her new aunt talking quietly so as to not disturb his lordship who was dozing next to his wife. Jane would have smiled at that pleasant picture of contentment if she was not pretending to focus on the latest issue of *Ackermann's Repository*.

The Marquis was the first to declare he was retiring for the evening. He bid good night and bowed to all, but before leaving he cast a last glance at Jane.

Jane curtsied, and her spirits lightened immediately after his departure.

Lord Roxburgh was next to take his leave. Coming up to his host and hostess, he bowed gallantly. "Countess, I had a wonderful time and never have I enjoyed the company of so many beautiful and graceful ladies as I have this evening." His last words were directed to the now flustered Miss Nelson.

Jane pitied her. Though she and Margaret had often been declared beauties of the town, they never paid heed to such talks. True that while Miss Nelson was not considered a beauty, she did have pleasant features, and though Jane had been annoyed with the girl, she understood society's expectations and shortcomings. The young woman was no different from other ladies of lesser or no consequence, all desperate for attention, especially from a handsome and eligible bachelor.

Roxburgh bowed to his hostess before turning to speak to his lordship. "Charles, I welcome the opportunity to reciprocate and invite you, her ladyship, and the young ladies to Walston Manor for dinner. Of course," he turned to the gentlemen, "the invitation is extended to your gentlemen guests as well, if they wish to attend."

"Thank you, Gerald. It would be an honour."

"It's settled then. I shall send my man over tomorrow with an invitation." Roxburgh, nodded, pleased at the acceptance, and turned toward Miss Nelson. "My dear lady, would you allow me the pleasure of escorting you and your companion home?"

Miss Nelson readily accepted.

"My apologies, Roxburgh, but Miss Nelson has agreed to allow me to escort her and her companion back home. Better luck next time, old boy," Sir Hugh interjected. Placing a hand on Miss Nelson's arm, he led her back to the drawing room while he went in search of Biltmore.

Jane saw Miss Nelson glow with pleasure. Having two men vie for her attention had been alien to her. Most likely she could not wait to run home and tell her mother all about it.

Jane thought she caught Roxburgh glaring at Sir Hugh's retreating form before turning his attention back to her and Margaret. But the flare in his eyes had been so quick that she was unsure and chalked it up to fatigue.

"Lady Jane, Miss Renard, until we meet again. I bid you all a good evening." Roxburgh bowed as the ladies curtsied and left with flair.

"I am retiring, for I am exhausted," Jane said. With a good night to everyone, she went upstairs, her glance resting a bit longer on Margaret, who had decided to go home Jane hoped she would change her mind and stay. They had much to discuss.

However to Jane's disappointment, Margaret could not be dissuaded and once again turned down her ladyship's invitation to spend the night. At least Margaret had agreed to let Biltmore and a footman escort her home for extra protection.

Sir Hugh followed the trio out as he left to see Miss Nelson home, bidding the lord and lady of the house a good night

Jane hovered at the top of the stairs watching their lone overnight guest bid her parents good night before returning to the drawing room, murmuring something about staying up a bit longer to review legal papers for a client.

For some reason knowing that Latham was in the house gave Jane a sense of added security. By the time she reached her room, Jane was determined she would take a long walk the next day to sort everything out, but she feared the solace of her mother's gardens would not be able to provide the comfort she needed.

Chapter Nineteen

The next morning Lady Crittenden waylaid Jane to confer on household and kitchen matters. She wanted to make sure that another faux pas, like last evening's, was not repeated. The discussion lasted well into the afternoon, leaving Jane exhausted from boredom and frustration. Obviously they had different opinions on how things were to be done. Jane had managed the house for years without thinking too much about it. She didn't put menus down on paper or make elaborate plans. She made simple lists or talked to the cook.

After tea Jane excused herself and retired to her room, but unable to rest, she chose to take the walk she had contemplated the previous evening hoping the fresh air would do her some good.

Once downstairs, she made it to the foyer, relieved it was devoid of inhabitants and saved from explaining why she needed to go out. Wrapping her cape around her, Jane decided a brisk walk to the village would be the ideal way to spend her bottled-up energy rather than walking the gardens, and made a mental note to be back before sunset, to avoid being missed.

After sometime Jane realized that the way was a little further than she'd remembered. Then again, it had been a long time since she ventured there on foot.

She saw several acquaintances and greeted them with pleasure, though their faces said plenty as they realized she was alone. Unlike Margaret, who made it her mission to break social rules, Jane usually followed them but was known to break a few of her own, and this was one of those times. It was improper for a young lady of her status to be out without a chaperone. And being such a small village consisting of little more than a market for produce, another for meats and fish, a small book store and a fabric store. Jane was sure the scandal of her unescorted walk would soon spread like wildfire. Such was the state of a small village.

Not caring what they thought, she continued on absently going in and out of the shops. Her thoughts were in constant turmoil as she pondered the vicar's murder, and Sir Hugh's ever-changing behaviour.

As the day grew cooler, Jane realized the sun had begun to set and she had stayed out longer than she had intended, she turned her way home, picking up her pace. She hoped that the day would not prove to have been a mistake as she had ventured out alone. Jane prayed for a quick and uneventful return home. She added another part to her prayer—that her father hadn't yet noticed her absence.

Choosing to stay on the road instead of going through the woods, Jane found herself intercepted by Mrs Appleby, as she passed the elderly woman's house and before reaching the boundary of the village. As always, Mrs. Appleby was on a mission to ascertain the latest gossip from Wellington Manor.

Having no time for idle chatter, Jane remained reticent and bid farewell to a very disappointed Mrs. Appleby.

Once back on the road Jane berated herself for not letting someone know where she was going. Telling Sir Hugh may have been better than not saying anything at all or even leaving a note for Biltmore at the very least. Chiding herself, Jane picked up her pace, eyes trained for anything out of the ordinary, ears attuned to the sounds around her. Though she knew the paved road well, in her rush she stumbled over a rock. Unfortunately, by preventing a fall, her attention had been diverted.

As she resumed walking, Jane realized something was wrong. The woods had become quieter, and the air suddenly felt heavy. Looking around, she saw a figure trying to hide behind the trees, and remembered her conversation with Mr Latham about the difference between a professional killer and an amateur.

Panic rising; Jane moved her feet even faster. Glancing back she saw nothing. Relieved she began to slow some, when a hand suddenly covered her mouth and another circled her neck. She tried to scream, but no sound came. Finding it hard to breathe, Jane gathered enough strength to kick and claw, but her assailant was much stronger.

Remembering her reticule, Jane swung it with all her might, striking the figure on the side of the head. She heard a male voice grunt as her assailant staggered, loosening his grip. Taking advantage of the opportunity, she turned and ran. Jane's knowledge of the roads kept her on the path home, but she knew she was still far away. Speed was of a necessity at this point, and propriety be dammed. Pulling up her skirt to free her legs, Jane took off as fast as she could. Within moments she heard footsteps closing in from behind her.

Hands gripped her shoulders, shoving her down. A heavy body landed on her, knocking the breath from her. A big hand forced her face down into the dirt; another hand closed around her throat. Jane saw where her reticule had fallen and tried to reach for it, but attacker pushed it further from her grasp. Gasping, Jane was fast losing hope, despair mingling with horror at the thought that perhaps this was her time to die.

Abruptly the weight was jerked off her, and fresh air rushed into her lungs. Through the loud buzzing in her ears, Jane could vaguely make out sounds of a struggle. She rolled over and saw Sir Hugh wrestling with a black figure, landing a punch squarely on his opponent's jaw.

The figure grunted and staggered backward, then pulled something out from beneath his cloak. Something long that glinted silver in the moonlight slashed towards Sir Hugh cutting a ribbon of red in his left arm. Sir Hugh growled, landing another hard blow to the figure's face. The assailant went down but quickly recovered scuttling away into the bushes like a frightened crab.

Sir Hugh hesitated after taking a step in the direction the man had taken, then turned back towards Jane.

Panting she watched him with a mix of fear and relief noticing how pale and grim his handsome face was as he took her hand.

"Can you stand?" he asked his voice rather shaky.

"Yes, I think so." Jane could barely speak above a whisper. Her throat hurt terribly. With his help, she was able to stand.

Jane wasn't sure if her light-headedness came from the momentary lack of oxygen or if it stemmed from how tightly Sir Hugh wrapped his right arm around her waist.

"Excuse me," Sir Hugh said, carefully, slowly stroking her upper body, probing her ribs. "But I must make sure you haven't sustained any broken bones before we start moving." A mask of calmness covered his troubled face.

Jane didn't mind in the least. In fact, she felt safe, and comforted. She staggered slightly at the realization, of how she was thankful for him. She felt his hold on her tighten, probably fearing she would faint. Instead, she sighed and tucked her head down on his shoulder. His left hand was still for a moment, and then she felt him stroke her cheek. It was a tentative touch, a tender stroke so gentle that she wanted to cry.

The hand moved away and, for an instant, she felt what could have been Sir Hugh's lips on her forehead. He was caring with her and she felt safe. And for the moment, it was all she wanted. He had saved her twice. Twice and all she had ever done was be mean to him.

She even had gone far enough to pray for the investigation of the vicar's killer to come to a close so that Sir Hugh would go back to his life in the military. England was his first love and how could she compete with that? With that thought Jane felt a sharp pain in her chest, causing her to shiver and take a deep breath. Not ready to face the thought that she was in another type of danger.

Sir Hugh put his hand under her chin and lifted her head. His face was still grim, but his dark eyes were soft and moist.

She felt a lump rising in her throat, and her heart began pounding—she was tempted to lean in and feel his lips on hers—but dear lord she was tempted. They stared at each other for an interminable amount of time. A minute or an hour, Jane had no idea. Moving her hands to his arms Jane touched something damp on his sleeve and remembered that he was bleeding. "You're hurt."

"Oh, I've seen worse. We'll make it back to the manor," he responded with a husk to his voice. "Can you walk? My horse is over there.

She nodded and slipped her arm around his waist and let him guide her towards the stallion.

After settling her onto the saddle, Sir Hugh swung himself up behind her. Jane leaned back into his arms, feeling him lean forward as his right arm encircled her waist. She sensed his breath in her hair, and at the moment she didn't care whether it was appropriate or not. Oh, how thankful she was for his breath, for her breath. Tonight it could've been taken from them. She leaned further into him. They were safe, and that was all that mattered.

With one hand on the reins, Sir Hugh put the other around Jane's waist and set the horse to a steady canter. Jane was sore, but she steadied herself against Sir Hugh—their bodies rising and falling in unison with the horse's movements, all the way back to Wellington Manor. Just as she was drifting into the darkness, she felt him kiss her on the top of her head or was it a dream?

Chapter Twenty

Sir Hugh couldn't resist placing a kiss in her hair. He'd come too close to losing her. He shifted slightly to protect his wounded arm, keeping a good grip on the reigns and a better one on Lady Jane who had dozed off. A sudden shakiness came over him at the image of the assailant's body on top of hers, pressing the life from her. The images replayed in his mind's eye. The shock of seeing the breath drain out of her before he'd jumped on the bastard had nearly killed him. A soft sigh from his passenger brought him back to the woman leaning into him. That she trusted him so brought him some comfort. He liked the feel of her against him. With a breath his shakiness lessened some and air filled his chest for what seemed like the first time since the struggle.

Other than when his father had been abusive to his mother he had never felt such an emotional reaction towards a woman as he felt now with Jane at this very moment. If he had to be honest with himself, the idea scared him. He'd been a fool to believe that he could enter her life, do his job and leave when the time came as though he felt nothing for her.

The horse whinnied, alerting him that they were approaching Wellington Manor. As the grounds came into sight Sir Hugh reluctantly pushed his emotions down. He needed to keep a clear head and focus on his mission, even if it meant never discovering where his heart lay where she was concerned.

Still dazed, Jane registered strong arms around her and a buzz of commotion. Evidently they had arrived home. The buzz of noise turned into an uproar when Sir Hugh carried her into the hall.

She immediately spotted her father emerging from the drawing room, his face blanching at the sight of her dishevelled appearance. Only once he was reassured by Sir Hugh that she was merely in shock did his colour return. And while she welcomed her father's embrace as Sir Hugh handed her over, Jane felt a sense of reluctance as he let her go.

Moments later she awakened to find Biltmore entering her bedroom with her stepmother walking closely behind. Catching sight of her condition, the Countess gasped but remained true to her calm countenance immediately instructing one of the servants to fetch the local doctor and another command for someone to bring Margaret.

After checking in on Jane, her ladyship excused herself for a few minutes to ensure that Sir Hugh was well.

Annoyed at all the fuss, Jane took the opportunity to close her eyes for but a moment before her stepmother returned with her maid to help remove her clothes. Every stain on the cloth reminded Jane how close to death she and Sir Hugh had come. Even now, in the safety of her home, she couldn't help but wonder if her attacker was out there lurking in the dark.

The doctor arrived in short order and after requesting that one of the maids stay behind, he ushered the Countess from the room so that he could examine Jane unimpeded. The Countess took exception but was reassured by her husband waiting for her in the hall. The doctor was an old family friend, having visited often when Jane was a child and required medical treatments, giving some right of familiarity.

An examination revealed no broken bones, although a great many bruises. With a nod to the maid and Jane he prescribed bed rest for the next few days and then went to check on Sir Hugh.

In due time Doctor Harrison sought out his lordship to give him a report.

"Your daughter is in need of a few days rest and some warm compresses on the worst of her bruises," he started accepting a glass of port form the Countess. "Sir Hugh's wound was deep but fortunately the blade did not sever any vital veins. I've bandaged him up and administered a dose of laudanum for the pain. Both are resting comfortably right now."

Lord Crittenden was thankful for the diagnosis, but there was one important question that plagued him, grasping his wife's hand for support, he asked, "Doctor, was she—"

Her ladyship gasped, knowing full well what her husband was asking.

Instinctively he pulled her into his arms.

"No," Doctor Harrison answered with an air of relief. "She remains untouched."

"Thank God." His lordship released a sigh, as his wife released tears she had been holding back.

"Now, now, dearest, you heard the doctor. Our girl is fine. Soon this will all be a bad memory. Though I do want the cretin who did this to her to pay. Tomorrow I will contact the magistrate and perhaps even put out a bounty for any information leading to his capture."

"I must be going, your lordship. I have another patient to visit."

"Yes, of course. Thank you, Harold, for everything."

"You are most welcome. I did leave her some laudanum to help her sleep, at least enough for tonight and perhaps tomorrow. You know where to reach me should you need anything. I shall be back in two days' time to check on them," said the doctor bowing before leaving.

The following morning brought an entourage of gentlemen callers inquiring after Lady Jane. In a small town, like Dover, gossip got around quickly and it seemed her horrifying ordeal was the talk of the village.

Many of the gentlemen had vied for her attention at one point or another, so his lordship wasn't surprised when he entered the parlour to find several of them glaring at one another.

One of them cried that the assailant was very lucky he had not been the one that came upon him, for he would have killed him with his bare hands.

Another young man declared he would have hung the man from the nearest tree, although this was also rather unlikely since he was afraid of heights.

Lord Crittenden, ever the gracious host, welcomed each and every one of them, ringing for tea, and reassuring them that his daughter was well and would attend the following week's ball at the Marquis de Faucheaux' mansion. With few comments they took their leave, but not before giving his lordship letters addressed to Jane.

His lordship had a feeling his daughter would have cared less for any of these pompous creatures and tossed the letters into a drawer in his writing desk.

Jane was not one for taking medicine; she had been difficult since a toddler, but for once, was grateful for the laudanum to help her sleep. The memories swirling around in her head left her with little choice.

She tried to put on a strong front for her family and for Margaret, who arrived in a frenzy of concern and insisted on not leaving her side. But inside, Jane had been terribly shaken, and her efforts to understand what happened only brought back a sense of panic. In the end she decided not to try to think too hard, confident that once the initial shock wore off, she would be able to piece together the events more clearly and perhaps find a reason why the violent act occurred.

Sir Hugh refused to leave her room taking up his vigil in a large chair across from the bed. When asked if one of the maids wouldn't be better suited to watch over Jane, his declaration of 'propriety be damned' ended all further discussions on the matter.

Jane found herself touched by his protectiveness, even though it cost him any comfortable position. He was under doctor's orders to rest, to which he stubbornly refused.

Margaret also stayed with her, admitting to Jane how amused she was that society dictated that she needed a chaperone even in such a situation. Really, as if Sir Hugh would try to take advantage of her weakened state.

Jane smiled slightly, having her friend and Sir Hugh as her self-appointed protectors, along with Bridgette. Her feline's loyal and loving presence snuggled near her on the bed, made the days after the attack bearable.

Tension was at its worst when her father and mother visited. It wasn't that she didn't appreciate their presence, but their own fears for her safety made it difficult for Jane to concentrate on getting better.

As if noticing her mistress' tension, Bridgette rubbed her head against Jane's cheek and then settled down once again by curling up tighter against her side.

Chapter Twenty-One

Two days after the attack Doctor Harrison returned and declared both Sir Hugh to be healing splendidly and Lady Jane well enough to leave her room unless troubled by continuing soreness.

Still refusing to leave Jane's side, Sir Hugh stood looking out the window of her room. Dark clouds filled the sky, offering a menacing mood. Thankfully all were home safe and sound, but for how long? Thinking of Jane and what could have happened to her had he not come when he did made his heart twist. It would be up to him and Latham to make sure that nothing else occurred. With purpose in each stride Sir Hugh strode over to the seat that had become his station since that dreadful night and took his place as her protector. *Where in the blazes is Latham?* Thinking of the solicitor was his last thought as he slipped into a restless sleep.

When Margaret did not receive a response to her knock, she slowly opened the door to Jane's room. Quietly looking into the room, she found her friend lying awake in her bed, seemingly deep in thought. Sir Hugh, on the other hand remained sleeping in his usual position I the big chair.

Joining her friend on the bed, Margaret spoke in a whisper not wanting to disturb Sir Hugh. She felt now was the appropriate time to find out what had happened. "What were you thinking, going to town on your own?"

Jane responded just as quietly with a glance to her guard "I had a headache and wanted some fresh air." She ended with a small rasp indicating her throat was still sore.

"You could have been killed," Margaret hissed.

"Please, I've already got a scolding from Papa and don't need another, especially from you."

"I am sorry, Jane." Margaret paused, taking a deep breath. "This whole ordeal has gotten the best of us all. I would never intentionally hurt you, but the thought of losing you...I just couldn't." She took Jane's small and gentle hands into her own. She swallowed a cry as her friend smiled at her—a smile filled with love and understanding. "Were you able to get a look at your attacker?"

"No. It happened too fast," Jane whispered harshly. "He appeared to be wearing some sort of mask, or had his face blackened. The suddenness of it was really the scary part. No warning. And he was so strong. I fought back as hard as I could, but he easily overpowered me. That was a terrifying feeling, Margaret, to be in the power of someone else and unable to help yourself."

Margaret glanced over at Sir Hugh, who seemed to still be asleep. For the first time in days he'd finally relaxed. Poor man had exhausted himself standing guard over Jane. For a moment she followed the rise and fall of his chest and wondered at the importance of such a simple act.

"Goodness, I remembered something," Jane cried sitting up pulling Margaret from her musings. "My reticule, I left it in the woods."

"Jane, I hardly think I would be so concerned over a reticule after having been attacked. Please don't worry about it, when we visit Bath in the spring, we can buy you another."

"No, no," Jane whispered as emphatically as she could. "You don't understand. I put the key in the bag."

Margaret remembered the key they had found in the vicar's study. Losing it would pose a problem. "Early tomorrow morning I'll go and fetch it."

Letting out a breath of relief, Jane leaned back into her pillows. "You mustn't go there alone. Please promise you'll take Biltmore with you," she begged.

Normally, Margaret would have argued with Jane about whether or not she needed protection, but after what had just happened, she decided not to argue with her. "I promise I will take Biltmore with me." In hopes of moving the subject away from her own safety Margaret said, "What a blessing that Sir Hugh was nearby and able to come to your aid. Has he explained what he was doing riding out that night?"

"No," replied Jane with a huff. "He won't discuss it with Papa or Mama either. I do intend to find out, though."

Margaret noted the fatigue closing in around Jane. "What's wrong, dearest?" she asked, concern that her friend had perhaps been playing down her physical ailments.

"Oh, just a sudden headache is plaguing me, that's all," Jane said closing her eyes.

Margaret waited. She knew there was something more that Jane was not telling her. "Jane?"

When Jane opened her eyes Margaret could see shadows of resignation dancing in their depths.

"It's just, there's so much we don't know, and sometimes it seems impossible we will be able to discover anything about the horrid events of this past month."

"That's not true, Jane." Margaret clutched her hand tighter. "We know the Marquis was uncomfortable when the men were talking about the vicar's murder. Furthermore, we know that the key has a French motif and as the Marquis is French there must be a connection." Her confidence waned slightly and she let out a slow breath "Though I must admit it is all circumstantial."

After a few moments of quite Jane declared, "I'm sorry, but I'm a bit tired. I need to rest. Would you please go check on my father and mother? They'd probably be very glad for your company. And get some fresh air. Take a turn in the gardens. You look rather pale, but don't go alone."

Margaret was reluctant to leave her friend's side, "Take a nap, and I'll be here when you awake."

"No, I insist. You need your rest as well. And you must tend to your own household, you know." Taking a deep breath, Jane closed her eyes again, her voice becoming soft, "I just require a little time to rest my eyes. I will see you later."

Margaret watched her for a few seconds longer before deciding what to do next. She then kissed Jane gently on her cheek and tiptoed toward the door. Looking back over her shoulder Margaret realized how quickly life could change. One day they were silly girls reading about mysteries they wished they could solve or discussing fashion designs. Then, like the ever-changing wind, they were in the middle of a murder and several attempts on her and Jane's family. Life was fragile. She turned once more to check on Sir Hugh, ever grateful that he had happened by to save her friend. Margaret then slipped through the door.

Not long after Jane heard Margaret leave, there was a soft knock at the door. She heard Sir Hugh rise from his chair and stride across the room wagering that he had only pretended to be asleep. Not wishing to alert him that she was awake she kept her eyes closed.

"Latham," Sir Hugh said his voice low. "Where in the devil have you been?"

"London. I was checking into some of those questions we had after the dinner party. It seems the Marquis' fortune has not been inherited from his family. He has business ties with several London merchants, but from the facts I gathered, not all of them are of the best quality. In fact, I am beginning to wonder about some of his associates. They have been linked with smuggling rings operating in the north of England, and you would not believe—"

"I will wager my entire fortune you are about to say we have a bit of smuggling here in Dover."

"Yes. Wager your entire fortune?" asked Latham dubiously.

"The devil," Sir Hugh said, ignoring the question. "There has got to be some connection between the Marquis and the mishaps in this village, and us in particular. I could swear that the attacker was Binet, the Belgian—short and squat, and strong.

Jane dared to open her eyes and watch the men talking in the doorway. Bridgette lay purring by her hand as long as neither of them moved she could continue feigning sleep. She couldn't see Sir Hugh's face from where she lay, but Mr Latham had a furrowed brow and worried look.

"Binet? Are you sure?" Latham asked.

Sir Hugh gave a slight nod. "I smelled that peculiar snuff scented with roses that he takes. Of course, that is not a positive form of identification since surely he isn't the only one who uses it, though it is not a very common brand."

"Any idea where it is commonly sold?" asked Mr Latham.

"Unfortunately, Latham it is a common snuff and therefore sold everywhere."

Jane noticed Sir Hugh rubbing away the pain on his arm.

"I find it hard to believe. After all didn't he return to France in disgrace? I did hear the Marquis vouched for him at the trial last year after that wrecking incident on the Dover coast, but his legitimacy as a merchant was severely damaged here. Who'd do business with a man like that?"

"Indeed," Sir Hugh said. "And the bigger question is why would the Marquis vouch for him? And why would they have business in London?"

"A day and a half ride is not so very far if there is money in it."

"True," said Sir Hugh. "We must keep our eyes and ears open. Once I have ensured things have settled here, I'll go to London myself. There is someone I need to talk to, someone who might be able to explain a great deal about what has been going on. Have you talked to the vicar's widow lately?"

"Yes, before I left for London. And she knows nothing."

"Then we must find people who do. Stay vigilant and I shall be in touch."

"Right," Mr Latham said. He glanced over at the bed and turned slightly with a sigh. "She is most fortunate that you were there. As a matter of fact, why were you in the vicinity, when I recall you saying you were off to Hastings?" Latham asked.

Fearing he might be heard, Sir Hugh mumbled his reply. He suspected Lady Jane was awake and straining to hear their conversation. Done speaking the men split up. Sir Hugh returned to Jane's bedside and Latham was off to his next task.

Sir Hugh's dark brown eyes had been staring down at her, when Lady Jane opened her eyes.

"Sir Hugh, your arm..." she said sleepily and then drifted off, again.

He took a strand of her golden locks that had fallen across Jane's cheeks and tucked it back. "The devil with my arm," he whispered. "Even in sleep your beauty astounds me." A creak from the hall made him turn towards the door. There was no danger to Jane here, unless one counted the embarrassment of someone finding him standing over Jane whispering words of emotions he was not ready to deal with. Reluctantly he returned to the damnable chair that was wreaking havoc with his back, and with a loud thump took his seat. Closing his eyes he muttered to himself, "I wonder what secrets you two are hiding from us?"

Chapter Twenty-Two

When Margaret returned she was surprised to find Hugh looking at her as she quietly slipped into the room. "Ah, Sir Hugh," she said softly. "I hope you're feeling stronger. May I do something for you? Fetch you something?"

"I'm fine, thank you, but I wondered if you'd mind staying with Lady Jane until my return."

"But of course, I'll be happy to stay," Margaret said.

Thanking her, he was at the door when Margaret called to him, "Sir Hugh?"

He stopped, hand on the door knob, and turned with a questioning brow.

"Thank you," Margaret smiled at him, standing as if holding a raw emotion in check.

"I'm only grateful I was there in time to prevent any real harm." He offered her a weak smile and then gently shut the door behind him.

With Jane still asleep, Margaret took the chair Hugh had just vacated and read until she heard Jane stirring.

Refreshed, Jane looked at her friend. "Margaret, how long have you been here?" she asked, eyes wandering around the room and finally settling on the door.

"Oh, about an hour or so. I thought Hugh would like time to get some of his things done." Margaret couldn't tell if Jane's wandering glance was an indication that she wanted to discuss something private or if she were missing Sir Hugh.

"Is everything all right?"

"Jane, pray do be still, I am fine—everyone is fine. You are the one convalescing, remember?" Margaret reminded her.

"True, but being a convalescent does have advantages." Jane lifted herself to a sitting position. "I happened to overhear a conversation between Sir Hugh and Latham before I fell asleep."

Moving to the bedside Margaret took some pillows and began fluffing them for Jane's use.

Jane continued. "Didn't you mention once of an old estate manager of your father who had stolen from him? You said you heard him and his attorney, Mr Latham Senior, discussing the man. Binet, I believe his name was."

"Binet?" Margaret was startled. "Yes, my father had business with him once. What does he have to do with this?"

"I overheard them discussing the attack, and Binet's name was mentioned. That's all. Perhaps you could discuss it with Latham. Bring it up casually during a conversation."

Margaret gave one of her unladylike snorts. "Indeed I shall not. I am not about to share anything of my family's history with him. Why would you suggest such a thing?" She turned away from Jane and let her thoughts slid back to what she knew about the man.

"Oh...maybe because the man saved your life not so long ago."

When Binet had worked for her father on one of their properties in Dover, a monthly audit revealed that the Belgian had been stealing. The man had been immediately dismissed.

Margaret also remembered that the land manager had been angry over her father's leniency, allowing Binet to repay some of what he had taken, and begged him to press charges and put the man in prison, but he had refused. Now Margaret wondered if her father's generosity had allowed a violent criminal go free.

Could Binet be the vicar's killer? Margaret's heart skipped a beat as a new fear clutched at her. If the vicar had financial problems and owed money, Binet would be the sort of person to be involved in such shady dealings. But was he capable of murder? "Do they think he could be involved in the attack on you and the one at the funeral?" Margaret asked returning her attentions to her friend.

"I cannot say. His name came up, and they were disturbed. I think it is a lead we need to follow."

"I'll check into it by going through my father's papers, although I am sure father sent Binet away. Now rest or uncle will be vexed with me for disturbing you." Margaret placed a kiss on Jane's cheek. "Will you be all right if I leave now? I'm sure Hugh will be back shortly."

"Please stay a little longer, if you can."

Margaret sat on the edge of the bed, taking Jane's hand. "Why don't I read to you for a while as you rest?"

"Yes, please," Jane said and settled back.

It did not take long for Jane to drift off to sleep again. Still smiling Margaret closed the book and sat quietly for a moment.

"You fool! You could have seriously hurt her. You're lucky you're alive!" Vane yelled kicking the unconscious man on the ground before Binet pulled him away.

"This is the second time he's failed me," he yelled at Binet. "How dare he put his filthy hands on her! If he fails me one more time, I swear to you, cousin or not, he will die. Do I make myself clear?"

Binet's own anger was slowly rising, but this was not the time. "May I remind you that you sent him?" was all he managed to say.

"A mistake I shall not make again. I should cut off his hands for touching her." Vane began to pace. He needed to move things quickly. Too many incidents and all it took was one more mistake and his whole plan could fail. No he had come too far for that. Failure was not an option. "Have the final plans been set in motion?"

"Yes," Binet said. "All the men were paid and have returned to their homes until we need them again. Will you be returning to France?"

His temper cooling, Vane was lost in thoughts of his impending future with his bride-to-be. With her beauty and his money, they would conquer all of Europe, starting with England.

"My lord?" Binet knew that look on his face. It was one of a person going deep into a reverie, a mad one.

"I think I should meet with her again. It is time for our courtship to begin."

Binet wondered what would become of the lady if she refused him. Smuggling was one thing, and killing a man or two another, but tampering with a Lord's daughter was downright suicidal. He had to make his exit from this business, or at least from his partnership with the devil, while he still could.

"Binet?"

"Yes, my lord."

"I need you to do one more thing for me. Find out all you can on Hugh Cameron and Phillip Latham. The men have insinuated themselves into the lives of the young ladies, and I am quite interested in them. Find out all you can and let me hear from you as soon as possible."

Without waiting for a response Vane stormed from the room.

Binet stood silently, contemplating the dangers that his lordship was bringing to the formerly simple smuggling operation.

Chapter Twenty-Three

Sir Hugh found his cousin in the drawing room leaning over a desk writing a letter. He cleared his throat to announce his presence.

Lady Crittenden raised her head and, finding her young cousin in good health, ran into his arms. "Hugh, I am so happy you have somewhat recovered. I was so afraid—."

"Hush, cousin. As you can see, I am well."

"It was a blessing that you happened per chance on Jane." She sobbed, tears flowing freely. "What could she have been thinking walking on her own…and without a proper chaperone?"

"I'm afraid, my dear that as much I respect the man I must say that your husband is to blame."

Her ladyship withdrew from Sir Hugh's embrace with a gasp, "Now, Hugh…"

Just at that moment his lordship entered from the library. "Now, now, dearest, you mustn't upset yourself. Hugh is correct. I've spoiled the child. Margaret too."

"Charles, what are we going to do?" asked her ladyship fearing her husband would take drastic measures.

"I am going to do whatever I can to see them both married. Let some other poor chap worry about them for once."

Her ladyship released her breath. "Now there I can be of assistance. As her new mother, I can arrange for parties with local mamas whose sons are considered worthy of our girls." Turning to Hugh, she added, "And Hugh can assist with making sure these gentlemen are of good countenance and fortune."

Hugh who had been smiling suddenly stopped and stared at his cousin. Once his mind began to work again he feigned fatigue and excused himself. Leaving the room and closing the door, he leaned against it—his heart beating like wild wings. Memories of his heartbroken mother resurfaced threatening to swallow him. Taking deep breaths, he willed his nerves to calm. With his next breath he vowed to get to the bottom of this business and leave as fast as it was humanly possible. He had trouble picturing Lady Jane in love with another man.

As promised, Margaret and Biltmore returned to the area where Jane had been attacked. Even in the bright light of day, the area of Jane's attack remained gloomy and smelled of rotting foliage due to the shadowing trees. The moisture made it feel colder than it actually was, and it looked like rain was almost upon them. As much as she hated to admit it she was thankful for Biltmore's presence and assistance.

Images of Jane fighting for her life played vividly in her mind and Margaret shook them away. Together she and Biltmore should have been able to make a quick search of the area and head back to safety before true dark settled in, yet the reticule remained absent.

Margaret was just about ready to admit defeat when a male voice startled her.

"Looking for this?"

Margaret let out an uncharacteristic scream, which brought Biltmore running with his pistol drawn.

Several yards away stood Hugh, Jane's reticule dangling from his good arm.

"Sir Hugh, you frightened me," Margaret admonished.

"My dear lady, you should be frightened. You took a big risk coming here. It was a foolish thing to do and all for a reticule."

Margaret bristled at his acerbic tone. "The bag means much to Jane. It was her mother's," she snapped. "I promised I would come back to fetch it for her and as you can see I am not alone."

"I am fully aware that you are not alone. Had I ill intentions, however, I assure that both you and Biltmore would now be dead." He turned to look pointedly at the manservant.

Margaret's cheeks reddened. *How dare he!*

As if reading her mind, Sir Hugh added. "I meant no disrespect to Biltmore. I am sure he understands that which I speak of."

Biltmore nodded in agreement.

Ignoring the apology Margaret stepped forward, "And what are *you* doing here?"

Hugh swung the bag teasingly. "I heard you and Lady Jane speaking about the reticule, and I must admit it piqued my curiosity. It dawned on me that perhaps there was something of great importance in here. Since I could not hear the rest of your conversation I came here early this morning. You can imagine my surprise when I found a rock inside of it." He smiled mischievously. "At first I thought this must be a trick, but then I felt something else."

Margaret drew in her breath.

"There was a key in one of the folds," declared Hugh. He waited challenging her to tell the truth.

Panic heated her blood. The key was their only clue and to lose it to Sir Hugh and Mr Latham was unthinkable. "The key is very important to Jane for reasons that do not concern you." She blurted out, desperate for an explanation they would accept.

"Come now, Miss Renard. I never thought of you as someone inclined to twisting the truth, not even in desperate circumstances," he replied with heavy irony.

Margaret nervously shifted her weight. *Am I that obvious?* The thought that he could read her was unnerving. She and Jane should have known better than to underestimate him.

When Margaret offered no further explanation he let out a long breath. "It really distresses me to know that you still don't trust me."

This cut deeply. Margaret really did trust him and thought highly of him. Exhausted, she gave in. "Very well, we found the key in the vicar's office, underneath his desk."

"I see," he said standing silently, waiting with an expectant look on his face.

Compelled to reveal more she added "The manner in which it was hidden told us that it was of great value."

Sir Hugh came closer, weighing his words carefully he said, "This is not a game or contest about who gets to solve the case first. Every moment, every piece of information that we come upon helps us put the pieces of the puzzle together, hopefully bringing us closer to catching the murderer before he or she strikes again."

Now she wondered if maybe they had been wrong in not uniting with the men to discover who had killed the vicar. The problem, however, was not that they did not want to band with the men, but that the men wanted them out of the whole investigative process. An aspect that was simply not acceptable. Although on some level she could not blame them, until the attack she and Jane had been acting as if this was a game. They needed to pull together, forget their differences, and find the killer before it was too late.

"Perhaps you are correct. I—"

"I shall never fathom why women should feel they must compete with men," he said as he ushered her and Biltmore out of the woods handing the bag with the key to her.

"If women felt equal to men, they would not have to continually work hard for their freedom and knowledge," she hissed back.

"I am afraid, that will never happen, at least not in my lifetime."

Just as she was about to vehemently disagree, he cut her off, "You realize that you might be holding on to a possible clue as to who may have murdered the vicar." His tone dripped with accusation.

She would never admit he was right, especially on the heels of his reprimand. "We checked the vicarage and found nothing," Margaret said to assure him that while they had withheld a clue from them; it had not been a waste of time.

Bag in hand Margaret turned to head home, not caring whether he or Biltmore followed her. After a few tense moments she could hear the crunch of their footsteps as they stepped on the drier leaves lying beneath the warm sun. For once, pleased that she was not alone.

After being escorted back to the manor, Margaret wasted no time in going directly up to Jane's room.

"What do you mean he knows about the key?"

Margaret explained what occurred in the woods, and expecting Jane to be angry, was pleasantly surprised when she appeared relieved.

"I'm glad," Jane said. "It may be that both he and Mr Latham will now become our allies and help us with the case rather than trying to lock us away."

For Jane to readily agree to needing help from Latham and Sir Hugh suggested her friend's encounter in the woods had left her more affected than originally imagined.

"Look Jane, it's raining." Margaret pointed to the window.

"I'm glad. The garden needs it." Jane smiled, though not with the joy or innocence Margaret had often delighted in, in the past.

"Well it may be good for the garden but it has brought us a chill." Rubbing her hands, Margaret stood up and rang for a maid, who rekindled the fire making the room warm and toasty.

Settling in, Margaret offered to read and Jane welcomed it. On the shelf were several of Ann Radcliffe's books, but considering her friend's recent experience, Margaret felt they were too dark, and so settled for Jane Austen's *Sense and Sensibility*. She had barely made it to the second page of the novel before Jane had fallen asleep. Enjoying the story, Margaret kept on reading until her own eyelids began to feel heavy and she too succumbed to the oblivion of dreams.

Chapter Twenty-Four

It rained for three days and while her mother's garden was gravely in need of it, Jane now wondered if it was in danger of over soaking and killing many of the exotic flowers and plants.

Sighing she returned to the labyrinth of her thoughts; there was nothing that could be done about the garden now.

Life was no longer as simple as it had been only a few weeks before. Though she prided herself on being capable of facing whatever challenges confronted her, Jane had to admit that her former carefree spirit had vanished. Complicated circumstances, such as her new mother and the resulting presence of her cousin, were one thing, but violence directed not only at the vicar but at her own family as well was quite another.

And what of Sir Hugh? Her feelings for him have changed. She considered him a friend. She was grateful he had come by when he did. She shuddered to think what might have been her fate had he not been around to rescue her.

Taking another deep breath, she willed her erratic emotions that ranged from gratefulness, to fear and finally utter respect for someone other than her father. Finally exhausted she remained by the window watching raindrops slither down the glass pane, picturing dozens of tiny snakes, sliding down the glass urging their way into the sanctuary of her room until she heard a gentle knock at the door pulling her from her dark musings.

"Come in."

Her father frowned as he entered. "Dearest, come away from the window." He quickly walked over to her, gently taking her arm and directing her to the settee. Sitting next to her he added, "The weather has grown chillier. You will catch a cold."

"Oh, Papa, there's no need for you to fret over me," she said smiling half-heartedly.

Softening, his lordship gently pulled her into his arms. "Darling, oh my darling, it is my privilege as your father to always worry over you."

A raw and primitive grief took hold of her—tears began to flow down her cheeks. She reached a hand up to wipe them away before her father noticed.

"Dear one, you are safe." He promised lovingly tilting her face up to his. "Oh, my baby girl, if something should have happened to you, I have no idea what I'd have done. If Sir Hugh had not shown up when he did, I —"

"Please, Papa, I'm fine." Jane touched her father's face and looked into his eyes finding that they had suddenly aged in the past few days.

His lordship smiled at his daughter, and leaning over he planted a gentle kiss on her forehead. "Are you up to talking about what happened? Sir Hugh told me his portion, but if possible I would like to hear from you what happened before his arrival."

Jane knew her father would not give up until he'd been told everything. She quickly described the walk to town and how she lost track of time and started back later than planned. A slight shiver she could not contain began to crawl up her spine as she recounted the attacker emerging from the darkness alongside the road. She could feel her father tensing as he listened.

"I am extremely grateful to Sir Hugh. You should have seen him when he brought you home. When I tried to take you away from him, I could have sworn he was prepared to fight me as well."

Jane remembered their ride back to the manor and how close he held her, how safe she had felt. In truth she wanted to remain in his arms forever. The man she swore as her enemy had now become what? The very thought made her question her feelings. Having closed herself off to the possibility caring anyone other than those she called family for so long she was no longer sure what she felt. Perhaps she was confusing gratitude for admiration, but how could she tell the difference?

"Father, if you don't mind, I don't want to talk about it anymore. I would like to rest a bit before dinner." She patted her father on his knee and rose from the settee to settle once again in her bed, her father just steps behind.

Once Jane settled herself, her father looked down on her, smiling.

"Why are you smiling?" Jane asked taking his hand.

"Oh, I'm just remembering the many times I tucked you in as a child." Clearing his throat he pulled the blanket to Jane's chin. "Well, there now, pleasant dreams, my dear." After another small peck on her forehead, he left the room.

As the door opened Jane thought for a moment she heard a quiet sob.

Later that evening, upon fetching his daughter for dinner, his lordship encountered Sir Hugh, Margaret and Latham standing around Jane's bed arguing about a trip to London. "There now," he said loudly as he let the door swing open. Sir Hugh and Latham pulled away from the bed to stand casually away from it. Margaret took the chair by Jane's bedside, picking up the book she had been reading to Jane

There was a great deal of hanging heads and shuffling feet.

"Now, now…what is all this. I am come to visit my daughter and I find you all arguing about riding off to London at present. Well, I won't hear of it," Jane's father declared sharply. "We need some time together as a family. I thought since we still have neighbours that have yet to meet Amelia, we would do some entertaining. I think a nice dinner and an evening of whist would be just the thing," he continued, looking apologetically at Jane, remembering her dislike of card games. "I know of one family that has two very beautiful daughters we could invite, eh, Hugh, Philip?"

Jane and Margaret glanced at each other.

"My lord—" Sir Hugh began.

"No, no, I will hear of nothing more. I shall ask Amelia to begin planning it immediately." He turned to his daughter. "No offense, my dear. You may certainly have a say in the menu and anyone you may care to invite, but we will have enough couples with the guests to make neat sets for whist, and I do not want to worry you with it. You must rest and get well."

Margaret noted Jane's distress, though unclear as to the exact cause. "I would be pleased to help with the arrangements," she said hoping that would ease some of her friend's stress. Seeing the pained expressions on Sir Hugh's and Latham's faces Margaret imagined that they feared being trapped into an evening better suited for middle-aged spinsters and church-goers rather than the young baronets and lords, that they were. Silently she had to agree that a polite dinner and a card game was not all that entertaining and thought to object until a new thought entered her mind

She squeezed Jane's hand, "I've been thinking, uncle, about how interesting an evening as you proposed that could be, indeed."

"Then it's settled. For the evening after next," his lordship declared gleefully turning to leave. "I shall invite the Hollinghams. They have been long overdue for a visit."

Chapter Twenty-Five

Disorder took over Wellington Manor as the Hollinghams arrived an hour earlier than they were expected. This threw the cook, kitchen and house staff into a complete frenzy.

Her ladyship having had quite a bit of entertaining experience, along with her slightly flustered husband, smoothly led their guests into the parlour. To her surprise Lady Crittenden found her cousin and Mr Latham standing by the fireplace, speaking in muted tones, large glasses of port in their hands. When Mrs. Holligham laughed at something her husband had said Sir Hugh and Mr. Latham instantly drew apart, their conversation was best left for another time.

"Hugh, Mr Latham," her ladyship called to them. "I would like to introduce you to Mr and Mrs Ronald Hollingham." Amelia continued, "Sir Hugh Cameron is my cousin, and is our trusted solicitor, as well as a friend of the family. His lordship, Philip Latham, is the Duke of Stanton."

"A duke?" repeated Mrs Hollingham. "My, we are deeply honoured, your Grace." The lady was no doubt pleased at having not just one unmarried young man, but a duke in mist of the eligible bachelor pool for her daughters to choose from.

"Gentlemen," Mr Hollingham was the first to speak, "it is a real pleasure to make your acquaintances. In turn, please allow me the pleasure of introducing my son Robert and our eldest daughter, Estella."

Chatting quietly to each other, Jane and Margaret made their entrance just as Sir Hugh and Mr Latham bowed slightly to a beautiful young woman dressed in the latest London fashion of pale pink with white lace, dropping into a perfect curtsey.

Margaret couldn't help notice how the young lady's eyes brazenly met Mr Latham's when she rose, and how they lingered on him, as if she was looking at a dress in a shop. For some strange reason she felt a compulsion to drag Mr Latham away as if he needed to be rescued.

Before either she or Jane could say a word Mr Hollingham revealed his other daughter, "And this is our youngest daughter, Mariah."

Though not quite as beautiful as her sister, Mariah was certainly attractive enough. She wore a yellow dress with short, puffed sleeves. The young girl dropped a curtsey seemingly directed to Sir Hugh and no one else.

Margaret could not miss that she too wore a hungry look as she smiled sweetly at him.

Feeling somewhat put-out by the blatant stares from the Hollingham sisters, Margaret snapped her fan open.

"Ah, and here are our girls," his lordship announced proudly. Everyone turned to the door, allowing Jane and Margaret to take advantage of making a grand entrance.

"Papa," Jane said, holding out her hands and going to her father. "How excellent, our guests have arrived. Please do make the introductions."

Margaret, on the other hand, was unable to act quite graciously as she noticed how the girl in pink continued to stare at Mr Latham. However, as difficult as it was she was able to retain her dignity.

Ever so gracious a hostess, her ladyship ordered sherry for everyone and managed to offset the tense atmosphere as the family and guests entertained each other.

After the young women exchanged curtseys, Margaret could not ignore the hardness she saw in the eyes of the newcomers. She recognized that look--these girls were on the hunt, and Sir Hugh and Mr Latham were their prey. *Have the town of Dover suddenly gone man-hungry? Was there really such a shortage of men that every single young lady they met set their sights on*

305

them? Unable to exchange private thoughts on the subject, both Margaret and Jane merely exchanged glances and a slight shrug.

Robert Hollingham, on the other hand, appeared indifferent to their presence and barely acknowledged them with more than a polite nod. He carried a gloomy air about him that drew away from his striking good looks, and his manners were of no consequence, though his countenance exhumed proudness. He seemed almost bored to have been included in the party.

Jane's hope for an uneventful dinner proved merely a wish that did not come true. The Hollingham daughters seemed incapable of eating, speaking, and staring at the men all at the same time, choosing instead to merely gaze and giggle as if they could communicate without speaking.

After returning from the dining room, Jane's father and Mr Hollingham announced a game of whist, to the dismay of several members of the group.

Lord Crittenden forced Latham and Jane to play against Robert Hollingham and Margaret.

Although Robert Hollingham initially appeared uninterested in playing, his mood soon changed for the better. He seemed to enjoy Margaret's tenacity at wanting to beat Mr Latham. Laughter and amused accusations of prowess quickly sallied across the table.

Free from the game Estella and Mariah surrounded Sir Hugh by taking seats on his left and right.

Jane noticed him squirming in his chair, and though they had just finished eating, she had the strange sensation that the girls thought he was dessert. Strangely she did not find humour in his discomfort as the girls nearly sat on his lap. He jumped up, complaining of a leg cramp. Sir Hugh then strode to the fireplace, explaining his muscles "often needed to be stretched."

Jane, pleased he had risen from his seat, tried suppressing a giggle, but with no luck. She received an annoyed glare from three sets of eyes.

After the Hollinghams had said their farewells, Margaret decided that she too should be going home, eager to search her father's papers for any information on Binet.

Jane however did not want her to go. "Really Margaret, must you leave tonight? I would feel so much better if you stayed and Biltmore took you home in the morning."

Margaret, whom usually gave in to Jane's whims, stood her ground. She'd much rather be doing something active to find the Vicar's killer rather than just fretting about it and the dark cloud that now seemed to hang over Dover.

"Don't fret. I shall be back as soon as possible. I must look into my father's study for any clues on Binet and the sooner the better."

"But—"

"Jane, your father is here." Margaret took Jane's hands in her own. "You are safe. Besides you have Sir Hugh and Mr Latham staying here as well. Even Mr Latham is spending the night."

Jane's eyes widened, "And pray, how did you come by that piece of knowledge?"

Margaret chuckled. "I have my ways."

Jane tilted her head, waiting for a complete answer.

"All right," Margaret relented with an exaggerated huff, "I heard your father ordering Biltmore to get a room ready for Mr Latham."

The girls stood for a moment staring at each other in silence. Then Jane began to laugh, a second passing before Margaret joined her.

Chapter Twenty-Six

Despite hearing that the roads were in poor condition due to the recent rain, Margaret felt that she had no choice but to order the stable hands to have Buttercup saddled and ready to go. From their disapproving expressions, Margaret knew they thought it wasn't safe for her to venture out, but she had to return to Wellington Manor and speak with Sir Hugh. Mrs Roth will have her followed anyway.

The fortnight she'd spent at home tending to her own affairs had done little to distract her from the recent violent events.

She arrived at the manor shortly after lunch without a drop of misfortune and handed Buttercup over to the shocked stable boys as she made her way to the kitchen entrance.

Mrs Hoyt, the Bartholomew housekeeper received her with distress colouring her voice "Goodness, Miss Margaret, though I am pleased as always see you, it's a dangerous period to be out and about riding alone and in this horrible weather."

Margaret smiled. "Mrs Hoyt, please do not fret. I was followed by one of my footmen. Mrs Roth always sends someone after me, though she suspects my ignorance in the whole. And Buttercup knows these roads and she is good with mud."

With a disapproving sniff, the housekeeper took Margaret's coat, gloves and hat.

"You well know, Mrs Hoyt," Margaret continued ignoring the house keepers dower expression, "that I'm not one to abide by convention. I wish to see Sir Hugh for a moment. Is he in?"

"Why, yes, miss. He was in the library last time I saw him. Why don't you settle yourself in the parlour, and I shall have tea sent over as soon as I can."

"That would be lovely. Thank you."

Suddenly unsure of her decision to speak with Sir Hugh, Margaret remained standing as she waited in the familiar room. Its comfortable burgundy furnishings and mellow wood did not give her a sense of security or ease on her nervousness.

Sir Hugh entered the room and strode over to Margaret's side. With a bow he asked, "And what brings you out on such a nasty day, Miss Renard, and unescorted as well from what I've been told?"

"Sir Hugh." Margaret bobbed a curtsy. "Please call me Margaret."

Sir Hugh inclined his head. "It will be an honour, Margaret, but only if you call me Hugh."

Margaret nodded with a smile.

"Since, that's settled, it was unwise of you to venture out alone, you know," continued Sir Hugh, "but it has been my observation you do pretty much as you like. I suppose that is from having a lack of parental guidance. Must I remind you that just weeks ago whilst out walking alone your friend was attacked?"

"I did not come here to be lectured on how society believes I should or should not conduct myself," Margaret said defensively. "There are more important things to discuss don't you believe?"

"Indeed." Hugh nodded a smirk on his lips. "And since I am a gentleman, the lady may go first."

"Do you know a man named Pierre Binet?"

Sir Hugh took in a deep and resigned breath. He had learned all about Pierre Binet from his superiors. The man was a petty thief, whom when fired for embezzling, decided to get involved with smuggling. He was smart and swift with a knife but not likely the one who killed the vicar. He was little more than a puppet, in the scheme of their investigation.

So the question remains as to who is pulling his strings? *Was it the Marquis?* He must admit the Marquis was an enigma. The man held allegiance to France and rightly so, it was his country of birth, but yet, he spent most of his time in England. There was no proof as to whether the Marquis had been spying for France, and that disturbed him. Or perhaps that disturbance was more about the man's infatuation with Lady Jane. His heart jumped at the mere whisper of thought that the Marquis could have been involved in the attack.

"Hugh?"

Images of what he would do to the Marquis, should his involvement prove true dissipated slowly as his eyes refocused on Margaret's concerned face.

"Why do you ask?"

"Jane overhead him mentioned in a conversation you had with Mr Latham. Do you believe he's involved in the recent events in Dover?"

Sir Hugh swore under his breath before answering. The thought that he needed to monitor his future conversations with Latham was just another intrusion on the ladies' part in their investigation. "I believe you should ask Latham. As a solicitor, he holds such records."

"I choose to speak with you instead. I know I can trust whatever you say to me to be the truth and nothing more. Not long ago you exhorted us not to keep secrets from you and Mr Latham. We agreed to join resources with you. We have no time for games or social niceties. Not anymore. Please tell me, what do you know of Binet?"

Sir Hugh stared at her a moment longer weighing his options. "All right," he said finally, offering a seat, which Margaret promptly ignored. "Binet has been known to dabble in all types of criminal activities, smuggling of late, especially off the Cornwall and Dover coasts. He and his associates smuggle wine, fabrics, and perhaps people, into England. These goods are sold to those who have plenty of money and ask few questions. That is all we know for certain at present. How do you know of him?" he asked her.

Margaret turned and looked Hugh in the eye. "He worked for my father. And for a very long time, he seemed to be an asset to the management of our properties. But eventually, greed got the best of him, and he stole a large sum of money. After he had been caught, it was only by my father's generosity that he escaped prison. Now I am beginning to wonder if my father's kind nature clouded his judgment. Perhaps he allowed a violent criminal to go loose when he thought he was showing mercy to a mere thief."

Not speaking, he only gave a slight nod, and then looked past her, out the window to the grey, dripping trees.

"And you came to your knowledge of his illegal acts how?" asked Margaret stiffly.

Sir Hugh hesitated for less than a breath, "He's been under surveillance"

Margaret stared at him, aghast with the revelation. "You mean you have been watching him for a long time and said nothing?" She paled, anger rising, remembering that her friend could have been killed and thinking that perhaps that could have been avoided had they been told the extent of Binet's power.

"I am sorry, but there are certain things I can't disclose at this moment." Hugh said regretfully. "I swore an oath to King and country, and nothing would have me go against that."

"I see," Margaret said, understanding all too well oaths to King and country, but not when it concerned family or friend. "Now I will ask another question and the devil take you if you lie to me."

He didn't flinch at her unladylike language.

"Something does not add up. For example, why would Binet take interest in Jane? Should he want revenge against my father, it should have been me he'd come after."

"I don't know, but I promise you this, he will never get another chance to lay a hand on her or you again. There is a reason for the violence inflicted upon this family and the vicar. Latham and I will do what we can to protect you, but you must help us and act with caution."

"I'll do just fine without Mr Latham's protection. But I thank you for your advice."

Pausing, she enquired, "What do you know of the vicar's murder and what are you not telling me?"

There was no hesitation this time as Hugh gave her a hard, angry look. "We know Binet was involved in the vicar's death. He may very well have been the killer, or he may know who it was. And until we find out for sure who is responsible, you must take great care. I can't play nursemaid to you and your friend, but I will do my best to watch over both of you, even if you and Lady Jane do not appreciate my efforts."

"Thank you for your concern, Hugh. And I must say; I do not think you realise how much Jane does appreciate your valiant efforts on her behalf."

He gave an odd, twisted smile. "I cannot fathom what is in her ladyship's head."

Before Margaret could utter another word, he added, "Latham can be of more help to you than you know. You should trust him."

Margaret snorted. "I fear, since we have joined our causes, that I have no choice but to trust him."

"You won't be sorry. Now if you please excuse me, I have some business to attend to. Remember what I said. Do take care, and please do not let Lady Jane venture out alone again." With that final warning, he turned and left the room

Margaret walked slowly toward the fireplace. While flames offered warmth, she felt a chill creeping over her. Though she didn't frighten easily, at the moment, she was afraid and found it odd that she was trembling.

Moreover, what an odd thing for Sir Hugh to say about Mr Latham, since the beginning, he'd made his contempt for her clear, all because she was not a conventional female member of society.

Margaret moved to the settee, perching on the edge as she considered her various, if somewhat limited options. Shaking her head, she determined that she would concentrate on helping Jane recover and discover what connection Binet had with the attacks in Dover. She was certain they could discover the truth without the men.

With that in mind, she resolutely headed toward the stairs only to be brought up short by a loud disturbance in the hall.

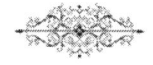

Latham's horse came to a complete halt in front of Wellington Manor. He was exhausted beyond belief, and glad to be back. The heaviness of his frustration over yielding no discoveries on the vicar's murder or Binet's involvement weighed on his shoulders. He was in need of a long bath and a good night's sleep. Knowing he would be too tired after he meets with Cameron to go home, he accepted his lordship's invitation, prior to his departure, to spend a couple of nights at the Manor.

Rubbing Morpheus' neck he admired the beauty of the Manor. Soon he reminded himself, he would have his own home. The purchase of land was in process and he'd already contacted a reputable company in London to take on the construction. He could just picture his mother and sisters living in the new manor, but just then the image of a fiery red head invaded the scene. His gut quivered as he saw himself running to her and taking her into his arms, her lips sweet and full. *Dear God! What has happened to me?*

Fortunately, at that moment a stable boy ran up taking charge of his stallion's reins, shaking him from the dangerous reverie.

His stallion whined in resistance as Latham dismantled. He grabbed the reins back from the boy and turning Morpheus' head to face him; he looked at his horse straight in the eyes. Latham then leaned over to whisper something into his left ear. The horse's head and mane shook as if in agreement to what Latham had whispered in his ears.

Latham then gave back the reins to the boy, who gladly walked the horse away

About to venture up the manor steps, Latham turned hearing another horse galloping towards him.

"Latham!" his lordship cried in excitement as he reigned in his own grey beauty. "Good to have you back."

"Thank you, Charles. I am looking forward to a few days on solid ground."

"Well, I am sure the young ladies will be pleased to have you around. At least one of them anyhow," said his lordship chuckling.

As his lordship handed his reins over to a stable boy they heard a commotion coming from around the manor.

Chapter Twenty-Seven

Margaret turned to see two stable boys carrying a lifeless body of a man, the identity of the man a temporary mystery. Taking a deep breath, she willed her nerves to remain steady, wishing, praying, that the person was just unconscious and not dead. Otherwise, this would make her first corpse. Perhaps sleuthing wasn't as glamourous as they thought. Making her way toward the back room, she came face to face with Latham.

"Miss Renard, I had no idea you would be here, my apologies." He cleared his throat. "That is to say, I heard from Hugh that you were here, but I thought you would be upstairs with Lady Jane."

"Don't fret. I'm truly not as weak as you think," she said looking past him as the stable boys carried the body to a back room "What happened? Who was that man?"

"I'm afraid these matters don't concern you. The magistrate and a doctor have been sent for. Until they arrive, his lordship has requested that we bring the body inside and the doctor has determined the cause of the gentleman's death."

Margaret gasped at his attempt to make the situation more palatable for a lady, "The gentleman! You speak as if he just stopped by for some tea, as opposed to being found dead, no doubt murdered." Her nerves were on edge.

Just as Margaret was about to comment further on Mr. Latham's manners, Jane appeared at the top of the stairs, preparing to make her way down.

Mr Latham and Margaret acted quickly, both seemingly to have come to the same conclusion—that Jane, in her weakened state, would not be up to discovering that a dead body had been brought into the manor.

"Lady Jane, look who's come for a visit with you." Mr Latham, grabbing Margaret's elbow, wasted little time in ushering her toward the stairs.

Margaret gave him a look of open disgust and, had it not been for her friend's appearance, would have wrenched free from his grasp.

Dampening her temper Margaret pasted on a smile. "Yes. Here I am, come all the way from home and alone. The rain stopped, and I've come to enjoy a chat with you." She tried her best to sound cheerful. She turned to the departing Mr Latham. "Perhaps Mr Latham would be so kind and request Mrs Long to bring us some sandwiches and tea."

Mr Latham scowled over his shoulder but responded pleasantly, "Of course, dear ladies, it would be my pleasure." He swung around toward the kitchen without another glance in their direction.

"I thought I heard some noises," Jane said, descending the remaining steps, heading toward the parlour.

Margaret followed closely behind her, thinking it best to have Jane out of the way when the magistrate and doctor arrived. "Ah, well. No doubt you actually heard me and Mr Latham arguing."

"Why you continue to argue with him is beyond me. He's a very agreeable man." Jane patted Margaret's arm as they entered the parlour. "However," she continued, "I do know the commotion I heard had nothing to do with your argument with him, but rather something about a dead body."

Margaret wanted to laugh. Leave it to Jane to be unaffected by a dead body. "How did you know?"

Jane's answering shrug indicated just how much she disliked being treated as a child or some delicate creature who swooned at the sight of a dead body. "I saw the whole procession from my bedroom window. Margaret,

I fear the living more than the dead." Plopping down on the couch, she let out an exasperated sigh.

Following her example Margaret took a seat in the chair opposite the couch, "I'm sorry. My only goal was merely to protect and look after you."

"I know, but really, I am not one of those simpleton maidens who faint at the mere sight of a dead body," Jane said. "And while I appreciate your efforts to protect me, it's time we all gave some effort to looking out for ourselves, as well. You would do well, as would I, too seriously examine who are our allies and who are not."

Margaret, suddenly finding herself exhausted and not wishing to argue further with Jane, chose to close her eyes and calm her nerves.

They remained silent as darkness crept into the room, gradually falling upon everything, quietly as a petal from a dying rose falling onto the ground, so lost in thought they were that both startled at the gentle knock.

Mary, Jane's maid, entered the room and gasped in surprise at finding the young ladies sitting alone in near darkness.

Margaret smiled at her, hoping to calm her shock but could not find energy to do more.

Without comment, Mary lit a fire and several candles throughout the room bringing the girls out of the darkness, surrounding them in dancing lights that created menacing shadows throughout the room.

Chapter Twenty-Eight

Jane felt her heartbeat blending with the steady tempo of the clock, marking time in a universe suddenly gone terribly wrong. The sofa surrounded her and she became part of the shadows. Glancing at Margaret, she found her eyes riveted on the carpet, captured by her own thoughts.

She wished there was something she could do, not simply watch and wait as others took action. But while men were in the nasty business of bodies and murder and violence, women were relegated to sit quietly, sew and always look pleasing.

A dead body here on their grounds was no coincidence. Her family was under attack, and she had no intention of idly allowing the disaster to happen. She gave herself a shake and stood.

Margaret looked up, startled. "What's wrong?"

"An overwhelming sense of uneasiness is what's wrong. I am determined to find out what's going on in my own home." Jane swept out of the room, her skirts swishing around her ankles, the back room containing the body her destination.

Margaret followed close behind.

Immediately stepping forward and straightening her shoulders, Jane lifted her chin and addressed the elder man, whom she recognized as the magistrate. "Sir, have you discovered the identity of the victim and the manner of death?"

"Yes, was it a stranger on the property or one of the staff? I believe all of the family is thankfully accounted for," Margaret interjected.

Somewhat taken aback by the onslaught by the young ladies, the magistrate harrumphed, looked down at the floor, shuffled his feet, and glanced at his lordship who at that moment was looking at his daughter with pride.

It seemed to Jane that the hall's grandfather clock's ticking had never been so loud. For some reason, she glanced at Sir Hugh, expecting him to be furious. To her surprise, he was steadily gazing at her with an expression that, on anyone else, would indicate pride. She felt absurdly pleased.

The magistrate coughed and, after another glance at her father, finally spoke. "Um, well, my lady, I do not believe such matters need concern you or Miss Renard. They are harsh and best handled by men."

Margaret snorted. "And why is that? Do you not think—?"

Jane gripped Margaret's arm. "Very well, sir. I am sure you know your business. We thank you for your service." She nodded her head slightly but made no move to leave

When the men realized the two women were not retreating into the parlour, the gathering broke up with brisk hand-shaking and farewells. The magistrate promised that the body would be removed by that evening as soon as his men could navigate the muddy roads to the manor. He then glanced at the young ladies, confusion in his eyes, nodded politely as he passed them, making a hasty retreat.

Noting his reaction, Jane realized that people, no matter how long they'd known each other, never lose the power of surprising one another.

Perhaps they could use this to their advantage as they investigated the vicar's murder.

"What the devil?" Sir Hugh said, as soon as the door closed behind the departing men. "What do you think you are doing?"

"Yes," Mr Latham added sternly, "what game are you ladies playing?"

Jane ignored them and addressed her father. "Papa, are you well? This has been a harrowing day for you."

His lordship smiled at his daughter. "You have your mother's courage and her stubbornness as well and always use it for good. I am fine, my dear girl, but I worry about you. I have been thinking about that trip to London the gentlemen spoke of earlier. I should like to write to my aunt Charlotte in London to request that you and Margaret be allowed to stay with her for a few days of shopping and relaxation. Would you like that?"

Jane looked away. She did not particularly want to leave the village at this time, but she had no idea how to tell her father that she and Margaret were deep in the middle of investigating the vicar's murder and the recent acts of violence. Although that fact might prompt him to pack them up and take them to London himself.

"I think that is a wonderful idea," agreed Margaret.

Jane hesitated for a breath before agreeing. "Yes, Papa, that would be lovely. Thank you." She suddenly remembered the upcoming ball to be hosted by the Marquis. "Papa, will we not miss the Marquis' ball?" Jane asked, and then quickly added, "That would not be looked upon very kindly by most," though the thought of not attending the ball pleased her.

"My dear, these are extraordinary times and circumstances. I should think the Marquis would quite understand that we are not up to an event like a ball, at this moment in time. And if he does not, well, devil take him. Now if you'll excuse me," his lordship said, leaving the four of them standing in the hall.

Jane could not miss how pleased Mr. Latham and Sir Hugh looked at the possibility that she and Margaret would soon be out of the way, and out of the investigation.

Looking away from their smug expressions Jane watched her father climbed the stairs at a slow pace. He seemed very tired and heavy-hearted. It made her heart ache.

Jane sighed loudly, then, instead of addressing Mr Latham, turned to Sir Hugh. "Whose body was it?"

Sir Hugh stared at her, his brown eyes inscrutable. He took a step toward her. "Do you really want to know?"

Firmly returning his look, she lowered her voice. "I am not one to use words lightly, Sir Hugh. If I say or ask, I mean every word."

A slight smile erased the shadow momentarily from Sir Hugh's features, "An admirable quality indeed." He again grew serious, "Chapman the stable master."

"Why would anyone want to kill Chapman?" Margaret blurted out, eyes searching first Sir Hugh, then Mr Latham.

Mr Latham looked long at Margaret, and glanced at Jane before speaking. "It is, ah, a delicate matter. No, no. It is more of a dangerous matter, and the less you know the—"

"The devil," Sir Hugh said, cutting him off. "Tell them, Latham. We had this conversation before, and we're to work together on this. They already know more than you think. I told them about Binet."

Mr Latham frowned. "Very well, Chapman and Binet belong to a smuggling ring. It seems Chapman may have been Binet's inside man. Binet helped transport the goods from London to Italy, Poland, and France. We've yet to discover how the goods arrive in the village and where they are stored, but it is highly suspected that smuggling via Dover and France is the way. Two deaths and two attacks have occurred, and we have no doubts they are connected."

"So you believe that Binet is the person responsible for the vicar's death and the attempts on my family?" asked Jane. She noticed Sir Hugh still focusing his attention on her and to her dismay, felt her cheeks grow warm.

"What they are telling us, Jane, is that he is involved, but not necessarily the man behind the orders," said Margaret a smile playing across her face.

That Mr Latham seemed pleased with, and though he would never admit it, it brought some pleasure to Margaret.

"Perhaps," began Sir Hugh, "it is a good idea that you both leave the village for a while, although I must say, it will be dreadfully dull around here without anyone to quarrel with."

Before Jane could reply, her father reappeared at the top of the stairs.

"Hullo there," he said rather loudly as he descended. "What is this, still conferencing in the hall? You do know there is a parlour fifty paces to your left where you can sit and discuss matters in a civilised manner. Perhaps even have tea."

"Oh Papa, we were just...catching up on everything."

"Yes, exactly," Margaret chimed in. "We were chatting about all the happenings in London."

"Yes, well" his lordship replied, a smug smile tugging his lips, "I have noticed what good friends you've been of late. I've just spoken with Amelia, and she has agreed that a visit to my aunt would do you two some good," he said, looking at the girls. "Let's go into the parlour to discuss the details."

The four glanced at one another and then dutifully followed his lordship out into the hall.

The men's gloominess gave Jane an uneasy feeling. The men definitely knew more than they were letting on and this made her believe they knew something that she and Margaret did not.

Jane took a seat beside her father on the sofa, Margaret in one of the armchairs and Mr Latham in the other. Sir Hugh walked over to the fireplace, pretended to stir the fire and then faced the group, choosing to remain standing.

"I have already dispatched a messenger to take a note to her ladyship. Though she will be in an uproar since I've not given her plenty of time to prepare, I believe she will be pleased with the idea of having you all for a visit."

Sir Hugh stiffened.

"I think we could all use some tea," his lordship said, ringing the pull-bell. "Now, as I was saying, your mother and I talked about the visit to London, and agreed that with all of the recent events, the girls shouldn't go alone. Therefore, we are requesting that you gentlemen accompany them," his lordship finished, eyes calmly fixed on the two stunned men.

There was a moment of silence caused by mere shock and then four voices distinctly cried out in disbelief and denial

"If he's going, then I'm not," Margaret said, gesturing at Mr Latham.

"Well, I had no intention of going," Mr Latham said, standing up. "Business, you know."

Sir Hugh chimed in, "If Latham is to go then there's no reason for my going."

"Oh no," Mr Latham said. "If I must go, then so do you."

The others sat quietly as they watched Sir Hugh and Mr Latham bicker. The young women were more than amused.

The men abruptly fell silent as they realized they were the only ones talking, and unintentionally providing entertainment. They coughed and reddened, unable to hide their embarrassment.

"Here, here," Lord Crittenden said, standing up. "This is unbecoming behaviour in you young people. This trip is meant to be a diversion, not a trip to the guillotine. I want the girls out of here for a few days, and I wish for you gentlemen to accompany them."

His sarcastic emphasis on the word "gentlemen" wasn't lost on his daughter nor, did it seem, on Sir Hugh, who appeared ashamed as he glanced down at the floor.

"I trust no one to do the job of delivering and watching out for them more than you," Lord Crittenden admitted as he returned to his seat. A moment later, he rose once again from his chair with a slap to the armrest and left the room without another word.

A silence hung like a heavy curtain between the remaining occupants, but not for long.

Before the second had of the clock could make a full circle the room was again filled with raised voices.

Mr Latham claimed Sir Hugh, being an actual relative of the family, should be the one to escort the young ladies.

Jane mentioned Sir Hugh possibly not being able to go due to his own business, while Margaret ploughed in talking loudly to Mr Latham until Sir Hugh begged for silence.

Jane caught herself realizing things had gotten out of hand. Her friend and Mr Latham were quite angry, impossible to say whether with each other or the circumstance forced upon them. She then looked at Sir Hugh, and the two shared a brief glance, almost of understanding. *Surely not*, Jane thought.

"Please," Jane begged. "Let us not argue any longer and try to make the best of things. I'm sure that it will work out for all of us. We needn't be in each other's company the entire time, you know."

Margaret took a deep breath.

Mr Latham strode to the window, his back to the room and the others.

Jane glanced over at Sir Hugh again, but he studiously avoided looking at anyone.

Chapter Twenty-Nine

The carriage carrying them to London left the manor at precisely nine o'clock the following morning. The previous night the servants were thrown into frenzy as they were commanded to pack the young ladies' trunk for their trip.

Her ladyship and lordship stood out on the driveway waving good-bye at the solemn girls.

The men, equally sombre, followed on their horses.

As the carriage rocked along, Jane and Margaret sat facing one another. Each occupied with their internal thoughts—some thoughts to do with the vicar's murder and the calamities assailing the formerly quiet village while others involved their trip and the two men who followed them on horseback. They could make out the clomping of the horses' hooves over the rattle of the carriage wheels.

Margaret finally broke the silence. "As much as I hate to admit this, I believe it is time we depended on our companions. They seem to have good knowledge of what is going on."

"Oh, I agree that we must regard them less as enemies and more as allies. I do confess, though, that Sir Hugh can be so stubborn and ridiculously mysterious at times, as a character out of a novel."

"You know, in all the excitement of the trip I forgot to mention that Mr Latham stopped by as I was packing to tell me that my papa's investment lost 500 pounds but that the income from his property in Antigua has doubled. I am rich, and to add insult to injury, he warned me of unsolicited suitors eager to dip their greedy paws into my inheritance. I certainly gave him a piece of my mind."

"What did you tell him?"

Margaret ignored the question, "As if I needed his assistance and offer of protection! True, I may not have my father or the Senior Latham anymore, but my steward is reliable. I trust I have not yet bankrupted the estate. I am sure Sir Hugh urged him to offer his services. He is always saying I should give Mr Latham a chance."

Jane sat quietly. Margaret continued in nervous chatter.

"Then, and you will find it hard to believe, almost as soon as Mr Latham left, Sir Thomas Galle's son arrived at the manor with flowers in hand to—" Margaret finally drew in a breath.

"I am sure—" Jane managed to get out before Margaret interrupted her.

"—to declare himself in love with me and propose marriage. Honestly, I didn't even know Sir Galle had a son. I was surprised almost to the point of shock, but I quickly yet politely turned him down. I mean really, Jane, the nerve of the man."

"Sir Thomas' son?" Jane asked.

"No, Mr Latham!"

"Oh," was all Jane could say.

"You know what?"

"What?" Jane replied in anticipation.

"It is all too complicated, is it not? Why should the sexes play such difficult games with one another, and one woman be pitted against another, all for a man's favour?" said Margaret.

"You are correct. Since we must acquire a husband, we are put in a precarious position where we run into the danger of marrying an unscrupulous man seeking our fortunes. And while society allows this, our spirit or mind can never be taken from us. It is important we keep reading and learning. Education will free our souls. Someday, women of all cultures will be free, perhaps not in our lifetime, but I feel it, Margaret, thanks to women

338

like Mary Wollstonecraft and her *A Vindication of the Rights of Woman*."

Margaret smiled and nodded. "You are beautiful and wise, dear friend."

"As are you! Now as for Mr Latham, I am sure he meant only to warn you in the kindest of ways. I do think he feels something of a responsibility for you, such as a guardian might. I am very glad that you have your money, it allows you more choices in life."

"I know you mean well, Jane. Unfortunately, I cannot fathom him doing anything out of kindness."

"That's due to your pride and his having wounded it. Margaret, if you are ever to marry, then you would do well to be more patient with men."

"I will never marry. You saw what marriage did to my father. He could not deal with her loss and that killed him. No, my dear friend, I shall remain single, besides, what about you? You cannot bear to be in the same room with a man who has done nothing but save your life on several occasions and watch over you. You are barely civil to him."

"That's not true. I may have not been kind to him initially, but I have softened in attitude towards the man." Jane declared barely audible in a whisper.

Margaret raised an eyebrow. "Softened?"

"Yes, if you haven't notice I barely argue with the man. Why yesterday before you arrived," Jane finally said, "I dropped my handkerchief and he picked it up. I thanked him."

Margaret rolled her eyes. "Oh, that was very kind indeed."

"You are one to talk. I merely mentioned Mr Latham's name and off you go into hysterics."

"That's not true!" Margaret's voice rose a tad higher. Controlling emotions was not one of her fortes.

"I merely mentioned his name because he was kind to advise you on your financial matters, and how do you repay him?"

"You know this all started because I said Sir Hugh—"

"Oh, I doubt that, my lady," Sir Hugh said through the carriage window, startling the girls and eliciting a small shriek from Jane.

Jane's temper flared, causing her cheeks to burn brightly red, her heart pounding.

"Sir Hugh, how long have you been there?"

"A while," Sir Hugh said, and then laughed.

Even in her anger, Jane realised that she'd never heard him laugh and as if things weren't confusing enough, she liked hearing the sound of it. She turned back to Margaret, willing herself to ignore him.

"How much further to London, do you think?" She asked Margaret.

"I pray you both excuse the interruption, I merely wanted to advise you ladies that we will be approaching our first stop for the evening at an inn."

Jane carefully controlled her anger, albeit with great effort. She now wished she had something to throw at Sir Hugh. Perhaps the book Margaret was reading? No, that wouldn't do, for it was dear to her and she loathed parting with it, especially with a long trip ahead of them.

Sir Hugh dropped back, and the girls heard laughter. They could have sworn Mr Latham joined in, and they began to regret their agreement to work with the two men.

In the dark caverns, the smugglers worked furiously. The nature of this business never provided a prolonged period of rest. A sliver of light seeped past the almost-closed door.

Vane spent most of his time negotiating the smuggling operation. Today he was going over the log of goods when one of his men, the one called Jones he believed, approached him. He could smell the fear in the man, and it pleased him, a good mood washing over him.

"Yes? Out with it and get back to work," he rapped sharply.

"Sir, how much longer will this operation be?"

Vane rose ominously to his feet. "Are you questioning me? Because if you are, you shall come to deeply, regret it, I can promise you."

The man backed away, mumbling, "No."

"Good. Tell Binet I leave for London tonight."

"Yes sir," the man managed to say. He backed off, as if afraid of being shot should he turn his back.

Vane smiled. Nothing would interrupt his plans.

Chapter Thirty

The Duchess of Stafford's townhouse on George Street was grand, as was her greeting full of warmth and joviality. His lordship's aunt was eighty years old though she did not quite look it. She was tall with full white hair and barely revealed any other signs of aging. She dressed elegantly for a woman of her status. She married her first husband at nineteen and had since then been married four times. None of the marriages yielded any children, and so when the opportunity presented itself for both Margaret and Jane to visit with her, she'd completely spoiled the young ladies.

To the girls' surprise, Aunt Charlotte offered an especially gracious welcome to Mr Latham and Sir Hugh, apparently privy to what had been happening in Dover and extremely grateful to Sir Hugh for his rescue of her only grandniece.

"You gentlemen are always welcome," she declared, walking over to Mr Latham and Sir Hugh. The men offered their arms as they escorted her to the largest drawing room they had ever seen. "Come have a seat. Dodger will be here shortly with tea and cakes."

The room was one of Jane's favourite. Painted in a sage green, it exhibited three large windows that faced the main street. It was here the girls would often sit and invent stories based on the strangers passing by. Once, there was a homeless old man who had been the King of France and having been dethroned by his greedy children he had no choice now, but to wonder the streets of his enemy.

Aunt Charlotte chose a large settee, the girls seating themselves next to each other on a large green velvet sofa.

Jane wondered about her aunt's pleasure with Sir Hugh. Perhaps it helped that he was a baronet in addition to rescuing her. She still contemplated a large sherry instead of the tea.

After tea (without the sherry), Aunt Charlotte insisted they take a walk around the gardens. "Come," her voice commanding, "I am sure a walk will do you good, especially after spending several days in a carriage."

Margaret was the first one to rise. "I agree, a stroll sounds delightful."

Aunt Charlotte chose Mr Latham to escort her out to the gardens, leaving Sir Hugh with a dilemma as to whom he should escort. The issue was solved when Margaret moved to his right side, and Jane took his left.

Jane's grand aunt, like her mother, had a magical hand with the greeneries and flowers in her garden. She smiled, remembering that the Duchess' tastes were impeccable as well as extravagant.

Though the sun shone bravely over the lovely finery of yellows, blues, pinks, reds and lavenders in the garden, a chilly breeze diminished their already wan enthusiasm.

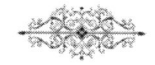

The first few days were spent visiting many of Aunt Charlotte's friends and acquaintances.

Social etiquette, much to the girls' dismay, demanded that Aunt Charlotte return the gesture by inviting families with their eligible sons. The girls, however, were not clueless to Aunt Charlotte's matchmaking attempts. They both laughed about it; whenever alone and pretended interest when Aunt Charlotte went on about the eligible bachelors.

Although she Aunt Charlotte had already deduced that the young ladies and gentlemen had already developed feelings for one another, but were too stubborn to admit it and thus avoid attachments—men always being the last to admit it. This was even obvious when the gentlemen often exhibited uneasiness and foul moods whenever in the presence of other young men.

Jane and Margaret, on the other hand, were further confused by their hostile replies to attempts of wit from the many young men bombarding Aunt Charlotte's home since their arrival.

The next morning Jane happened upon Sir Hugh, who had been breakfasting alone in the dining room, having risen earlier than everyone.

He glanced at her with a strange smile. One could almost call it a smirk, Jane thought.

"So, Lady Jane, are you enjoying the attention from all of the London fops? It would appear you have many choices for a potential husband. The prospect must thrill you immensely."

Feeling more playful than combative, she simply shrugged. Something she rarely did, since her father pointed out many times how unattractive it was for a lady to do so. "Oh, indeed it does. It's wonderful to have choices. Do you not agree, Sir Hugh?"

At first he was quiet. Frowning, he said, "I suppose. The more the merrier."

Jane raised her brows.

"It would suit a young lady to have many to choose from, though a witless lot, if you were to ask me," he added.

She was about to reply when Sir Hugh continued, "Will you excuse me? I wish to eat my breakfast and be gone. I have some business in town."

Jane bit back her tongue, turning her attention to her own breakfast, wondering what had gotten into him.

Sir Hugh ate his eggs and sausages in silence. Once done, he rose from his chair, turned to Jane and bowed. He almost ran into Mr Latham as he left, continuing without a greeting.

"I say, what's troubling him?" Latham asked.

"I haven't the least idea. If you'll please excuse me, I have things to do." She hurried off.

Confused Mr Latham opted to eat his breakfast alone.

Grateful for having avoided running into her aunt, Jane reached Margaret's room panting, taking several deep breaths she gave several excitable knocks on the door, barely giving Margaret a chance to open it before ushering her quickly back into the room.

"Jane, what is the matter?"

When Margaret heard Jane's recount about her exchange with Sir Hugh that morning, she asked, "What could he be going into town for?"

"I can only assume it has something to do with the recent wave of violence. Perhaps he has contacts, and we'll soon know more," Jane answered.

Later that day, while having tea and cake in the drawing room, the Duchess was advised she had visitors.

"Oh, do show them in…Hodgkin." Aunt Charlotte commanded excitedly. Rising from her chair, she straightened her dress and fiddled a bit with her hair.

Jane and Margaret who had been reading raised their inquiring eyes, before getting up from their places and following Aunt Charlotte's cue.

"My dears," she said Aunt Charlotte in danger of the vapours, "Lady Ashfield and her daughter, Emma are here. Lady Ashfield is a dear friend of mine. Her daughter is a London beauty, though I wished her—"

The door to the room opened, Hodgkin entered leading the guests into the room.

Aunt Charlotte walked over to her friend and gave her a huge hug.

Lady Ashfield was very tall and slender. Her hair high was of the colour grey. But that was the only thing that gave the woman's age—it was not possible that she was more than forty years old.

Lady Emma Ashfield was indeed a beauty, and with head held up high, the eighteen year old was a mirrored image of her mother.

"Victoria, I want you to meet my grandniece, Lady Jane Bartholomew and her very dear friend and someone we consider a member of our family, Miss Margaret Renard."

Lady Ashfield was the first to step forward to greet the girls. "Lady Jane, it is indeed a pleasure to meet you. I have heard so much from her ladyship, as I have heard of you as well, Miss Renard."

"The pleasure is ours," said Jane on their behalf.

The younger Lady Ashfield took in a deep sigh—

Was that boredom? Margaret, appalled, wondered.

As if she had forgotten her offspring, Lady Ashfield made excuses and introduced her daughter.

"Please," said Aunt Charlotte, "have a seat. Hodgkin will be here shortly with some sweets and tea. Hilda has outdone herself today. She has made it her mission to spoil the girls while they are visiting by making all types of sweets, including Margaret's favourite—baked apple pudding."

"That is lovely indeed," declared Lady Ashfield. "However, I would rather speak with you privately, if you do not mind. The young ladies can get well acquainted with one another—I am sure there is talk of fashion to be had."

The Duchess was willingly led to the other side of the enormous parlour.

Jane taking the role of hostess said to their visitor, "Emma, please come have a seat."

"Thank you, Jane," said Lady Emma barely glancing at Margaret as she took the seat being offered.

Jane had not been clueless to the snubbing of her friend, and this angered her. But this being Aunt Charlotte's home and she calmed herself enough to continue playing a gracious hostess. She could tell, however, that her friend was having a difficult time trying to control her temper. "Tell us, how do you find London society?" Jane asked hoping to ease the sudden drop in temperature.

"I find it quite amiable and exciting. My fiancé is Lord William Branscombe. His father is the Duke of Cornwall. One day I will be the Duchess of Cornwall.

350

Mama says it is quite an accomplishment." She quizzically looked at Jane and Margaret as if daring them to defeat such a triumph."

"Then felicitations are in order," said Jane. She looked at her friend for a second and then back to Lady Emma.

Margaret remained silent. She was taught if one had nothing nice to say then quiet one should remain.

"Thank you. William is quite the most handsome, richest and eligible bachelor in London society. Until I ensnared him, that is. One would hope to achieve such an accomplishment," said Emma with great pride and stressing the word "accomplishments". "I am sure such success would be lacking in the country."

Goodness thought Margaret. A mental image of a spider setting up a web to catch her prey came to mind. "How so?" asked Margaret, no longer able to remain silent.

"Well, country life being so confining, it would be difficult to make agreeable acquaintances." When none of the girls made an attempt to support her theory, Lady Emma added, "don't you agree?"

What Lady Emma Ashfield meant that her chances of finding a suitable match that would only be comparable to her own next to impossible, if none at all —*was she that conceited?*

"I do not, Lady Emma. As far as I am concern country life is the centre of the universe."

"Yes, I guess you would." She said brushing an imaginary piece of fuzz from her dress.

"Pray, what do you ever mean by that?" Margaret asked, her colouring turning from a soft pink hue to shades darker.

"Only that I find country life small and uncivilized," said Lady Emma not bashful with her opinions and her not so hidden meaning.

"Uncivilized?" Jane asked, dubious of what she had heard.

"I fear you heard correctly, Jane. Lady Emma perhaps pictures country life to be of savagery. Like when we assisted in the birthing of a calf? Remember when all that blood poured out from the belly of the cow?"

Lady Emma's pale cream skin began to turn a green hue.

Margaret, who would normally begin to feel sorry, decided the girl deserved it and so much more. "Oh," she added, "Jane, remember when we went to see where the vicar had been murdered and we traced the form of his body?"

"Mother!" screeched Lady Emma startling both her mother and the Duchess. She rose from her chair and nearly stumbled trying to reach her mother.

Lady Ashfield welcomed her nearly hysterical daughter into her arms. "Dearest, what is the matter? Are you ill?"

Looking at Jane and Margaret with seething eyes, Lady Emma refused to give the girls further satisfaction, "I do not feel well, mother. May, we please go."

Aunt Charlotte concerned for the girl, called Hodgkin to escort the ladies to their waiting carriage. "Oh, dear," she began, "I do hope they make it home, the poor girl looked as if she was approaching a faint." Eyes narrowing she turned to the girls, "Now I wonder what really did happen to cause Lady Emma to approach the vapours?"

Both girls giggled at the silliness of Aunt Charlotte's concern for such a vile creature.

Aunt Charlotte had not been a fool. "I am disappointed in you both."

"Disappointed?" Jane cried. Never in her life had she questioned any of Aunt Charlotte's idiosyncrasies, until now.

"Yes, disappointed. Lady Emma deserved your compassion. It was badly done Jane."

"But why would she, a young woman of good fortune, about to make a fortune through marriage and with such snobbish pride deserve compassion. She did nothing but insult me from the moment she walked into your home." Margaret said in Jane's defence.

"I agree Aunt Charlotte, Lady Emma did not behave any better than Miss Caroline Bingley, from Jane Austen's *Pride and Prejudice*."

"This is not a story Jane," scolded Aunt Charlotte. "And Margaret, dear, I know Lady Emma can be quite proud; however, I expected better from you."

Margaret started to feel bad indeed. Perhaps, Aunt Charlotte was correct. She knew better and because of that she was at an advantage toward the small minds of society. "I am sorry, Aunt," said Margaret.

"I for one am not sorry. She got what she deserved. Believe me, tomorrow it will be just a memory and she will be back to insulting someone else she believes is beneath her," said Jane walking out of the room, leaving her friend loss for words.

Aunt Charlotte merely shook her head and left in the same manner as her grand-niece.

Chapter Thirty-One

After a few days of reading and sitting or walking around in the gardens, Jane and Margaret had enough of the peace and quiet, and much to their disappointment Sir Hugh's visit to the town had not yielded any results, at least none that he had shared with them.

Setting out in search of Aunt Charlotte, they found her reading in the lavish drawing room.

Always in good humour and having forgiven them for their ill-treatment of Lady Emma, Aunt Charlotte was easily persuaded to let Margaret and Jane visit some of the nearby shops. Christmas several months away called for them to take advantage of their respite and go on a shopping spree.

"Very well," Aunt Charlotte said, "but you will not go alone. I would be most comforted if both gentlemen accompanied you instead of one of the footmen. I have one of my horrible headaches and will be of no use to anyone at the moment." Pulling the service cord, she returned to her settee.

Hodgkin, appeared, bowing to the ladies he addressed her ladyship. "Yes, my lady."

"Oh, Hodgkin, would you be kind as to fetch Sir Hugh and Mr Latham and bring them to me?"

"Right away, milady," he said.

The girls were not pleased with her ladyship's suggestion, but it never helped to argue with her.

Despite protests from Sir Hugh and Mr Latham, the carriage was readied for the next morning's shopping excursion. Jane and Margaret sat side by side, facing the two men. Conversation among the young people was non-existence as well as eye contact.

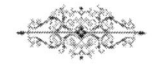

Once they were dropped off, the foursome agreed to split up, despite Aunt Charlotte's obvious meaning for them to stay together.

Margaret sensed Sir Hugh was anxious to be elsewhere, and Mr Latham seemed a bit nervous. She and Jane glanced at one another, remembering the men's individual trips to London for business matters. If their solo wanderings moved the murder investigation forward, then they approved.

"Very well," said Margaret, cocking her head towards Jane. "We'll meet you at this spot at the appointed time."

She turned to leave and stopped when Jane didn't follow.

Margaret hoping for a diversion was none too pleased in realizing that their excursion would consist of nothing more than shopping. What she would rather do was go with the men. She knew they were most likely continuing with their investigation. And as part of it they would be going into places a woman of society would never be allowed to go. Confounded society! Reluctantly admitting defeat, she moved to Jane's side.

"Remember," Sir Hugh said to them, "stay on Market Street. There are plenty of shops there to keep you occupied. Latham and I won't be gone for long."

The men waited until they were sure the girls were on the right footpath and out of hearing.

"Are we letting them go alone, after all that has happened?" Margaret heard Mr Latham ask.

Straining to hear anything else they said, Margaret walked slowly, hoping to catch something more, but, unfortunately, she couldn't hear Sir Hugh's reply.

"In actuality, we aren't," Sir Hugh said. "While everyone packed, I sent word to a friend of mine. The young ladies are being followed as we speak. My friend's job is to guard them at all costs, and should he fail; it will be because he's dead. To make sure, there's a back-up to take his place."

"Brilliant, Cameron. I wish I'd thought of it myself."

"As much as the ladies are more trouble than I care to acknowledge, you don't think I'd willingly let them out on their own without any protection?"

The girls walked along the busy streets, Jane giddy with joy at the prospect of shopping and Margaret trying her best to get into the mood. The numerous shops, lined up in an unregimented fashion, seemed to go on and on. Cigar shops, book stores, and fabric and millinery shops in varying styles clustered along their way. Most were decorated with fir and colours of greens, reds, blues and yellow in celebration of the upcoming holiday season.

Men tipped their hats at them as they walked by.

The girls merely smiled neutrally and continued on. Further acknowledgment of their greetings would be highly improper.

The frenzy of people shopping increased the ambience of the holiday spirit. Street urchins singing holiday songs were given a shilling from passers-by, and the girls were no exception. Reminded of those less fortunate, they readily gave when they had the chance.

"I'm glad we managed to get out a bit," said Margaret, the music and joviality of the spirit of the holiday finally helping her join Jane in her good mood. "I should like to see some lovely fabrics. I haven't worn anything new in a long time."

"What do you mean you haven't worn a new dress in a while? Besides, why would you care?"

"As a woman, cannot I want to look nice, because I can?" Margaret asked, rather irritated. "Besides, have you not heard? I am quite rich now."

"Of course," Jane said, smiling and linking her arm in Margaret's. "I was just teasing. I must say I would love to find some fine silks as well." It pleased her to hear Margaret's desire to shop. It was times like this when she experienced complete happiness. It is as if all was normal. There were no deaths or proud young men to contend with.

They spent the next half-hour going through several millinery and jewellery shops. Jane ordered a necklace for her stepmother and Margaret bought a pin for Jane's birthday which was after the holidays. Smelling the enticing aroma from a chocolate house, they decided to indulge themselves with a nice hot cup of chocolate.

After their drinks, the girls headed out to visit the fabric shop next door which displayed beautiful exotic fabrics in different designs and colours.

"These are unusual," said Margaret. Leaning closer to the window, she added, "I, wonder if they are made locally."

"I agree," Jane replied. "Very pretty indeed, although their extraordinary style doesn't indicate they're local products. I wonder how the shopkeeper could afford so many expensive fabrics."

Giggling, Margaret added, "Perhaps she engages in a bit of smuggling."

"Really, sometimes your imagination goes to extreme lengths."

The girls laughed as the bell over the door rang and a plump woman with a round face came from a door behind the counter.

"Good afternoon, ladies."

"Hullo. We noticed the silks in the window and would like to see some in lavender and blue colours."

"Of course, miss," the shopkeeper said excitedly. She had yet to make a sale today and was hopeful that the young ladies would shop and walk away with at least a month's worth of earnings for her pocket. "The fabrics are some of the finest you will find in this area."

"I see. How did you happen to come into such an array of foreign cloth in London?" asked Margaret offhandily.

Eyes narrowing, the shopkeeper asked, "What are you getting at?"

"What my friend is trying to say is that you must be fortunate to have come to such delightful fabrics through your trading connections."

The frightened shopkeeper suddenly stiffened when the bell over the door jingled and someone else entered the shop.

For a moment, Jane wondered if Sir Hugh had walked in on them. It would be just like him to show up and take the glory of discovery. Turning around to confront him, she came face to face with the Marquis de Faucheaux.

Jane gasped as she stepped back into Margaret.

"Lady Jane, Miss Renard, how do you do?" he said, bowing to the startled young women.

"Marquis," Margaret was the first to recover. "It is a pleasant surprise indeed."

Ignoring Margaret, the Marquis shifted his attention to Jane. "It is I who am pleased beyond belief to discover your presences in this delightful shop. I have but recently arrived in London and was looking for fabric for my goddaughter's birthday dress."

He stood closer to Jane, taking advantage of the opportunity to lean over a little, bringing himself much closer to her.

Margaret heard from Mrs Appleby that the Marquis was a good friend of Lord Hastington and that he had baptized his lordship's daughter. So how dangerous could he be, especially to her friend? Margaret wondered. She knew the Marquis to be completely smitten with Jane, only a fool would not have noticed. Yet, there was something mysterious about the man. Something about knowing more than he was letting on, but what? She made a mental note to ask Sir Hugh about him. She doubted he would offer her any information, but it was worth a try, especially when it concerns her friend.

"I heard about your attack. Do you remember anything?" he asked, allowing a brief moment of genuine concern to show across his face, before pulling himself together.

Taken aback at the closeness, Jane could see how dark his eyes were. She instinctively stepped back up against the counter. Feeling cornered like a trapped animal, she raised her chin. "I am sorry, sir. But, I do not wish to discuss what happened. It was a very frightening experience."

Like a tigress protecting her cub, Margaret said coolly, "Please excuse me, Marquis, for I do not wish to be impolite, but Lady Jane is my dearest friend, and I do not want to put her through unnecessary angst."

It took several seconds, though it seemed an eternity to Margaret, before the Marquis gave her friend space.

"Pray do forgive me, ladies. I meant no harm and surely it wasn't my intention to upset your ladyship. Like you, Miss Renard, I am most grateful she was unharmed. Had I had been the one there to rescue her, I would have made sure the fellow did not have the chance to escape." He turned to Jane who was using the counter top to support her wobbly legs. "Well then, I bid you farewell and safe journey home."

"Good day, sir," Jane said, inclining her head.

Bowing, the Marquis said, "By the by, I have decided to postpone the ball till you are both back. I look forward to a first dance with you Lady Jane, if I may be so bold."

364

Jane remained still. She had hoped to have escaped the ball, but alas the man was devious indeed. "It will be an honour, Marquis."

The Marquis bowed and the ladies curtseyed.

Neither spoke until the bell over the shop's door stopped ringing.

"Well, that was interesting," said Margaret, clearing her throat.

The shopkeeper, not wanting any trouble, had moved to the other side of the store.

"It's awful how he can be so intimidating when he is quite handsome," Margaret sighed deeply. "Come, Jane, I think we should proceed a little earlier than agreed to meet back with Mr Latham and Sir Hugh. If you want we could revisit the chocolate house. Maybe we can buy Aunt Charlotte some chocolate."

Jane liked that idea. Aunt Charlotte favoured chocolate as one of her greatest desserts. Even Sir Hugh's presence would be a welcome diversion. However, it would be a pity if they had come all this way to London and not done some Christmas shopping. She decided then and there not to allow the Marquis the power to make her quiver in her slippers. "You know what? I'm no longer exhausted and believe that we should take this opportunity to continue with our Christmas shopping. What say you?"

"Aye, says I," Margaret concurred, her imitation of a pirate bringing a smile to Jane. Taking Margaret's arm, she ushered her friend toward the other shops, chocolate house temporarily forgotten.

Chapter Thirty-Two

After leaving the girls to their shopping, Mr Latham and Sir Hugh proceeded to one of the seediest pubs in the town, unaware they were being followed.

The Red Devil played host to the more infamous sorts of criminals. Sir Hugh ventured there on many occasions when working for the government. Once he was stabbed trying to stop a brawl between his informant and a debt collector. Saving the rascal nearly cost him his left lung. Luckily he was young and healed quickly and completely.

"I am still not sure it was wise to leave the young ladies to amateurs, especially after Lady Jane's attack," declared Latham.

"Trust me, Philip. My friends are far from amateurs. Many have killed and died in the name of England."

Mr Latham could tell Sir Hugh was in a foul mood. It was funny how his moods changed like the wind. He wondered if Lady Jane had something to do with it. Lord knows Miss Renard had the ability to make him go from a calm countenance to one of sheer annoyance.

"Here, put this in your pocket." Sir Hugh handed him a small revolver.

Mr Latham did not believe in killing, so carrying a weapon was never part of his wardrobe, let alone his character.

Sir Hugh noticed his hesitation, "Listen carefully, Philip. We are entering one of the most dangerous pubs in the entire country. The men in there are likely to kill you soon as you look them in their eyes and without a moment's notice. I need you to watch my back and I shall be watching yours."

Mr Latham merely nodded, holding the weapon as if he was holding waste.

Sir Hugh took the gun from him, dropping it inside Mr Latham's coat pocket.

Latham realised the risks. There were times when a man living in dangerous environment had no choice but to take those risks. He needed to remain alert. Many lives were at stake and not just Miss Renard's or Lady Jane's and her family, but his family as well. Should something happen to him, what would become of his mother and sisters, he wondered painfully. Fortunately, he would leave them with a small fortune; however, he was not a fool and knew his family required the protection of a man. Especially his sisters—young ladies of fortune often fall prey to men of less fortunes and even lesser honour. While he did defend society, against Miss Renard, he was not blind to its many faults, though he would never admit this to her.

Giving Sir Hugh an expression that went from hesitation to determination, Sir Hugh said, "That's a good man. Remember, it's either them or us" giving him a hard thumped on the back making him wince.

How could such a small fellow pack such strength?

The two men entered the pub separately. If there were going to be any elements of surprise, then it best be their side.

The dank smell of the pub nearly knocked Latham over. The smell of beer, smoke, sweat and probably bodily fluid was overwhelmingly strong, and he envied Sir Hugh who seemed to have a better constitution for it. He prided himself on believing he was a man of the world, but he definitely would not claim any part of this one. A man who looked familiar remained unperturbed as he ordered a pint. He knew his father would probably applaud him for stepping out of character from society's narrow expectations of normal "upper class" behaviour to that of the slums of London.

The person Sir Hugh sought, Maxwell St. John, was seated away from the bar in a dark, quiet corner.

St. John was not a man with whom to trifle. Even Sir Hugh respected his ability to kill without hesitation. He did this for a living, and on many occasions Sir Hugh hired him on behalf of his superiors.

Sir Hugh knew the moment they had stepped into the pub that they were being watched. He was not a fool to believe that St. John would allow him or Latham to walk in without any form of protection. He also knew more about St. John than he let on.

The tall red-headed young man drinking his demons away had been born Anthony Thorpe, son of the late Duke of Archstone. He had been born to privilege, including loving parents who worshipped the ground he and his five year-old sister, Miranda, walked on.

Sir Hugh had found out that the young man had once had a happy constitution and believed in honour, very much to his father's pride and joy.

But all had changed when his parents, returning from a ball, had been waylaid and killed by a group of highwaymen. Vowing revenge, the sixteen year old sent his sister to live with an aunt in Edinburgh. He sought a group of highwaymen and joined them. Working his way up the ranks, he became an expert shot and swordsman. When he found the highwaymen responsible for his parents' death, he killed them all and celebrated his success by giving himself a new name and identity:

Maxwell St. John, mercenary for hire, and of the worst kind, had been born into the world. St. John sold his services to the highest bidder; whether it was for murder, espionage, or thievery, it mattered not to him. He owed no allegiance, not even to his country, unless of course it was she that offered the highest bid. Ten years after setting out to find his parents' killers, St. John had become a rich man and made many enemies.

There were many reasons Cameron admired St. John. The most important one was for his love of and dedication to his sister. The young girl had been spoiled beyond belief and lacked nothing. Sir Hugh believed there was more to his personae than that of a ruthless killer, but only St. John was privy to that personae and on any other given day, he no doubt felt he and the red-headed killer would have been the best of friends.

St. John watched Cameron come in, a dark-haired gentleman following closely behind, no doubt a cohort of his. Cameron was not fool and while they often fought on opposites sides, St. John believed he would have made an excellent partner—in this business a trustworthy fellow was worth his weight in gold. He signalled to Sir Hugh, who acknowledged him with a nod.

The other man who he believed came with Cameron settled himself at the bar, facing the establishment's entrance. Though it was too early for a drink, he had ordered one nonetheless.

"Well, it took you long enough to get here," St. John growled, taking a gulp of ale before wiping his mouth with the sleeve of his expensive coat. The heavy drinking from the night before had left him in a foul mood. The chit he spent it with stole his money and left quietly before he had roused from his heavy drinking and partying. Even Cameron, whom he liked, seemed to do nothing to lift his mood.

"Sorry, old chap, but one cannot be too careful these days."

With most of the men he had dealt with, St. John could always detect fear in their voices, but never with Sir Hugh, and because of this he admired him. Well, that and the fact that Sir Hugh had become the man he was not.

"So what can I do for you?" St. John asked, coming directly to the point.

"Pierre Binet. Have you heard of him?"

Taking another drink, St. John belched, "From Belgium—a little man with wandering fingers. Started working for the landed gentry as an estate manager until money kept disappearing. He was working for a Monsieur Renard in Dover. Left quietly one night and disappeared. Had some people asking me for him but couldn't offer news on his whereabouts. Last I heard he was dealing with some unsavoury characters. An acquaintance saw him several weeks ago at a local inn handing out pound notes like they grew on trees. Of late, rumour has it he's in with a smuggling ring."

"I suspected as much," Sir Hugh said.

A waiter brought him a glass of ale before hurrying off to his next customer.

"Any idea where we can find him?"

St. John finished his drink with one gulp. "No idea, but if I hear anything, I'll send you a post."

"Let me give you the address to where you can send it. I—"

"Don't bother. I know where you put up. I'd not mind staying there myself, having the chance to be surrounded by such lovely ladies. The beauties of Dover, from what I hear."

Sir Hugh paled, and then turned crimson. "I know what makes a man like you tick, St. John, but try not to confuse my admiration for cowardice. I respect you, and I hope you will respect the young ladies and their families. They are off limits to the kind of worlds you and I have frequented."

The menace in his voice did not escape St. John. Admiration followed by laughter. "Not to fear, Cameron. I have a sister who is a young and as innocent as your ladies. And if I were to ever find myself in their presence, I shall be the epitome of gentlemanly behaviour."

"And I shall do the same for you."

"Oh, I am counting on it." His kind of job was not one of the safest and he was a fool to believe he would die of old age. Cameron was an honourable man, and a promise made is a promise kept. He loved his sister dearly and wanted her to have a good life. Until she was happily married to a gentleman of honour, and one she loved, he planned to ensure she was guarded against men of his type. He had seen to it that she had gone to the best schools and made the right connections. A man like Sir Hugh was one of those connections.

They bid farewell with an understanding. Sir Hugh had gotten his confirmation, met Latham at the bar, and together they walked out to look for the girls.

The other man who had sat quietly watching Sir Hugh and Latham emptied his pint and followed them out, carefully trailing at a distance.

Chapter Thirty-Three

"What are you getting Mr Latham for Christmas?" Jane asked. Their encounter with the Marquis temporarily forgotten, her cheerfulness had returned. They were now browsing in a comfortable, well-lit milliner's shop.

Margaret was looking at some cufflinks for Jane's father. "I shall get him a sense of humour, or perhaps a sensible disposition," she said rather flippantly.

Jane giggled. "Silly girl, the man has one of the best humours in town and an excellent disposition, I might add. It is you who lack in sensibilities."

Margaret decided to ignore the whole subject of Mr Latham and prayed Jane would, as well. She found a beautifully knitted shawl in lavender—one that would suit Jane's stepmother.

Jane picked up the cufflinks Margaret had looked at earlier and decided her father would love them. She felt decidedly happier they had chosen to do a bit of shopping, always a good antidote to the doldrums, including their encounter with the Marquis. If luck held out she would soon have a gift for everyone on her list.

"Jane, if it were not for my father's money, where do you think I would have ended up?"

Examining a gift for Mr Latham, Jane looked up and quickly answered. "What made you ask that question?"

"I don't know. I guess I often wondered what it would have been had it not been for my fortune."

"Well, I think you should stop worrying. Papa and I would have adopted you. You would have been my sister, silly. Don't concern yourself with dreary thoughts like that."

Margaret was touched by Jane's dedication. She wiped a deceitful tear away before it trickled down her cheek.

"I've thought of the best gift for Mr Latham and Sir Hugh," Jane said.

Margaret, who was holding a pipe, set it down and turned. "What?"

"A pug!"

"A pug? Why in heavens would you want to put an innocent animal in the hands of a man like Mr Latham? It would be inhuman."

"I am serious. We each get them a pug."

"I don't know. It just doesn't feel right," was all Margaret managed to say. She tried to picture the self-centred Mr Latham caring for anything other than himself. She could see him now, stiff and uncomfortable, with a bubbly puppy following him. She then feared the poor dog might die of hunger. That would lead to her having its death on her head. It might serve him well to be discomforted over another's welfare.

Sir Hugh, on the other hand, would love the pup. He'd end up spoiling it, and in return, it would love him unconditionally. The dog would most likely grow to dislike Mr Latham. Now that was a very comforting thought.

"I like it," declared Margaret. "Pugs for the two of them it will be. I'll contact one of my footmen to inquire about a breeder."

Jane agreed. She felt Mr Latham's loyalty would benefit with the care of a small pet of his own, but the joke would be on Sir Hugh. She pictured the small dog being a nuisance, chewing on his favourite shoes or unravelling his clothes. The more she thought about it, the more she liked the idea.

After having purchased several gifts, the girls crossed Bailey Square to a small bookstore called "The Dignified Poet." Books made the ideal gift and perhaps, if they were lucky, they would find some for themselves.

Jane found her father a copy of Sir Walter Scott's *Waverly*. Sir Walter Scott was a favourite of his.

Margaret discovered two copies of Jane Austen's *Mansfield Park*, only just published the year before. She knew Jane would love a copy. They had their own special Christmas morning ritual. When all the gifts were opened, they retreated to Jane's bedroom to open the gifts they had for each other. Often it became a contest between them as to who could outdo the other in the uniqueness of their gifts. But their generosity toward one another had always been in the best spirit of friendship and fun.

"Don't wish to sound alarming, but I do believe we're being followed," Mr Latham whispered.

"I know. I noticed him at the pub." Passing a window, Sir Hugh caught a brief glimpse of their follower. He had seen this man before, but exactly from where? The man's hat made it difficult for him to recognize the man.

Upon entering an intersection, Sir Hugh and Mr Latham agreed to separate and flank their follower, hoping to take him by surprise.

The man, content with how well his mission was going, suddenly lost sight of his quarry. Casting around hastily for any sight of them, he was more than startled when they appeared at either side of him. Mr Latham grabbed and pulled him aside into an alley. "Who sent you?" he demanded.

Nervously, the man sputtered and removed his hat. "Please, sir, 'tis I, Palmer, milady's footman. It was milady who asked me to follow you. I meant no disrespect. You see my mistress, she can be, well, you know, quite—."

Sir Hugh recognized him. "Stubborn, tenacious, pig headed..." He called out, a frown marring his pleasant features.

Palmer gulped. "I am afraid all of the above, sir. And if you do not mind me saying so, when Miss Renard is with her, they tend to become a force to reckon with."

Sir Hugh laughed. Poor Palmer, he understood all too well what they had to put up with.

"I must own, they are the most provoking women I have ever met, and I hope I shall never meet two of their kind ever again," spat out Latham.

"Aye, governor," Palmer agreed.

Palmer's dilemma all too understandable, Latham gestured. "Very well, you may go."

Sir Hugh was still incapacitated with laughter as Palmer took off as if his shoes were on fire.

"When I see them again, I shall give them a tongue-lashing they will never forget." Latham said, gritting his teeth.

"Now, now, we are not going to say anything about this. I prefer to have them think they have the upper hand. That is until Palmer tells them differently. Then it will be wonderful to watch them squirm."

"You have a devious mind, old man."

"And just imagine, when they are done squirming, they will realize we have foiled their plans."

Mr Latham finally caught on. "They will be exceedingly vexed, I grant you that, because, as men, we have outsmarted them once more." It was Latham's turn to heartily pat Sir Hugh on his back.

"Now that," Sir Hugh declared, regaining his composure "is worth more than my entire fortune."

On the way back to meet with the girls, the men thought they spied the Marquis de Faucheaux sliding quickly into another pub of questionable repute. Because the time was near their appointment, they couldn't take the chance and follow him.

"There you are," Jane said, catching the gentlemen by surprise.

"Was that the Marquis?" Margaret asked her arms as full of packages as were Jane's.

Sir Hugh turned to Margaret. "Where did you two come from?"

At the mention of the Marquis, Jane shivered, which didn't escape Sir Hugh. "Did you see him earlier?" he queried, distracting her sufficiently to take three of the packages before she could protest.

As if on cue, Mr Latham tried to take some of Margaret's packages, but had no luck in prying them from her tight hold.

"Yes, we did," Margaret said casting one of her "I can take care of myself" looks to Mr Latham. "We met him at a fabric shop, no less. Rather peculiar place for a single man to visit, do you not think?"

"He did claim he was there to shop for his goddaughter." Jane had no idea why she came to his defence, other than to perhaps annoy Sir Hugh.

"And which fabric shop would that be?" asked Mr Latham.

"The one called La Fleur de Paris," Jane said. "Margaret and I noticed some very interesting silks."

Mr Latham and Sir Hugh looked at the girls. Their stance had gone from relaxed to alert.

Perhaps, Margaret smiled; their male sensitivities were threatened by the choice of topic. Even if totally ridiculous, they should at least pretend to be interested in the conversation. Normally she would enjoy their misery, or at least Mr Latham's. But somehow this did not feel the time for that.

"What Jane meant to say was the fabrics were very expensive and not from this area. We, therefore, surmised they were perhaps, smuggled goods?"

The men nodded in acknowledgement of the possibilities that the clothes could have very well been smuggled into Dover, though they were clearly pleased to have escaped from discussing the types and colours of the fabrics. Without speaking, they exchanged a look that the young ladies interpreted to mean La Fleur de Paris would be the subject of further investigation.

Margaret and Jane were pleased with themselves on having provided the men with some valuable information.

Chapter Thirty-Four

Back at Aunt Charlotte's house, the girls retired to the drawing room, the most recent subject of interest, as to whether the Prince Regent would attend their next ball, having been thoroughly dissected.

Jane picked up a book from the shelf, recalling she had started the book from a previous visit but never quite finished reading it. Interest renewed, she settled by the window intending she would try to finish the book. She felt, however, that a nap would be in order, as she was suddenly exhausted.

Margaret stretched on the couch, and propping her head on the sofa's arm, she closed her eyes and sighed contently. Several minutes later she had completely dozed off.

Jane watched her friend fall asleep. Chuckling at her friend's lack of stamina, she soldiered on with her book.

An hour later a loud knock startled the girls. Embarrassed, Jane realised she too had fallen asleep—so much for stamina in either of them.

Entering, Palmer reported his failure in following Sir Hugh and Latham. It hadn't been a complete waste of effort, since he was able to recount the meeting with a man by the name of St. John and their conversation about a man by the name of Binet.

Jane paid him a shilling and thanked him for his efforts. Before taking his leave, he admitted Sir Hugh and Mr Latham had ambushed him and forced him to return home.

Margaret stomped her foot in frustration. "I am afraid we sent an amateur and have now been found out. What do you think the consequences will be?"

Jane did not reply, but remained silent as questions swirled around in her head. *Who was St. John? Better yet, why would this man have information on Binet?* "I can only deduce that the men were looking for information, and this St. John person was able to provide it. But why not tell us?"

"I meant the fact Sir Hugh and Mr Latham didn't confront us about Palmer."

"I know, I know," Jane murmured as she began to pace the length of the room. "Let's not assume the worst," she said, trying to sound confident, when, in fact, she felt the opposite.

"It will look as if we did not trust them, especially when we agreed to work together."

"I think you are correct. We should find them and apologize before it escalates to a shouting match, which I have no doubt it will." Jane felt quite badly about the whole business. Had she thought out the possible ramifications, she would not have sent Palmer to follow the two men.

Calmly, Margaret proposed that she and Jane have dinner in their rooms and leave the confrontation for the next morning.

Jane agreed. They were not really afraid of Sir Hugh and Mr Latham's tempers, but believed waiting till morning would give them a chance to accept what they had done. They quickly made their exit, first to Cook with their dinner choices, and secondly to find Aunt Charlotte and make their excuses, Margaret claiming fatigue and Jane a pounding headache.

At the start of dinner Sir Hugh and Mr Latham found they were dreading the empty evening that lay ahead of them, both in denial that the cause of this was due to the young ladies' absence.

The Duchess had made their excuses for taking dinner in their rooms.

Sir Hugh and Mr Latham of course knew what really ailed the young ladies. During the first course conversation was very light.

Aunt Charlotte asked questions concerning parents and siblings, receiving only one or two word answers from them. She had not reached the ripe old age of fifty and eight without learning a thing or two about relationships and their dynamics. She could tell by watching Sir Hugh swirl his spoon in and out of his soup and a fidgeting Mr Latham with a faraway look in his eyes that both men had their own problems. They were missing the young ladies. It pleased her there was romance developing between them, though they had yet to realize it. She believed Mr Latham a suitable match for her niece. He was a proud and honourable man and reminded her of Jane's father. She was certain he would keep her niece from being under Margaret's influence, especially the foolishness about women and their suffrage.

She did love Margaret but felt the girl needed someone with a spirit to match hers. Her heart told her Sir Hugh would be the ideal partner. As an ex-military man, he would command order, something Margaret has been lacking due to the absence of her parents. She was never wrong where matters of the heart were concerned. After all, she had been married four times.

By the time they were through the second course, the evening had taken a turn for the better as Aunt Charlotte proved to be a charming hostess.

She told them tales of her many exploits as a young woman, which included her marriages and a most recent affair with the Prince Regent.

Both men found them far-fetched but entertaining enough that before they knew it the evening had come to an end. They each kissed Aunt Charlotte good night and headed to their chambers.

Discussions about their meeting with St. John and the young ladies were best left for tomorrow. Besides, it was going to be fun watching them squirm.

The following morning the men followed the young ladies' lead and visited the fabric shop, only to discover it had been emptied out.

"How peculiar," Sir Hugh said, peering through the windows. The entire front part of the store had been completely cleaned. Not even a piece of paper on the floor. He was beginning to hate the thought that perhaps the girls had been accurate. What if the goods were smuggled? He groaned at the sight of Lady Jane's knowing smile—a pretty smile, he corrected himself.

Mr Latham circled the building, hoping to find someone who might provide them with information, but it was too early for patrons to be about. He came back to the front of the store, peered inside once more, and to his surprise found Sir Hugh rummaging around inside the store.

When Sir Hugh saw him peering in, he walked over to the door and opened it for him.

"I swear, Cameron, you never cease to amaze me."

Sir Hugh smiled. "I wish I could have amazed you even more, but I am afraid I've found nothing of value."

"I found nothing in the back either," admitted Latham.

Every time they took a step forward they ended up going several steps back. "I think we should return to the house and develop a new plan." A frustrated and angry Sir Hugh strode out the front door.

"I must say, the Marquis being a step ahead of us is wearing thin on my nerves," Latham said, impatiently removing his hat, running his fingers through his dark hair and putting his hat back on.

The men returned to the Duchess' house. Hodgkin escorted them to the drawing room where Aunt Charlotte and the young ladies were having their morning tea.

Each reading a book, they presented a picture of calmness, indifference and beauty.

"Good morning, ladies," Sir Hugh said, bowing mockingly low.

Jane and Margaret readied themselves for the onslaught, but nothing happened.

Sir Hugh was the epitome of gentlemanly behaviour, although sarcasm emanated from him, which seemed to have escaped Aunt Charlotte, still engrossed in her book.

Mr Latham dropped into a chair and began rubbing his head, either to alleviate a painful headache or erase the urge to burst out laughing.

The tea, cakes and sandwiches laid out beautifully on a buffet table in front of the double windows facing Aunt Charlotte's garden issued a beckoning welcome.

Silence ticked solemnly away, indicating no one wanted to be the first to rise and pour the tea.

Margaret refused to lift her eyes and look at the gentlemen. She feared her eyes would give away her thoughts as she waited with little patience their onslaught from having them followed.

Jane began to fidget in her chair and then offered to serve the tea. "Should I pour, Aunt Charlotte?"

"Oh, yes, please do." said Aunt Charlotte, ignorant to the tension and silence in the room.

Rising, she poured the first a cup for Aunt Charlotte, then one for Margaret. She took a cup to Mr Latham, smiling, but did not get one in return.

Standing up, he took the cup, nodded his thanks and walked over to the buffet, where he selected a cucumber sandwich.

Blasted men, why did they have to be so irritating? Jane thought. It was not as if she had lifted his wallet or insulted his family.

"Tell me, Sir Hugh, what do you think of today's weather?" asked Margaret.

Sir Hugh, who declined tea, choosing to read the paper, instead picked up on the charade. "I believe it is a fine day indeed Miss Renard." He replied without looking up from his paper.

Latham finished his sandwich and slowly sipped his tea. His next remark took the entire room by surprise.

"This is enough of polite conversation. I think what the young ladies did was despicable."

"I believe, Sir—," Margaret started to reply, but was interrupted.

"What you believe is inconsequential. You both are guilty of not trusting us after you agreed to work with us. Imagine how we felt when we learned of your deceit."

Jane could not believe Latham's remark and said coolly, "Your tricks were no less demeaning."

Mr Latham remained silent.

"Do you care to comment?" Jane asked looking at the solicitor straight in the face and then turning to Sir Hugh.

"You knew we had you followed?" Latham asked slowly trying not to sound too incredulous.

Jane knew they were being followed but had never given even a hint to Margaret.

"It was really elemental, Mr Latham. Sir Hugh may be a cad—"

"Why thank you, Lady Jane," he said, inclining his head to her.

"You are very welcome. Now as I was saying, Sir Hugh, who may be a rake —"

"Thank you, but I think you said cad, just a few seconds ago."

"You are very welcome. Now, let us see, so far a cad, a rake —"

"I believe you have made your point, my lady," Sir Hugh said. "If you cease from your deductions, then we can perhaps enjoy the rest of the day."

Aunt Charlotte, who had remained silent during this interchange, suddenly spoke up. "Here, here. Of what deceit do you young people speak? Who is following whom? The young gentlemen are here to protect you, and Margaret. Why are you trying to pick a quarrel with them?"

Jane merely smiled at her aunt, "I suppose a bit of a headache is making me rather out of sorts this morning—my apologies to the gentlemen."

"Then I suppose we are even," Sir Hugh said smoothly as he stood up, bowed and left the room.

Mr Latham, however, did not make such a fast exit. "I believe women have no place in this kind of business."

"I should very much appreciate knowing what business you mean," Aunt Charlotte said.

Mr Latham looked at her. "My dear lady, it is only a childish wager amongst the four of us. It is nothing for you to worry about." He too bowed before leaving.

Margaret went over to Jane. "Bravo," she said, hugging her friend. "But how did you know they had someone following us, and why did you not tell me?"

Jane smiled. "I know your temper, Margaret. If I had told you, you would have confronted them."

"I am speechless. I have done the one thing I promised never to do and that is to underestimate you," declared Margaret. "I would have still appreciated knowing," she added, crossing her arms and lifting her chin.

Jane felt awful for hurting her friend's feelings. Perhaps she was correct. As partners in solving crimes, they needed to trust each other. She could have told her and convinced her to remain silent. "I do apologize, dearest. You are correct. I should have."

Margaret smiled and all was forgiven.

"We need to go and get ready for tonight, Aunt," Jane said as she and Margaret made a graceful exit.

"Very well," Aunt Charlotte said, and looking up, saw an empty room. "My word, are the young people nowadays so rude?" She then turned back to her book.

Chapter Thirty-Five

Jane and Margaret descended the stairs together to meet Aunt Charlotte, who dressed in all her finery, stood in the hall's mirror fidgeting over her dress and jewels—the diamond crown sitting prettily in her grey hair.

The girls hoped to have a wonderful time at Lord and Lady Radcliffe's ball. They learned from Aunt Charlotte that the young gentlemen were waiting patiently in the drawing room.

Jane had chosen a teal gown with sewn dangling pearls around the cuff of the sleeves. Her hair had been pulled up with curls also dangling in cascades down the back of her head, looking very much like the goddess Diana.

Margaret wore a pink gown with white pearls intertwined with embroidered ribbons to create pink rose petals. A few loose curls rested lightly on her shoulders.

Long-time friends of Aunt Charlotte, Lord and Lady Radcliffe, were thrilled to learn that the Duchess of Stafford's niece and friends were visiting and insisted upon having a ball to introduce them to their circle of friends. Their manor on the outskirts of central London was ideally situated for entertaining.

The ladies were soon joined by the men.

Upon seeing Sir Hugh, Jane became shy and unsure. Did the blasted man have to look so handsome in his evening attire?

Margaret's own stomach did some somersaulting as Mr Latham joined them. His coat of dark green and stiff cravat were of fashion, overall she admired his evening attired, but wished his stiff cravat wasn't so stiff, it reminded her of the man.

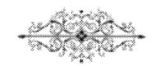

<hr />

They rode in silence to the ball. Hurdled together there was warmth throughout the carriage. Arriving at the manor the ladies were assisted as they alighted.

Upon entering the ballroom, the girls were taken aback by both the grandeur of the room's size and decorations. The presence of many members of England's noble and rich families gathered in clusters, busily chatting.

"Oh, my," Margaret said, continuing to absorb the ambience of the party.

"I know," Jane said.

After several minutes, both were inundated with introductions to eligible bachelors and invitations to dance. Mr Latham and Sir Hugh found themselves equally overwhelmed with several invitations to family estates for sporting events or dinner from some of the older men with ulterior motives of ridding themselves of their single daughters. They had no choice, for they were besieged by their wives to solicit such invitations from the young men.

Rumours that the Prince Regent might be attending had Aunt Charlotte practically over the moon, having bragged that the Prince once wept over her when she refused his advances. The girls found it hard to believe, since Aunt Charlotte was ancient, but who were they to argue over someone as respected and loved by society as Aunt Charlotte.

Margaret found a place to stand a little apart from the other guests to gather her wits. Then she saw Lord Roxburgh. She was surprised to see him, having no idea the extent of his connections. For tonight he was an eligible bachelor, handsome and very rich, though not as handsome as Mr Latham. *Heavens, where did that come from?*

As if sensing her eyes on him, Lord Roxburgh turned to her, inclined his head in greeting and raised his glass. Margaret quickly recovered, curtsied, and moved slightly to the side to look for Jane. She found her standing across the room talking to a rather tall, thin woman dressed in a lavish red dress of silk and chiffon.

"My dear, I am so pleased that you have come to stay with the Duchess," the woman said.

Joining Jane, Margaret was promptly introduced to Lady Ackerton. Known for her opulent attire she was famous for her connection to the Prince Regent. Rumours circulated that she was his latest conquest. Astonished by the woman's beauty, Margaret did not find it difficult to believe.

"Miss Renard, it is indeed a pleasure to meet you. Your lovely friend here," gracefully gesturing toward Jane, "did not exaggerate in her description of you."

Margaret blushed at the compliment.

The music stopped long enough for the musicians to take refreshments. A violinist provided background music as conversations throughout the ballroom continued.

To her surprise, she saw Mr Latham approaching the group.

"Lady Ackerton, I trust you are enjoying yourself," he said, bowing to the ladies.

"Indeed I am your lordship. I trust your mother and sisters are as well as can be expected, considering the circumstances." There was sincerity in Lady Ackerton's comment concerning his family's loss.

"I thank you, they are."

Turning to Margaret, "Miss Renard, would you do me the honour of the next dance?"

Speechless, Margaret smiled stiffly, not finding the words to turn him down gently, she merely stared at him.

Taking her silence to mean her agreement, Mr Latham inclined his head, and excusing himself, strolled off.

Intrigued, Lady Ackerton recognized the signs of a fledgling romance. Herself a romantic at heart, she decided to give it a little help. She leaned closer to Margaret and whispered, "I hear he is quite a catch and comes with forty-thousand pounds a year."

Jane and Margaret smiled politely.

Margaret knew that Mr Latham was comfortably well off, but she had no idea the worth of his estate, nor did she feel it was her business. Once again she was reminded of society's small-mindedness. Lady Ackerton, a woman of high social standards, had nothing better to do than gossip about people's personal affairs and perhaps try her hands at matchmaking.

Margaret turned toward the dance floor, in time to see Mr Latham dancing with Lord Hemsworth's daughter,

Lady Sarah Ashworth. Many of the young gentlemen in attendance were eligible bachelors. Sir Hugh, Mr Latham, and Lord Roxburgh were no exceptions. She was certain none would lack female companionship though there was a small pull on the thought of Sir Hugh and another young lady. Realistically she knew that the single young ladies would flock around the men throughout the evening, in hopes of inspiring a marriage proposal.

Not finished, Lady Ackerton added, "I also heard he's opening a law practice and hopes to find a new home in Dover."

Margaret and Jane glanced at one another, smiling neutrally, neither one revealing their surprise at the news. *Was there anything the woman did not know about the Lathams?* Margaret's mind began calculating the possibilities of them living nearby. True, since she'd met Mr Latham he had acquired several new clients and she could see why an office would be needed, but a home in Dover? She knew their home in Whitfield was several hours north of Dover, and perhaps he found the ride to and from too much to handle. *Was he planning on settling down?* She attributed the sudden rush of heat in the pit of her stomach to an upset from lack of food. She wondered if his mother and sisters would be joining him. Perhaps they would. As the only son, it was his responsibility to take care of them. Margaret knew he would do that, proud and responsible as he was.

Mr Latham broke her reverie as he appeared at her side to claim his dance.

Another young man made his claim for Lady Jane.

A slow waltz began to play.

Putting one arm around Margaret's waist, Latham he took her right arm just as they began speaking at the same time.

"You first," Mr Latham said.

Margaret could now better appreciate how elegantly he was dressed. For the first time in her life, she found it hard to think of something to say—never had she been so close to a man. "Wonderful evening," she finally said, her voice low. Her heart threatening to burst, perhaps she was beginning to catch a chill—she shivered.

Mr Latham did not do much better. "Are you cold?"

"No, thank you." she said. Discovering they danced well together, she decided the less said the better.

A long silence between them followed.

"I've heard the Prince is to make an appearance," Latham was the first to speak.

"Really?" Margaret responded as if she hadn't heard the rumour earlier. She glanced up at his face when she heard him take a deep, sharp breath. "I am sorry. Did I skip a step?"

"No, you were perfect," he said, swirling her around.

They moved in perfect unison with the other couples and yet both were in their own little world. It wasn't until the music had stopped and they began to hear murmurs that they realized the dance had ended some time ago.

Margaret laughed and blushed. "My, we must both be either tone-deaf or not attending closely enough."

Mr Latham gave her a rare smile and escorted her off the floor, to where Jane stood, recovering after finishing a dance with a young man who had a propensity for stuttering and two left feet.

Back with Jane, Margaret looked beautifully flushed. She had to admit, if only to herself, she had had a wonderful time dancing with Mr Latham, and this perplexed her.

Jane had used the opportunity to watch her friend dance with a man she claimed she utterly detested, yet while dancing she could have sworn she saw Margaret look at Mr Latham with high regard, just as Mr Latham smiled down at her.

Her partnered skipped a step bringing her attention back to him. Earlier in the dance he had stepped on her left foot. She loved dancing but not when her partner had two left foot.

"Lady Jane," he began. The young man had a slouch even when standing straight. He seemed to have more teeth than he needed. Jane felt bad for him and tried to compensate by being an attentive dancing partner.

From where he danced, Sir Hugh watched as Jane's partner held her a little closer than he liked. He then heard Jane laugh at something that was said. He felt a knot form at the pit of his stomach. Any closer and he hopped to run his fist down his throat. He could use losing some.

The music ended and another dance was set to begin. Sir Hugh chose this moment to claim a dance from Lady Jane. He walked over to where the girls stood. Jane had been facing away from his approaching form and thus was surprised when he appeared.

"Lady Jane, may I have this dance?"

His years in the government taught him to read facial expressions and from Lady Jane's face he could see her react with shock and then pleasure. Placing her hand on his arm, she went willingly with him as he escorted her to the dance floor. This would be the first time since rescuing her that he would get the chance to be close to her—memories of her warm and curvaceous body next to his reminded him of his desires.

"You look very lovely, tonight." He declared. He stared intently into her eyes, noticing something else in them. There was a spark of amber in them. The chit had developed feelings for him. At first, it pleased, but then he remembered who he was and why he was here. A young lady of Lady Jane's repute deserved a proper husband to be. Someone to love her unconditionally, to appreciate her wit and intelligence, to be the perfect caregiver for the children, unfortunately he was not that man. Going rigid with caution he caused Jane to miss a step. *What was wrong with him?*

"My apologies."

"I believe, madam, it is best if you rid yourself of those thoughts."

"Pray, what thoughts?" Jane asked confused, turning a vivid scarlet.

"I will not be domesticated, madam. As soon as I find out who killed the vicar, I am gone." He declared with contempt. He grabbed her by her arm, pulling her away from the unfinished dance and escorted her back to where Margaret stood talking to an old dowager.

Jane swallowed hard trying to find an answer to his accusations. "Sir, I do not understand your meaning."

Coming to an abrupt halt, Sir Hugh said, "Then pray let me explain it to you, my lady, since you seem clueless to my meaning. It is clear that your feelings for me have changed, perhaps because I saved you. I live the life of a confirmed bachelor and my kind of work leaves little time for anything more, hence the dreams of domesticated bliss is not for me. So I suggest you find some fop to marry you and give you all you desire.

Blood began to pound in her temple; Jane raised a hand to steady her head. Her embarrassment turning into fury, she stood in place seething with rage.

Margaret noticing something was wrong, quickly rushed to her friend, "Jane, Sir Hugh what is the matter?"

"You should remove your friend to a private room, I believe she is about to have the vapours." He glowered and turned way. *Women, was marriage all they ever thought about?*

Margaret escorted Jane to private room across from the ballroom. Thankfully no one seemed to notice what had transpired. As soon as they entered the room, Jane broke down in Margaret's arms, vowing that she hated the man.

After Jane had recovered, they spent the rest of the evening dancing till they were ready to faint from exhaustion. Jane was determined not to give Sir Hugh, the satisfaction of having hurt her so deeply to where she would not have been able to enjoy the party. However, truth be told it was definitely the most difficult thing she has had to do and only when she realise she had not seen Sir Hugh for most of the evening—a sudden pang hit her heart, reminding her of the pain he had caused.

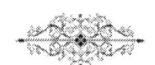

The week after the Radcliffe ball flew by, and it was time to return home. Several offers of marriage from the parade of young men who visited them in the wake of the ball had been rejected, causing Aunt Charlotte much dismay. She had hoped to have the girls married by the end of their visit. All of their belongings packed and loaded, the group was ready for their several days trip back home.

Jane and Margaret stayed clear away from the men. Jane needed time to recover from the pain caused by Sir Hugh's rejection, though there was doubt she would ever, but was determine to try her best.

The morning of departure saw Aunt Charlotte much in the vapours. She bid farewell to all and became teary eyed when it came time to hug and bid her grand-niece goodbye. "My dear, I can't tell you enough how much I am going to miss you. Promise, you will take care and stop this foolishness of investigating missing horses and catching murderers."

Jane listened politely, to assure her aunt that she would take her request under advisement. However, she had no plans of giving up their investigation.

The journey home was long and uneventful. Neither of the young ladies had been inclined to conversation nor were their escorts, especially Sir Hugh who for some reason or another had since the Radcliff ball, been in a foul countenance. The gentlemen remained on their horses till they approached their first stop.

Once inside the inn they ordered their meals to be taken in their rooms where Jane and Margaret would eat together.

During their meal, Margaret stared on her friend, hoping for any signs of improvement over her disappointment of Sir Hugh, "Jane?"

Jane who was about to take her first bite, stopped and surprisingly found that she was hungry, "Yes?"

"How are you?"

"I am fine, Margaret. And please, I do not wish to discuss Sir Hugh," she said, her eyes flickering with pain. She had spent the evening prior, pondering what had gone wrong and it wasn't long till she discovered she had indeed fallen in love with Sir Hugh. Had she discovered it first she would have hidden it from him.

"Very well, I shall be pleased when this trip is over."

The men chose rooms on each side of the young ladies. They thought it best to flank them in case they found themselves in some danger. They continued travelling in this manner. The men were exhausted and frustrated, knowing that once back at the manor, the violence of the vicar's death and the attempts on their lives would return to haunt them, so they thought it best if they gave the young ladies their space. Finally, late in the evening on the fourth day, they arrived at Wellington Manor.

His lordship was the first to be on hand to assist them alight the coach.

Jane hugged her father and kissed him on the cheek. "Oh, Papa, it is so good to see you. Where is mother?"

Staring at his daughter's face, his lordship found her a little pale, causing him to hold onto her a little longer – attributing the condition to the journey. "She has gone to bed. She has been ill of late." Reaching with the other arm, he helped Margaret descend and pulled her into a hug, as well.

Turning back to his daughter, "dearest, are you well." He asked in an odd but gentle tone.

"I am fine, father." Jane declared leaning into him.

"Now, you all must be tired, so we shall talk tomorrow. Your mother had the maid clean both your rooms. You have clean sheets, pillows fluffed and cups of hot chocolate waiting for you. I have also instructed baths prepared in case you wanted to take one before retiring for the night."

Jane and Margaret looked at one another with raised eyebrows and then burst into laughter. "Uncle," said

Margaret, "it seems a certain someone missed us terribly."

His lordship reddened at the openness of his feelings, especially in front of the other gentlemen. "Well in actuality, your mother has missed you both and wanted everything perfect." He admitted in his defence, "I merely did as I was told."

Invited to stay, Mr Latham chose to go back to his home.

Sir Hugh welcomed the thought of sleeping in his bed. Taking the horses to the stables, he instructed the new stable boy to take special care of his stallion, Dante. He hoped that by the time he got back the young ladies would be in their rooms. Besides the more time he spent away from Jane the better things would be.

Over the next few days, Sir Hugh would make several mysterious trips. And when home for longer than a day, he'd lock himself in his room for hours. On occasion, he would resurface for sustenance and then back to his room he'd go. This confused and frustrated Jane for she suspected him and Mr Latham of holding back any developments on the vicar's murder investigation. On the hand she was only too pleased for the time away from him, since the night of the ball when he tore her heart to shreds.

Chapter Thirty-Six

Christmas was fast approaching, and, despite their private worries, the girls helped decorate the manor.

Jane asked Margaret to stay with her through the holidays. Not having a family, Margaret was only too happy to accept. She trusted her servants to keep the house and send word to her property manager to call upon her at Wellington Manor should she be needed, and requested her renters be provided with whatever they lacked, including gifting them each a turkey for Christmas. Knowing that her father would have been proud of her was the only gift she needed.

The Bartholomews were pleased to have everyone back and the manor full of festive life. They issued an invitation to Latham's family to spend the Christmas holidays at Wellington Manor. Though still in mourning, her Grace, the Duchess of Stanton graciously accepted.

Another invitation to a ball hosted by the Marquis de Faucheaux arrived, which Jane and Margaret thought odd. The ball had originally been planned during their London visit. Jane had been wishing she could miss this particular event, and was filled with dismay when her parents accepted. According to her father, some business had called the Marquis away, necessitating the ball to be postponed after all. Jane and Margaret already knew this.

Ensconced on the divan in the drawing room, Margaret looked up from her reading when Jane came in. Brows creased, she sensed her friend seemed troubled. "What is it?"

Taking a chair across from the divan, Jane said, "It's this confounded ball the Marquis is having." She knew an outburst like this was not acceptable in society, but she was with Margaret, and as far as she was concerned, society could take a giant leap backwards.

"Dearest Jane, rare is the man who can keep his wits about him in your presence," declared Margaret. She wanted her friend to face the fact that perhaps the Marquis did have genuine feelings for her. Though she found while handsome, his countenance held a wicked element she could not easily shake off.

Jane smiled. "Beauty is not everything. You know that, Margaret. Look at Miss Nelson. Plain as she is, her hope of finding a suitable match depends on the needs of the man. And while her only grace is that she is rich. But, if she is not careful, she will fall prey to a penniless and greedy man. Who will marry and squander her fortune."

"I agree. I merely spoke of inner beauty as the key—"

"Goodness." Jane rose from the chair. "The key!" she yelled. "Oh, Margaret you are brilliant."

"I am? I mean, I am." Margaret wished she knew what Jane meant by the key.

When Jane offered no more, she began to tap her foot, a sign of her waning patience. "Very well, I surrender. Now, please tell me about the key."

Jane laughed. She knew patience was not part of her friend's list of attributes, "The key with the fleur-de-lys for a motif—a French motif." And waited to see if Margaret caught on, but she wrinkled her nose in confusion.

"Margaret, think, the fleur-de-lys, La Fleur de Paris and the Marquis!" Pleased with herself, Jane tied the clues together and aligned the pieces of the puzzle that would lead to solving the vicar's and Chapman's murder.

"Oh my, you're correct. Of course, it all fits now. He arrived about the same time the vicar was murdered. He's been following us every step of the way. He showed up for dinner and then at the fabric shop."

"It explains his discomfort when the men were all in the parlour the night of our dinner and the murder was brought up," Jane said.

"I still would like to know how the vicar came by the key," Margaret reflected.

"Perhaps he visited the Marquis' home, found something in the armoire and took the key for evidence."

"That could be a good reason for getting killed." Margaret began to pace. She always paced when she needed to think. "Somewhere in his home an armoire is missing a key. We can take the key with us to the ball, slip away from the party and make our way to the Marquis' library and see if we find a match."

Jane hugged her friend. "You're brilliant."

"We are brilliant," insisted Margaret.

The girls laughed, then instantly sobered.

"Mr Latham and Sir Hugh!" cried Margaret.

"What about them?" Jane said.

"But, we promised to tell them—"

"I know we did, but I've been thinking, let's just keep this to ourselves. Since they will most likely attend the ball, should we discover anything we will discuss it with them," said Jane—as always, the voice of reason.

"You are right. I think this is something we should do ourselves. We need to prove to them that we are as capable as they are. Did they not go to the pub and leave us to go shopping?"

"Yes, they did. And think when the whole town gets word of our solving the biggest crime in Dover's history. We would be the first true women crime solvers!"

Jane nodded, looking ready to cry. "I am, however, really exhausted and afraid. I mean this whole business of murder and smuggling, I want our lives to go back to the way they were," she said, tears spilling down. Tears for the loss of a fledging romance.

Margaret hated to see her this way. She too wished they could go back to when the most complicated things they had to decide were which dress to wear or what to eat for dinner. She knew her friend had changed but had refused to see it up until now. *Was it selfish of her to still want to make a difference in a man's world?*

She held Jane gently, caressing the small of her back while whispering words of comfort.

"Jane, let's see this through till at least the Marquis' party. If we do not find a match to the key, then we will let Sir Hugh and Mr Latham have the key back and let them look for the lock to which it fits. You and I, we can travel if you like. What do you say?"

Jane looked at Margaret and knew her friend was giving up a lot for her, and this made her love her even more. "Oh, Margaret, you really are the best friend in the whole world."

Margaret laughed and teased, "I thought your father, your step-mama, and then Bridgette, in that order, headed the list of your favourite people. I even believe Mr Latham is in there somewhere."

Jane was about to argue, but then she held back.

Margaret laughed again. "Now you better not agree with me," she admonished, one finger pointing at her. It was so ridiculous that Jane burst out laughing, and it felt good. She took Jane's hands into hers. "There. You are very welcome, love. Now please cheer up. We mustn't let your father see your red eyes or else he will lock you up in your room and never let you out."

Jane smiled. Margaret's remark was not too farfetched. Already on edge, the last thing she wanted was for her father to go to such extremes to keep them all safe.

Chapter Thirty-Seven

Mr Latham returned to Wellington Manor in search of Sir Hugh. He had acquired some interesting information he couldn't wait to share. Encountering a servant, he was told that Sir Hugh was in his room. He took the stairs two at a time. Once he reached the landing he walked in long strides, taking the corner at high speed, only to be stopped by nearly colliding with Jane.

"Lady Jane, pray forgive me," he apologized.

"Mr Latham! Goodness, I wasn't expecting you."

"I have but just arrived and must seek Sir Hugh on some urgent matter."

"He's in his room. It is lovely to see you again. I hear your family is coming to stay with us for the holidays. Till then you must stay with us. All this travel to and from our home must be quite exhausting." Jane realized she was babbling. Mr Latham's declaration that he needed to see Sir Hugh on an "urgent matter" had her wondering how she could find out what had him so excited.

"Thank you. You are very generous. I am looking forward to spending time with our families. Christmas is one of my favourite holidays." Realizing he too was going on about mundane matters, he sketched a bow before proceeding to Sir Hugh's door, knocking sharply. The door opened slightly, and he slid in.

Unable to resist, Jane quietly moved over to the door, glancing up and down the hallway. Seeing no one, she put an ear against the smooth wood.

"Cameron, I have interesting news. It seems that the vicar's home had an unwanted guest in the middle of the night. The culprit was searching for something, destroying everything in his path. Mrs Bostwick, apparently hearing noises, surprised the intruder, who escaped through the large double windows, the same he way he entered. This further confirms the vicar had something someone else desperately wanted. And more than indicates he was involved in some sort of disreputable dealings."

"The devil," Sir Hugh said. "How did you hear about this?"

"I met the magistrate on the road this morning, and after some prodding, he reluctantly shared the information. He cautioned this family should be extra vigilant since the intruder must still be lurking about and no doubt may attempt to search Wellington Manor."

Not wishing to get caught eavesdropping Jane slipped quietly away from the door. She needed to find Margaret as soon as possible but was delayed when Mr Latham unexpectedly came out into the hallway.

Surprised to see Lady Jane still there, Mr Latham wondered if she had heard their conversation.

In an effort to cover up any suspicion that she'd been eavesdropping, Jane quickly said, "I almost forgot to ask. Will you be staying for lunch?" She rather doubted he would accept after hearing what he'd just told his friend.

"Alas, I cannot stay, but I thank you for the invitation. I shall return this evening for the Marquis' ball."

"Then I have a favour to ask you."

Mr Latham smiled. "I am at your disposal, my lady."

"Would you please take a blanket out to Margaret? I saw her from my window. She's sitting on the bench by the oak tree reading, and she looked rather cold."

Before he could reply, Jane said, "I will only be a moment." Darting over to her room, she quickly returned with a thick green blanket.

Mr Latham had waited, looking uncomfortable and shuffling his feet as if he was press for time.

"Thank you very much," she said, handing him the blanket.

Mr Latham nodded, walking away with the blanket. The thought of being alone with Margaret caused his stomach to tighten. He hadn't seen her since their return from London and had to admit he had indeed hoped to run into her during his visit with Sir Hugh. And now the thought left him uncomfortable. He had not been himself of late. Even colleagues noticed his black moods. One cited his unpleasant disposition, as another said something about his absentmindedness, all because he could not keep a certain young lady out of his mind.

Margaret sat on the bench wrapped warmly in her woollen shawl, but she wished she had brought something for her legs. The book offered no solace in her attempt to block a certain young man from her mind.

"Good afternoon," Latham said, announcing his presence. He had come upon her very quietly, admiring her long graceful neck, her head bent over the book she was reading. While she seemed engrossed in her book, he couldn't help but notice her face changing with each passing thought. He would wager and win that Miss

422

Renard was not enjoying her book, for her thoughts were elsewhere.

"Mr Latham," she said, rising and letting go of her book. Their hands touched when both bent to retrieve it. Margaret felt herself flush, and was the first to withdraw her hand. Wondering if she found his touch repulsive, he reddened in annoyance. He was a fool to believe they could be friends.

"Lady Jane thought you might appreciate a blanket," he said, placing it on the bench, ready to stalk away.

Margaret, sensing she had somehow missed an opportunity or hurt his feelings, impulsively said, "Forgive me, I was merely startled. I was so engrossed in my book that I did not hear you arrive."

Latham stopped and his expression softened. "No need to explain. I had but only just come when Lady Jane recruited me to deliver the blanket."

Nodding, he turned to leave. She wondered if he was thinking of the brief touching of their hands. She forgot to give a thought to any other reason that might preoccupy a man of his serious nature.

"Mr Latham," she called after him. *Why in heaven's name would she do that?* "How are your mother and sisters faring?"

Swivelling, he took two long strides to stand in front of her. "My mother and sisters are well. Thank you for asking."

Margaret smiled, causing more than great confusion within the gentleman. He smiled back. "Good day, Miss Renard."

Margaret returned to the manor, more exasperated than ever. *Did the man believe her to have the plague?* She found Jane waiting anxiously for her in the parlour.

"I must speak with you. Let's go up to my room." Once safely cloistered in her bedroom, Jane told Margaret what she'd overheard.

"But, this is horrid news. Poor Mrs Bostwick, as if she has not endured enough." Margaret was appalled.

"What could they have been looking for?" Jane's cat sauntered over to where she stood and gently rubbed around her legs.

"Jane, they were looking for the key."

"Goodness that would make sense. It was the only piece that was suspiciously hidden in the vicar's office. Mr Latham thinks they might try searching Wellington Manor." Jane wanted to solve the mystery as much as Margaret, but they had to first endure the Marquis' ball.

Suddenly the thought of being surrounded by danger terrified her, and she knew she would much rather stay at home doing needlework than step foot into the Marquis' home, even if it meant the lock to the key was there.

However, there was nothing to be done about it now. Despite her dread, Jane tried to immerse herself in Margaret's excitement for putting an end to the sinister events in their quiet town by discovering the piece of furniture belonging to the key. And thereby finding out who killed the vicar and Chapman. Their attitudes were much more positive than the ones apparently adopted by Sir Hugh and Mr Latham.

That evening after everyone had gone off to bed, Jane decided to keep vigilant in her room, watching and waiting for any unfamiliar noise. She stayed up reading and when that threatened to put her to sleep she paced her bedroom. If only Margaret had stayed up with her.

When she told her of her plans, Margaret immediately denied such worries and wanted no part in protecting the house. "Seriously Jane, with Uncle, Hugh and Bilty you'd think some fool would attempt to break down our doors and make their way through the entire household looking for a key?" she teased. "I think not. I am going off to bed where my beauty sleep will do me some good." She kissed her friend on the cheek and left her musing in her own thoughts.

At precisely the stroke of midnight, Jane heard a thump. Putting on her robe, she quietly tip-toed to her door. Opening it she peered out into the hallway. Thankful for the dim light, from the moon, coming in from the window at the end of the hall lighting the hall all the way down to the other side—of the hall, where her father's and Sir Hugh's room were located. Some bodyguard he turned out to be, probably in slumber dreaming of battlefields and his bachelor life. She prayed he got shot, at least in his dream. A nightmare or two will please her.

To the left of her room was where Margaret stayed when she visited. Stairs after her room led to the servants' quarter. Hearing some shuffling, Jane ran back to her room and picked up her rock laden reticule and ran back out to the hall. She will teach the intruder whose house they were messing with. She heard the same shuffling noise again. It was coming from down the hall toward her right. Holding her bag tightly she crept against the wall passing her father's room. She stopped trying to attune her hearing to the silence. Another sound was heard from her right. It was definitely coming from the upstairs. No doubt the intruder was probably trying to come in from one of the windows. Passing Sir Hugh's room she stopped to listen again. She heard a click and then someone was beside her. Blasted! The intruder had caught her. Knowing they were unaware of her bag, she turned swiftly and stroked the figure on the head, his body hitting the floor in a loud thump. "I got you!" she whispered.

Her father came out of his room. "What in the blazes is going on?" he asked in a whisper, afraid of waking his wife.

"I caught an intruder, father," declared Jane only too pleased with herself.

Margaret had now joined the group in the hall, closely followed by Biltmore who came with his gun.

"Careful, father, he might be dangerous." Jane cautioned her father as he approached the lifeless body.

"Nonsense, child, it is Sir Hugh."

Jane turned to Margaret, a huge smile on her face. "I heard a noise…Sir Hugh?" She turned incredulous to her father. "Are you sure?" It can't be…

"Quite sure," said her father helping a stung Sir Hugh to up on his feet. "Are you all right?" he asked.

"I heard a noise, so I came out of the room and then something hit me." Sir Hugh said, daring his hand to touch the growing lump on his head.

His lordship hoping to avoid a misunderstanding, "Biltmore, please go and search the premises for an intruder." He winked at Biltmore who strode away shaking his head.

Jane hid her reticule and decided to escort Margaret back to her room. Once inside the others could hear laughter coming from the room.

The household awakened the next morning to gently falling snow and a world hushed and still, almost as if it held its breath waiting for an unknown darkness to descend.

Sir Hugh was checked by the doctor and was pronounced well enough to continue with his daily activities. Thankfully he suffered not from a concussion.

Jane, was more upset that her intruder proved to be Sir Hugh, though it pleased her to have hit him with the rock, it made up for his behaviour the other evening, well just a little. She watched the snow fall from her room, praying the weather would be so severe that it would put an end to the Marquis' ball, discouraging him from ever planning another. Taking a deep breath, she stood a little longer by the window and gazed at the flakes drifting down. Then she let the curtain fall back into place and began a brief morning toilette.

Across the hall, Margaret watched out her window, admiring the scene before her. Poor Jane and Sir Hugh, though he merited it for treating her friend badly. She believes the man loves her friend but his fear of attachments has wiped all senses from his head.

A snowflake landed on the window. She had always loved the snow. Normally at this time of the year, they would be planning their sleigh rides, but the murders yet to be solved banished the joy of riding in the snow. The innocence of even one's favourite pastimes had vanished. Unlike Jane, she eagerly anticipated the ball. This was a chance to investigate the Marquis' library and office for a clue. She knew Jane was taking this whole business to heart and would be glad when it was over.

Finally the night of the Marquis' ball had arrived. By five o'clock in the afternoon, Biltmore had two carriages brought to the front of the manor. His lordship and ladyship were to ride in a separate carriage, an arrangement that increased Jane's apprehension—just why she wasn't certain.

Both girls wore their hooded velvet cloaks over their fine dresses. Jane wore a deep green gown while Margaret chose a red gown that highlighted her red curls.

When they reached the bottom of the stairs to the foyer, they were met by Biltmore with an invitation in hand.

"This has just arrived, my lady."

Jane took the invitation and read it. "Strange. There seems to have been a change with the location of the party."

"An error? Whatever do you mean?" Margaret asked.

"Well, the invitation says the ball is now taking place at Walston Manor."

"Walston Manor? Isn't that Lord Roxburgh's home?" Margaret's forehead wrinkled in confusion. She reached for the invitation to read it herself. "Lord Roxburgh does have the largest ballroom in the whole county. Perhaps the Marquis asked if he could use it." Handing the invitation back to Jane, Margaret added with flair, "You know how flighty the rich are."

"My, but your sense of humour is sharp sometimes. As if all of us are flighty. That would also include you, you know." Jane said.

"Nay, my fair friend, I am but merely a pawn in a game of social chess." Margaret declared laughing.

Jane shook her head—noting her friend was silly indeed. "Well, let us get on. Papa and Mama will follow. Sir Hugh and Mr Latham plan to come in their own carriage." Jane gave new directions to the coachmen, but the change remained unknown to anyone else at Wellington Manor.

"Shouldn't we wait for them?" Margaret asked.

"I should say not. If we stay behind we prove to them that we need them or are afraid of what has been happening around town. I am not going to give them the satisfaction, besides this will give us a head start."

"Very well, let us go then." Margaret led the way out to the first carriage. Placing one foot on the first step, she stopped, causing Jane to bump into her. "How did you hear about Mr Latham and Sir Hugh's intentions?" asked Margaret, a foot on the carriage and one on the ground.

Jane was beginning to think they might be late to the ball. Frustrated and without answering the question, she gave her friend a push. The invitation fluttered from her hand and fell unnoticed onto the ground. Margaret landed with a thump on one of the seats. Jane entered the coach, flustered, and also made an unladylike landing across from Margaret. The girls looked at each other for a moment in solemn silence and then burst into laughter.

Mr Latham's carriage pulled to a complete stop outside of Wellington Manor at half past five. Seeing the family's coach parked close to the manor's entrance, both men relaxed somewhat. They felt relieved that the family had not yet departed.

Sir Hugh was the first to alight. Latham followed close behind, his mind preoccupied with figuring out how to tackle his next task. Considering the several attempts on their lives, Sir Hugh was cross he hadn't found a way to convince the young ladies that it would be wise for them to ride with him and Latham. He knew there would be opposition, but he was prepared to argue with them to get them to see reason.

Walking up toward the three steps leading to the main door of the manor, Sir Hugh's right foot slipped on the icy snow, nearly causing a tumble. Looking down to get his footing, he noticed a piece of paper lying by his foot.

"Why, what trickery is this?" he said, frowning and passing the paper to Mr Latham, whose face grew alarmed as he read.

"It's strange, Cameron. We best go inside and find out if the family is aware of this. It could very well be that the location of the ball has indeed changed."

Once inside, Sir Hugh inquired after the family. Biltmore told them that his lordship and ladyship were preparing to leave for the ball, whereas the young ladies had already departed.

Charles and Amelia Bartholomew were descending the stairs leading to the foyer when they noticed Sir Hugh, Mr Latham and Biltmore in deep conversation.

"Sir Hugh, Mr Latham. I thought you at the party, but since you are still here, perhaps the girls can ride with you."

Amelia noticed something amiss. "Hugh, what is it?"

"We found this outside," Mr Latham said, turning the invitation over to his lordship, who frowned as he read the invitation.

"I don't understand at all," his lordship remarked. "Are we to go to Roxburgh's manor? But I saw the Marquis earlier today, and he was looking forward to our being at his home."

"Are you sure he said his manor and not Roxburgh's?" Sir Hugh asked.

"Biltmore gave me a second invitation this evening confirming the party at the Marquis. Dear God, what is going on? Are the girls in some sort of danger?" his lordship asked, turning pale at the thought.

"Perhaps it is a misunderstanding," his wife soothed. "The girls are probably upstairs in their rooms getting ready."

Lord Crittenden ordered Biltmore to go upstairs and check when Sir Hugh stopped him.

"I am afraid, Lord Crittenden, that Biltmore has confirmed he gave them this invitation and that they left early in the hopes of getting to the party ahead of us."

"But why leave without a chaperone?" her ladyship exclaimed. "They know better!"

"I'm afraid I am to blame for that," Mr Latham said. "I teased Miss Renard about women and gambling, and wagered that she had to abide by society's rules and avoid traveling alone without an escort. I believe Miss Renard wanted to prove something to me, and I fear Lady Jane has become her accomplice."

Doing his utmost to stifle the rising panic, his lordship said, "Do not place blame on yourself, Phillip. Margaret and Jane have been a handful ever since I could remember. I have indulged them far too long. Wandering alone in the countryside or on shopping expeditions must be prohibited. I have given them too much freedom. From now on they are not to go anywhere without proper chaperones. But what is to be done now?"

"We have no time to waste," Sir Hugh said. "I promise you, sir, we will race with the wind to fetch them. No harm will come to them, I bet my—, I mean, I promise you."

"And I shall come with you," declared his lordship. Her ladyship blanched, looking ready for the vapours.

"No," Sir Hugh said. "I need you and Amelia to remain here in case they return. We will go and bring them back unharmed, we promise."

His cousin gave him a grateful smile.

Taking notice of his wife's pale complexion, Charles put his arm around her waist. "Come, dear," he begged, pulling her close to him, her body providing him with comfort.

"Biltmore, please bring some sherry for her ladyship."

"I prefer a glass of water, Biltmore."

Biltmore, feeling extremely guilty, bowed and withdrew.

As lordship continued to escort his wife upstairs, he remembered something. Turning to the young men he said, "In the library I have my weapon collection. The key is in the left drawer of my desk. Take all you need. Please bring the girls back to us." He added in a whisper, "Unharmed."

The men nodded solemnly. They went into the library, found several small pistols in the collection, and took them.

Back outside, Sir Hugh and Mr Latham quickly unharnessed the horses from the carriage. Thankfully it had stopped snowing and they could travel quickly. Every second mattered.

To say that Sir Hugh was angry was an understatement. "I blame myself for this whole mess," he growled.

"Come now, Cameron, we were all fooled into believing the Marquis was the culprit."

"The girls were purposely deceived and for what reason?"

"I've been thinking about that, and it strikes me that Roxburgh has been after Miss Renard. I understand from my cousin that Miss Renard rejected him a couple of seasons ago. Perhaps he seeks vengeance," said Latham, his stomach tightening at the thought of Roxburgh harming the girls.

"Cameron, let's be off as fast as we can."

"As soon as we get there, we should split up. We can cover more ground that way."

"I agree." Latham's lips were set into a grim line, dark thoughts swirling. If Roxburgh harmed her...them... there would be hell to pay.

As if reading Latham's mind, Sir Hugh concluded, "There is a great possibility Roxburgh will not live to see another day," and then with a kick, he urged his horse onward.

"Faster!" Latham commanded over the wind urging his horse.

437

Chapter Thirty-Eight

Walston Manor sat up on a hill, like a statue from Greece mounted on a large foundation made out of marble. The manor was grand and beautifully kept, yet tonight, in the dark, it was quietly menacing, with no lights or other carriages in sight.

Their carriage came to a full stop in front of the wide steps leading to the manor's massive entrance.

Jane was the first to speak, "Strange."

"What is?" Margaret asked.

"Listen."

Margaret stiffened as she struggled to remain calm. Total silence surrounded them. Not even— "No music."

Jane nodded. She wished they had waited for her father. Even Sir Hugh would be a welcomed distraction just about now.

"What could this mean?" Jane asked a flicker of fear beginning to course through her.

Margaret shrugged her shoulders, "It could be our first clue to run." It was meant to be a jest but somehow it didn't come out that way. Not wanting to frighten Jane, she added, "I haven't the slightest idea. The only way to find out, it would seem, is for us to go inside. Perhaps we are late in arriving and everyone else is already here, with the exception of our group," she theorized, but she too wished they'd waited for the others.

Cautiously they exited the carriage, looking around, but found and saw nothing.

Taking several steps up the stairs, they could finally see the doors leading to the main entrance of the manor. They were shut. Once they reached the landing, the closed doors began to open, the rusty hinges emitting a high pitched menacing squeak, giving the girls chills. As the entrance became wider a well-lit entry hall was revealed. Stepping inside, the girls relaxed a little, believing that if there was light further down one of the rooms at the end of the hall, and then perhaps there would be others there waiting for other guests to arrive. An antique round mahogany table stood in the middle of the entry hall with a large Chinese pot proudly centred on it.

At another time, the beautiful decorations would have impressed them, but at this moment their fear began to crowd out all else.

"Hullo," Margaret called out.

Other than Margaret's voice echoing back to them, they heard no one.

In the semi-darkness of the hall, Jane reached out and found Margaret's hand. They continued down towards the lit room, looking into the rooms prior to the last one in the hopes of finding people but instead found the rooms empty. When they finally reached the last room they found it to be an abandoned formal living area. Its furnishings had seen better days. The fabric on the settee and matching chairs were worn from time and dust. Another candle had been lit and was placed on the fireplace mantle. Flames danced around the room, mocking them for coming to the party that no one planned to attend.

They quickly exited the room and crossed the hall to a room they had passed earlier, realizing it had been a library at one time or another. From the hall they could see that the room now stood empty with the exception of the countless shelves covering the length of the room. Some of the shelves had been emptied, while others contained leather-bound books, filled with dust.

"I really do have a bad feeling about this, Margaret."

"It's going to be all right," Margaret insisted. "We are so close, Jane," Margaret said, showing no signs of defeat.

Jane feared her friend was beyond reason. "No, Margaret, I think we should leave this instance. We could come back in the morning, when it's daylight. We could bring Biltmore." She begged, hoping that by adding Biltmore into the trip back, Margaret would agree.

"I'm sorry, Jane. I have been very foolish—foolish, indeed. Let us go. We may not have a ride back but I think I would rather face the walk home in the dark than to stay here and wait for something or someone to find us."

Relieved, Jane let out a deep breath. Not wasting any more time, she began to lead the way, anxiously hoping to make it to the entrance of the manor, when she heard a noise. Margaret heard it too, for she pulled Jane back into the library room.

Several seconds passed by, though to the young ladies it seemed an eternity. When nothing happened they began to feel safe enough to begin their journey home.

This time Margaret led the way, but immediately felt a tug from Jane. Turning back, she could discern that Jane had been pointing at something. Following Jane's direction, she could barely make the shape of something large. It had originally been covered by the shadows in the room, and therefore had been hidden from their view. As they got closer they realized they were now facing what seemed an antique armoire, overbearing in its size, with a lock shaped in a fleur-de-lys design.

The shock of discovering the armoire had the girls frozen for a moment. It was Jane who brought them out of their stupor by removing the key from her bag. Funny—she never noted before how heavy it was. Inserting the key it into the keyhole, she turned it until there was a soft click. The girls exhaled deep breaths, unaware they had been holding them.

Hands shaking, Jane thought it best if she tried steadying her nerves before opening the doors to the armoire. Whatever was being stored in the French armoire, it cost two men their lives—two that they had been aware of. Taking another deep breath, she opened the doors to the armoire. Fabrics of French silk almost poured out of one shelf. Bottles of wine were neatly stacked side by side, along with several bags of gold coins.

Jane and Margaret were stunned with the knowledge that the culprit had been Lord Roxburgh all along and not the Marquis de Faucheaux, as they had originally thought.

Jane had been wrong about many things in her young life, and if she lived to be ninety, she would never forget how wrong she had been about the Marquis. Her prejudice against him had been over the simple reason that she had been too proud to ever consider a man like him as her equal. If they made it back, she would make sure to apologize. "It would appear his Roxburgh has been involved in some illegal activities," was all she could muster to declare.

"And perhaps murder," Margaret added as she ran her fingers over the silks.

All this time they had feared the Marquis, yet here was the truth staring implacably at them. Jane belittled herself for not taking Mr Latham's conversation with Sir Hugh into account when she and Margaret set off this afternoon with no chaperone.

Not wishing to spend another second in the house, Jane grabbed Margaret's hand and turned to leave when they halted at the sudden darkness awaiting them outside the room. While making their discoveries something had snuffed out the candles. Not feeling any draft it both girls knew someone had done it.

"What are we going to do?" Jane whispered.

"We need to leave. I fear, the longer we stay, the more danger we are in."

"You're correct, but how are we to proceed in the dark?" Jane said, blindly leading the way. She would rather face the wilderness of the cliffs than be cornered like a hunted animal. She held on tight to Margaret's hand as they tiptoed into the hall.

She was about to say something else when a silent and abrupt attack divided them from each other, sending them crashing to the floor. The wind knocked out of them, they had no time to scream. Jane scrambled to her knees in time to see Margaret fighting from being pulled away.

Margaret's eyes took a little longer to adjust to the darkness, and she was still unable to see her assailant, who had instantly wound his arms tightly around her. Though she fought hard against the person, she stood no chance to prevent being dragged down a long spiral staircase. Once at the bottom of the steps, she was thrown into a dark, dank, cold room. Finding the smell overwhelming, her stomach threatened revolt. She would welcome a dead faint about now, though she had in the past mocked the weakness of some women. She thought of Mr Latham. If she got out of this mess, she would never admit to him that she had ever called her gender the weaker sex.

It then dawned on her she was not alone. A man's figure loomed over her in the dark. She wasn't sure, but could have sworn she had seen him before. "Hello, Miss Renard. Remember me?"

"Binet?" So it was true, Binet had been the one working all along with Roxburgh. She knew him to be a thief, yet she had never truly believed him capable of murder. "How dare you drag me down here? Where is Jane?"

"I think, Miss Renard, that at the moment you should be more concerned for your own safety," he said, his eyes conveying fury within him.

"Why are you doing this?" she asked. Panic like she'd never known before welled in her throat.

But Binet only laughed.

It was the laughter of a mad man that sent chills to course through Margaret.

The icy terror melted, and with her head clearer, Jane tried to flee, but the figure that separated her from freedom moved quicker than she. Jane felt an arm reach out of the darkness, pulling her close up against a firm body, and another covering her mouth.

"Not so fast, my dear," Lord Roxburgh's voice said in her ear. She could smell the liquor on his breath.

"Lord Roxburgh, I am so glad to see you," she said, hoping to convince him she still believed him innocent of any wrong doing. "We are in dire need of your assistance. Margaret has been taken and I was left to—"

"I am afraid, Lady Jane, that I cannot offer you the arm of a hero. You see, it was I who commanded you be brought here." He dragged her into a room off the hall, probably the living room she and Margaret had seen earlier.

"You 'commanded' me here? I do not understand. What have you done with Margaret?" The fear in her voice betrayed her outer calm. "If you harm her, I swear that I—"

"You swear? Really, my dear, I cannot have the future Lady Roxburgh speaking in such a manner. I am afraid Margaret has been a bad influence on you."

Jane gasped. "Lady Roxburgh? You can't be serious. I thought your affections laid elsewhere, Sir."

Confusion registered for a second on Roxburgh's face and then it became clear of whom Jane spoke. "Please, do not insult me, our Margaret is an abomination. She was never good enough for me. It has always been you. I did it all for you. And naturally the fact that you are far richer than her played a role in my plans of making sure you became my bride."

Jane knew Roxburgh to be indulgent, always ready to enjoy the lavish things society offered, but never did she suspect him of violence or insanity. Icy fear twisted from within.

"What... what 'all' did you do for me?" she asked, dizziness threatening to overwhelm her.

When he didn't answer, she grew more frightened. "What makes you believe I would consent to marry you?" Jane added, although she feared his response.

"Because if you do not marry me, your precious friend will come to an unpleasant end, and we must not have that. Not that I would mind," he said with a wave of his hand, as if he was dismissing a servant. "She has been more trouble to me than I care to say. I was not going to involve her in this, but she had to meddle in business that did not concern her and to make matters worse, she pulled you into her foolishness."

"Pulled me in?"

Lord Roxburgh released his hold on her, his face a glowering mask of rage. He began pacing about the room, giving her an opportunity to study her surroundings. The room had two windows, but she could see they were barred. There was only the one door though which they'd entered. It was closed, and Jane suspected it was also locked. There was a desk with one lit candle. Shadows danced menacingly around the room, taunting her.

"She nearly ruined your reputation with all the meddling in affairs that did not concern you or her."

Jane swallowed hard, trying to manage a feeble answer, "The vicar was murdered. Something had to be done."

"The scoundrel deserved to be killed."

"You surely cannot mean that. He was a man of God."

Roxburgh laughed. "A man of God, you say? He was trying to blackmail me! He gave in to the sin of greed. I had little choice but to do deal with him. His greed almost ruined all of my plans, destroyed all I was doing for you. For us! I knew a lady like you would wish to continue with the lifestyle to which you have been accustomed. You are spoiled, but your beauty makes amends for that. I have to give you and our children a beautiful home, money, and a title."

The thought of having his children nearly caused her to faint. But she knew she had to keep her wits if she and Margaret were going to make it out of this alive. She needed to discover a way out and find Margaret. The thought that no one knew where they where did nothing to quell her rising panic.

The ride toward Roxburgh's manor felt like an eternity to Sir Hugh. He chastised himself over and over for rejecting Jane, for churning away the love she was willing to give a scoundrel like him. He felt sorry for Latham who blames himself for Margaret and Jane's predicament.

"Confounded, the rake is dead set on marrying Miss Renard for her fortune." He told Sir Hugh on their way to Wellington Manor. "Men like Roxburgh, ruthless and murderous did not take well to rejection."

Sir Hugh had agreed. They had also discovered that suspicions laid on Roxburgh for the death of his father. More stories surfaced in their investigations that tied

Roxburgh to a number of other crimes—the man was definitely insane.

Arriving at the manor, no lights or music greeted them as they drew rein, stopping mid-way along the drive.

"And now," Sir Hugh said, "it looks as if Roxburgh hopes to force Miss Renard into marriage by ruining her reputation, as well as Jane's. Confounded society! I have no liking for it." No two finer women, with the exception of his cousin, walk this earth. They had to save them—his Jane. He had to save her…He loved her and was a fool in believing he could go on with his life as if nothing had changed once his mission was over. He had hurt her the day of the ball and did not want another minute to go by without her knowing that he, Sir Hugh Cameron, a fool of a man, who had rather face the barrel of a pistol than to love, had fallen in love with her and wanted to spend the rest of his life making it up to her.

Latham was about to say something, when Sir Hugh added, "Quiet now. We don't want to announce our arrival."

Latham nodded in agreement.

Sir Hugh sensed Latham's own hell of guilt. He felt sorry for him. In reality had the ladies stuck to tea parties, gossip and marriage, they would now be home safe—a sudden image of Margaret holding an infant coming to mind and as quickly as it appeared he willed it away.

"Are you all right?" asked Sir Hugh.

Latham nodded once more.

Coming from the side of the manor where trees gathered, they silently slipped off their horses, and tethered them to an adjacent tree before creeping along the drive until they came to the dark, Gothic door.

"Cameron, do you hear what I hear?"

Sir Hugh stiffened, "The Sea?"

"Could be why he was never caught in the act."

"Clever man," at any other time, Sir Hugh would have found Roxburgh an interesting opponent, but for now his fear for the girls' well-being left him feeling strangely vulnerable and frightened. He recalled many soldiers in the battlefield confronted with that. "He will probably try to escape by sea, perhaps taking them with him."

Drawing their pistols, Sir Hugh said, "I will go to the left. At the back of the building there is a slope that will probably lead to some of the caves. You take the right side."

Latham nodded and was off.

Sir Hugh felt for the knife strapped around his left ankle and sprinted around the left side of the building, down toward the cliffs.

Latham turned to see Sir Hugh disappear around the manor's bend. He made his way to the back of the house without hearing anything, coming to halt facing the end of a long cloistered hallway. He turned around trying to get his bearings when the air was rent by a scream from somewhere below the first level of the house. At first his feet felt like lead, but then he picked up momentum, running faster and faster toward the stairs, taking several at a time.

"You waste your time screaming. No one knows you are here. I made sure that the Marquis de Faucheaux was seen as the culprit, allowing us the time to get away," Roxburgh said, tying Jane's hands and feet. Once done he lifted and carried her down a flight of stairs, then through several long tunnels that ended in a large, outdoor clearing.

Ocean waves rolled in, cliffs looming above them. Jane had heard there were multiple levels of caves along the cliffs and wondered if they were on the ground level.

But if they were still higher up, the chance of plunging to her death was a definite possibility. Not that she wished to die, but perhaps it was a better fate than being married to a monster. She wondered about creating a distraction to buy them some time for rescuers to find them, positive that both she and Margaret would have been missed by now.

They had all suspected the Marquis of killing the vicar and Chapman, yet he had been completely innocent and misunderstood. Jane felt sorry for the way she had treated him. She had let her fears create a prejudice against a man whose only crime was having fallen in love with her. In return she had suspected him of crimes he had never committed. It was so very unfair of her and would gladly welcome the sight of him, if only say how sorry she was for her ill treatment of him.

It was all unreal with the exception of her fear. She hated fear and felt no one should ever have to fear anyone or anything.

Suddenly the thought came to her of the little children of the poor and their fears of hunger and the elements. That, she felt, was a justifiable fear. Her fear was not! She was bolstered by this realization, and as her anger began to distend within her, she found the strength to control the sheer panic threatening to overcome her.

Roxburgh could see thoughts flitting across her face. She was so beautiful. He could take her here and now, but she deserved a wedding, and not having one would hurt her more than anything. Society would shun her and him, though he would recover much more quickly than she would ever be able to. She was not like the many whores he had dallied with. No, not his intended—she was pure and innocent. A lady.

Smiling he said, "You are quite a spirited woman. I love that about you. I also know that you are loyal to those you love. But in time you will forgive me for all and perhaps come to love me as I love you."

With her legs bound, all Jane could do was take several hops backwards to create a barrier, at least a mental one.

"Well, Lady Jane, will it be marriage to me or your friend's death?" he asked as he began his approach.

Jane heard about women being forced to marry men they did not love because of their unfortunate circumstances, but this was not the case with Roxburgh. He was going to ruin her reputation in the hopes of forcing her to marry him, not to mention his threats against Margaret. But what she could not understand was why he was doing all this? He was handsome and rich. Any woman would proudly claim him as her husband, yet he chose to pursue her, and in the process he had killed and smuggled. She shuddered inwardly.

She needed to create a diversion in the hopes of delaying his plans. Taking a deep breath to steady her nerves, she said, "Tell me something, please."

Roxburgh blinked, surprised at her calm demeanour. "Anything, you have but only to ask. Of course, letting you go is not an option," he added, teasing.

"Why? Why the vicar, the smuggling? I don't understand."

"Why, my dear, for money, of course. As I mentioned earlier, he tried to blackmail me. He had been out on an evening's stroll when he heard my men during one of our operations. He followed my men to this very cave, walked in as if God would protect him, and demanded money in return for silence. He wanted money for the church, he said. No doubt for his own pockets, as well, and he threatened to reveal me if I didn't give it to him. I had a plan, and couldn't let him destroy all that I worked so hard for."

"You committed murder for money?"

"Ah, my lady... thy vanity is wounded. Of course, I did it all for you," he laughed, mocking her.

"Do not patronise me, my lord. I am merely confused, for you possess money and a title. Why commit yourself to a life of murder and smuggling?"

Taking a deep sigh, Roxburgh explained, "On the contrary. I do not possess a title. Shortly before his death, my father revealed to me that he had a son out of wedlock. This older brother was entitled to all of my inheritance. For years, I put up with his constant delusions of grandeur. He would taunt me about my brother, declaring at every chance he could 'he's a better man than you'. Of course I did not believe him, but I tolerated it, hoping for the day he would finally die and I would inherit the lands, title, and money." Roxburgh began to pace, stopped and glanced at Jane before he resumed pacing.

For the first time since Roxburgh's arrival, Jane was seeing the shy young boy she had first met. But now she faced a desperate man who had lost everything—including his honour and a firm grasp on reality.

Jane feverishly cast around for a means of escape. First and foremost she had to free herself from the ropes that kept her immobile.

Roxburgh continued, "When I realized the old man was telling the truth and I was not his legal heir, I wanted to strangle him but couldn't bring myself to do it. Instead I hoped to prove he had erred."

"There is nothing wrong with hoping that your father did love you," Jane said, trying to keep him talking.

"Love?" he screamed, the sudden outburst causing Jane to tremble. "The bastard knew nothing of love. I wanted to hate my brother as well but couldn't find it in me. If he had been raised by my father, then he too would have suffered at his hands."

"I regret your pain. But—"

"You know," he said, "it's strange that after all that, I still believed I could prove him wrong, that I was the capable and strong son he'd always wanted."

He paced around, looking lost, "Oh, I tried my hand at all sorts of plans, but nothing worked out. I even began to court Margaret. Though she had no title, I believed the old man would have been thrilled at my being married and acquiring her fortune. But instead, he was pleased when she turned me down."

He violently punched the trunk of a nearby tree, raising a shriek from Jane. "I hated him...he continued to hold my failures over my head. On the day of his death, I came to bid him farewell and inform him I was going abroad. He was strangely furious that I should abandon him. He began taunting me once again about my brother. 'He is the better man', how my brother would become lord of all his property..."

He stopped pacing and turned to Jane. "You can imagine what happened next." Roxburgh began to laugh as the memories of that night overwhelmed him. "The bastard begged for his life, and with his last breath, he smiled. His last taunt was a smile."

He looked at her as if wondering what she was doing there. He began to shake. "I wanted to cut him piece by piece, but I couldn't. I had to make it look like an accident."

Jane could hardly breathe. The images were too much and tears began to trickle down her cheeks. She realised getting out of this situation wouldn't be as easy as she had initially thought.

"What about Chapman? Why did you kill him?"

"I hired him to keep an eye on you, and like the vicar, he too became greedy." His face had changed from a crazed expression to that of a man who believed himself in love. "My life was ugly, my lady, until two summers ago, when I came upon you and Margaret riding. It was like the knife all over again, but this time it was slicing my heart. I was astonished you had bloomed overnight into a great beauty. My heart became yours forever on that day."

"But you left." More time, more time was needed.

"I had to leave," he said. "I needed to ensure I was not connected to my father's death. And I had to make money. That was when the smuggling opportunity arose."

"And who was the man who attacked me?"

"I swear to you, the man paid within an inch of his life for touching you. It was Binet's cousin. He thought he could earn extra money by bringing you directly to me. But then that pansy, Sir Hugh, showed up. At first, I wanted to get rid of him myself, but I thought that would have stirred up too much suspicion. But who is here now with you? It is I. We will sail away to France, where we will be married. After a year, we shall return to claim your inheritance."

The thought of being married to him nearly dissolved her courage. Fighting for control, she asked about his trip to America. But he was not to have any of that.

"Enough, I am done with talking. Do you think me as daft as not to realize that you wish me to ramble on in the hope someone might arrive to rescue you? My dear, no one is coming. I made sure of that." Roxburgh moved toward her.

"Wait," she said, disregarding the desperation creeping into her voice, "The day of the vicar's funeral, when the horses were startled. Were you responsible for that?"

"No, I would never have endangered you. I was furious when I found out."

If he was not responsible, then who was? Was there another force at work here?

Roxburgh advanced slowly toward her and in his face she read his desire. Jane was bound, helpless to defend herself. What could she do?

Chapter Thirty-Nine

Sir Hugh heard a scream come from a tunnel off to his left. For a moment he felt as if his heart had stopped beating. *Confounded, am I too late?* But then immediate relief overcame him as he heard his lady yell something unbefitting a lady.

"Damn you, Roxburgh! Take your filthy and murderous hands off me!"

At any other time he might have laughed. If they should live through this, he promised himself to talk to her about her use of such language. But for now he would be content eliminating the man responsible for everything that had been happening to them all.

He picked up speed as he ran through the bushes leading to the voices. He came to a sudden halt and ducked behind a large rock, a horrifying scene before him as he saw Lady Jane laying on the ground, feet and hands bound, and her mouth gagged. Roxburgh surely intended to carry her off to the shores below, where a ship would most likely be waiting for them.

"You must cooperate, my sweet. I shall make you very happy and in time you will learn to love me."

It was here that Sir Hugh realised Roxburgh's interest had always been in Jane and her money, and never Margaret. He prayed that wherever Margaret had been taken too, that Phillip would find them in time, before any harm came to her.

Roxburgh continued, unaware that Sir Hugh was watching them, "I love these cliffs. You know Shakespeare wrote about them in *King Lear*. I have often spent time here wondering about the future and where it would lead me." He looked at Jane but his face was emotionless, his eyes blank.

Sir Hugh began silently creeping toward Roxburgh, who had his back to the rock where he had been hiding. The full moon's cold light fitfully illuminated the scene, allowing Sir Hugh to silently edge forward, closer to Roxburgh.

Jane collapsed with relief when she saw Sir Hugh. He could have sworn a smile played behind her gag. Signalling to her to remain still, Sir Hugh stood behind Roxburgh. Shooting out his arm, he wrapped it around the other man's neck in a steel grip, his other hand holding a knife now pricking his throat. "It seems your future is looking rather bleak, Roxburgh."

Taken by surprise, Roxburgh nevertheless reacted quickly, jabbing his elbow into Sir Hugh's ribs.

Sir Hugh's reflex jerk allowed Roxburgh time to whip out his own knife.

"What have we here? Is this an attempt at playing the warrior rather than the fop you usually play?" Roxburgh asked.

"You chose a clever guise, convincing us all that the Marquis was the villain."

"Once I am rid of you, the world will continue to believe that the Marquis was responsible for all of the murders, including yours." Roxburgh thrust his knife forward and slashed Sir Hugh's arm.

Sir Hugh heard Jane whimper, but ignored her. He needed to keep is attention focused on his opponent.

Jane feared the worst when the knife cut through Sir Hugh's sleeve. She closed her eyes for a second before gathering the courage to open them—her heart threatening to leap right from her chest. Realizing that the attention was no longer on her she began to struggle with her ropes, managing to loosen one hand.

"You won't get away with it, Roxburgh. I'm not the only one here, nor am I the only one who knows about you."

Roxburgh laughed, "No matter, I shall be long gone before anyone else comes for me or Lady Jane."

Sir Hugh lunged, his own knife striking Roxburgh in the shoulder. Roxburgh roared from pain and rage. "I should have disposed of you when I had the chance!" he cried.

"It's a pity you didn't. No doubt it would have been a poor attempt on your part."

Roxburgh's level of venom rose. He had underestimated the man and vowed never again to let anyone interfere with his plans. "I'll have everything I ever wanted, and no one, including you, will be able to stop me," Roxburgh declared.

"Care to wager on that? You committed murder and thievery out of greed?"

"It was my right. I deserve it all—the money, the title, and the beautiful and rich wife."

"I am afraid that's not going to happen," Sir Hugh said quietly, never taking his eyes off Roxburgh.

"You are a conceited rake, Cameron. She will never see you for the man that I am."

"It is not about whom she sees, Roxburgh. It is about the injustices the world sees when someone breaks the law and commits murder."

Both men, although bleeding, began to wrestle. The larger Roxburgh dragged Sir Hugh forward toward the cliff's edge.

Jane managed to tear off her gag, unbind her feet and angrily aimed her clenched fist at Roxburgh's face. Since the men were violently thrashing her blow unfortunately landed squarely on Sir Hugh's head.

She yelped at the pain, convinced she now sported a broken hand.

"Comport yourself, madam," Sir Hugh yelled at her, only to turn back to Roxburgh in time to welcome his fist landing squarely on his jaw. He took a few steps back. *Bloody hell—concentrate, Cameron or you'll get killed!* He willed himself.

"I was merely trying to help you!" Jane cried.

"I don't need your confounded assistance," he shouted, turning to look at her.

Taking advantage of the opening, Roxburgh sent another blow, this time to Sir Hugh's stomach.

"Very well, devil take you," she yelled, her aching fist this time finding its target hitting Roxburgh in the jaw.

Grunting in pain, Roxburgh turned to her. One look at her eyes and he could see something in them that told him more than he wanted to know. "So, your affection lies with him, does it? You ungrateful chit! Had I known earlier, I would have killed him."

Jane screamed again as Roxburgh's knife sliced through the air.

Recovering from the blow, Sir Hugh circled his opponent. He could hear the waves coming closer, but he kept on fighting. He gave a mighty thrust and his blade slashed into Roxburgh's chest.

Roxburgh grunted and flew at Sir Hugh, pushing him forward again, the pounding waves growing nearer and more deafening.

A savage thrust from Roxburgh stabbed Sir Hugh's chest. Pain and confusion registered on Sir Hugh's face as Roxburgh sliced upwards with all of his might. Sir Hugh grunted, staggered, and Roxburgh rushed him. The two fell on the ground, rolling for what seemed an eternity until finally, they both went over the cliff's edge and nothing but air embraced them.

From the distance Sir Hugh could hear Jane's desperate, agonising scream as his feet gave way to nothingness.

Mr Latham found a door leading into a deserted tunnel. He clambered down several flights of stairs leading to a lower level, emerging into a large room that looked like a wine cellar. In the centre an unconscious Margaret lay on a table. Her hands and feet were bound, and the rope twisted around her body, making sure she could not get up if she awakened.

He couldn't bear to think of the alternative. He rushed forward, thankful he had taken Sir Hugh's cue and strapped a blade to his ankle. He whipped it out now, frantically sawing at the thick bindings until they fell away. He prayed she had suffered no major injury and had merely fainted.

Having finished untying her, he checked for a pulse and found one. He began to breathe more easily. Energized by hope, he began to check for any broken bones. He was working on her arms when, from behind, a thin wire whipped around his throat.

He grabbed at it, getting his hands behind the wire before it completely cut through his skin. He painfully gasped for air as he pushed his whole body against his attacker. Turning around, he came face to face with Pierre Binet—Roxburgh's second in command.

Drawing out his knife, Binet advanced. Latham danced to the side, disconcerting Binet's attention. That was all Latham needed to grab and flip Binet behind him, immediately twisting to face him, "You are not very smart, Binet. You could have gotten away with everything."

"I couldn't leave things as they were," Binet said, pearls of perspiration slowly forming on his forehead. They manoeuvred in anticipation of each other's attempts to attack.

"I understand your greed, but not your interest in Miss Renard."

"A small matter of revenge—her father dishonoured me."

"Yet it was you who dishonoured him by stealing from him."

"I was merely borrowing. I had intentions of putting it all back."

Binet launched himself at Latham. They struggled, but Latham was stronger. Sensing that he would lose the battle because of his opponent's large, strong frame,

Binet gripped his knife more firmly, aiming at Latham's heart. He missed, stabbing his shoulder instead.

Latham gasped but jumped away, only to shove Binet backward. Losing his footing, he quickly regained it and charged at Latham again, grabbing to pull him down to the floor. A miscalculation on Binet's part, for Latham landed on top of him with his weight forcing a shift in Binet's position. His arm moved up to deflect Latham, but it was too late. Latham's hand still gripped his knife, and as he landed, it sank into Binet's heart. The little man exhaled briefly and was gone.

Pushing to his feet, Latham saw Margaret stirring awake. He helped her off the table, and when he assured himself she had regained her balance, he put two fingers under her chin, tilting her face up to look into her eyes. "Are you unwell? Can you walk?"

In her confusion she cried, "He's here!" and began to thrash her arms.

"Hush, Binet won't come after you or anyone else for that matter," Mr Latham promised her as he tried to keep her from looking back where Binet's lifeless body lay.

But it was too late. When she saw Binet lying in his blood, Margaret cringed back into Latham's arms.

Realizing that Latham had saved her life she asked, "How did you get here?"

"No time for questions. We must search for Sir Hugh and Lady Jane." With one arm circling her waist and another holding one of her hands, he guided her to the stairs and back out of the manor. Straining to hear, they caught a scream echoing from near the cliffs.

Releasing Margaret, Latham ran as fast as he could. He arrived in time to see Sir Hugh and Roxburgh go over the cliff.

Chapter Forty

Jane and Margaret waited anxiously outside the bedroom as the doctor saw to Sir Hugh's injuries. Her ladyship had taken to her room, ill from the sight of the blood covering Sir Hugh's body when he was brought in.

The doctor promised to check on her after he'd finished with Sir Hugh. That statement gave everyone hope, as it implied Sir Hugh would recover.

His lordship was reluctant to leave Jane and Margaret alone as they kept vigil outside Sir Hugh's room. Once Margaret assured him she wouldn't leave Jane alone, he left to join his wife.

"Oh, Margaret, if he should—," started Jane.

"Stop talking nonsense." Margaret put her arm around her friend. "Sir Hugh is strong and too stubborn to die. After all, with whom would you argue if he did? I believe Sir Hugh is aware of that and will fight for his life. He won't let you get away so easily." Margaret finished, hoping she sounded confident. Her thoughts were elsewhere. She longed to see how Mr Latham fared, but it would have to wait until the laudanum wore off.

They were alive, thanks to Sir Hugh and Mr Latham. In the midst of last night's turmoil she realized her feelings for Mr Latham had changed from dislike to admiration for his strength and courage. He had been prepared to die for her and Jane.

Jane impatiently rose from her chair and went to the door, peeking in to see if the doctor could give them word on Sir Hugh's condition. He didn't.

Having finished attending to Sir Hugh's injuries, Doctor Harrison filled the family in on his status and firmly insisted that he be allowed to rest. Once he reassured them of Sir Hugh's condition, he left to examine her ladyship.

Jane took advantage of the opportunity to visit Sir Hugh while the doctor was with her mother. Tiptoeing, she approached his sleeping form and saw he was quite pale from blood loss. She dared herself to touch his skin and it felt cool. Twice now he had been hurt in rescuing her.

There were bandages tied around his torso and left arm, but she still found strength in him, even in his weak state.

He almost died because of her. This man whom she initially dislike, proved to be a man of honour, strength, courage and dedication. But he had emotional scars. His father was abusive to his mother. No doubt he felt he could not love a woman because he was not worthy to love one. She loved him…the thought did not shake her to the core. She didn't even wondered when it had occurred, for it had been building up gradually. The realization did not come until she thought she had lost him. She found that she loved him and if he chooses to run away from that love, then she will just have to run after him. For this man, had come to mean more to her than she could have ever imagined a man would.

Her hand traced along his arm and then up to his face. She felt a heat that welled from the pit of her stomach.

Sir Hugh stirred and inhaled softy. His skin had become warm to her touch, as if her touch brought him back from the brink of death. Not one to believe in romantic ideals, she realistically acknowledged that a fever normally followed injuries like his. In his weak state, she didn't know if he would survive and prayed no infection would flare up.

Jane gasped when he opened his eyes. "Jane?" he whispered. "I must be dreaming. Otherwise you would not be here by yourself. Highly improper, you know."

She shivered at the way he said her name. "Hang propriety," she said softly through tears. Touching his forehead again, she grew more concerned as it seemed to have gotten warmer.

Sir Hugh tried to sit up, but inhaled sharply as pain coursed through his body. "I'm sorry I did not rescue you, dearest heart."

"But you did. You and Mr Latham saved us!" Jane affirmed fervently. She needed to get the doctor.

"Are you well? Did he hurt you? I am sorry I was too late, for I let him put his hands all over you—"

"Do not think of such horrible thoughts. Because of you, both Margaret and I are alive and unharmed. Hush, now and don't fret. I must fetch the doctor. You are too warm."

"I have failed, for you are here with me in death. Oh, how sweet death is after all."

Tears streaming down her face, she nonetheless kept her voice steady. "No, you're not dead, foolish man. I will get the doctor and he'll make you better, I promise."

Sir Hugh began thrashing from left to right. Afraid for him, Jane ran to the door and called out for the doctor.

Doctor Harrison, who had left a sleeping ladyship just moments before, rushed into the room, Margaret and his lordship following closely.

No one mentioned or acknowledged the fact that Jane had been alone with Sir Hugh.

The doctor hastily drew a syringe and a small bottle filled with clear liquid from his medicine bag and called on his lordship to help hold Sir Hugh still. He injected the serum and several seconds later, Sir Hugh began to quiet down.

"It is as I was afraid. He has a fever. The next twenty-four hours will be difficult for him," the doctor said to his lordship, avoiding Jane's eyes.

Jane knew what he was not telling them. Sir Hugh had developed an infection. This was too much. All of the pent-up emotions and experiences of the past several weeks surfaced, and Jane broke down in her father's arms. He led her out and straight into Margaret's arms.

The doctor followed the girls into Jane's room, where he gave her a sedative. "This will help her sleep," he said. "She will awaken refreshed, and hopefully by then we shall have good news regarding the young man."

He smiled at Margaret and then turned to leave the room.

"Doctor, will he make it?"

"He is young, and therefore has a chance—a small one, but a chance nonetheless. I am afraid that is all I can tell you for now. Lord Crittenden has been gracious enough to offer me a room. I must notify my man that I will be staying here at least for tonight. Should another emergency arise, he will know where to find me. Pray excuse me."

"Thank you, doctor."

Margaret turned to check on Jane. There were trails of tears trickling down her friend's cheeks, as well as her own. She fetched a wet cloth and wiped Jane's face. She then knelt beside the bed to pray. She prayed for Sir Hugh and Jane. She prayed for Philip Latham. They had both saved them. *How does one ever repay such a debt?* She tightened her eyes shut, hoping to close out the images of their captivity, but to no avail, so she settled for a book instead.

A gentle knock on the door startled her. Making sure Jane was still asleep; she rose to answer the door. To her surprise Mr Latham stood on the other side of the door.

She had a strange urge to run into the annoying man's arms but stopped herself just in time. Stepping out of the room, she gently closed the door.

"How are you? Why are you out of bed? Was your mother informed of your latest adventure?" She wished she hadn't wept so much, certain her eyes were red and puffy.

"Thank you for your concern, but I am fine. Fortunately, the knife entered mostly through flesh and didn't sever any vital arteries. The doctor changed the bandages and claimed my wounds not life threatening. His lordship sent word to my mother. Thankfully she is not easily given to the vapours. I understand that Cameron, on the other hand, is having a bit of a rough spell. I know he will make it. He has good reason to want to live."

He mistook her blushing, little knowing she had been thinking of how close he came to dying because of her. She was ridden with guilt—he too could have easily died from his wound had it been more severe. Those seconds after she had awoken to find him bleeding were the longest she had ever experienced.

She gave up trying to be brave. It was all too much for her. She leaned against him and began to cry. He gently held her, neither of them caring about social improprieties.

"I'm sorry," was all she managed to say after several seconds. As the torrents of pain and anguish left, she realized how exhausted she was.

Mr Latham sensed her fatigue and insisted they sit on the chaise in the hall between Sir Hugh's and Lady Jane's room.

Margaret broke the silence between them by saying, "So your mother and sister are well?"

"Yes, from her note I could tell she had been overwhelmed with relief to learn that I had escaped with minor injuries. I believe she took the news in exceptionally good order."

Margaret reached out and took his hands in hers. She had an urge to lean into him, but the butler announced tea. Thank God, this near death experience has made jelly of her.

Mr Latham looked surprised for a moment, but he tightened his grip on Margaret's soft hands.

That evening after she had awakened from her deep sleep, Jane asked for a bath, but only after inquiring after

Sir Hugh. Dressed in a soft muslin gown and hair combed, she quietly entered Sir Hugh's room. She excused the maid who had been assigned to watch him. She could tell she wanted to protest, but Jane was beyond caring what society thought.

After bathing his forehead, Jane took a chair and moved it closer to the bed. She made herself comfortable and began to reminisce about the first day she met him. It wasn't that long ago, yet it seemed like ages. The man she met then and the one she had come to know were as different as night and day. Sir Hugh first seemed selfish and ill-mannered. *Or had it been all a ruse?* Perhaps it was part of his cover, since she discovered he was a Guard of the King. The man she had come to know was pleasant, humorous, bright and brave. Her lips curved into a small smile, remembering he had called her 'dearest heart,' even if he had been in a feverish state.

She dozed off and started when a sound awakened her. To her delight she found him watching her. "Hullo," she said with a heartfelt smile.

Blue warm eyes were staring at her. "I have been ill," Sir Hugh mumbled his tongue thick from thirst.

"Yes, you have. But you are much better now, and it's a glorious day."

He looked past her to the window and noticed it was dark and grey. "It looks like rain to me," he declared.

"Foolish man, must you always argue with me..."

"Water," he said very weakly.

Jane felt guilty for teasing him, rushed to pour a glass of water and helped him lift it to drink. He drank, choking a bit, "Thank you."

Jane smiled lightly.

"I must be on my deathbed. Is that why you are being so kind? After all those terrible things I said to you. How could you be here tending to my needs."

Jane did not know whether to scream or laugh.

"No, you stubborn man, you are not dying. I would not let you have the satisfaction of abandoning me so that I would never have anyone else to argue with," Jane said, sniffing back tears.

Sir Hugh pulled her to him with his good arm. The closeness might prove to have a detrimental consequence for their reputations, should they be found like this. Jane gently pulled away and hurried to find the doctor. She refused to get her hopes up until the doctor had a chance to confirm that Sir Hugh was out of danger.

Once the doctor examined him, he confirmed Sir Hugh was indeed on the mend. He was ordered to remain in bed for at least five more days, much to his patient's chagrin. But to Jane and the others, all was well with the world, at least for now.

After the doctor excused himself to check on her ladyship, Margaret and Jane stood near Sir Hugh's bed, Mr Latham choosing to sit by the fireplace.

"So did they find Roxburgh?" He wanted to say "the body", but wisely used the man's name. The girls needed no extra stress from their ordeal.

Latham came over to Sir Hugh's bed, "You and Roxburgh went over the cliff, and by the grace of God you were spared, barely hanging on to the root of a tree. Lady Jane and I were able to get to you before you let go. It was a certainty you would have plunged to your death.

"I could have sworn that it was Margaret he fancied. But it was me, or actually, my title," Jane said.

"Vanity, thy name is woman," Mr Latham teased, causing everyone to smile.

"But he had a title," Margaret interjected, confusion registering across her face.

Sir Hugh spoke first, "In actuality, he didn't."

"No title... what about his family's fortune?" Margaret asked in surprised astonishment.

Mr Latham shook his head in response.

"It all now makes sense," declared Margaret. "It is terrible and I sort of feel sorry for him. His greed was based not on love but on materialism." She knew that whether rich or poor, she could never marry someone unless she truly loved him. But she need not worry about that since she will never marry.

"I see, so all of your so-called business trips were really to gather information," Jane accused Mr Latham.

Latham nodded and smiled sheepishly. "Having a title is what he wanted everyone to believe, but Roxburgh had an illegitimate brother living in America, and that is why no one ever knew about him. Granted, Roxburgh had the money to support the title, but he needed more."

"It is common to hear of penniless women marrying into loveless marriages for the sake of having a home, but more uncommon is the man who finds himself in that same predicament."

"I would marry a penniless man if our union was to be one out of love," Jane declared, and then blushed when she realized she spoke openly on such a personal matter in front of the gentlemen.

The others waited to see if Margaret would agree, but she remained silent.

Both Sir Hugh and Mr Latham stared at the young ladies as if they were seeing them for the first time. Perhaps they had underestimated them and they were not as pampered and spoiled as they were first led to believe.

Jane was the first to break the silence, "I must apologize to you and Mr Latham. I was too proud to have listened to reason." She looked at Sir Hugh and realized that it must be hard for a man to surrender to illness and not be in command of his environment.

"I know it must be hard not to be in control—"

Sir Hugh threw his hands up as best as he could, considering his wounds, "No control? Your ladyship, if you think that my ego is wounded out of lack of control, then you do not know me."

Mr Latham and Margaret looked at one another and simultaneously moved toward the door. No doubt Sir Hugh was on the road to recovery, and Jane was back to making sure she stood up to his tempers and normal behaviour.

Closing the door, they heard Jane say something about if he continued being a bear she would leave. Then there was silence.

Margaret and Latham grinned.

"Jane, my dearest and loveliest, Jane."

"Hush, you must rest." Jane said barely in a whisper. Hoping the low tones of her voice would lure him to sleep.

"Not before I say what I must."

Jane had given up on the hopes of keeping him calm. "Very well, say what you must and then it will be rest for you or I will be forced to call the doctor."

He smiled. Already she was acting like a wife—his wife. He liked the sound of that. "I was foolish to believe that my life could go on as if nothing had happened or changed. I lied to you when I told you that I did not need or loved you. My parents' marriage was not what you would call ideal. I hated my father for the misery he caused my mother—"

"You are not your father." She declared, hope surging through her.

"I know that now. I had convinced myself that I was like him. That all men were like him, but after seeing the love your father has for my cousin and how I feel about you I know now that I am not or would I ever be like my

484

father. I have been running ever since. I know now there is no need to run. I can be who I want to be without fear."

"I understand," Jane said. The hope she felt moments ago, gone. Despair, overtook her heart. She understood what he was trying to say. He is changed and can now be a government agent at peace, no longer running from himself. She loved him enough to want him to be happy and that meant that if he needed to pursue his profession then who was she to stop him. After all loving someone does not come without sacrifices.

Sir Hugh could see pain in her eyes. Blasted he was doing a poor job of explaining things to her. "Jane, I love you and I would be honoured if you became my wife."

"I don't understand, what about your profession? You said that you could not have a wife and lead the life you have been leading. That King and country was the only thing you loved."

Sir Hugh tried to rise from his bed, but only managed to cause himself pain.

Jane gently pushed him down and moved a pillow under his wounded arm to support blood flow.

"I know what I said, but I was wrong. Nothing is more important to me than you. I was a selfish and proud brute. I hurt you that day and the things I said were not true and cruel."

Jane began to shed tears…tears she had held inside since that night when he kissed her so passionately and then he told her she meant nothing to him.

"Jane I can't take back the things I said, but please know this, they were not true and I am so sorry, I said them. It was fear talking, for I had fallen in love with you and felt as if my peaceful and carefully planned life was unravelling. I am only sorry that it almost took losing you to make me realize that I could not go a moment longer on this earth without you besides me. I promise you I will spend the rest of my life making it up to you."

"Oh, Hugh, my dearest love, you do not have to make it up to me. All that matters is that you love me and I love you. Yes, I would be honoured to be your wife." She threw herself at him and only pulled away when he winced, but he refused to let her go. The pain he felt was minor compared to the emptiness of his arms of late. She was the only cure he needed.

Finally releasing her, he said, "Now, please go fetch your father, I have a final and most important mission to complete on behalf of my being—" He said.

"Mission?" Jane said confused. "Oh, yes right away." She laughed. She could tell he was in need of sleep, but also knew he would not rest until he completed his most valuable mission—that of asking her father for her hand in marriage. She leaned boldly and kissed him on his soft and warm lips.

A fire had been lit in the drawing room. Though still daylight, the wintery grey darkened the room. Margaret, Jane and Mr Latham had come in after Sir Hugh fell asleep.

After the excitement of her friend's engagement, Margaret decided to finish her book, while Mr Latham went through some legal papers. Not wanting to be alone in her room, Jane chose instead to lay on the chaise lounge closest to the fireplace, the happiest she has ever been. Sir Hugh loved her and she loved him. They will be married in the spring, though he could not understand the delay, but he had obliged her, her wish.

The doctor visited Lady Crittenden once more, and before leaving, gave his Lordship some instructions.

Assuring himself that his wife slept, he went in search of the others. He needed to share some news and God only knew he was in need of a drink.

He found Biltmore in the hall, and was told that everyone had retired to the drawing room, enjoying their afternoon tea and cakes.

Jane heard her father come into the drawing and immediately noticed his odd expression and hurried over to him. "Papa, is Mama unwell?"

"No, no. All is well," he said, looking at Jane, his features softening as colour returned to his face. What a gift Jane had been when she was born. When his late wife had told him they were expecting their second child he was beyond thrilled. But then he had lost them both and never in a million years did he imagine he would wed again and have another child. That is until now...

"Would you like me to pour you a port, sir?" Mr Latham asked.

"Yes, a drink is in order."

"Did the doctor have a chance to check on Lady Crittenden?"

"Yes, he did. You won't believe the diagnosis." He took a long drink of the port Latham handed him. "It seems that we are expecting."

"Who are we expecting?" Margaret asked. Surely it could not be Mr Latham's mother? That would make her arrival earlier than expected.

"Really Margaret, there are times when I truly do worry about you." Jane stared at her father. She remembered the time when both her parents had told her about a new baby brother or sister. They were ecstatic at the news, but then her mother and infant brother had died. It had taken both a long time to overcome the loss. Life had a funny way of coming full circle.

"A baby! Oh, Papa, this is wonderful news." Jane hugged her father in rapture. "Margaret, I am going to have a brother or a sister," she cried, hugging her, and letting her go, she hugged Mr Latham. In one day she managed to get engaged and become a big sister, well that latter she had no part in it, but it felt great.

"Uncle, I am very happy for you," Margaret said, hugging him as well.

"I must go and tell Hugh," Jane hurried out of the room with Margaret quickly following in pursuit.

Lord Crittenden did not want his worries to dampen the joyous celebration of the girls' safe return and Sir Hugh's and Latham's recovery. He must have faith that his wife and child would survive. After all, in a fortnight was Christmas, a holiday of miracles.

Left alone with Mr Latham, he raised his glass, "A toast. To life."

"May I be the first to congratulate you, Charles?" Mr Latham said, raising his glass. "And if I may, I should like to add 'To love.'"

~Finis~

Made in the USA
Charleston, SC
06 October 2014